Brighter Than Her Fears

Brighter Than Her Fears

Lisa Ard

Also by Lisa Ard

Children's Books

Saving Halloween

Fright Flight

Dream Team

"And one day she discovered that she was fierce, and strong, and full of fire, and that not even she could hold herself back because her passion burned brighter than her fears."

—Mark Anthony, The Beautiful Truth

Published in the United States by Creative James Media.

www.creativejamesmedia.com

978-1-956183-14-6 (trade paperback)

First U.S. Edition 2024

Interior artwork by Molly Ard.

Dedicated to my mother Nancy,
who comes from a long line of strong women,
including Alice

Chapter One
Asheville 1882

"AT ASHEVILLE!—For two days past the Iron Horse had made his regular trip to Asheville depot..., It is a great event, this opening of railway facilities to the heart of the mountain region."

The Farmer and Mechanic

The dressmaker probably saw every kind of bride—joyful, nervous, excited, even frightened, yet rarely two sisters on the same day and seldom ones of our advanced age. At thirty years old, I'd long since abandoned the idea of marriage. The War had ended when I was thirteen and with battlefields turned to cemeteries, the marriage prospects in the South had dimmed considerably. I didn't favor the title spinster, but I valued my independence. Especially now, as it slipped from my grasp.

"Shorter, Miss Harris?" Miss Shackton asked. "You might wear it after the wedding."

"Yes, thank you. It'll make a fine church dress." My cheeks warmed at the suggestion for thrift. My thoughts thundered over my family's losses. A hastily arranged marriage to a man I barely knew was my only option.

While Miss Shackton circled to pin the dress's hem, my eyes swept the neatly kept shop. It was narrow, not two wagons' breadth across, with a front counter crafted from a rich, dark slab of wood laid on top of postmaster shelving. The many nooks and crannies held the dressmaker's tools of the trade: threads, spools, pin cushions, bolts of fabric, scissors, and more. The orderliness soothed me.

"I'm almost finished here. Be with you in a minute," Miss Shackton announced to my sister.

Jennie slumped on a faded settee and dabbed her eyes with a damp handkerchief. She'd always been delicate and our rushed marriages, and that of our two sisters, Louise and Ina, didn't help. From my earliest years, I'd taken care of Jennie and my other siblings, filling in where our mother and father had fallen short. *Who would look after my sister?* The shop's mirror reflected my sour expression.

Jennie twisted her kerchief. "It's getting late. I could come back another day."

The dressmaker opened her mouth to reply, but my words stabbed the space between us.

"There's no getting around it, Jennie. Best get it done." My eyes prickled. I exhaled long and hard.

A fire in the corner wood stove pushed away the late winter draft seeping under the front door. The shop's exposed brick walls held no adornment, not a picture nor sign nor frame, which told me more about the seamstress than the organized tools. The storefront faced Asheville's Main Street, and I watched passersby through the wide front window embellished with *Custom Tailoring, Elizabeth Shackton, Proprietress.*

I'd never met a woman with her own business. How liberating it must be to earn one's own way, to not depend on a man to provide. The young seamstress circled the fabric, billowing against the wooden floorboards with deliberate, efficient movements. She was girlish with her curly golden hair and a modest dress of blue-striped cotton. Her only decoration was the various pins and needles poking out of a wrist cushion.

The bell jingled as the shop door swung open, drawing in the smell of the livery stable across the road, the noises of the street traffic, and a composed young woman. Her pale, smooth hands held a stack of papers. I clutched my rough, sun-worn hands behind my back.

"Good day, Miss Elizabeth. I've brought the flyers for the meeting."

"Good day as well, Miss Margaret," Elizabeth said. "You might put them on the counter. I'll get them out this evening." She stood and smoothed her skirt.

Margaret's peculiar dialect piqued my curiosity. I glanced between the dressmaker and her acquaintance until Elizabeth put her work aside and introduced us.

"Miss Alice Harris and Miss Jennie Harris, Miss Margaret Petersen of Boston, Massachusetts." We exchanged curtsies and smiles.

"Shall I read it to you?" Margaret asked.

The sudden coloring of Elizabeth's cheeks startled me. Many didn't know their letters, but I expected a woman in business to read.

"The Women's Home Missionary Society Meeting, Wednesday, seven o'clock at the Methodist Church. Come support efforts to fund public schools." Margaret Petersen looked at me. "Are you a supporter, Miss Harris?"

I'd scarcely thought about promoting public education. The War had curtailed my schooling. In those years when I should have walked the red-earth road to the country schoolhouse, I kept our household together and our inn running—until I couldn't. At the end of the War, with the schoolhouse burned down and our family scraping by, my father's concern for our education had gone by the wayside. Our hardship forced Jennie and me on a singular path toward financial security—marriage. With a better education, we'd have had more choices.

"I support your efforts, Miss Petersen." I also welcomed a diversion from our wedding preparations. "Jennie, we must attend the meeting."

"Thank you, Miss Petersen, for the invitation," Jennie said. "Alice, we'd best speak with family before we commit." My sister clasped her trembling hands behind her back.

"Cousin Mary will be asleep not long after dessert," I said. "We are two engaged women in each other's company. I shall chaperone you and you me." I accepted a flyer from Miss Petersen. "We'll meet you there at seven tomorrow evening."

Jennie's eyebrows rose in response. I recalled her reproachful words three days ago, when we'd left our home for Asheville.

Jennie had jutted out her chin. "Honestly, Alice, you're only four years older than me."

"And?"

"And it means you expect to have your way, whether seeing to the packing, scheduling our trip, or getting the first pick of our grooms." Jennie had crossed her arms and refused to talk to me for the rest of the carriage ride. I'd ignored the outburst, knowing time and distance soothed her best. Clearly, she was bitter about marrying the older of the two men.

The dressmaker's suggestion brought me back to the invitation at hand. "You might come for the last fitting at six o'clock, then we'd go to the meeting together," she said.

"We'd be delighted, Miss Shackton." I excused myself to the curtained-off area to change. After Jennie had her wedding dress fitted, we left the shop arm in arm.

My sister's exasperation didn't last, and I chose a roundabout way to our cousin's home. Jennie and I were free to stroll on our own under the open sky, unencumbered by wedding dresses, obligations, and demands. We sauntered over to Court Square, its stately green stretching before the Buncombe County courthouse and the heart of the city. Our long hems swished across the stone paths toward a commemorative plaque announcing Israel Baird's land grant to the city.

"Smell that mountain air," a tall man in a bowler hat said to the woman on his arm.

She let out a sigh of satisfaction. "This is truly—what is that wonderful expression one hears? The land of the sky."

I hadn't read the novel, but I recognized the famous title the railroad used to advertise Asheville.

"Now it is," the man stressed and dropped his voice. "It wasn't long ago they sold slaves on those very steps." His outstretched arm pointed toward the courthouse entry. The woman's lips curled in distaste.

The imposing courthouse towered over the square, a focal point with its distinctive curved roofline and wrought-iron widow's walk. I marveled at the three-arched entry and the way the masons repeated the curves atop each window. Where these visitors dwelled in the past, I glimpsed the city's growth and bright future.

"A despicable trade." The woman held her palm under her bosom. The couple glided away.

Jennie snorted. "I think Mr. Baird would hardly recognize Asheville."

"Not the disapproving visitors, nor their unusual

fashions." I eyed the woman's oversized bustle from a distance. I was glad I didn't wear a garment emphasizing my backside. The visible boning of the woman's corset squeezed her waistline into an unnatural smallness that pained me. I pulled in my stomach.

We wandered the stone pathways, bare and wet from the afternoon warmth after last night's dusting of snow. Constant noise plied the busy thoroughfares, with wagons rumbling, horse hooves clopping, people chatting, vendors shouting, and shop doors jingling.

Asheville showed off sturdy brick structures built to last, planked roadways, and crowds of people dressed in their finest. In contrast, my family's land presented falling down farm buildings, empty roads, and the pinched together necessities of our home. Asheville's progress distracted me from the countryside's demise, or maybe I should say, our family's ruin. In admiring the city, I avoided considering my role in our downfall.

"I bet that woman has a lady-in-waiting and doesn't fix her own hair or attach her own hat."

"Alice, that's petty." Jennie gave me a conspiratorial smile. "But true."

I was determined to squeeze out these last moments with Jennie. In a fortnight, my younger sister would move with her husband to Hendersonville, several hours away from my new home in Democrat, North Carolina. She'd been my constant companion in running our household and my confidante. I would miss her terribly. Our linked arms held fast to one another.

People hurried between storefronts, ducking under the colorful awnings shading the shops' interiors. Many windows above street level were cracked open, ventilating the upper level warehousing space or living areas.

Our time in town freed us from our cousin's great interest in our comings and goings. I'd explained more than once, we were engaged to be married, as we had the licenses. However, our mother's cousin, Mary, viewed us as single women needing her guardianship, since the banns hadn't been read as they would have been in her day.

"The town is bustling," I said.

"Yes," Jennie murmured.

"And Miss Shackton and Miss Petersen are most interesting."

"Hm."

My arm tensed to keep ahold of my sister, to stop her from drifting away. Jennie's spells came unexpectedly. No, that wasn't right. Jennie distanced herself when I pulled too hard, pushed too much. Unfortunately, that was my nature.

Our grandmother often reminded Jennie that a lady should be quiet, not aloof. She'd taught Jennie fine stitching to keep her present in company. Without an embroidery hoop to thrust in her hand, I challenged my sister. "Oh Jennie, you've barely said a word since the betrothals."

Her words poured forth like a broken dam. "Our family is broken apart. Ina is already married and gone to South Carolina. What will become of us?" Jennie choked back tears.

I pulled Jennie onto a park bench and gave her my handkerchief. My sister's light blue eyes were her best feature, both for their color and the ability to see the good in every situation. Apparently, that attribute was hard to muster today. The question she posed I'd asked myself countless times. I'd sustained our family through the years, but I couldn't figure out how to do so now. *If I couldn't hold my family together, how would I do so with another?*

"Hendersonville is not far away from Democrat and we'll visit one another. The beginning of new families isn't the end of our family." I almost convinced myself. I stood and brushed off my skirt. It was an act of stoicism I believed I'd perfected. Jennie wouldn't have noticed the tears I'd shed at night, and I pretended not to hear her quiet sobs as she wept in the darkness of our shared bed.

Chapter Two

"The influence of what has already been effected [sic] in railroad construction was immediately manifest. Permanent settlers poured in..., to unite their fortunes with Asheville."

Asheville Citizen-Times

Our steps slowed as we approached our cousin's home. Jennie and I had left the busy streets of the city behind, but the sweet smells of cured tobacco trailed after us.

The prominent neighborhood suited our cousin, Mary. Her husband, Stewart Tate, had moved up with the Western North Carolina Railroad four years ago, and was second-in-command to the chief engineer, Colonel Thaddeus Coleman. He'd managed the recent opening of the Asheville-to-Salisbury rail line. While his work often called him from home, Mary assured us we would enjoy Stewart's company for the entirety of our stay. I steeled myself for another lengthy conversation this evening on the benefits of the railroad and the progress it had brought to Asheville.

We passed several Queen Anne style houses with their hipped roofs, rounded towers, and wrap-around porches, before reaching our cousins' home. The style was all about standing out, yet theirs had a reticent quality. Its low front hedge denied entry from the street. The house said: look at me, but don't come in. That standoffishness conflicted with Mary's demeanor. She'd welcomed Jennie and me for a week-long stay.

We followed the side path to the front entry where a maid answered the door and took our gloves and hats. Jennie and I climbed the elegant central stairway to the guest room to freshen up for dinner.

"Do you think Cousin Mary lifts a finger around the house?" I asked.

"Tsk, tsk, Alice. For someone who knows very well how we got here, you are showing more irritability than usual."

Jennie's broad smile irked me. I knew she was right. Irritation bubbled up in me like an underground spring, breaking forth at every opportunity. My sister teased me, but how would my husband react? *My husband.* Those two words conjured every negative connotation: bondage, servitude, and control. A husband represented the loss of my freedom and my choice.

Jennie smoothed back her hair before replacing her hair combs. "Besides, Cousin Mary is engaged in many civic duties, and a household this size requires help."

"So, the maid welcomes guests, cleans the house, and serves meals. A boy runs errands and tends the wagons and horses. With the likes of supper last night, I don't suppose the cook ever leaves the kitchen."

"For which they are paid," Jennie shot back.

"Freedmen come cheap." I looked away, unwilling to

engage in a fight I knew I could win. I could bicker and beat her down, but Jennie wasn't the source of my anger. Mother, Father, the War, cotton prices, weather, railroads, myself—all were more to blame for my reversal of fortune.

I focused instead on my outfit. My linen dress looked plain and drab amidst the richly colored furnishings. Its beige fabric was sun-worn and faded. There'd been no money for a new dress for the last two years. I'd scrubbed away stains and patched any tear, hopelessly trying to keep my wardrobe looking its best. In the absence of a dinner gown, I would make do by adding a ribbon to my hair and a brooch to my neckline.

"No doubt Mary will put us in our place by appearing in a fancy gown with her best jewelry."

Jennie's rebuttal came quickly. "Alice! Mary and Stewart have welcomed us into their home."

Heat rose in my neck and face. Not for the first time, I wished I had one-tenth of Jennie's sense of propriety. When a storm gathered, Jennie sought cover, safeguarding what people thought of her and her situation.

She turned away from me and pinched color into her cheeks. I admired my sister's fair complexion and hooded eyelids, her soft jawline, and slender, graceful neck. If not for the shortage of men, Jennie would have had plenty of suitors. I cupped my rigid jawline and jutting chin. My temper and my outspokenness were equally strong. Unless I managed to dampen those, my marriage would be rocky.

Over supper, I turned my admiration to our cousins' elegant dining room. The long mahogany table gleamed in the light from the wall-mounted gas lamps. A cream linen table runner lay smooth and crisp. I shuddered to think of the hours spent sprinkling water and enduring a stove's heat to warm the iron. A burgundy-striped wallpaper and ivory-colored wainscoting dressed the walls. It was a striking room that implied tradition and wealth, although I knew the latter to be rather new to this family.

Mary's mother and our grandmother were twins, and they couldn't have raised more different daughters. Where our mother was slender and tall, Mary was short and plump. Mother took the reckless path, marrying a man who would 'never amount to much' according to Grandmother. Mary made an advantageous match with Stewart Tate, whose prospects as an engineer proved helpful when the railroad clamored for skilled men to extend the rail through the mountains, connecting the coast to Asheville, on to Tennessee and farther west.

Mother attributed her cousin's marital success to Mary's family climbing back more quickly following the War, thanks to fewer battles in the mountains. But the War was long after our mother made her fateful decision to marry Father. Despite their differences, Mary was fond of our mother and us.

"My, what healthy appetites you girls have," Mary said.

She was one to talk.

Stewart cleared his throat and addressed his wife. "Now Mary, Alice and Jennie are paying you a compliment for the fine food you have assembled."

"It's delicious." I smoothed the linen napkin across my lap after dabbing the corners of my mouth in my best impression of a lady.

"I thank you," Mary replied. "I do hope we can keep this cook longer than the last one."

"Is it difficult to find servants, Cousin?" Jennie asked.

"Since Durham's tobacco mills started offering work to Negro women, all the good help is moving on."

"What of the cotton mills? Those are closer," Jennie said.

"My dear, the cotton mills wouldn't hire Negro girls. They draw many poor white women from surrounding farms. The good Lord knows those are aplenty." Mary shook her head and stabbed at her chicken.

"*Ahem.* Farming has always borne risks." Stewart shifted in his seat and reached for his wine glass.

Jennie's eyes glistened. No doubt Jennie's thoughts, like mine, lingered on our losses this past year. First Father, then our brother Leander, taken from us too soon. With a quick clearing of my throat, I pushed the conversation in a new direction.

"Miss Shackton invited us to a Women's Home Missionary Society meeting tomorrow evening."

"The dressmaker?" Mary's fork clattered across her plate.

"The Methodists highlight our great need for public education," Stewart said. "If we're to continue with modern advances, we must have educated people. The railroads require engineers, and the mills need mechanically inclined workers."

Here was my cousin in his most comfortable role, master of the table and the conversation. I rolled my eyes at Jennie, and she threw me a biting look.

Mary encouraged him. "With Asheville's growth, we'll need more doctors, lawyers, and teachers."

"However, I would not go as far as reviving the Freedmen's Bureau," Stewart said. "President Johnson made the right decision to veto their funding. Educating the Negro violates state rights."

"You are surely right, Husband. We know what's best and educating people beyond their needs—why, the expense of it!" Mary's outburst left her grasping for her fan.

"Although those Negroes in the eastern counties could have used some education, at least for governing." Stewart had one elbow on the table and shook his fork with the other.

"Why is that?" Jennie looked from one end of the table to the other.

"Why, the Negroes are in great numbers in the eastern

counties. They controlled the elections and selected their own kind. They ran up substantial debts."

Stewart welcomed questions when, and only when, they allowed him to expound his world view. In our two evenings together, I'd come to understand that once offered, his word was final. Jennie modeled the perfect guest, asking the question, staying quiet and allowing our cousin to have his say. I could take a lesson from my sister. Tonight, Mary could as well.

"Thankfully, the General Assembly stepped in to appoint commissioners rather than allow an ignorant people to elect incompetent men," Mary said.

"Yes, *ahem.*" Stewart commanded our attention. "The legislature selects only from the White race, and I must say, those men see the value of the railroads and keeping our taxes low."

"Indeed." Cousin Mary waved her fan and batted the maid away before she could remove her plate. The young Negro woman shrank back to stand in the corner. Her skin was uncommonly light, a factor I supposed helped her secure such favorable work.

"Well, I dare say Elizabeth Shackton has made a name for herself with her dressmaking amongst the ladies of Asheville and the visitors. I wish her every success," Mary said.

Stewart harrumphed. "Times are changing, what with women owning businesses."

The outing was approved, thanks to Mary. Jennie and I exchanged discreet smiles.

After supper, Stewart withdrew to the library for his pipe and paperwork. Aside from the kitchen, it was the one room I had not been in. I longed to see what books he might have in his library. With not much schooling, books and newspapers had been my primary sources of learning, besides Mother's rudimentary lessons.

Jennie and I lounged in the parlor with Mary. Jennie embroidered, but I found it difficult to concentrate on my novel with the volume of our cousin's snoring. Mary's breathing gradually increased to such a pitch she woke herself. Her chin lifted off her bosom, only to come to rest and start the cycle again. I kicked out my foot to gain Jennie's attention, lifted the small book in front of my face, and mimicked the noises, rising in strength until Jennie laughed and Mary shuddered forward.

"Oh, my dear girls, you must be tired after such a trying day of wedding preparations." Mary dabbed at the drool on her chin.

Jennie turned her laugh into a yawn. "Quite trying, Mary. If you'll excuse us, we'll turn in for the evening."

Behind the closed door of the guest room, we giggled like schoolgirls. The oil lamp had been lit and the bed warmer placed and removed by a servant. We changed into our cotton nightgowns and climbed into bed, eager for the warmth and comfort of its down cover and crisp linen sheets. For years we shared a bed, although nothing as luxurious as this, just as our sisters Louise and Ina had. Soon we would lie with our husbands. I wouldn't think of that now, knowing I had few precious days remaining with Jennie.

"I will miss our bedtime talks," I said.

"Me too." Jennie held my hand. "Mother will make sure the wedding is lovely. I'm glad we'll share the ceremony."

"Two for one, as Mother would say. Always one for economy."

Jennie rolled onto her back and stared at the ceiling. "Did you mean it today? Will we find a way to remain close?"

"You have my word. I'll write and we'll visit as often as possible." I stared at my sister's profile. "Jennie, you're my dearest companion. I will need you more than ever." I knew this to be true. My fears, my dreams, my hopes, my transgressions—these I'd always shared with Jennie and she with me. If not in person, then I'd reveal myself through letters.

"Alice, you won't *need* me. We all know how capable you are." Jennie turned her face toward mine. "I wish I was half as able."

I squeezed my sister's hand, trying to make everything okay again. Through these past weeks I'd convinced Jennie of our lasting bond and our expanding family, but I'd no assurance of that. My husband or hers might forbid visits. They might be callous, mean, or even tyrannical, and we should obey them.

"What you need and what you want are two different things," Jennie said. "Someday you'll recognize that."

Times like these, Jennie seemed to be the older, wiser one. For many years, I'd thought Jennie shirked her chores to search the muddy creek side for the wildflowers that inspired her stitching. After our engagements, her wanderings increased, and I realized she needed those escapes to ease her mind and heart. I wondered how long it would take me to define what I needed versus what I wanted.

"Is my tendency to criticize a need or a want?" I asked.

"Tendency?" Jennie smiled. "Yes, you might work on that." Her smile dimmed, and her eyes drifted to the ceiling again. "I hope Mr. Cannon will be kind."

"With you as a wife, he will be."

"And Mr. Carter will be a careful husband," she said.

Not handsome, not dashing, but careful. The Carter family had maintained their significant land holdings, unlike our father. My groom, Jasper Shuflin Carter, was fifty some years old and known as an honest farmer. Beyond that, I knew little of him. In our three days of chaperoned walks at the Methodist camp, I'd done my best to assess my prospective husband. He appeared well-fed and in good health. He stood a few inches taller than me, which was something considering I had what Mother called 'unfortunate height.' His sun-worn face peeked out from behind a neatly trimmed gray beard. Mr. Carter spoke of his land, the home he could offer, and his previous marriage. That hadn't shocked me, for it was uncommon for a man of his age to be unmarried. His first wife had died in childbirth and his son, Robert, was eleven years old. With no cause to object, I was betrothed.

I wanted to believe Mother when she said we'd have years to get to know one another. I turned down the lamp, pulled up the covers, and sank into a restless sleep.

Chapter Three

"A little detail may be useful in stating some of the work done by Northern Christians for our colored people. Among the chief of the societies at work in the South for the help of the colored people is the 'American Missionary Association.'"

Our Brother in Black: His Freedom and His Future, Atticus G. Haygood, Southern Methodist Publishing House

Jennie and I spent the morning traipsing through Mary's backyard and neighbors' gardens, taking evergreen and holly cuttings for the Flower Mission, one of our cousin's many charitable activities. The oozing stem cuts left my hands sticky and grimy. I missed my sun hat, hanging on a hook back home. The morning tested my patience. I was unaccustomed to wiling away my time with something as trivial as ornamental gardening. By the height of the sun in the sky, it'd be many more hours until we escaped to the public education meeting.

"You girls are such a help." Mary laid the branches in a flat basket held in the crook of her servant's arm. The maid arranged batches of spruce, holly and magnolia stems in water pails hauled from the houses and placed the buckets in crates lining the carriage floor.

We delivered the greenery to Asheville's elderly shut-ins and sickly residents. The boy drove the carriage and jumped down to lift crates out at each of our stops. Past the Eagle Hotel, we veered off on Sycamore and the streetscape changed with shrinking storefronts, unlit roadways, and less permanent exteriors. I wedged my feet between the buckets and leaned my face toward the window to avoid the overpowering scent.

"We don't go into the East End." Mary gestured toward a neighborhood filled with neat wood-frame cottages packed side by side. "That is the colored neighborhood. Hold up, Boy."

The wagon stopped before a small steepled building. A stooped Negro woman swept the stairs leading up to the arched double doors. Another woman with white nubby hair used a corn broom on the dirt path and yard.

"I want to show you the Freedmen's Chapel, in case you think from last night's dinner conversation that I resist the education of the Negroes."

"You don't?" I asked.

Mary pursed her lips. "No, Alice, I don't. I agree with the founders of this chapel. The Martins considered it their duty before God to bring education to the Freedmen and thereby spiritual sustenance. Carry on, Boy!"

Like Stewart, Mary issued her statement, and it was final. *What purpose did Mary's declaration serve? Did she wish to appear progressive? To prove her Christian faith?* She'd drawn her boundary, taking us to the church but not beyond. Before meeting Elizabeth and Margaret, I'd never met a person who supported teaching the Negroes. They'd challenged my thinking.

Mary's arm slackened around the wooden donation box the farther we drove away from the East End. "Place any donations right here. I'll judge whether we ask for a contribution because I know the circumstances of all we visit." The box remained firmly in Mary's lap.

"Of course, Cousin. Alice and I appreciate your guidance. What kindness you offer in service," Jennie said.

When I rolled my eyes at my sister, I expected, and got, her stern look.

Mary patted the box lid. "Oh, but they will be happy to see some fresh faces."

Fresh and young like produce on display at the market.

We made the rounds through Asheville, dispensing the flowers and sacred readings for the less fortunate. Despite a sense of being on display, I enjoyed our afternoon and the obvious gratitude from those we visited.

"The donations are coming in. Won't be long before we have Asheville's first hospital," Mary said. "Modern amenities, educated doctors and nurses, and care for all of Asheville's citizens."

"All the citizens?" I asked.

Mary puffed up with pride. "Yes, Alice, all. Whites and Negroes will be cared for."

Jennie raised her eyebrows and mouthed: Whites <u>AND</u> Negroes.

I pressed my lips together to stifle a laugh.

Following the long day of deliveries and another lavish supper, we excused ourselves and left for Elizabeth's shop. Through the storefront window, we saw her adjusting a dress draped on a mannequin.

"Good evenin'." She tucked her pins in her apron and got off her knees to greet us.

At the back of the shop, where a curtain had been drawn, was a small table and bed.

"My livin' quarters." Elizabeth showed no embarrassment at the frugal space.

"I thought you lived above the store," I said.

Elizabeth shook her head. "Rent's plenty and I don't need much room."

"It's a charming space and you keep it so tidy." Jennie motioned toward the fitting space and front counter.

"It's taken me two years to get here." Elizabeth removed her apron and, once folded, tucked it under the counter. "Started in the mills at fourteen, picked up the means to dye and pattern fabrics. Figured I could leave the twelve-hour days behind and hang my own shingle."

Her candor astonished me. "You make it sound easy."

"Hardly so. I's lucky." Elizabeth rolled a bolt of cloth and slid it into a cubbyhole under the front counter. "Resort needed a dressmaker and inquired at the mill. I went along. Fashioned a spa outfit for a New York woman. It pleased her, and the resort owner called again. Took a liking to me and helped me set up my business." She grabbed a broom and swept up the loose threads on the floor. "'Course, she avoided the commission owed the mill owner that way."

"My goodness, I don't understand what all that means," Jennie said.

"Miss Harris, laws are changin'. Women got more opportunities. Single women got the right to earn a living. Need that same right for married women."

My frown spread like spilt syrup, languid and unstoppable. With no prospect of employment, I had not considered the legal rights I was giving up with marriage. From the look on my sister's face, she hadn't either.

"Expect a few dissenters tonight. Not ever'body favors public education," Elizabeth said.

"Some think educating Negroes will give them ideas of rising above their station," Jennie said.

"'Tis a common view, Miss Harris." Elizabeth contemplated her next words. "I'd remind those people the law says both Whites and Negroes need educatin'. Plenty of need. My only learning was dressmaking. Without it, where would I be?"

Working the mills, I thought, or marrying to survive as my sisters and I were forced to do. Elizabeth Shackton might have little education, but she possessed the smarts and ambition to support herself. I had more formal schooling than this young woman, but she had something to teach me.

"Your mother sounds like quite the force," I said.

"Was. Orphaned at fourteen. Had to make my own way." Elizabeth covered her mouth with her hand. "Speakin' my mind again. Forgive me. Let's get these dresses fitted and be off to the meetin'."

I stepped forward to try on my wedding dress. Elizabeth knelt on the floor, tugging on the hem to check her handiwork. She stood behind me and checked the bodice. I glanced in the standing mirror and saw how the dress highlighted my trim waistline without emphasizing the breadth of my hips. The collar's stitching drew the eye away from my prominent jawline.

"Alice, you look lovely." Jennie breathed out her words.

I did. I'd never considered myself pretty. Practical, hard-working, competent—I knew myself to be, but lovely?

Elizabeth stood on tiptoe to peer over my shoulder. My smile joined hers in the mirror, while my hands smoothed the darting below my breasts and the finished stitching along the waistline. I liked the dressmaker and the more I learned of her, the more I wanted to know.

With the dresses boxed and tied, we had them delivered to the Tate home. Elizabeth pinned her hat in place and donned her gloves before setting off. Along the streets, many greeted Elizabeth as she strode forward at a pace surprising for her small stature. She lifted her skirts to avoid the mud and debris between the planked roads. Jennie and I hurried to keep up.

The lights within the Methodist Church and its open double doors beckoned men and women, White and Negro, into the sanctuary. I counted the pews leading to the altar. I couldn't imagine worshiping in the size crowd this church could hold. Thankfully, far fewer would attend our weddings in our little country church.

"Miss Harrises, please." Elizabeth ushered us toward a front pew. "Be back shortly. They might need me at the pulpit."

The front of the church filled with men and women of plain stock and simple fashions. There were no well-dressed visitors or wealthy citizens in attendance, but then they already had options for schooling their children. With the growing white crowd, the Negro men and women, with children in tow, sat or stood uneasily in the back half of the church.

"Ladies and gentlemen, please take a seat." Elizabeth's voice carried further than expected.

She tensed when handed a slip of paper. Her eyes landed on Margaret, and she thrust the paper toward her, scurrying to join us in the front pew. Elizabeth might not be embarrassed about her living space, but she was ashamed of her inability to read. Margaret stood at the altar and read the introduction for the guest of honor.

A stout woman stepped onto a wooden stool to see across the lectern and address the gathering. The woman's dark auburn hair twisted back to rest above her lace collar. Her skin was fair, like a good gentlewoman, but her cheeks held color, either from the warmth of the crowd or from her nerves of speaking before such a large group.

"Good evening. My name is Mrs. Hannah Dawes, and I have the honor of presiding over this meeting. The president of our Women's Home Missionary Society, former First Lady

Lucy Hayes, sends you her regards and thanks for coming to hear of our important work. Further, I would like to tell you more about the Society and the purpose of our gathering here tonight."

A few latecomers scuffled into the pews.

"No doubt you have noticed from my speech that I don't hail from the South." Mrs. Dawes's mouth drew into a slow, lopsided smile as the crowd chuckled and nodded. "I come from Ohio and that is where this story begins. Some time ago, a woman named Jennie Hartzell chose to make a difference."

I leaned forward. A woman with a choice was a story I wanted to hear. Jennie inched forward on the pew.

"Mrs. Hartzell traveled from Mississippi to Cincinnati to ask our church to send missionaries and teachers to improve the situations of freed men and women. Now the fifty women who met her that day heard of the lamentable conditions of southern Negroes, the widespread poverty and immigration of Whites and Negroes, and they cried 'no!'"

Voices rang out, "Here, here."

Mrs. Dawes lifted both hands face out. "That very day, those good Christian women founded the Women's Home Missionary Society to serve all people, to loosen the chains of ignorance and poverty."

With this crowd of working white people, it was unlikely that any had owned slaves. She was smart, or well-informed, for the reference to loosening chains would not offend Whites and it would bolster those in the back half of the church. I glanced over my shoulder and was surprised to see my cousin's maid nodding along to Mrs. Dawes's words. For a moment, I couldn't place how she looked different. It was her eyes, looking straight ahead, eager and determined. The crowd's applause continued unabated, and it drew my attention back to Mrs. Dawes, who quieted the people with a tamping down of her hands.

"Your fine state recognizes the need for schools. The Legislature has approved a State Board of Education, the opening of common schools for Whites and for Negroes, and the creation of Normal schools to provide teacher education. Yet, they have so far failed to implement the taxation needed to support these efforts."

The crowd rumbled.

"Industry counters that increased taxes will put them at a disadvantage. But I ask you, how will businesses grow and modernize without employees that can read, write, do sums, and reason?"

"True enough," someone shouted.

Cousin Stewart wasn't the only one predicting the need for an educated worker.

"I won't pay any taxes to school no Negroes!" An older woman stood and addressed Mrs. Dawes. The woman glanced toward the back of the church with disdain. Mumbling emerged from the crowd and a few nodded in agreement.

"The Women's Home Missionary Society, working alongside the Freedman's Aid Society, will work to fill the gap by bringing educated teachers to the South."

Mrs. Dawes managed the concern with aplomb, placating those worried about Negro schools by mentioning the Freedmen's Aid Society. She avoided the woman's concern about taxes supporting colored schools. Not only was this Ohio woman an adept speaker, but she was also well-versed in Southern concerns around public education. I had my suspicions about who might have educated her. Elizabeth's head bobbed up and down.

"This is a new beginning. Today I am pleased to introduce our first teacher and missionary for Buncombe County, Miss Margaret Petersen." Margaret, seated on the other side of Elizabeth, rose.

Jennie whispered, "How can one teacher make a

difference? Look at this crowd. They'll need many more teachers."

I shushed her and Jennie elbowed me.

"Our first classroom will be at this very church," Mrs. Dawes continued. "To continue and progress, we must band together to solicit members and donations for the society, to seek land to expand with dedicated schools. We must speak out to our local businesses, our state legislators, Governor Jarvis ..."

Elizabeth jumped to her feet and called out, "Mrs. Dawes, if ya please, the votes have come down against taxation three times. How do you propose we fund schools?"

"Just as Mrs. Hartzell made a difference, so must everyone in this room," Mrs. Dawes responded. "She was one. We are many. All of us must become promoters of the cause."

The warmth of the sanctuary increased with the clapping of hands and stomping of feet. Mrs. Dawes inflamed the people, firing them up for the fight.

"Mrs. Dawes!" Mary's maid stood and raised her hand.

"Yes? May I have your name, please?" Mrs. Dawes squinted at the back row.

"My name is Miss Amanda Jane Smith. I hear your call to promote public education and I stand ready to do just that with the Negroes of Asheville."

A sea of emboldened darkness swelled toward the young woman. Elizabeth rose in her seat and acknowledged Amanda with a wave.

My jaw dropped at the young woman's announcement. Mary's maid spoke, and she spoke well. I hadn't considered whether she could or would. Until now, I hadn't known her name. Jennie elbowed me again. I hastily closed my mouth and turned to the front.

"Education will move this mighty country forward," Mrs. Dawes continued. "Industrialization demands a new worker.

Rapid advancements in farming require knowledge of changing practices. We must not leave any behind!"

The enthusiasm in the church hit me like a hurricane makes landfall, spinning my thoughts and twisting my intentions. I longed to join Mrs. Dawes on the altar. I wished to convince others that education would give boys and girls choices and save them from what awaited me.

"Come together to convince the good people of Buncombe County of the value in uplifting the downtrodden by supporting taxation for public education." Mrs. Dawes yielded the lectern to the next speaker.

Elizabeth eyed the crowd. I suspected the timing of her question had been planned, even coordinated, with Mrs. Dawes. The dressmaker knew how to get her way.

Had Elizabeth invited me here with a purpose? Had she sized me up and concluded I was unhappy with the role I must soon take on? With my former life gone, I yearned for a choice in my future and a purpose. Public education might have come too late for Jennie and me, but it would help others. I'd been led like a good horse to marry. Perhaps it was time for me to lead.

Chapter Four

"The tide of women platform speakers is rising upon us. We turn for relief to Paul's letter to Titus, and read that he was instructed to charge the "aged women" to teach the "young women to be sober, to love their husbands, to love their children, to be discreet, chaste, keepers at home."

The Biblical Recorder

The graded school meeting concluded, but the crowd remained. Many hovered in the church alcoves, speaking in animated tones. Men and women turned to neighbors in the pews to discuss the missionary group's efforts. I stood amongst them, jittering from the energy this mission evoked and my growing sense that I must be a part of it.

"Your counsel made all the difference," Mrs. Dawes said.

"Y'all are too kind," Elizabeth said. "Your words will spur many on. It was just the kick our cause needed."

Margaret stepped forward and aligned herself with

Elizabeth. "Miss Shackton stands at the front of Asheville's public education efforts. She's a true crusader."

Elizabeth and Margaret were unlikely to have ever met, if not for this common cause. Margaret's speech and attire indicated education and wealth. I admired her finely woven wool dress, the evergreen fabric custom tailored. The broad lace collar lay flat across the neckline, complimenting her fair complexion. Southern charm evaded Margaret, but she mastered Northern refinement. She'd likely never thought about her next meal or whether she'd have a roof over her head. From what Elizabeth disclosed earlier, she'd likely worried about both, being an illiterate Southerner and an orphan.

Society judged Elizabeth's uncouth manner, but I didn't. She spoke honestly and plainly. There appeared to be room in this fight for women of any means if one had conviction.

"Mrs. Dawes, may I present Miss Alice Harris and Miss Jennie Harris of Rutherford County." Margaret continued, "The sisters are soon to be wed. They've taken an interest in public education."

"How wonderful. It's the women that will invoke change. Movements are underway to push through the vote for women, and once that happens, they will hear our agenda."

"What agenda is that, Mrs. Dawes?" Jennie asked.

"The agenda of half the people in this country, who currently have no say."

Jennie squared her shoulders. "That is a worthy agenda."

"There are women's associations right here in Asheville working for the women's vote. Perhaps you'll attend one of their meetings?" Mrs. Dawes looked at Jennie, then me.

We both bubbled with enthusiasm. Jennie clasped her hands before her chest, her face bright, her eyes darting amongst these women leaders. I supposed I appeared equally inspired. It took all my efforts to portray a refined, mannerly gentlewoman.

"We will ask our cousin," I said. "She's very involved. Jennie and I worked with her this morning on the Flower Mission. They hope to open Asheville's first hospital."

"Then Asheville will need doctors and nurses. The demand is there. With the growth in sanitariums and health resorts, Asheville has drawn educated medical staff from the North. It's time the South educated their own to meet the people's needs."

She'd left the pulpit, but Mrs. Dawes still preached the cause. Strong words flowed from this short, middle-aged woman like a Southern rain on a rooftop, drenching us in her message. White visitors drew closer to Mrs. Dawes, while the Negroes kept their distance. Margaret waved them up, and a few inched toward us. The Whites pressed forward, eager to maintain the invisible, unwavering barrier.

Asheville didn't have a large Negro population, unlike the eastern part of the state, but they represented almost half of this crowd. Elizabeth said the need was great, and their attendance at the meeting showed it. From the little I'd seen in terms of Asheville's neighborhoods, business owners, and sheer numbers, persuading Whites to approve taxes would be critical to funding schools. Yet, the Negroes had the vote. Mary had said we didn't go into the colored neighborhood. But her maid Amanda lived there and stood ready to help.

Elizabeth cocked her head and clasped her hands behind her back. "Resorts need all kinds of workers. Schools for industrial studies are a start in educatin' Negroes to provide services." Her confidence added inches to her slight frame. Several White bystanders nodded. Elizabeth had bridged the racial divide.

The meeting delegates dispersed, and we wandered out of the church. The streetlights blazed, the gas hissed, and the flames bounced off the glass enclosures. Shops and storefronts were closed, but people spilled out of hotels and others poured in to hear live music, enjoy a meal or drink, or spend the evening. The buzz in Asheville bolstered the hum in my chest.

Only later would I consider that Mrs. Dawes's call to promote public education appealed to me precisely because I controlled so little in my life. I'd run my family's household and lost it. I'd controlled who I ate with, worked with, laughed with, and slept with. Now I faced a lifetime dependent on a stranger.

"The flyers worked. We had a good turnout this evening," Margaret said.

"And Mrs. Dawes spoke eloquently of the need for education." I paused under a streetlight, lingering before we went our separate ways. Jennie stood on the balls of her feet. There was no drifting away tonight, no quiet cloud enveloping her and carrying her off. We'd both been wrapped up in our undoing and were keen to think of anything else.

"When do you start teaching, Miss Petersen?" Jennie asked.

"I already have." Margaret smiled at Elizabeth, her first student. "I will begin with daily classes this coming Monday and I've been working all week to ready my classroom. The reverend kindly helped me acquire furniture through donations and from what the church had on hand. The Society brought supplies from Northern benefactors. I've been planning my lessons, although I must wait and assess the abilities of my pupils before doing much more."

"Miss Alice," Elizabeth said, "your cousin's workin' for Asheville's first hospital. Mrs. Dawes's right, that'll take many skilled workers. Would your cousin help us?"

In addressing me by my given name, Elizabeth not only invited me to join her in the public education cause, but to accept her friendship. It was unusual given our brief acquaintance. She probably didn't know better, given her upbringing, or perhaps it reflected her doggedness.

"I'll find an opportunity to speak with her, Miss Elizabeth." I returned the familiar address. Within the week, I would depart Asheville and arrive at an uncertain future. I'd need a friend.

We said goodnight, and before Jennie and I left for our cousin's home, I watched Elizabeth striding toward her shop in the same way she pursued what she wanted—with purpose.

Chapter Five

"The CITIZEN heartily endorses..., the policy of using the convicts to aid in the construction of [rail]roads in various sections of the State, rather than keep them in the penitentiary at Raleigh to be fed and fattened in idleness at the expense of the taxpayers of the State."

The Asheville Weekly Citizen

Cousin Mary bustled into the breakfast room, with her skirts swishing back and forth and her hands moving constantly through the air. "Girls, take your breakfast, then I will need your help."

Only Mary called us girls, and it rankled me. I'd long been a woman, albeit an unmarried one. And I wasn't used to being at another's beck and call, especially before breakfast.

Jennie took a seat and hastened to butter a biscuit. She fumbled with the knife and almost spread butter on the tablecloth. "Cousin, whatever is the matter?"

"Senator Vance is coming to supper. The Senator!"

Cousin Mary braced one hand on her hip and fanned herself with the other. "Lord o' Mercy!"

"Senator Zebulon Baird Vance is coming? Here?" The thought of meeting North Carolina's favorite politician enthralled me.

Mary's fan stopped midair. "Yes, Alice, here. And why not?"

Jennie shot me her mind-your-words look, which dissolved into a smile at Mary.

I clamped my lips together, then mustered a reasonable answer. "I didn't know he was in Asheville. As a senator, I thought he'd be in Washington."

"He often returns home to the mountains and is lovingly received by the people." Mary's face softened, and I stopped holding my breath. With that crisis averted and the excitement of the Senator's visit, I joined Jennie at the breakfast table and girded myself for Mary's requests.

Jennie gulped her coffee. "Why the sudden invitation?"

Mary moved to the windows and ran a finger along the sash. Her nerves were as catching as a fever. I turned a critical eye to the room and what needed tending.

"Colonel Coleman planned to host Senator Vance. However, Mrs. Coleman is not well, so the task falls to Stewart as his second in command." Mary huffed and her corseted bosom heaved. "Well, if she would have had the good grace to become ill a few days ago, I would not be in such a pickle." She hurried off to the main entry. "Boy! Sweep the steps and the porch!"

Jennie and I were caught up in the preparations throughout the day. I itched to go outside for a walk but remained bound to the kitchen or parlor or dining room or entry—any part of the house the illustrious senator might visit. Mary, Jennie and I talked through the menu, sorted the linens to be used, selected the serving utensils, and determined which needed polishing. Mary wanted our advice on her evening wear, and she assessed and approved our dresses, with the addition of some borrowed jewelry and other accessories. In the afternoon, we escaped the house by offering to shop for the table centerpiece.

"It's early in the year for flowers." I pulled my shawl over my shoulders. Clouds passed over the mid-afternoon sun and the air cooled considerably. We set a brisk pace toward Main Street.

Jennie carried the shopping basket plus the coins Mary had pressed into her palm. "If not flowers, we'll make do with an urn of fruits and magnolia trimmings."

We purchased some golden pears and shiny red apples from a grocer. Jennie swayed her basket to dodge the other shoppers. Afternoon traffic rumbled along the street, with horses tied up steps from storefronts, boxes and shipments lining the road, wagons parked every which way. On our return, we passed Elizabeth's shop.

"Let's stop and say hello," I said.

"Alice, we shouldn't dawdle. Mary will be on a tirade."

"She's rarely not."

Jennie shrugged. "Too true."

I pushed open the shop door. The bell jingled, and Elizabeth glanced up from her work.

"Good mornin', Miss Alice, Miss Jennie. Hope everythin's alright with the dresses?"

Warmth from the corner woodstove and the fragrance of fresh-brewed tea permeated the small shop. It was impeccably tidy, with not a dust mote to be seen in the sunlight streaming through the wide front window. After hours of putting the Tate home in order, I was aware of any disarray. I loosened my shawl in the cozy interior.

"Oh yes, Miss Elizabeth, the dresses are perfect. Jennie and

I came downtown to purchase flowers and thought to stop by," I said.

"You've no flowers." She gestured toward our basket.

"No, and our cousin will not be happy, as she's entertaining an important visitor at supper tonight." Elizabeth did not inquire, so I forged on. "Senator Vance will dine with us."

Elizabeth moved swiftly toward us. "Oh my, that'll be interestin'. Did y'all know Senator Vance supported public education while governor?"

Jennie rested our parcels on the counter. "How so?"

"The Superintendent of Public Instruction came 'bout under his watch." Elizabeth took off her bib apron and rounded the counter. "Might you ask the Senator his opinion on pushin' the movement forward?" Elizabeth's gaze landed on me.

If the meeting invitation had been a furtive appeal to join the cause, here was a direct invitation. I should have been thrilled, but a wave of insecurity washed over me. Elizabeth was the crusader, not me. I intended to help the public education cause by handing out meeting flyers or speaking with Cousin Mary, not in discussion with one of the most powerful men in the state.

Jennie nudged me. "Alice?"

I cleared my throat. "I'll do my best."

The honored guest paraded into the dining room and was none the wiser for the effort behind this supper. Senator Vance and Colonel Coleman circled the table.

"I thank you for hosting supper on such short notice,"

Colonel Coleman said. "It disappointed my wife to not welcome y'all."

Mary batted her eyes. "It is no trouble."

My eyebrows hitched upward while Jennie kept her face placid. Mother often instructed me to hide my temperament. I hadn't mastered that, and there wasn't much hope that I would.

"Senator Vance, please honor us at the head of our table." Stewart guided Mary to the other end.

Jennie had proposed the seating chart with Mary earlier in the day. She maneuvered me to sit to the left of the senator and she took the seat across from me. Jennie nodded ever so slightly.

My sister believed in me. Now I must believe in myself.

I glanced at my target. Senator Vance was handsome, more so as a man of fifty-two than in his earlier years. In his official portrait, some twenty years ago as North Carolina's Governor, his face wore the stress of those war-torn years with his dark, brooding glance and lined brow. His hair, once dark and unruly, was now white, short and tamed, and his mustache much subdued.

The maid served wine, and the boy took each guest's napkin and draped it across their lap.

"What a fine home you have, Mrs. Tate." Senator Vance raised his glass. "When we agreed to meet to discuss the future of the railroad, I'd no idea that I would be in the company of such lovely women."

Jennie had advised me to use my feminine ways, for everyone knew the senator liked women and they adored him. His political rallies attracted just as many women as men. My sister batted her eyelashes, and I mimicked her. I probably looked like I had something in my eye.

"Oh Senator, you are too kind," Mary said. Our commanding cousin had been replaced by an unassuming version of herself. I followed Mary's lead, figuring her experience in Asheville society with men the likes of these had taught her a few things.

The servants hovered at the room's edges after delivering steaming dishes and platters to the table. My stomach grumbled at the sight of roasted pork, rubbed liberally with salt and pepper to form a crispy crust and sliced to perfection. A side dish held chunky applesauce, and I imagined smothering a thick slice of pork with it. But then there was also the tomato catsup, the bottle proudly placed on the table, which I was curious to try. The day's activities had taxed me, and I was eager to eat.

Senator Vance's words called me away from the food. "I'm sorry that my wife did not accompany me. She surely would have enjoyed the female companionship. I understand the two Miss Harrises are soon to be wed?"

"Yes, Jennie will wed G.W. Cannon of Hendersonville and I'll marry Jasper Carter of Democrat." I looked across at Jennie, and she gave me an insistent look. I directed my attention back to Senator Vance and his response.

"Ah, I am familiar with the Carter family. I stay at their inn every time I tour through the mountains. I'm afraid I've worn down John Carter's porch boards with my political ramblings, but then I cannot leave a crowd wanting." Senator Vance sipped his wine. "Jasper is younger than John."

Not exactly young.

"A fine man and a prosperous family." The Senator, who had begun to cut his meat, stopped with his knife and fork suspended in the air. "Did you know his brother John named the town Democrat after his favorite political party? I like to take some credit for that."

"I should think so. Don't you agree, Colonel?" Stewart said.

"Yes, indeed. I concur." Colonel Coleman raised his glass.

It teetered when he lowered it in his rush to return to his supper. His plate was nearly empty. With the way his jacket hung on his shoulders, I wondered if his wife bothered to feed him.

The Senator turned to Jennie. "I've had occasion to visit Mr. Cannon's general mercantile in Hendersonville on my travels. I know a little of his family from before the War, when they sent their livestock on the Drover's Road. My family had a stand in Lapland along the French Broad."

"Our family ran the Harris Inn farther down the road toward the coastal markets," Jennie said. "While our father tended the animals and Mother greeted guests, Alice supervised everything else."

Actually, Father hired the men who tended the animals. Mother approved the menus I proposed, the purchases I made, and the staff I managed. My parents enjoyed being innkeepers, with none of the work involved in making it successful. Of course, I would not divulge that. Jennie bragged on my behalf.

"Of course, the Harris Inn! I heard many Drovers speak of your mother's pies," the senator said.

My pies.

"As a boy, I spoke to all the men driving livestock along the road. The quality of an inn's food determined where many stopped." Senator Vance passed a platter to me. "I dreamed once or twice of joining them just to partake in those pies."

"You would have been most welcome, Senator, although you would have had to fight for a slice with Jennie and me. I must warn you, with three brothers, we learned to tussle." *Oh goodness, why did I say that? As a war veteran, would the senator think I was mocking him?* The room felt awfully warm. I must limit my wine.

The Senator laughed. "I don't doubt it."

Stewart raised an eyebrow. Mary chuckled. Jennie let out her breath. The colonel sought any stray crumb on his plate.

"Colonel Coleman, how does the line progress toward Tennessee?" Mary asked.

Before the colonel could answer, Stewart intervened, "Now Mary, let's enjoy our supper and leave the business discussion to the men afterwards." He raised his glass of wine. "A toast to fine company and fine food. May they always go together."

The maid arrived with freshly filled bowls of mashed potatoes, gravy, and more boiled vegetables. Dusk departed and the room's gas lights put a glow on the wavy glass panes in the floor-to-ceiling windows. Jennie tilted her head toward the senator, signaling it was now or never.

"Senator, while governor, you took steps to further public education. I wonder if you might enlighten us on more recent efforts?" I presented an earnest face, and Jennie posed an inquiring look toward the senator. I'd practiced this line in front of the mirror with Jennie until it rolled off my tongue.

"Alice and Jennie attended the Women's Home Missionary Society meeting last night," Mary offered.

The senator paused before assuming the position of orator, for which he was famous. "You may be aware, as governor I encouraged the legislature to found, and fund, normal schools for both Whites and Negroes. To not all my recommendations, but to this particular one, the General Assembly complied." He paused to use his napkin. "Those institutions have assisted with improving teacher education, which has long been a problem as the lack of standards results in uneven learning." He interlaced his fingers across his rotund form. "More recently, the Superintendent of Public Instruction identified other areas for improvement."

"What might those be, Senator?" I patted the hairline at my neck, drawing attention to my borrowed jewel earring and my long, slender neck. I gave my best impression of a woman in need of instruction. If Mary and Jennie could act a part, so could I.

Senator Vance cleared his throat, rested his arm on the dining table, and leaned toward me. "In the latest report from that office, the superintendent deemed several areas critical. First, teacher pay is too low. This attracts a less qualified individual."

The senator knew he commanded the room. Whether at the head of a table or on stage, he was at ease. "It can also lead to a shortened school term," he said. "The constitutional convention designated a four-month term some fourteen years ago, but currently school averages closer to ten weeks per year."

"Now, that's a shame." Stewart turned to Colonel Coleman and shook his head.

The colonel looked up from his second or third serving and put down his utensils. "Why, indeed it is."

The boy stepped around the table, removing dishes and cutlery from each guest's place. The maid placed dessert plates.

"Second, there is a need to invest in school buildings," the senator said. "Many were destroyed in the War or fell into disrepair. Another need is textbooks, which are in short supply considering the growing number of students."

"The main fix to those issues is funding, is it not?" I asked.

"Miss Harris, you state the matter plainly," Senator Vance said.

"Alice, perhaps the senator would like to sample the pie."

I could not ignore Stewart's hint to leave our estimable guest alone. I squinted and forced a smile at my cousin. Jennie's grip tightened around her dessert fork. Mary opened her mouth to speak, then shut it. I wickedly hoped Stewart might choke on his next bite of pie. Fortunately, Senator Vance helped me.

"It looks delicious." The senator tucked in closer to the table. "Florence, my wife, would advise me to abstain from the pie, but not from the concerns of a constituent." The senator did not pass up dessert or discussion. He took a healthy bite. "Mrs. Tate, I commend you. This is a most delicious pie."

He turned his corpulent form to face me. "Miss Harris, the people of North Carolina have wanted, and needed, public education since well before the War. The creation of the Literary Fund back in 1825 is evidence of that." He hesitated to let that sink in, or maybe to keep us anticipating his next nugget of information. "As to current funding efforts, Governor Jarvis raised taxes last year to support public education. In addition, there is a poll tax. Under the law, if that sum proves insufficient, then a county may impose a special-levy tax."

"Taxes posed to the voters have been unpopular," Stewart said.

I wanted to gag Stewart with my napkin. He'd said he supported education, but it appeared not at his own expense. My brow must have furrowed, because Jennie kicked me under the table.

Colonel Coleman, whose dessert plate showed not a speck of pie filling or crust, interjected, "Yet, taxes on industry are even more objectionable. I, for one, want the taxes kept low on the railroads. We face extraordinary costs in extending the line through the mountains. Just last week we had a mudslide fill a gulch with twice the infill we'd cleared. That's manpower and money."

The senator placed his hands wide on the table and extinguished the men's misgivings like water dousing a fire—suddenly and emphatically. "The legislature will fill the labor need with convicts. That's been a promise the general assembly has continued to deliver on."

Colonel Coleman nodded and tugged the lapels of his ill-fitted jacket. For a man in such a prominent position, he really needed a better tailor.

"Gentlemen, the purpose of this pleasant gathering was to address railroad funding. I suggest we excuse ourselves from the ladies and retire to the library for that discussion." Stewart pushed his chair back and stood. "My dear, thank you for a lovely supper. My dear cousins, good evening."

All rose at the summons to leave the table. Senator Vance stood hastily and pulled back my chair. "Miss Harris, I have enjoyed the pleasure of your company. I hope we meet again, at which time I suspect I'll hear more about the state of public education here in Buncombe County." The senator kissed my hand. "In fact, with your obvious interest in the issue, it would not surprise me if you were educating me on how we advance the cause." He followed the men from the room.

My heartbeat drummed, and I wondered if Mary and Jennie could hear it. My cousins provided the venue, but I'd commanded the attention of the great Senator Vance.

Jennie grasped my arm. "Well done, Alice. You've just held your first debate on public education."

I tittered and covered my mouth. "I did, didn't I?"

Mary instructed the boy in the main hallway before leading us to the front porch. I shivered with the abrupt change from the warmth of the dining room to the cool darkness outside.

"My dears, let's sit and enjoy the silence of this evening."

This was a strange request. Mary had more than most to say.

She ushered us to one small loveseat against the house wall. The lantern remained unlit, and we huddled near one another on the dim porch. As much as I liked my sister and cousin, I preferred my own seat, and there were several comfortable wicker chairs and sofas available. Our strategic position became apparent when a small brown hand opened the library window facing the veranda.

"Gentlemen, a drink?" Stewart's voice reached us. His polite tone hardened in the company of men.

Mary smiled in satisfaction, closed her eyes, and leaned back in her seat.

"Let us come to the issue at hand." I recognized the cadence of Colonel Coleman's speech. "We cannot meet the schedule to extend the rail to Tennessee without further investment. Between slides, rain-soaked earth, steep grades and tunneling through solid rock, the progress has been slow."

The library's light filtered onto the porch floorboards, broken only by the movement of the men inside. The senator's enormous shadow momentarily blocked the light.

"The state has infused massive investment into this line," Senator Vance said. "May I remind you, five hundred convicts eased your labor issue. Gentlemen, the work must continue. Getting their crops to market is crucial to the livelihoods of the mountain people."

The men stopped to light their pipes and fragrant smoke floated through the open window. I was eager for their talk to resume and so was Jennie; she leaned forward on the wicker loveseat.

"I agree, Senator," Stewart said. "The convict crews have helped, but we've seen severe losses through construction. In completing the Swannanoa Tunnel, we lost one hundred and twenty-five lives. Plus, it required nine miles of track for the three-and-a-half-mile ascent. With the added cost of steel rails and nitroglycerine charges, we're tapped out."

I whispered, "One hundred—"

Mary put a finger to her lips and edged closer to the window. Gone was the naïve, accommodating Mary. Here was a better version, commanding and manipulative.

"Damn that Swepson and Littlefield!" the senator's lilting voice boomed.

Jennie and I gave Mary questioning looks.

Mary whispered, "While Vance was governor, they embezzled four million dollars in state bonds and fled the region, halting rail construction."

Mary knew about more than Asheville's charitable activities. This was the most fun I'd had in days. The three of us leaned into our act of espionage.

"I have spoken with Governor Jarvis about the need for additional laborers," Senator Vance said. "He assures me the legislature will direct local jurisdictions to round up the convicts required to complete the rail line. However, the state cannot muster the funds needed."

Someone inside set a glass down forcefully.

"Then we shall fail," Stewart insisted.

"Not if I can help it." The senator's shadow blocked the light, and Mary leaned away from the window to conceal herself. "I have proposed a sale of the state's ownership to William J. Best. He's agreed to our terms, which include continuing the line. Once we reach Tennessee, gentlemen, the mountains and markets will be bridged."

"That is good news," Colonel Coleman exclaimed. "When can we expect the sale to be completed?"

Mary sighed and collapsed against the loveseat's back. "Stewart's work is secure, as is our life in Asheville."

My measure of Mary had changed. I knew her to be generous, spending her time with ladies' organizations to better Asheville. She was loving and kind to Jennie and me. Tonight showed Mary's shrewdness as she finessed her husband's business and social connections. She'd presented an unassuming face to powerful men and discovered exactly what she wanted to know. What surprised me most was my false presumption of her security.

I'd been oblivious to the anxiety Mary carried and rued my self-absorption. Two days ago, I arrived in Asheville, bitter and disappointed in my lot. It was time to dispense with self-pity. After all, I'd met Elizabeth, who plotted her own course forward from an unfortunate position; Margaret, who moved miles away from home and family to pursue a cause; and Mary, who despite many visible advantages, was vulnerable, and strove to secure her position and better others' fortunes. These women pushed forward, like Asheville itself. Perhaps I was being shown a way forward.

Footsteps scuffled across the hardwood floors inside. "With the divestiture of the state government from the railroad," Senator Vance said, "additional monies can fuel the expansion of public education in the state, a need Miss Harris clearly illuminated at dinner tonight."

Both Jennie and Mary clasped my hands. Were it not for our secretive guise, I think we might have jumped up to dance. I couldn't wait to tell Elizabeth.

Chapter Six
Rutherford County, North Carolina, 1882

"Trustworthy information reaches the Observer that responsible capitalists in New York City propose to take the Western North Carolina Railroad off the hands of the State."

The News and Observer

Jennie and I returned to the farm, where the dingy white farmhouse appeared small and temporary compared to the city's manufactured brick buildings. Opportunity wore a shiny fresh coat in Asheville, the land of the sky.

Our mother clutched a porch column and steadied herself on the sloped floor that shed our heavy Southern rainfall away from the foundation. A hired man scraped the railing's peeling paint. Until now, keeping the house in good repair had fallen by the wayside. Our mother's pride opened her meager purse in putting on a show for the wedding.

I'd often wished Mother were more capable. She threw herself into the tasks she enjoyed, such as extending hospitality to guests, socializing with neighbors, or spending leisure hours with the family, while she neglected the day-to-day running of a household. My grandmother called her frivolous—said our mother displayed no sense in accepting a match with our father, that she spent her days in a purposeless, carefree manner. Easy to say after my father lost everything. I didn't remind Grandmother Gilkey that she had given permission for the marriage.

While they were lackadaisical in earning our keep and absent in parenting, Mother and Father doted on one another. In their thirty-two years of marriage, my parents had endured hardship and experienced great joys, and through it all, they had loved each other. If only I could be so lucky. I lumbered forward and kissed my mother's cheek.

"Oh, I'm pleased to see you." Mother embraced us. "Come right on in. I've supper ready and I'll tell y'all of the wedding preparations."

Jennie rolled her eyes at me. Our mother couldn't get rid of us fast enough.

On the morning of our wedding, the air was brisk and dew clung to the grass. Mother drove the wagon and urged the horses toward the church. Jennie and I sat rigidly on the spring seat, wrapped in our new finery, our hair coiled, curled and pinned. We'd hardly uttered a word as we readied for the ceremony, and the silence stretched on. I stared down the one-lane dirt road and let the bird calls and frogs croaking drown out my mother's incessant banter.

The wagon struck a bump and startled us. "Mother, slow down!" Jennie's words echoed my thoughts.

I'd give anything to turn around and go home. Better yet, to go back in time, when our toughest decision was who'd set the table or clean the floors, not who would provide for us, ensuring we had enough to eat and a roof over our heads.

The answer to that question had been found for our sister Ina. She couldn't attend our wedding, now that she'd settled in South Carolina with her husband. Louise, for whom Mother still sought a groom, and our much younger brothers, Ralph and John, rode with us. Mother babbled away over the arrangements at the house.

"I hope we have enough side dishes." Mother turned to Jennie. "The daffodils and crocus came early this year. Their blooms make for a beautiful wedding scene."

Jennie ignored Mother's happy sentiments. I held my tongue.

"Who cares about the sides? I want cake," Ralph said.

Fourteen years old and full of opinions. My husband's son, Robert, was just three years younger. I shuddered. Although I'd mothered my brothers, I felt unprepared to raise a boy I'd never met.

"How long do we have to stay at church?" John tugged at his collar. I reached over and smoothed my youngest brother's shirt front.

Everyone was in a hurry to reach the chapel, except Jennie and me. I held my sister's hand, limp and damp as wet laundry on the line. In the churchyard, John managed the wagon and horses while we headed to the chapel. I put one foot in front of the other. I'd agreed to this. There was no other option. Family and friends smiled and welcomed us. I let none of them witness my reluctance. In an hour, it would be over.

The church I'd visited all my life brought some comfort. Its stout brick walls and squat design spoke to its steadfastness. The steep shingle roof didn't have a steeple, and I liked it that way. This house of God was a house first, welcoming rather than imposing. Passersby recognized it as a church by its entry; the white door and a painted wood panel above it formed the vertical beam of the Cross, while panels to the door's left and right represented the cross timber. Until now, I'd attended church cognizant of my Savior's life offered for my salvation. Today I entered thinking only of my own sacrifice.

Windows lined the side walls, so until I crossed the threshold, I didn't know how many people already filled the pews. Our neighbors had turned up early to adorn the altar—as I had done for others. Evergreen boughs tied with white ribbons perfumed the sanctuary and the glass panes glimmered as the sun climbed above the wooded hills to penetrate and warm the interior. Mother led Jennie and me to the altar, and our grooms.

Did Jennie's heart beat as fast as my own?

Mr. Cannon placed my sister's hand in the crook of his arm, and she shrank in size next to her burly groom. No doubt he could swing an ax with those broad shoulders. His suit barely buttoned over his belly. I gave him credit for attempting to comb down his curly silvered beard that spread beyond his collar and as wide as his ears.

"Please be seated." The minister's booming voice ordered anyone left standing to find space on a pew. "From Genesis 2:18, 'And the LORD God said, It is not good that the man should be alone; I will make him a help meet for him.'"

They would reduce me to a helpmate. My knees almost buckled. Despite the breeze wafting through the open windows, perspiration trickled down my back. I focused on the top of the minister's forehead, unable to face his eyes, unwilling to watch his words tumble out. I'd heard these words countless times for others and never considered the ramifications.

Jasper reached for me with his warm, dry hand, rough from his labor. While he spoke his vows, I searched his dark blue eyes for hints of the type of man to whom I'd be bound.

"Alice Harris, the Bible tells us 'Wives, submit yourselves unto your own husbands.'"

My thumping pulse drowned out my pledges. Jasper slid the gold band on my finger, a symbol of his ownership like a brand on cattle. The ring was tight, heavy, and unwanted. I stared at my trembling hand. Jasper clutched it and offered a fleeting smile before turning back to the minister.

"What God hath joined together, let no man put asunder!"

Our separate lives began when we left the church, I was on Jasper's arm and Jennie on G.W. Cannon's. After the wedding party, we would depart for our new homes. *When would I walk arm in arm with my sister again?* Even with the crowd of neighbors and family, I felt desperately alone. A tear rolled down my cheek, and I forced a smile, hoping friends would interpret this show of emotion as one of joy. Jasper helped me up onto the wagon's bench seat.

Jasper introduced our driver and his companion. "My brother, Zimri, and his wife Susannah."

"Good afternoon, Mrs. Carter." Zimri tipped his hat. He shook the reins and moved the horses along.

I stifled a sob. In the course of an hour, I'd given up my sister, my family, my name. No one voiced concern or noticed my distress. Either I was a wonderful actress, or they preferred not to see it. Oh, I longed for Jennie, for someone to hold on to other than this stranger beside me. My husband.

Jasper's son sat next to his uncle and aunt. He shifted around. "Good Mornin', I don't rightly know what to call you."

"How about Alice?"

"Yes, Ma'am, I mean, Alice." Robert faced forward and the matter was settled.

I was a stepmother, but I wasn't ready to be called 'Mother.' Besides, if I perceived little of Jasper, I understood even less of Robert. He was tall for eleven and coming up on his formative years. He'd soon have a tremendous appetite and shoot up and out, as Ralph and John had both done in the last two years.

It was a short drive from church to our farm and the caravan of wedding guests rumbled down the familiar road, worn smooth over years of use. I considered the mountain laurel nestled in the wooded areas, and the blooming white stalks of black cohosh pointing us toward my childhood home. A sleek falcon soared above us on the lookout for his next meal. Some things didn't change.

The house appeared inviting, with the fresh porch paint and the wildflower carpet rolled out to welcome guests. Wagons parked side by side and people gathered in the yard, bringing dishes of vegetables, salads and other family specialties to share. Warm biscuits and butter made my mouth water. I'd been unable to eat this morning.

We heard the fiddlers' tune before we saw them. This party would be the last celebration in the only home any of the Harris children had ever known. Mother would move with the boys and Louise to Chimney Rock, where she would be the new postmistress. My mother's family name, Gilkey, still carried weight in this county, allowing Mother the position. The two rooms above the post office would be tight quarters for Mother, my brothers and Louise until my sister married. The Harris home would stand empty of people and possessions. Once an inn, then a farm, and soon a shabby house on a barren field.

I turned away from our undoing to face my future. We stood before the porch steps, welcoming our guests and directing them to the side yard, where wooden benches and chairs encircled an open grassy area. Our neighbors, dressed in their finest attire, took advantage of these leisure hours. The Cannon family had come the day before to bring the pig and build the roasting pit. I thought I might faint from hunger as the men pulled the pork. The rich savory smell hung in the air like Spanish moss draped on a live oak tree.

Mother mingled in the crowd and grinned as if spring arriving early in the mountains had been her doing and all a part of her planned decorations. Or perhaps, Mother celebrated three daughters down and one to go.

A round-faced, red-haired young woman curtsied. "My very best wishes."

"Cousin, may I present my intended, Miss Frances Whitson."

In the rush of my marriage, I'd quite forgotten that my cousin, James Gilkey, had become engaged. I introduced Jasper.

Jasper pumped James's hand. "My congratulations. I hope you'll both be very happy."

His hearty well wishes and the way his beard lifted when he smiled caused me to relax. Jasper glanced at me and his eyes crinkled with yet another smile. I returned the smile and bowed my head, unfamiliar with the sensations he aroused in me.

Carter family members crowded the receiving line. John, Jasper's eldest brother, and his wife Caroline arrived with their children and grandchildren.

"Welcome to the family." Caroline took my hands in hers. "Every Sunday afternoon we gather at our home for supper. I look forward to visiting with you then."

A smartly dressed, dark-haired woman lingered as Caroline moved on.

"Alice, I'd like you to meet John and Caroline's daughter, Harriet, and her children, Rollelia, William, John Edward, and Cornelia." Jasper cupped the toddler's chin, and Cornelia batted his hand away.

Harriet leaned forward. "His favorite niece."

Jasper laughed. "Aye, not too loudly now. I don't rightly know how many other nieces I have here today, but I suspect they might take offense."

Harriett bounced the baby on her hip and shooed her other children on with her parents. She gave me a quick wink. "Don't let him tell you any different, I'm responsible for your match." Harriet cast her eyes down and muttered, "We, however, will not boast beyond measure."

Harriet's pious gesture surprised me. Of course, I was familiar with the verse from 2 Corinthians. I'd recited it often enough.

"I hope it will be a happy union." Harriet hurried off after her little ones.

I turned to question Jasper. Before he could answer, the receiving line swelled with the McCalls, the Lees, and Mrs. Jackson. I relaxed and enjoyed the family, friends and acquaintances in attendance until Mary Ellen Cooper approached with her husband and two small children in tow.

"Miss Alice, did you ever envision this day? And to such a mature gentleman?" The men exchanged pleasantries. "When you were my Sunday School teacher, I said to the others, 'Miss Alice is made for the teaching life, you'll see.'" Her mouth smiled, but her eyes did not. She rounded up her babies and led them away.

I'd never liked Mary Ellen, a know-it-all from her earliest days. My lips curled, remembering the smug little girl leading a pack of followers, whispering behind my back, and issuing insincere smiles when caught in the act. I wouldn't be sorry to leave Mary Ellen behind.

At fifteen years old, I'd started teaching Sunday school, and I counted several amongst the wedding attendees as former pupils, including a few of Jasper's nieces and nephews, the ones who lived closer to Chimney Rock than to the larger Carter family contingent in Democrat. That gave me a head start on learning the names of Jasper's many siblings, their spouses, children, and grandchildren. Most of Jasper's family attended the Methodist church in Democrat, although our churches were on the circuit, served by the same saddlebag minister.

The receiving line drew to a close, and Jasper and I joined the guests on the lawn. Smiles surrounded us, and a few men applauded. The jaunty music slowed to a waltz and Jasper led me to the cleared area. Extending his hand was invitation enough, but Jasper added, "My wife, will you dance with me?" as if I had any choice in the matter. His arm went about my waist, and I cringed at the thought of what touches awaited me tonight.

"I shall care for you, Alice," Jasper said, stating the very reason for this marriage. I would have a home. Everything else that defined my life fell away and what remained of me, I would soon find out. I looked into his eyes, nodded, and edged closer.

Chapter Seven
Democrat, North Carolina, 1882

"MARRIED..., On the 16th inst., by Rev. G. W. Ivey, Mr. G. W. Cannon, of Henderson, to Miss I. Jennie Harris. By the same, Mr. J. S. Carter, of Buncombe, to Miss S. Alice Harris.

Our young friend, J. H. Gilkey, attended the ceremonies, in order, as he says, to nerve himself for the trying ordeal which he hopes soon to undertake on his own account—provided, 'don't you understand.'"

The Rutherford Banner

We chatted on the late afternoon drive to Democrat, in a wagon train of Carter families headed home after the wedding. Jasper distracted me from the tearful goodbye with my family by telling tales about our guests, and some about himself. I dried my face and listened to his boyhood pranks.

"Remember when Jasper tried to roll the cow?" his brother Samuel yelled forward.

"Aye, now, don't be revealing my secrets," Jasper called back.

"Pa was hopping mad!" Zimri said.

Jasper chuckled. "Until he wasn't! Fell over laughing at my stupidity."

I welcomed the stories, even if they reminded me how little we knew of one another. We'd lived in distant towns and attended different churches. He'd grown up before the War. I was a child when he was a soldier. I shifted on the wagon bench, trying to find a comfortable position. Jasper had a sense of humor. We both came from large farming families. We'd both known loss—Jasper with his first wife, while I'd lost my father and brother. Surely I'd discover more commonalities in the days to come and hopefully few differences.

The hours-long drive seemed impossibly short when we waved goodbye to John and Caroline, their daughter Harriet and her children, Zimri and Susannah, and the other Carter families. Jasper and I remained frozen on the front porch. The sounds of the wagons grew fainter, and the night edged in, silent, cool and endless.

"Might I?" He hoisted me in his arms and we crossed the threshold. I wondered if my much older husband should attempt such a feat.

Once inside the house, the enclosed space stifled conversation. I loosened my arms around his neck. He put me down, fetched my case from the porch, and lit a lamp. The oiled wick glowed like a firefly. With the glass chimney in place, the light diffused, but didn't reach the corners of the large living area. He handed me the lamp and moved through the darkness with ease to add wood to the kitchen stove. My reflection shone in the window, soft and shimmering. I lifted the light, and an upholstered chair appeared alongside a shelf holding several stacked books. We had reading in common. I released the breath I'd been holding.

"I'll bring in the rest of your things and see to the horses," Jasper said.

In his absence, I explored my new home, starting with the living room with its broad fieldstone fireplace. I stoked the embers and added a log from the hearth. The fire crackled and sputtered, shooting light upward as the flame caught the dry, red bark. A good supply of cherry logs and branches stacked nearby promised fruit trees on the property. With winter not yet behind us, the house would need a fire overnight. I imagined sitting before the hearth on the sofa's low-slung seat, stretching my legs out toward the flame. I fingered a newspaper and a book lying on the table, finding it a cozy spot for winter evenings spent inside. The table lacked any decorative cover, but then I'd expected as much from a widower.

I walked through the living area to the kitchen at the back of the home, where a simple square table and four ladder-back chairs stood. Two side-by-side windows over the sink promised a view of the farm, although tonight they mirrored my sober face.

By the looks of it, the wood stove was a recent addition, as cooking pots hung from the fireplace's arms and hooks. *Had Jasper purchased this modern convenience with me in mind?* I drew my finger along the edge of its warmth. Perhaps my husband wanted to impress me. The idea of sharing this nervousness lessened mine.

Drifting back to the front door, the hallway's polished wooden floors shone in the lamplight. I wondered who had prepared the house for my arrival. Come warmer weather, propping open the hallway's top window would let nighttime breezes travel through the home, cooling the hall and the rooms off it.

I peeked into the first room on the left and came upon a roll-top desk and chair—Jasper's office to handle the farm's affairs. The second door revealed Robert's room with its single bed and a bookshelf lined with primers and books. Thankfully, my stepson stayed with John and Caroline tonight. One room remained. My feet padded across the planked floor to the last open door. A colorful quilt dressed the wrought-iron bed and its log cabin design showed off shades of blue, purple, white, and green. I touched the dainty stitches and snooped around the unfamiliar room in which I would sleep the rest of my nights and wake for the rest of my days.

"The privy's out back." Jasper stood in the doorway, blocking any escape. "I brought in your case but left your other things in the front room." He filled the water basin on the dresser. "Is that a banjo I carried in?"

I nodded. I couldn't play my banjo as fast as my heart pounded.

"Be nice to have music in the house." Jasper shifted from one foot to the other. He folded a small towel and tucked it alongside the basin. "I'm up early to see to the milking. I'll have a pipe on the porch and let you settle."

Alone in our bedroom, in the house I would live in until death do us part, my breathing quickened. I unlatched my case with shaking hands and unpacked a nightgown. I folded and sorted my belongings into two empty drawers until I could no longer delay.

The soft cloth and icy water felt heavenly against my flushed skin. Washed and wrapped in my familiar gown, I drew back the quilt and climbed into bed. At the sound of Jasper's footsteps in the hallway, I closed my eyes and prayed for courage. I smelled his sweet tobacco before I saw him in the doorway.

Jasper drew off his shirt and pants and arranged them across the chair. The male figure without clothing was not a mystery to me. I'd raised younger brothers, diapering them in their first days, dressing them as they grew, and mending all manner of scratch and cut. I knew the various parts of the male physique—I just didn't understand how it all worked. I'd witnessed farm animals together. *It couldn't be like that?* I'd never dared ask Mother about marital relations. When my courses began, Mother warned me to preserve myself. When I'd asked how to do that, she told me to keep my skirts down. I'd pieced together a little more by listening to hushed conversations and overhearing disturbing noises through the walls of my parents' bedroom. I wondered if Jennie lay with the same fears this evening.

At the dresser, Jasper washed his face, hands, and forearms. No doubt he'd bathed this morning as I had. With just his union suit on, I glimpsed his gray, curly chest hair. His arms were sinewy from labor and his shoulders strong, but sunken with age. His stomach rounded against the front buttons, but not as much as Mr. Cannon's. I said a silent prayer for Jennie.

Jasper climbed into bed and pulled me to him. The bed creaked and groaned with the movement, falling silent as he wrapped his arms about me. "Have you been told what to expect?"

I shook my head, unable to answer or to meet his gaze.

Jasper lifted my chin and looked into my eyes. "It can hurt at first. I'll take my time."

My husband turned down the lamp, and we were blinded to any shy grimaces, nervous twitches, or embarrassed glances. In the dark and quiet, I focused on the unexpected gentleness of his touch.

Jasper's lips met mine, and he paused when they quivered. I pressed mine together, willing myself to reach forward and touch my lips to his own. His palm curved around my face and sensuous kisses fell across my mouth, neck, collarbone and elsewhere. With his tender caresses, my body softened. My husband took his time exploring the length of my body, discovering its hidden places. In the light of day, I was large and cumbersome. Tonight I became light and shadow. A flooding warmth replaced the earlier heat I'd experienced. No one had told me what to expect and yet I knew what to do.

Chapter Eight

"A Table of the Altitudes of Western North Carolina Mountains That Everybody Will Want.

VALLEY OF THE BIG IVEY CREEK.

Dillingham's house below Yeate's Knob, or Big Butte... 2,568

Junction of the three forks..2,276

Solomon Carter's house..2,215"

Asheville Citizen-Times

Roosters crowed in the yard and sunlight streamed through the window near the bedroom ceiling. Jasper's half of the bed lay empty and in disarray. I brushed my fingers across my lips, remembering my husband's touch. My skin felt increasingly warm as I recalled the night's lingering caresses, heavy breaths, and passionate embraces. I covered my face with both hands. I'd feared this and I'd been so wrong.

I dressed, straightened the bed linen, and hurried to the kitchen to unpack the few parcels Mother had sent from home: a jar of strawberry jam, a fresh loaf of bread, and a modest bag of coffee. The measly contribution reminded me of how little I brought to this marriage.

I fastened my apron and fingered Jennie's decorative stitching along the bottom edge. *Where had she wandered to find the Dutchman's Breeches in this design?* Her tiny stitches created dainty shapes and the green background highlighted the white blooms. I smoothed the apron skirt and hoped that Jennie fared well this morning.

With no time to brood over Jennie's absence, I welcomed the tasks before me. I'd had weeks of anxiety and melancholy around leaving one home behind and awaiting a new, unknown one. Today I would return to what I did best, running a household. I'd inspect the stores, garden, and outbuildings plus make a schedule for my chores. A slim kitchen door opened to a pantry, put up with jars of vegetables and dried fruits, a barrel of flour, cornmeal and syrup, a bag of coffee, and other necessities. An abundance of dried brown apple rings strung up by the door smelled faintly sweet, and the roasted coffee beans emitted a rich aroma. A second door revealed the cool air of a springhouse. The clear, gurgling water kept two forms of butter on the shelves, cold and firm. Later, I'd look for a smokehouse to assess the meat supply. Either a cellar or an outdoor pit held the root vegetables. I'd ask Jasper about that. The convenience of a springhouse, the orderly pantry, and the clean, bright kitchen pleased me.

Closing my eyes, I paused at the window and let the sun's first rays strike my face. I listened to the farm waking up—the hens clucking in the yard, hogs grunting, and a barn door knocking shut. My new home offered pleasant surprises, including last night's. My thoughts drifted to the tenderness Jasper had shown me and the unexpected sensations he aroused.

With coffee brewing on the stove, I sliced thick wedges of bread and stacked them beside the jam and cutlery on the kitchen table. Jasper came through the back door carrying a jar of strained milk. While he stashed the milk in the springhouse, I fumbled with the coffee mugs.

"Is that strawberry jam?" Jasper tucked himself into the table and slathered on a layer. "Why, that is mighty fine."

I placed a coffee before Jasper and sat down to break bread with my husband. My face was warm, and I suspected its color matched the jam.

"After breakfast, we might tour the farm. Get you acquainted with the place."

We walked out to the plowed fields with their dark, rich earth stretching in every direction, like an ebony picture framed to the west by Sugar Creek, to the north by Big Ivy Creek, and by tree-lined hillsides all around. Beech, yellow birch, and chestnut trees rose tall and thick on the foothills of the Blue Ridge mountains, grappling with the dominant white pines. Grasses and vines flourished under the tree canopy. If Jennie were here, she'd name all the flowers, bushes, and trees. The familiar flora and fauna comforted me. I was not terribly far from my old home. The state of this farm, with its well-groomed fields and tended outbuildings, was a welcome change from the one I'd left behind. We strolled to the northern property line and worked our way back toward the house.

"The corner of our farm is at the junction of the two creeks," Jasper said. "Zimri farms the fields across Big Ivy." He turned and pointed to the fruit trees lined up in three rows along Sugar Creek. "We got peach, apple and cherry trees in the orchard. Should bloom in another five or six weeks. Aye, it's been a mild winter, so maybe sooner."

My skirts grew heavy, soaking up dew off the deep orchard grass. Jasper glanced at my hemline's spreading dampness. He reached for me. I slipped my hand into his and our eyes lingered on one another, matching sight with the touches and sounds of last night. My mouth watered, and a strange form of hunger overtook me. Jasper was the first to look away.

"I'll bring the scythe out and mow this week," Jasper said.

I held on to my husband, picked up my hem, and brushed through the tall, wet grass.

The unbroken golden field covered a small amount of the fertile valley. The winter wheat spikes would tawny up closer to cutting, losing their brilliant yellow cast. With no breeze this morning, the shafts stood sharp, tall, unbending.

"Zimri and I'll harvest our wheat before the end of the month. Robert helps me tie the bundles and set them to shocks." Jasper clasped my elbow and assisted me over an uneven patch of ground. "Before they're dried, I'll get to John's store to leave word for the threshing man to come by. Our acres should yield a decent crop."

The lines on Jasper's forehead softened when talking about the land. His gait grew steady and slow while drinking up the views of all he'd accomplished. He was proud of this productive, well-kept farm with its pruned orchard trees, mended fences, and weeded fields. Here was the 'careful' farmer I'd married.

"With the crop threshed and dried, I'll clean the bedding, putting fresh straw in the ticks," I said.

Jasper nodded and touched the seed heads. "Kernels are full. We'll get a good supply of flour at the mill."

The Carter family owning the grist mill worked to our advantage. *How else did our farm fit within the larger Carter lands and businesses?* A hundred questions begged to be asked, but our leisurely wandering placated me. There'd be time for inquiries later.

We walked on, past withered corn stalks. "Short on rain when we needed it," Jasper said. "A sad corn return last year, but you should have enough cornmeal for cooking. I'll burn the field and plow it under before planting this year's corn."

"You're well provided for here," I said.

"Aye, we are."

We. This was ours. I was safe and secure. So far, all signs pointed toward a hopeful, happy home.

"Seventy-five acres," Jasper continued. "Most of it is woodland for grazing and fuel. In this patch, I'll plant cane in June. Neighbor over yonder makes syrup." Jasper threw me a sheepish look. "Robert and I both have a sweet tooth."

With his admission, I noticed the same squint of the eye and shrug his son had given me after the wedding. "There's a jar of syrup and dried apples in the pantry. Would a flat apple pie after supper please you?"

"That it would." Jasper smiled and fell into step beside me.

This is how it would work—we would lob each other nuggets of information, catch them, and throw another back. Over time, we would get to know one another and, I hoped, grow fond of one another.

We neared the backside of the barn where a corral contained a cream-colored horse, whinnying and jostling at our approach. Two shaggy gray mules stood docile and uncaring that a new person walked the grounds. Hens wandered in and out under the fence, pecking for their breakfast, with mothers guarding their chicks from the mule's clumsy hooves. Jasper steered me toward a paling fence that surrounded a kitchen garden.

"Harriet started the garden for us with peas, lettuce and cool crops. You'll be wanting to plant the summer vegetables you're partial to," he said.

"And what you and Robert like. I'll thank Harriet when I see her next." Hearing her name reminded me of his niece's boast. "How is she responsible for our union?"

Jasper hunched his shoulders and shoved his hands in his overall pockets. "Harriet's been a help to us since her husband passed two years ago. She came to the house every day. I'd say her children and Robert are more siblings than cousins." Jasper slowed his stride, and his eyebrows lowered. "The work helped with her grief. When she'd come to the other side of it, she told me it was time I did the same."

I wasn't used to my husband's rambling answers, giving me more than I'd asked for.

"She's very young. How did her husband die?" I asked.

"She was only eighteen when my brother invited John Swain to the inn. John and I served alongside him in the War and though I don't rightly know how, Swain found God in the midst of battle." Jasper gripped the fence top. "After the War, Swain started circuit riding. He always had a commanding voice, but I suppose it was the preaching during his inn stays that turned Harriet's heart. She joined him, preaching and visiting the people in communities, including your own."

"Of course," I said. "I remember Reverend Swain coming to the house." Mother took a liking to the well-dressed, devout man. With his smooth, pale-skinned face, she said he had a natural clerical countenance.

"Aye, Harriet kept up with the traveling ministers after Swain died and heard of your family's losses—when your father, and then your brother, passed." Jasper cleared his throat. "Harriet corresponded with your mother and first told me about you."

What had my mother said about me? Why had she chosen to write Jasper about me rather than Jennie? As much as I wanted answers, Jasper wasn't the one to give them.

"And Harriet's husband, how did he die?"

"Aye, right ... once the children came, Harriet stayed behind with her parents at the inn. She wrote letters for Swain to carry to the families along his route and she looked forward to his return every couple weeks until he didn't come home."

I waited while Jasper rubbed his beard and found his

words.

"Probably a snake but could have been a wildcat. Something startled his horse, and it kicked Swain off. Folks found the empty-saddled horse grazing alongside the road and his body in the brush. Neck broken."

"Oh, dear."

"Harriet's faith sustained her."

Jasper emphasized *her*, and I wondered if he envied his scripture-quoting niece.

"Swain swayed me to a deeper faith. I gave my son his name—Robert Swain Carter, in thanks for that gift. Then when Robert's mother died ... well, I lost faith for a time."

I didn't judge Jasper for his crisis in faith. I'd had a few angry words with God after Father and Leander died. Jasper's story revealed I wasn't replacing his first wife. I was taking the place of a favorite niece, one with strong faith, ready playmates for Robert, and a record of managing this home. My brows knit together. The sun warmed the dew, lifting it and creating a hazy mist along the ground. I kicked out my skirts, hoping to dispel this fresh worry as easily as I shooed away the fog.

Jasper led me away from the garden. He pointed to the fields with the raised rows. "When the soil warms," he said, "we'll transplant the tobacco seedlings yonder and in the field south of the house. I've gained that field at a favorable price. Our tobacco yield will double this year."

I figured the additional plot came about because of another farmer's failings, but I held my tongue. The Carter family already had expansive land holdings. I hadn't considered they were increasing them. These days, few families had the capital to buy more land.

"The mills in Asheville and Durham are competing for product with last year's invention of the cigarette rolling machine," Jasper said. "A miraculous thing. Prices will be good this year."

"Indeed," I said.

We walked side by side, but apart, and I showed great interest in the property while my husband looked me over. Despite last night's intimacies—or perhaps because of them, I felt shy in the light of day. We wavered between boldness and shyness, touch and distance, words and silence.

"You can see the new field from the front porch," Jasper said. "I've got an arrangement that includes the log cabin over there. The tenants are Negroes."

The tilled fields stretched toward a simple square home in the corner of the added land. A small garden showed signs of new starts, with rows of lettuce and climbing poles readied for peas. The meager house had a ramshackle lean-to for farm equipment. A sloped roof draped over the empty porch.

"They won't bother you none." Jasper's words had an abrupt edge, and he clamped his lips together. Since his family had been slaveholders, I imagined he wouldn't agree with Elizabeth about educating the Negroes. This wasn't the time to introduce that topic. Maybe there never would be such a time.

"My brother Samuel runs the sawmill on Big Ivy. Through this break in the grove, you can see the Solomon Carter house —my father's homestead, where I was born and where my brother Daniel and his wife Anna live."

Jasper pointed in various directions from our front porch, orienting me with the extensive family holdings. I followed along and put the men in birth order: John—Harriet's father, Jasper, Samuel, Zimri and Daniel, with sisters in between.

"Daniel farms the most acreage, and he runs the grist mill. Follow the Big Ivy Creek west to the Holcombe Branch and you'll see John and Caroline's home."

"And inn?" I said.

"Aye. They lodge judges, circuit riders, politicians and other travelers, all on their way between Asheville and

Burnsville. John and Samuel run the general store by the inn and John acts as postmaster for Democrat."

"The town he named," I said.

Jasper chuckled. "Ah, you've heard. John's the big man about town and Daniel vies for next in line."

While I questioned whether Jasper envied his niece's faith, his curt remark left no doubt he begrudged his brothers.

"The wives will be a source of company for you on a Sunday afternoon. The planting and harvesting keep us working dawn to dusk every day but the Lord's Day."

I was no stranger to work. I'd tended the family garden, kept the animals and taken care of household tasks and children all my years. However, I had never worked in tobacco fields.

"Tobacco farming is labor intensive," Jasper said. "Zimri and I share the work on our farms. Plenty to go around. Come fall, we'll bring the crop to the Asheville warehouse. Although you can get most everything you need at John's store, there may be some things you'll want from the bigger city stores."

A day ago I'd worried myself sick, wondering how my life would change and assuming the worst. I'd been silly, considering the home I'd left was no longer a working farm. If Jasper tended me half as well as he did this property, I would be fortunate. Gratitude filled me like an overflowing bucket of raw, warm milk. Plus, the prospect of spending more time in Asheville with Elizabeth and Margaret thrilled me.

"Will your brothers and their wives join us?"

It was a slight, but noticeable, pause.

"Not every Carter brother farms and only some work together," Jasper said.

He motioned me toward the tobacco barn, closing the door on the conversation. I looked toward the Carter homestead and wondered if, in getting to know Harriet, she might divulge the family divisions.

Chapter Nine

"Many persons suppose the worst is over, now that the Blue Ridge is tunnelled. Far from it."

The Raleigh News

The sun peeked over the horizon while Jasper milked the cow and I scattered scratch for the chickens and gathered eggs. I preferred the hour of first light, when the farm awakened, the sounds of the animals rising with the sunlight, the melting frost swirling along the ground, and the earthy smells becoming more pungent with the growing warmth.

Robert returned home the day after the wedding. The following morning, he rose early and met me in the kitchen. He made short work of two fried eggs and three slices of bread. I choked back a laugh, witnessing my son's Adam's apple bulge with every gulp. *My son.*

Robert didn't dawdle over breakfast. On late winter days, he carried hay to the hogs, following the clanking of their collar bells to the hollows where they settled.

"The hogs like the chestnuts and it saves us feed," Robert informed me. "We won't bring one down to the pen until six weeks before hoggin'. Pa says they taste better when they're finished on corn."

I've got a little teacher. "That so?"

"Yes, Ma'am. I best be off. I'll be back before dinner." The kitchen door thudded shut and Robert raced to the barn to load the hay onto the horse-drawn sled.

"I'll be waiting for you," I murmured.

Jasper's brother, Zimri, showed up to help with the farm work. His angular frame wandered toward our farmhouse. The wide-brimmed hat tamped down his unruly curls. Zimri loped into the kitchen and his broad grin appeared when offered a cup of coffee. Jasper was right behind him, in from the milking.

"Miss Alice." Zimri touched the brim of his hat. "My Susannah looks forward to visiting with you come Sunday at the inn."

Once Jasper finished his breakfast, the men left for a day's work of cutting and hauling logs. After a few mornings drinking coffee together, I anticipated Zimri's jokes and light banter. My laughter hung on until the men crossed the field. I hummed a song and cleaned up the breakfast dishes before turning to the deserted house.

It faced me like a death portrait, the silence pressing in, heavy and solemn. I walked to the fireplace just to hear the floorboards creak and stoked the embers to hear the logs rustle. While the fire poker clattered against its cradle, I rubbed the back of my neck and longed for a wind to buffet our home or a rain to pelt the rooftop.

Don't be silly. Keep busy.

Jasper and Robert had a sweet tooth, so I would brew them a tonic with the sassafras brought from home. While the roots boiled on the stove, I tested the milk in the butter churn, tilting it to the side. The clabbered cream held together and separated from the sides. The roots infused the water. The butter took form. But Jennie was not at the table, kneading the bread dough while I agitated the milk. My eyes brimmed, and I jabbed the dasher up and down, yearning for noise, movement, and companionship. I blotted my eyes with my apron.

I checked the tonic, stirring the simmering liquid and vigorously mashing the roots. Through the kitchen window, I watched the wagon pull alongside the curing barn. Jasper and Zimri unloaded the logs and stacked the timber under the barn eaves. Last night's conversation had explained the great need for fuel.

"Early spring, Pa stockpiles the wood needed for curin' tobacco," Robert had said.

"That's right," Jasper added. "Takes a great deal to run the barn stoves for a week."

"When will we plant tobacco?" I'd been embarrassed to show my ineptitude at tobacco farming, but I hadn't questioned my father when he'd attempted to farm cotton, and I wouldn't make the mistake of not understanding our livelihood again.

"We'll sow seed in April and when the seedlings reach about eight inches and the soil is warm enough, we'll transplant them to the fields, 'round about May," Jasper said.

With the logs stacked and the wagon empty, the men prodded the mules back into the woods. I set the pan to cool and wondered what to tackle next. I rubbed the tension from my neck and shoulders. The housework occupied my hands, but the gloominess of the house weighed me down. I had no sisters traipsing through the rooms. My brothers Ralph and John didn't peek in the kitchen, eager to sneak a bite of whatever I was baking. No one to scold for shirking their chores. I'd expected to miss my family. I'd feared this marriage, and losing my independence was still a worry. I pulled my apron to my face and wept, then sank onto a kitchen chair. Three days in the house and not a hope of change ahead. Long, lonely days threatened to build like a storm.

The worry I'd carried over the past weeks drenched me. While the wedding had solved my immediate problem of needing a benefactor, I was left with a husband who was a stranger. A kind stranger, but a stranger. My heart ached for my loved ones. I longed to confide in Jennie, to laugh with my sisters, to berate my younger brothers. I heaved myself out of the chair and entered the springhouse to splash cool water on my face.

Keep busy. I dried my face and returned to the kitchen. Tossing more wood into the stove, I prepared dinner. I peeled and boiled potatoes, pan-fried salt pork, and made a milk gravy. A jar of green beans from the pantry warmed on the stovetop.

At midday, Jasper, Zimri, and Robert washed their hands and faces at the porch tub before coming to the table. The pungent odors of sweat, mud, and pine sap competed with dinner. I clasped my hands together in prayer and Jasper touched Robert's arm to stop him from inhaling the meal. I wished the men would remove their hats.

"Heavenly Father, we thank Thee for these gifts. Amen." Considering the palpable hunger around the table, I kept the prayer short, and everyone fell to their food. I welcomed the company, even sweat-streaked, silent men with questionable manners.

Robert wedged in between his father and uncle. He tackled dinner like breakfast, with fervor. Jasper and Zimri kept up with him. Robert resembled Jasper in form, lanky and tall for his age. His mother must have been fair, given the boy's towhead and sun-kissed skin. Freckles crossed the middle of his face like a speckled bandage, striping his cheeks and nose.

"Robert, tell me about your schooling," I said.

The men's faces jerked up from their plates. Apparently, talking and eating didn't go together.

"I'm done with school this year, Alice," Robert said.

I regretted telling Robert to call me by my Christian name. It reminded me of my younger brothers clamoring for my attention. Funny how Ralph and John had annoyed me, and now I missed them.

"Children around here get six weeks of schooling in winter," Jasper said. "Robert got high marks for his reading and penmanship."

"That's not enough education."

Jasper threw me a lightning-quick glance, as sharp as my paring knife.

Hadn't Jennie warned me to think before speaking?

Jasper jabbed the pork on his plate and averted his eyes.

Zimri shifted in his seat. "I'll take some more potatoes. That's a fine gravy, Miss Alice."

Jasper gave me an almost imperceptible nod. This was a private discussion for later. We finished our meal in silence and I considered the trials of my first days in the home. I was busy and lonely, outspoken and silent, praised and chastised. I said a prayer for patience, for it would take time to settle into my new home.

The afternoon stretched out like the darkness in winter. I worked and waited and sighed, counting the hours on the wall clock. The sun sank and Zimri headed home. I welcomed Jasper and Robert at the supper table.

"How was your afternoon?" My voice rose unnaturally. "I caught glimpses of you through the kitchen window. You moved a lot of wood today." I poured the cooled, sweetened tea.

"Aye," Jasper said.

"What's this?" Robert asked.

"Why, it's a sassafras tonic. My mother believed a good dose of tonic in the spring kept the doctor away."

Jasper gulped it down. "Mighty sweet and tasty."

Robert sipped tentatively and squeezed his eyes shut to choke down the brown liquid. "That is peculiar."

Jasper scowled. "Manners, Robert."

"I expect it takes some getting used to," I said.

Jasper and Robert ate heartily. I should've accepted that as a compliment. Instead, I wallowed in my inadequacy with something as simple as making a tasty drink. I picked at the food on my plate and scraped off the remaining bits into the slop bucket.

After our evening meal, Jasper made another visit to the barn for milking and I warmed the wash water. Darkness fell outside like autumn leaves, floating into sudden stillness. I lit the lanterns.

"Pa says I'm to manage my chores and not expect you to cook supper and clean up after," Robert said.

"That's much appreciated," I said. "I'll write a letter."

"Who you writing to?"

"My sister." I remained in the kitchen doorway, reluctant to leave Robert and yet impatient to write Jennie.

"Must be mighty fine to get post. I bet she'll be happy to hear from you." Robert took the pot of scalding water off the stove and poured it into a basin. He fetched cold water from the springhouse and added it to the steaming tub. "Pa says my writing is near good enough to help him with the farm accounts. Not much more learning needed."

"More education will take you far," I said.

"Pa says I don't need to go farther than this farm."

"That may be. Then again, times are changing."

Robert nodded, but that didn't mean he agreed. It seemed I had some work to do within my own family to sell the idea of public education. I left Robert to do the dishwashing.

I set the lantern on the roll-top desk and sank into the chair. With a piece of paper and ink bottle before me, I hesitated to dip the pen. If I revealed my unsettled self to Jennie, she would worry. She couldn't fix it, just as I couldn't change it. I took a deep breath and began.

February 21, 1882

Dearest Jennie,

I am eager to hear from you. Please tell me about your home, family, everything about how you spend your days.

On my first morning here, Jasper and I toured the farm. We are well provided for, growing corn and wheat to take to Carter's Mill for our own use and tobacco to sell at market. It's the new Brightleaf variety that's very popular. There's a small orchard, a garden and two creeks that border our farm.

Our home is well-appointed, not small, not large, but just right, with nice amenities such as a springhouse—no hauling water! And a fine stove. Timber is abundant from the woods on our lands. Jasper has acquired additional acreage and a Negro couple will farm it. They keep to themselves.

Robert is a polite, energetic young man. He loves to read and I hope we might bond over that favorite activity. Robert's schooling has been limited and I'm already scheming for a school here in Democrat. Write to me if you hear more of the public school effort on your trips to Asheville. I envy your regular visits to the city to make purchases for the store.

After only a few days together, Jasper and I are finding things to appreciate in one another. You know I hate to say Mother was right ... well, time will tell.

Write to me, dear sister, and tell me about your married life.

Your loving sister,

Alice

Jasper appeared in the doorway. "You've got a fine hand, Alice."

"Thank you, Husband. I'm writing Jennie." My voice quivered. I capped the ink bottle. Jasper laid a hand on my shoulder and the tension I'd been holding onto eased. It was the smallest comfort after a long day of loneliness.

We retired to the porch where fireflies lit the blackening sky like so many small, flickering lanterns. I remembered catching the luminous insects in jars as a child. The rhythmic rocking of the chair soothed me, lessening the weight of the day. *Had I really thought Robert and Jasper could replace my family? That two strangers were a match for ten loved ones?*

I breathed in the crisp evening air and the coolness filled my chest. What I couldn't see in the low light, I could hear and smell and touch. I closed my eyes and listened to the night. The still air carried the scent of pine. My breathing slowed to the speed of the chair runners' creak on the porch boards. Under the cover of darkness, my thoughts and feelings flowed readily. I discovered my husband's did as well.

"Alice, you keep a fine house." Jasper puffed on his pipe. "I expect your mother had high standards in running the family inn."

"My mother liked to play hostess. That's for sure." My mother's finest moments came when she greeted guests. Ensuring the beds were ready, floors were cleaned, that another animal needed butchering—all the important duties of managing an inn and a household somehow escaped her attention. I kept those thoughts to myself, though, recalling Jennie's advice. "She was known for her hospitality and no drover left hungry."

"The herds could be large," Jasper said.

"Yes, sometimes thousands of animals. Father managed the animal pens and worked the fields to supply the feed."

"Until the War came."

Jasper wouldn't have known the details of the Harris Inn, but imagined, rightly, that the Union troops stormed through and plundered all in their wake. I remembered watching the blue-coated horde swarm over the hill, and Father rounding the family up to hide in the barn loft, saving us from God knows what.

"They took everything," I said.

"Damn Yankees." Jasper looked northward. "Sometimes it doesn't seem that long ago."

I swallowed the urge to ask about Jasper's war experience. The unexpected closeness we'd experienced in our marriage bed was hard to replicate in daylight. Moonlight streaked the porch and the dim setting provided an in-between place—a niche of cautious revelation.

"It was a hard climb back from the War," I said. "The inn traffic dried up when the animals could ride the rails."

"Faster to market, plus the benefit of dropping less weight," Jasper added.

"That's why my father tried to farm cotton."

Jasper puffed on his pipe and the smoke billowed around his head. "No one predicted the blight."

I was grateful for the kindness. Jasper hadn't mentioned Father's excessive borrowing, or lack of cotton farming experience, or greed in seeking a quick gain from the cash crop. Never mind, our land wasn't right for growing cotton. I rued my father's decision and my mother's compliance. The tinge of heartburn returned, reminding me of those perilous days when my anger over my acquiescence singed my throat.

Father had been so convincing. He'd sat at our kitchen table, waving his arms toward our empty shelves, and promised we'd use the profits to buy whatever we needed. I'd believed him. I'd managed the household, but I should have controlled Father's pocketbook. My stomach juices had roiled as blackness spread across the cotton leaves. The tattered leaves were a daily reminder of my ragged dress. When the blight destroyed the crop, he owed more than he could pay. The land was lost, and we succumbed to tenant farming. The loss was more than Father could bear. We laid him to rest that same year.

Jasper knew most of my story, and I was reluctant to relive it with the telling tonight. The rockers' creaking joined with the coyote's mournful call. The tale always ended in the same way.

"Losing your brother was surely hard," Jasper said.

"He'd hoped to pay off Father's debts." I stopped rocking. The rhythm was too close to Leander's rasping on his deathbed.

"Terrible thing, swamp fever." Jasper laid his pipe aside.

I'd nursed Leander best I knew how, but it wasn't good enough. It didn't take long for word of a family's demise to circulate. Creditors came. Gossip flew. A mother's need to marry off daughters traveled the circuit riders' routes. And a widower with an eleven-year-old son needed a wife.

In our few days together, I'd come to admire this man many years my senior. Jasper spoke honestly. Whether that was his nature or he valued having someone to talk to after so many years alone, I didn't know. To my inquiry into Robert's schooling, Jasper had issued a quiet rebuttal rather than provoke a confrontation. I slipped my hand under Jasper's and the gentle rocking of his chair pressed his hand against mine. The touch of his skin evoked memories of our nights together, the unexpected softness of his mouth, his skin against mine, and the heat that blossomed between us.

Jasper finished his pipe, and we retired upstairs, where we were becoming even more familiar with one another.

Chapter Ten

"The manufacturing interests of Asheville and Buncombe County, in spite of almost illimitable water-power, cheap labor, and convenient raw material, are still in their infancy; but a new era is dawning."

The Asheville City Directory and Gazetteer of Buncombe County

I rose and took particular care with my dress. Following church services, we would visit with extended family at the inn. Jasper's brother, John, and his wife, Caroline, ran a general store, the post office, and the Carter Inn. I was eager to see the place where Senator Vance held political rallies.

My dark hair held a nice curl, and I shaped it into a low, loose bun, twirling the strands with dampened fingers to frame my face. *What would the Carters think of me?* The dresser's mirror reflected firm features, much like my judgments. Working in the sun left my complexion a little too brown, but the color highlighted the light blue gray of my eyes. *Vanity is not a virtue.* I clipped a cameo brooch at my neckline and added a ribbon to my waist. My wedding costume was now a fine day dress.

After chores and breakfast, we set off for church. As the wagon bumped along the winding road, I admired the blooming wildflowers sprinkled amongst the tall grasses. Songbirds fluttered about, flitting between the stems, rising to circle us, and swooping down the lane. If Jennie was here, she'd recognize the bird calls and name each flower. I pulled out my handkerchief and drew my fingers across my sister's stitching.

"That's fine work," Jasper said.

"Not mine. Jennie's. While I read most evenings, she stitched." I pointed to the bright colored roadside. "These flowers remind me of my sister." My voice slowed and faded. I smoothed the closely woven fabric on my lap. I'd never attended church without Jennie.

Robert's bearing in the driver's seat and his intent expression distracted me from my sister's absence.

"Lucky for me, I have two escorts for Sunday services," I said.

Robert blushed and fidgeted on the seat.

"I enjoy the hymns," I added.

"Aye, and I like the singing," Jasper said.

"I just hope Preacher doesn't go on." Robert shook the reins, hustling the horses on. The clip-clopping of their hooves drowned out our laughter. His honest revelation pleased me. In only a week's time, Robert was more relaxed, sitting beside me to read in the evenings, enjoying my cooking, and helping with chores. We were blending together as a family, if not a fine linen weave, then a patchwork quilt.

Pulling into the churchyard, I spotted John and Caroline.

John strode over to me, letter in hand. "This came for you yesterday."

I recognized Jennie's writing, thanked John, and stuffed the envelope in my skirt pocket to read after services.

"Alice, you look well this morning." John's daughter, Harriet, fixed her hand in the crook of my arm and guided me toward the chapel. "Welcome to our congregation. No doubt you'll find many similarities to your family's church home, both being Methodist." Harriet pulled me away from the others. "Although I suspect your minister does not go on as long as Reverend Pope."

"So I hear." I glanced over my shoulder at Robert.

The white clapboard church rested on a hilltop overlooking Sugar Creek. It was a comely building and freshly painted, the white color clear and bright and without a speck of dirt or mold. Standing at the red double door, the reverend greeted his flock with a firm handshake and a blessing.

More wagons arrived and people milled about. This was the time to exchange gossip, share news, predict weather, and discuss farm crops. The conversation ended when the church bells rang and we filed into the sanctuary.

The minister droned on and I flexed my feet beneath my skirt to keep myself awake. Robert sagged against me. Jasper prodded him with his elbow from the other side. My husband pretended to smooth his beard, but I saw him cover a yawn more than once.

After services, I gathered our picnic basket and blanket, then followed the families to the creek's bank. Fresh growth on scattered oak trees promised shade come summer. I rested in the sun's warmth and in the company of others.

Harriet plopped down next to me while her children played nearby.

"Goodness, that was long. My husband would not have abided by such a lengthy service." Harriet arranged her skirts. "And my backside cannot take a wooden pew for so many hours."

"Oh, thank goodness," I admitted. I rubbed my lower back side. "I thought it was just me."

Harriet laughed. "How is your housekeeping coming?"

I assured her I had everything I needed and thanked her for the garden and the spotless home. Recounting all that Harriet had done for me, I blurted out, "I hope I can measure up."

Her face pinched. "Oh, not you too?"

"What do you mean?" I asked.

"Jasper ... nothing. I'm afraid I've spoken out of turn." Harriet closed her eyes and whispered, "He that refraineth his lips is wise."

Outspoken, pious, and apt to reveal the family secrets. *What could she tell me of my husband? And of the Carter family?*

Harriet pleated her apron deliberately. "And how do you pass the spare moments?"

"I enjoy reading and writing."

"You must have a fine hand," Harriet said. "I've been perusing my late husband's journal from his ministering during the War. Swain's been gone four years now, but I still hear his voice." Her eyes held mine, soft, soulful, and the color of aged whiskey.

"I'm sorry for your loss, Harriet." The children's laughter drew our attention away from the somber moment. Her four little ones and Robert rolled down the grassy embankment. "Your children must be a solace," I said.

"They are a joy and they keep me *busy*." Harriet rolled her eyes. "What other talents do you have?"

"I play the banjo," I said.

"Oh, marvelous! Then we must have a play party. Daniel's wife Anna loves to sing." Harriet continued, "but how not to include Uncle Daniel?"

"Is he tone deaf?" I asked.

Harriet laughed. "Oh, heavens, if only!"

I must have offered a baffled look because Harriet said, "My father brought you a letter. I'll check on the children and leave you to read it."

I ripped open the envelope and absorbed my sister's words. Then I read it a second and a third time. My hands fell to my lap, clutching the pages. I tried to read between the lines, to understand what Jennie was saying and not saying. My thoughts drowned out the sounds of the children and the return of Harriet.

"Not bad news, I hope?" She lowered herself onto the blanket.

"From my sister." I unfolded the pages and stared at Jennie's words. "I don't know what to make of it."

Harriet cleared her throat. "Might she find the first days of marriage ... trying?"

"She writes, 'It has been unexpected and G.W. is a devoted companion. Thankfully, Sunday approaches and it is a day of rest.'" My fist sprang to my mouth to stifle a choking sound. *Was my sister hurt?* Jasper said it could cause pain. Despite my promise to keep our correspondence private, I'd shared this intimate knowledge with Harriet. *What would she think of me?* I wanted to give G.W. a piece of my mind. *Why wasn't he gentle with Jennie like Jasper was with me?*

Harriet spoke softly, but firmly. "When I ministered with Swain on the circuit, I often talked with new brides while he tended to the husbands' spiritual needs. The early days of marriage can be a trial."

Why didn't our mother tell us a darn thing about marital relations? Why did our father ruin our family and put my sisters and me in these circumstances? I crushed the pages. *How could I not care for Jennie when she needed me?*

Harriet leaned toward me. "I recommended warm salt baths."

She didn't let propriety impede helping others. We were going to be fast friends.

Harriet kept her voice low. "And a woman might say her monthlies had arrived."

I gripped Harriet's hand. Jennie and I had been left with few choices. Here was a friend conveying options.

Jasper drove the wagon home after services, and we walked to supper at the Carter Inn. After our lengthy time on a pew, I fancied stretching my legs. Perhaps he sensed Jennie's letter weighed on me and an airing would do me good. Robert had left services with John and Caroline and a gaggle of cousins. We strolled the creek-side road.

Jasper fell in step with me. "What did you think of today's sermon?"

I didn't yet know my husband's mind around religion—he'd admitted to gaining faith and losing it after the death of his first wife. However, I knew the story of Job, having run across it countless times during Sunday school. I cringed at the memory of teaching this particular Bible story. Many were troubled by God playing with the life of a devout follower.

"The story of Job is difficult," I said. "We see God in an uncomfortable light."

Jasper rubbed his hand over his beard. "I'm curious why God deals with the Devil."

"Some believe the Devil is an angel of trickery, trying to test the limits of Job's faith."

"Is that what you believe?" Jasper turned toward me.

I believed my views would be unwelcome with marriage. *Could I trust that Jasper wished for my opinion? Was this a test of my vows? Hadn't Jasper pledged to love and honor me while I had promised to love, honor and obey him?* I entered this marriage expecting to be hobbled. I'd agreed to submit to a man I barely knew. Jasper's simple question offered an unexpected freedom, and I reached for it.

"I believe that faith is effortless when life is good," I said. "One's faith is tested with misfortune, and everyone faces hardship at some point." My words struck me like a match, igniting a worry I'd said too much again. I'd been thinking of my own misfortunes and hadn't considered all Jasper had lived through—the War, losing his father, brother, a wife. I bit my lip through the ensuing silence, casting sideways glances at my husband. With his chin tucked in, he studied his feet.

The short walk to the Carter Inn stretched interminably long. We leaned into the hilly road, leaving our home, Sugar Creek, and the Carter Mill behind. Bare tree branches curved up and over the dirt road, creating a tunnel for contemplation and an air of protection.

"And how is your faith today?" Jasper asked.

In the past year, my faith had been shaken by the loss of my father, eldest brother, and childhood home. Our household had dissolved. My three sisters and I rushed to marry for want of security. My steps slowed and narrowed the space between us. Our sleeves grazed one another.

"It is easy," I answered. "Today, my faith is easy."

The Carter Inn stood along the major thoroughfare, a large, well-kept building with wide porches stretching across its two levels like a broad smile on a welcoming face. Four guests sat and smoked on the upper-level veranda. We climbed the steps to the lower porch with its fine wooden rockers and wicker chairs, and a sideboard holding a cold supper. The upset of

Jennie's letter had caused me to skip the picnic dinner and my stomach grumbled at the hearty fare of ham, potatoes, pickled vegetables plus plenty of fresh bread and butter.

Caroline greeted us, and John nodded from behind his wife. Like all Carter men, he was tall and slender. As the eldest, I expected a prominent figure with a commanding air, but John was anything but that. John Carter, innkeeper, store owner, postmaster, and farmer, was the quietest of the Carter men, content to listen and observe.

I'd met most of Jasper's relatives at the wedding, and I tried my best to remember their names. Jasper's mother Alvira, widow and family matriarch, perched on a rocker with her grandchildren and great grandchildren running circles around her. She lived with John, Caroline, Harriet and the children. Brother Zimri and Susannah, the youngest brother, Daniel, and his wife Anna, and a dozen more, lined the porch railing.

Anna's smooth, alabaster complexion told me she did not work in the fields or the garden. Jasper told me that Daniel and Anna had the most extensive land holdings within the family, so much acreage that Daniel hired field workers and employed two servants in his household. I slipped my tan hands behind my back. Anna rose and curtsied. She was the picture of womanly beauty with her diminutive stature, fair skin and flaxen hair. When she offered the seat beside her, I detected the distinctive drawl of Georgia.

"How are crops faring?" Daniel stretched his arms across the railing like a politician readying for a speech. He was nothing like the expansive Senator Vance, who'd rallied voters from this very porch.

"We'll start harvesting the wheat next week," Zimri said.

"Good, good," Daniel said. "The grist mill is busy. I might add more men. Perhaps Robert will give me a hand?"

My husband bristled but said nothing.

It wasn't just the two brothers' mannerisms that were different. Where Jasper wore his hair cropped and his beard trimmed, Daniel had the look of a dandy with a slicked-back mane, a smooth-shaven face and a pin-striped vest. He flicked open his pocket watch, checked the time, and snapped it shut theatrically.

"Our supper is ready," Caroline announced. "Get it before the flies do."

The women helped the children fill their plates from overflowing platters. The men lingered along the railing, waiting for us to take seats on the porch before they stepped forward for their supper. Harriet moved beside me at the buffet. "Tell me more about how you're settling in."

I blushed, recalling how Harriet had perceived my sister's situation. I focused on the practical. "The kitchen was well stocked. Might I have you to thank for that?"

"Anna helped," Harriet said. Anna ducked her chin, giving me a quick nod. The crown of her head reached Harriet's chin. Standing next to me, Anna barely came to my bosom. I was large, unfamiliar, and out of place. Good manners were all I could offer.

"I thank you both. The house is a home already."

I studied the two Carter women closest in age to me. As a widow, Harriet lived with her parents, who helped raise their four grandchildren and undoubtedly had some say in Harriet's comings and goings. She'd been the woman of Jasper's house in the years following his first wife's death. Daniel's wife, Anna, appeared younger than both Harriet and me with her refined looks. She had no children, but she managed servants and a large family home. This was the sister-in-law who liked to sing.

"I'm glad to see more of you, Harriet," Anna said.

"And yet, the children and I miss seeing Robert," Harriet said.

My appearance had upset the family dynamics in more ways than one. "Harriet, I'd welcome your company," I said. "I admit I'm not used to being the only woman in the house. I'm tired of singing to myself just to hear some noise."

Harriet's face lit with delight. "Might tomorrow morning be too soon?"

"I'll see you then." I returned Harriet's smile.

Anna's eyes looked downward, but not before I detected a dolefulness. We filled our plates and seated ourselves at a narrow table with six chairs. The older wives, Caroline and Susannah, joined us.

"I suspect the farm and house have kept you busy, Alice," Caroline said.

"I have some learning to do."

The men stood around us and, between bites of supper, interjected into our conversation.

"We planned the wedding with this break in mind," Jasper said. "After the tobacco planting, we'll stay busy with topping and suckering until harvest."

"Once the harvest starts, there is no rest," Zimri said. "Every man, woman and child are in the fields pulling tobacco leaves."

"Shouldn't the children be in school?" I asked.

"Around here, school runs December and January, with time off for Christmas," Daniel said.

"That hardly seems enough," I said.

Harriet's eyebrows lifted. Her father, John, raised the corner of his mouth.

"It's sufficient for farm work. We need the children morning 'til night in the fields like everyone else." Daniel checked the time and snapped his watch casing shut.

"Not every child will farm," I said. "With the growth Asheville is experiencing, other professions might call, ones that demand a better educated workforce." Elizabeth's and

Margaret's ideas had lodged within me. The sights and sounds of Asheville convinced me that a new age was coming.

"Why Alice, you're living in the country now," Daniel said. "And this land provides food for those so-called educated workers. Best not forget the amount of work needed around here."

Daniel's smooth-skinned hands told me he did little hard labor.

"Which is why we rest on the Lord's Day," Caroline said.

My husband's jaw jutted outward and he would not meet my eye.

My shoulders sagged. *Would Jasper reprimand me later?* I twisted one hand over the other.

"And we look forward to the harvest's end and a few days in Asheville for the auction," Susannah said.

I sipped my tea and pressed a gentle smile on my face. I wouldn't let them see me grumble over the school conversation. Daniel wouldn't have the last word. I needed better ammunition, and I would get it from Elizabeth when I returned to Asheville at year's end. Figuring out how to deal with Jasper was another matter.

After supper, Robert ran ahead toward home while Jasper and I adopted a more leisurely pace. The day was ending and the setting sun glowed from beyond the ridge, shading the layers of mountains from dark to light. Birds and animals traded places, some rising and some resting.

"You'll not get many takers for prolonging education here, Alice."

"Speak your mind, Husband."

"Best take a cue from Caroline on managing the family

exchanges." Jasper looked far down the road and away from this conversation.

My opinions would be welcome sometimes, and only sometimes. I changed the subject. "Does Daniel accompany us to Asheville?"

"He doesn't come along." Jasper stopped to take the earth's temperature. The soil slipped through his fingers. "Daniel runs the grist mill, while his brothers work in the fields." He spit out his words.

"He farms too, right?" I asked.

"He pays others to farm his land." The edge of my husband's voice was sharp and clear, like a well-honed ax blade.

I smoothed the bodice of my dress. "I see."

"You'll learn soon enough." Jasper slowed his pace as if more deliberate steps aided in a careful telling of the family history. "As a young man, I worked in the grist mill alongside Zimri and our brother Garrett. We were all equal in our father's eyes until the War. When Garrett didn't return, my father never forgave us."

I laid my hand on Jasper's upper arm and my touch halted him. He leaned into my palm. In comforting him, I recognized my old self, capable and caring. My breaths drew even and long and Jasper's followed suit.

"Daniel came along later, too young for the War. He wasn't a reminder of Garrett or Zimri or me. Father placed him in the grist mill. As he aged, Father relied more and more on Daniel. Even had Daniel write out a will with his preferences."

"To benefit himself?" I asked.

"Father divided the lands and businesses unevenly. Couple more Sunday suppers and you'll figure who came out ahead." Jasper's explanation was curt, plain, and unyielding.

Did he, like Job, feel betrayed? Had he lost his faith in

family and God? My heart swelled at Jasper's hurt. "One's faith is tested with misfortune," I offered.

The line of Jasper's jaw softened and the tension in his shoulders and neck eased somewhat. We walked the rest of the way home in silence.

March 16, 1882

My dear Miss Elizabeth and Miss Margaret,

Today marks one month since my wedding and I'm adjusting to life on the farm with my husband and stepson, Robert. My time is much taken by managing the household and the garden. Seeing my propensity to write, Jasper has asked me to take over detailing our farm expenses. I hope this does not sound conceited, but I am proving a quick study of farm management. Why, just last night I documented the age of the hens and selected one too old to lay for a fine supper this evening. I find it valuable schooling, albeit a different education than what you are both working toward.

Every Sunday the Carter family gathers, and on our first evening together, I learned the schooling here is limited. I will keep you informed of any opportunities, and I welcome updates on your progress in furthering public education.

After the tobacco harvest, I'll accompany Jasper to Asheville. I look forward to seeing you both again this fall.

Your friend,

Alice

April 1, 1882

Dear Miss Alice,

It delighted us to receive your correspondence. Your letter proved excellent material (and encouragement) for Elizabeth to practice her reading. As you might expect, her penmanship is precise, which I credit to years of decorative stitching by hand.

My classroom occupies much of my time. I teach forty-six Negro children and I can hardly manage. We need more teachers, as I cannot admit all that applied. The children are sharing slates and chalk, primers, and even chairs. We will persevere. The gap is substantial and the enthusiasm of the pupils rewarding.

I hope I am not imprudent in sharing that Asheville society has not opened their arms to me. Whether it is my profession or my Northern ways, I don't know.

Miss Alice, looking back over this letter, you must think I am quite ill-tempered. Thankfully, I have Miss Elizabeth, my students, and your letters to keep me company.

With fondness,

Margaret

April 20, 1882

My Dearest Alice,

How glad I was to receive your last letter. You asked about Hendersonville. While it doesn't attract the numbers of travelers that Asheville does, the railroad arriving three years ago helped the town grow. We have a depot and a telegraph office.

The city has a fine main street that's one hundred feet wide! Mayor W.A. Smith welcomed me to town and shared that fact. G.W. was pleased that store traffic picked up with my arrival. It seems curiosity brought the ladies in. With several stores in town, we have some competition, but I like to think we offer goods the others don't. Our purchasing trips to Asheville help with that.

Last week, I met Mrs. Smith in the store. She admired my embroidered collar, and we fell into conversation easily. Next Tuesday evening I'm invited to her quilting circle. I'm excited to see the inside of the Smith-Green House, as it is a handsome addition to our town. A lawyer must make a fine living as Mayor and Mrs. Smith's home stands three stories high with many glass windows, including a set of bay windows on the second floor.

I'm busy in the store, serving customers, shelving items, and handling transactions. The hours fly by and I enjoy visiting with the townspeople. Our home requires little work. Our three rooms above the store offer plenty of space but require little to keep in order. When I need something, I can run downstairs.

As to my earlier letter, let me assure you that G.W. and I are coming to an understanding. You think of me as submissive. On my own, I'm asserting myself. I've had a good model for that.

Your loving sister,

Jennie

Chapter Eleven

"Mrs. Alvira Carter ..., is one of the most remarkable women of the country. She will be 83 years old in March next and is still an active old lady. Has had fourteen children, thriteen of whom lived to be married, ten of whom now live, Mr. John A. Carter being the oldest. She has over 200 descendants."

The News and Observer

The months flowed one into another like a brook to a stream to a river, rushing forward and quenching my thirst for stability. We divided six days of dawn-to-dusk work between the fields, house, garden, and barns. The setting had shifted, and the people had changed, but the routine was the same. I found solace in that.

One Friday evening, I picked up my banjo as twilight diffused the day's brightness. My notes joined the familiar nighttime sounds: crickets chirping, insects buzzing, and small animals rustling through the grasses.

"You play fine, Alice." Jasper rocked his chair to the

rhythm of my song. "How did you come to the banjo?"

I softened my picking to quiet the strings. "I first heard it played by a drover staying at our inn. The man noticed my infatuation with the instrument, and when he returned from the market, he offered my father payment with his old gourd banjo and a music book."

"That one looks store-bought."

"Father said when I'd mastered every song in the book, then he'd find me a lady's banjo." I stopped playing. "I don't know whether he was fed up with the few songs I strummed or thought I deserved a finer instrument."

Jasper pulled his pipe from his mouth and chuckled. "I s'pose the latter. I once saw Lotta Crabtree play in Asheville. She toured in 'Jenny Leatherlungs.' Perhaps we can take in a show when we go to town."

I strummed a new song. "What would you say to a play party, Husband?"

At the next Sunday supper, Carters of every age crowded around me as I picked and sang:

Frog went a courtin' and he did ride, uh-huh
Frog went a courtin' and he did ride, uh-huh
Frog went a courtin' and he did ride
With a sword and a pistol by his side, uh-huh, uh-huh, uh-huh.

He rode right up to Miss Mousie's door, uh-huh
He rode right up to Miss Mousie's door, uh-huh
He rode right up to Miss Mousie's door
Gave three loud raps, and a very big roar, uh-huh, uh-huh, uh-huh,

The children sang along while the adults tapped their feet to the familiar tune.

"Play another!"

"Yes, Aunt Alice, another song!"

"I need some more instruments," I said. "Put your hands together and stomp those feet." I tapped my foot and sang along with them. With all our noisemaking, I worried the inn guests might pack up and leave.

Harriet grabbed Anna, and the two spun around, singing and giggling. Anna beamed, a noticeable change from her usual modesty. Daniel's dreamy countenance revealed a glimpse of their courting days. I'd assumed Anna's sense of propriety fueled her quietness. I decided her marriage demanded it.

Harriet motioned to her grandmother to join in. Alvira waved the suggestion away until Zimri stepped forward, offered his mother an exaggerated bow, and invited her to the floor. I played a slow ragtime tune, and the family quieted and scooted back to clear a makeshift dance circle.

Watching Zimri lope across the fields most mornings, I expected a stuttering ability to dance, but he surprised me with his smooth graceful steps. Mother and son glided across the floorboards. Aside from my soft banjo playing and the padding of the dancers' feet, not a sound was heard. I strummed an extra chorus. As my song ended, Zimri spun his mother out on his arm. Alvira held her skirt to the side and dipped in a curtsy, beaming like a maid. Young and old applauded.

Everyone recognized Alvira Carter as the glue holding together the family—the sons competing and cooperating, the daughters far and near, the grandchildren and great grandchildren flocking to her side. *What must it be like to build a family and watch it grow?* I hoped to find out.

John Carter stepped forward with a song bow in his hand and motioned to the seat beside me. I nodded and John sat, licked the string, and placed the end of the curved sourwood branch in his mouth. He plucked along to my next tune, opening and closing his lips to resonate the sound. The twang of the bow added a regular beat to my banjo's melody. We swayed a bit, finding our rhythm.

The children's perplexed looks told me they'd never seen a song bow, or they'd never heard their grandfather play one. John stomped his foot and his brothers tapped along. Jasper caught my eye and grinned.

We played every song I knew. By the time parents loaded sleepy children into wagons, my fingers were worn out, and I'd never enjoyed myself more.

"Daddy, you haven't touched your song bow in years," Harriet said. "Alice, I hope you'll bring your banjo next Sunday." With a quick goodnight, she bundled her four little ones upstairs.

While Jasper said goodbye to his mother, the wagons cleared the yard and rumbled down the road. Daniel and Anna stood alongside their carriage. He loomed over her and clutched her elbow. I leaned out over the railing, but they were too far away to hear their words. Daniel's earlier dreamy look had disappeared. She'd disappointed him, or worse.

"That was a treat," Caroline said. She moved to my side and touched my upper arm.

I reeled back from the porch's edge. Caroline might have meant the music or her husband holding a prominent place in the family gathering.

"I enjoyed that, Alice." John offered me something between a nod and a bow.

Bit by bit, I was making inroads into the Carter family. My heart softened when John played music with me. I'd told Jennie we were starting new families, and for me, it was a good beginning. I turned back to the road, where the darkness swallowed Daniel and Anna's carriage.

Chapter Twelve

"'Bright Yellows,' which rival the famous Virginia leaf, is the leading variety; and very fancy prices, sometimes over one dollar a pound, are often obtained for superior grades in the markets of Asheville and other cities."

The Asheville City Directory and Gazetteer of Buncombe County

"Soil's warm," Jasper said one early May morning. "Time to plant tobacco."

I covered my day dress with a simple smock and trailed after the men to the fields. My bonnet's stiff brim shielded my face, and I tugged the ruffle down to cover the back of my neck. I did not look forward to the hours in the open field with the sun bearing down.

Robert worked the planting beds, removing the linen covers, exposing the small tobacco seedlings. He burrowed his hands into the moist dark earth, lifted the tender plants, and laid them on a wire-bottomed tray for transplanting to the field.

"Robert will show you what to do," Jasper said.

I grasped the corners of the tray. Robert stood on tiptoes to secure its wide strap around my neck. The extra soil fell through to the ground and the spindly plants with sprawling white roots lay ready for the taking.

Jasper and Zimri moved parallel to one another along the plowed rows, each gripping a tobacco peg. The men snatched seedlings and slipped the tiny plants into the ground where the dull wooden spike formed divots several inches deep. Step. Dig. Drop. I shimmied back and forth so Jasper and Zimri could grasp the tiny plants from my tray. Crawling along the ground after us, Robert packed dirt around the slender stems and watered each plant. Sand and mud matted his clothes and boots.

"I bet more schooling sounds good right now," I said. None of the men acknowledged me. "A young man should better himself by learning his letters and sums." I stumbled on the turned soil.

Jasper continued the repetitive motion of dropping seedlings into the soil. "Robert's learning what he's meant to do. He'll take over this farm one day." He reached for a seedling and avoided looking at me. The thrust of the tobacco peg, a gush of water, and the plodding of our steps replaced any further conversation.

My thoughts percolated, watching Robert labor from dawn to dusk like a grown man. Sweat and dirt streaked my stepson's solemn face. My brother had died from field work, contracting the fever rampant in the low-lying marshy areas. *Darn my husband's pride and wanting Robert to be just like him. Why couldn't Jasper see there might be a better way?*

I felt clumsy and slow throughout the morning. Come break time, I knew it was true when my husband reassured me by saying, "You'll soon learn the rhythm."

Robert hefted water pails on a pole strung across his

shoulders. He wouldn't be slight for long. I refilled the seedling tray and mopped my face. My skirt drooped with clumps of soil clinging to its hem. The mud marked the once beige smock with a pattern of dirty handprints and smudges. I could smell myself and it wasn't pretty.

Before midday, I escaped the fields to fix dinner. I simply could not cook in this state. I washed up and covered my filthy skirt with a fresh apron. The skin on my hands was dry and split. My head throbbed from the heat. I breathed deeply to calm the bitter thoughts directed at my pig-headed husband and his attitude about schooling.

Meat sizzled in the cast-iron pan, but the thought of eating it turned my stomach. The men had no such qualms. With the meal gulped down and the last dish scraped clean, Jasper declared 'no rest for the weary,' and we returned to the fields. The sun climbed higher and seized the dampness from the muddy plants to steam the air like a kettle on the stove. My dress clung to my back and under my arms. I loosened the collar buttons and tugged my bonnet lower.

Such were our days during tobacco planting season: long, hot, dirty, exhausting. Each night as my head touched the pillow, I dreamed the sounds of the fields, the peg striking the earth, the drag of my heavy skirt across the uneven ground, and the heave of my breath with each fumbling footstep. As the days progressed, I found my gait mirrored those of the men. My pace quickened. My stamina improved. I applied balm to my hands to ease the dryness. I had learned to plant tobacco.

By early summer, with the tobacco growing taller by the day, I spent more time with Jasper's niece. On a late summer morning, as Harriet's children played in the yard and we churned the butter and baked bread, Robert flung the kitchen screen door open.

"Did you bring it?" he asked.

"Pardon me?" Harriet stood with hands on hips.

"Good mornin', Cousin. How are you? And did you bring me a new Deadwood Dick?"

"That's better. Good morning to you, Robert. Yes, I left it in your room."

Robert dashed toward his bedroom.

"Thank your cousin!" I called after him.

"Thank my father for putting one aside is more like it," Harriet said. "These dime novels are so popular, he can't keep them stocked at the store."

"Adventure stories, tales of the wild west, cowboys and Indians—all very enticing to a twelve-year-old boy," I replied.

Robert ambled through the kitchen with his nose in the book.

"Watch your step, young man, and hurry back to help your pa," I said.

"This one's about Jesse James!" he cried.

"Robert, do you admire a known bank robber?" Harriet asked.

"Pa says he can't be all bad. He was a bushwhacker after all and fought the Union." Robert put his treasure on the table and bolted outside.

We raised our eyebrows at one another. Harriet and I had become close in our days spent together, sharing chores and confidences. I still missed Jennie, but the ache had lessened and my distress faded like sun-bleached cotton. Harriet's children warmed to me, for I was a Carter woman, free to mend a hurt, feed them, or give a cuddle. Memories of minding my younger brothers and sisters returned with more frequency, sharp and clear and without melancholy. My remaining family lay scattered across the Carolinas, in new homes and with new families. Loss had nearly crushed me in the months leading up to my marriage, and my new life astonished me with all I had gained.

I grabbed a basket, and we wandered out to the garden to pick our dinner vegetables. Harriet's youngest waddled behind her, while the other children ran to play in the barn.

"I've been thinking about Robert," Harriet said. "The boy has a keen mind and a love of reading. He's read all the books we have at the house more than once. I think he would benefit from more schooling, and I know you agree with me."

Dark red tomatoes hung ripe on the vine. Harriet crouched to find the hidden cucumbers, making a game of it with Cornelia.

"It's a shame we don't have a school," I said. "From our church attendance, we have enough children."

"From the Carter family alone, we have plenty." Harriet stood and stretched her back. "Although I shudder at the thought of teaching many of them." Under her breath, she said, "Let no corrupt communication proceed out of your mouth."

I'd become used to Harriet's audible prayer. Based on its regularity, I surmised it didn't alter behavior. She wasn't scolding herself as much as voicing her ideals. Perhaps it kept her preacher husband near her in spirit.

"Many parents 'round here agree with Daniel. Children don't need further schooling," Harriet said.

"A friend in Asheville tells me the Normal School graduates are in demand when towns find the means to support them."

"Around here, neither farmers nor business owners will pay that price," Harriet said.

"Yet schooling prepares young people for the manufacturing jobs at the new furniture factories or textile mills, commerce positions in Asheville's banks and stores, and engineering careers with the railroads, waterworks, or municipal functions." I nearly lost my breath spouting the vast opportunities available in Asheville.

"I couldn't agree more. But consider who controls the businesses in Democrat—my father, Uncle Samuel, and Uncle Daniel. The mills have all the labor they need without the added school tax."

Cornelia handed me a dandelion, her chubby cheeks swelling with her gap-toothed smile. I kissed the little one's hand, and she ran off in search of more *fow-ers.*

"Jasper doesn't favor a school, either. He kindly informed me that Robert *will* farm," I said.

"He likely will," Harriet said. "Even if you're blessed with children, Robert stands to inherit the farm."

My head swam with the thorny problem of encouraging this family to see it my way. "Surely your father wants the best for his grandchildren. Where does he stand? He is the eldest Carter brother."

"Father doesn't assume to be patriarch." Harriet snorted. "Uncle Daniel welcomes taking on that role."

I expected Harriet's self-rebuke, but none came. "Has he?"

"No, but Daniel won my grandfather's favor long ago," Harriet said.

She placed two more cucumbers in the basket and stood to face me. "Did you know Father and my husband were in the same regiment? John Swain captured more than one heart." A listless smile crossed Harriet's face.

Cornelia shoved a handful of dandelion tops at her mother. Harriet embraced her daughter as if she could squeeze out her lingering grief. Memories of my father and my brother brimmed beneath the surface. A year after their passing, grief surged inside me, often unexpectedly.

I searched for any remaining vegetables ripe for the

picking, and for the answer to the school problem. It took perseverance to reveal the fruits of a garden, or a solution to a dilemma. We loaded the basket and returned to the house.

"Grandfather Solomon considered Father's deepening faith a weakness," Harriet explained. "Grandfather was a religious man, but his faith took third place behind business and family. My father ordered his priorities differently, and I've always admired him for that." Harriet placed the tomatoes, cucumbers, and beans on the kitchen table. "Not long after Grandfather named Daniel executor of his will, Father acquired lands to make his own way."

"Where did the other brothers stand with your grandfather?" I asked.

The kitchen window framed Zimri and Jasper in the fields. At a distance, there was little to tell them apart. Daniel was different. His own father recognized it and sowed the seeds of dissension in this family.

"My John counseled Father, Jasper, Grandfather and the rest of the family as best he could." Harriet's shoulders slumped. "The War ripped families apart in more ways than one."

"It's all making sense. A father enables a son's gain and the others either leave or band together."

Harriet filled a basin with water. "Oh, don't count my father out just yet. He's a silent force in the community, with connections he does not flaunt."

I grinned. "A silent force? What's that?"

"I wouldn't know." Harriet leaned her shoulder against mine playfully.

Standing near the kitchen window, we snapped and trimmed beans. The chickens fluttered and squawked in the yard as the older children chased them. Cornelia toddled along behind them, never quite catching up. In a few years, these children would exchange chores for work.

"I'm convinced times are changing. I want Robert prepared." *And secure, not struggling for wages as a tenant farmer or subject to the whims of tobacco or commodity prices.* A few months ago, I'd stepped into the role of stepmother, uncertain and confused. It hadn't taken long to become a mother to Robert. My heart swelled.

"I want the same for my children," Harriet said. "Security can be fleeting."

Sorrow etched her face. I longed to ease Harriet's sorrow, but I knew that one's grief is singular. Sharing it might provide comfort, but it would not staunch it. I grasped Harriet's hand in sympathy and, if I was honest with myself, in fear.

Chapter Thirteen

"The lost cause has the associations which are among the holiest that ennoble human nature. It is a cause that perhaps will never be taken up again ... Yet it is a cause that will never be forgotten, one that will never be associated with shame, one that its adherents will always glory to avow."

Asheville Citizen Times

The other Carter women noticed my growing friendship with Harriet and asked to join us in our housekeeping tasks. My daytime solitude in those first weeks after the wedding disappeared. I welcomed my Carter sisters and the accompanying banter and laughter.

"Many hands make light work of canning." Susannah plopped down a basket of cucumbers.

Anna followed with a crate of glass jars. While one chopped, another washed. I cooked the brine on the stovetop. One filled and sealed containers while another placed them into the water bath on the stove.

Anna sliced the cucumbers. "I declare, I've never enjoyed canning more."

Of all my Carter sisters, Anna remained an enigma. She was refined, but could let loose, dancing or singing at Sunday suppers. She mothered all the Carter children but didn't have her own. Anna lived in the grandest house with the largest staff, yet she moved about the kitchen with ease.

Tightly packed in jars, the bright green cucumbers took on a subdued color and joined the beets, green beans and tomatoes to create a rainbow on my pantry shelves. I breathed in the kitchen air, hot from our four close bodies, and a simmering stock pot on the woodstove. A smaller pan added smells of vinegar and sugar. By the end of our endeavors, I might be pickled.

"Beats doing all this by myself, that's for sure." Susannah's frank tone contrasted with her husband's easy-going nature. I knew where I stood with Susannah, and I supposed her husband Zimri did as well. I couldn't say the same about Anna.

"You have a lovely voice," I said. During Sunday play day, Anna shined, whether singing the melody or harmony. I didn't care for her husband, Daniel. He was full of himself and voiced his opinions for all to hear. However, I gave him credit for admiring his wife's singing. His face softened and his body relaxed when she sang. "Have you had training?"

"My sisters and I all had a musical education, either voice or piano. Mother directed our daily practice, and we had weekly family recitals before our father," Anna said.

How regimental and formal. Utterly different from a childhood chasing chickens or exploring the woods. "If your sisters play half as well as you sing, I imagine those were wonderful concerts," I said. "Do you see your family?"

The even pattern of Harriet's chopping faltered. Susannah carried on, sliding glass jars into the canning pot.

"My parents and two sisters died in Savannah's yellow fever outbreak. My eldest brother was away on business in Gainesville and survived. He remains at our family home."

"I'm so sorry, Anna," I said.

"I haven't been back to the city since my marriage." Anna beat an even rhythm with the knife against the cutting board.

Harriet was widowed. Anna had lost most of her family. My own loved ones were dead or scattered. None of us moved on unscathed, independent of our pasts. My chopping slowed.

"This batch is done," Susannah said. "Ready for another dozen."

I edged next to Anna at the kitchen table, and we filled more jars. Our pasts hovered like the kitchen's steamy air—surrounding, cradling, and sometimes oppressing us. Yet, here we all were, carrying on.

"Friends who perspire together, stay together." Susannah dropped the last set of pickles into the water bath and wiped her brow and hands with her apron. "Lordy, I never want to see another pickle."

We laughed, but the air hung heavy with memory.

After supper that Friday, Jasper and I examined the farm accounts. I recorded expenses in the ledger while Jasper read from the newspaper—what prices were higher this season from the last, what was the same or lower, the yields of various types of crops, the outlook for the coming weeks. I learned about tobacco, and that my stepson came by his teacher tendencies honestly.

We finished our work and settled on the porch. Jasper filled his pipe. These evenings drew us closer together, with the day's labors done, when we could sit in each other's company, resting and contemplative. As I strummed my banjo, my husband composed the lyrics to my song.

"One imagines that war is all blood and noise, and aye, it is that." Jasper puffed and exhaled. "But there were also the evenings in the camps, when I was dead tired and fixin' to collapse in my tent. I wondered how many more nights I'd look at the stars." His eyes drifted upward.

The sky was inky black. Moonlight silhouetted an owl in flight, its broad wings as distinctive as its voice.

Now months into our marriage, with hints of family divisions and echoes of ghosts, my curiosity got the better of me. "What happened to Garrett?"

Jasper's words poured out. "Zimri, Garrett and I were all privates in Company K, 25th North Carolina Infantry Regiment. Like so many other patriots, we enlisted together back in 1862. We rushed into it with such aspirations. Foolish ones."

I picked at the banjo strings while Jasper plucked out his long-ago memories.

"Marching to the front, we were almost giddy. There we were, dressed in our gray uniforms, ready to fight the Northern boys for our way of life. Only took lookin' one of 'em right in the eye just before he fell to realize he was just as scared as us."

"You were young and idealistic." I laid the instrument across my lap.

"Aye, those two often go together. I was the oldest of us three. Even though we were men, we grew up during the War."

"I can only imagine."

The sweet scent of Jasper's tobacco surrounded us. Unlike these memories, the pungent smells dissipated quickly.

"Petersburg was the decisive battle in the War. We had to defend the Capitol, and the Union knew it. They were shrewd, striking us hard to disrupt the rail lines and supplies to

Richmond. We lost Garrett on September 29, 1864 at Chaffin's Farm."

Part of me wanted to end this retelling, to not hear of this loss, to not feel the burning ache that plagued my husband. Another part of me understood that until I knew of the event that transformed his life, I wouldn't fully know him.

"Until that day, we'd fought side by side, looking out for one another," Jasper continued. "This battle was too damn big —too many soldiers, too much noise and smoke. Muzzle flashes blinded me." He clasped his hands together and raised them to his mouth. His eyes briefly closed. When they opened, they glinted in the dim light. "Sometimes, I still smell the gunpowder."

Jasper stared into the darkness as if he could see beyond it to another place and time. I longed to reach out to him, but my touch would interrupt his reverie.

"The Union troops crossed the James River on a pontoon bridge they'd built without our knowledge. They attacked from the south and the north with a force much greater than ours. General Lee tried to replenish the units, but after all the deaths, disease, and desertions, we never stood a chance."

"What happened to Garrett?" More than my needing to know, Jasper needed to share it. I'd witnessed my husband bottling up his emotions with his brother Daniel, and seen the clear strain in a hardened jaw, stiff neck, or clenched fists.

"I found him, with a shot through his right eye." Jasper choked and cleared his throat. "Don't s'pose I'll ever not see that."

I gripped my husband's hand. Jasper's lips squeezed together as if doing so could compress his thoughts and bury his feelings.

"You were young, but you probably know the rest," Jasper said. "After Petersburg fell in April 1865, we lost Richmond.

General Lee surrendered at Appomattox, and we came home. At least some of us."

"It wasn't your fault, Jasper."

"Father didn't think so. Zimri, Garrett, and I were to all return. We were to win the War. Instead, we'd let them bury our brother in a mass, unmarked grave far from home. Our father, and our relationship with our father, changed forever." Jasper's eyes drooped.

No words would console my husband. My touch would have to do. His grip tightened on mine. Jasper chose me when I'd had no option but to find a husband and a home. Perhaps he'd needed me as much as I'd needed him.

"Father gifted Zimri and me our lands soon after our return. That kept us from his everyday life at the sawmill and grist mill. Samuel and John were in a different regiment, but they, too, felt the sting of our father's dismissal. Daniel was too young to fight. He and our younger sisters remained at home. I wrestled with my demons for a long time. Working the land helped."

"And then came Sarah," I said.

"After a while, yes. She was young, and we weren't married but a year."

Sarah had died following Robert's birth. I hadn't realized the brief time they'd had together. The trauma of war, his father's dismissal, losing his wife—all helped explain why Jasper hadn't married when faced with an infant to raise on his own.

"Swain saved me. Aye, and Harriet." Jasper scanned the sky rather than look me in the eye. "She cared for Robert when I wasn't fit to do more than till the fields."

I turned my gaze to the heavens, starlit and endless, dark and full of mystery.

"Your niece is dear to me," I said. "She's filled a gap."

"Your sister."

It wasn't a question, but a statement prompting me to tell my story. "I only remember running the household with Jennie at my side. From sunup to sundown we were together. While Mother and Father did their best to support the family, Jennie and I raised our siblings and managed our home."

I hadn't always thought my parents had done their best, but with time and separation, I'd come to appreciate their goodness. My own travels convinced me that life's course is unpredictable. I didn't know all the trials thrown in their path, but I could think of several, and my parents had faced them together.

Jasper smiled and stroked his beard. "I imagined as much, given the changes you've made here, adding your own touch to the ways things are done."

"I came prepared to run a household. Being a mother is more difficult." I could not deny that a certain coolness remained with my stepson. He was polite and appreciative, but he still called me Alice and maintained his distance. I'd tried to manage him much like the home, but Robert had his own ways. A stepmother seemed unnecessary. His pa and he did just fine.

"He'll come 'round," Jasper said. "The boy takes some time with change."

"I've tried to be a mother to him."

"Aye, but he's never really had one. Don't s'pose he knows what he wants or needs."

A familiar phrase. I hadn't answered my sister's question in the days before the wedding. *Had I figured out what I wanted? What I needed?*

Silence enveloped us like a warm blanket. The night sky revealed faraway stars as we unveiled our secrets. The smells of ripened plants and something sweet and musty infused the air, sparking an idea.

"Might you spare Robert for an afternoon?"

"I might. What do you have in mind?" Jasper asked.

"I'd like some berry baskets. I could use a strong young man to fell and split some white oaks," I said.

"If that means berry pie, then I believe I can spare Robert tomorrow."

Chapter Fourteen

"The Farmers of Buncombe County, although but few of them are rich, few are very poor, and they are, without doubt, thankful to that providence which has cast their lot in a land so highly favored by nature ... What more, on earth, could man desire!"

The Asheville City Directory and Gazetteer of Buncombe County

I hitched my skirts and followed Robert up the densely wooded slopes. We would check on the hogs before climbing higher in search of suitable white oak trees.

"I'm glad you've come with me today," I said.

Robert shrugged. "Bet Pa misses me. I'm a good worker."

"Oh, I know. You're such a help to me. I couldn't possibly fell the size tree we need and get it down the hill." I crossed my fingers behind my back at telling such a blatant fib.

The earth was stable in between the tree roots that curled along the path. I picked my way over loose soil in other places, while Robert moved nimbly over rocky outcroppings. He stooped to pick up acorns and lob them back into the trees.

The musty smell of decaying leaves hung heavy in the air, moving only when the breath of pine overpowered it. A breeze lifted the tree branches and sunlight dappled through, causing the waxy leaves of the shrubs to shimmer magically. Given a chance, my sister would lose herself in these woods and dream up a new design with her needle and thread.

"We're looking for a sapling 'bout five, six inches through and a straight eight or nine feet tall," Robert said. "It won't do to have knots or limbs on the trunk." Robert's pant legs ended above his boots.

I must let down the hem, if there's any left. "I knew you were just the one to help."

Robert glanced at me and I wondered if I was laying it on too thick.

"I've split oaks before," Robert said. "I wove the seat and back for your porch rocker."

That revelation stopped me flat. "You made my chair?" I'd walked by the three rocking chairs, and never considered there'd likely been just two before my arrival. I lifted my skirt to step over a fallen log.

"Pa finished the wood frame, and I wove the splits."

"Thank you, Robert. That was a fine welcoming gift."

He shrugged off the compliment. Hog bells tinkled, and we turned toward the sound.

Maybe I needed to learn more about Robert. *Maybe* I needed to learn more about this family. I'd made assumptions and been surprised. As we trudged higher, I considered my stepson's shoulders, broadened by the fieldwork, and his quiet, unassuming way. *So like his father.* Perhaps in the ways I'd grown close to Jasper—sharing our work and talking in the evenings—I might grow dearer to Robert. Today was just the start.

"This one will do real nice." Robert swung the axe.

Summer drew on like oil to a painting, brushing the tobacco leaves a rich green against a cerulean sky. Jasper, Zimri, and Robert started at sunup with the first harvesting. Perspiration soon sketched dark streaks down their backs. The men picked the ripening leaves from the bottom, leaving the younger ones farther up the stem for a later harvest. Robert followed along to grasp the lugs, the foliage spattered with sand from our drenching summer rains. He shook off the grit that clung to the sap-soaked leaves. The men piled the tobacco atop the mule-drawn sleigh and delivered it to us—the women loopers.

Susannah and I sheltered in the shade of the barn. I'd never felt so inadequate. Keeping house was one thing, but gathering tobacco leaves into bundles—called hands, and stringing them to a pole at the speed of Susannah was quite another. By the second harvest, when the next leaves had ripened, I could make one hand for Susannah's two.

"You're doing fine, Alice. Won't be long until we hang the poles and Jasper lights the furnace for the curing." Susannah tipped her chin toward the field where our tenants worked. "Hot work as it is, even worse when one's carrying a child."

I glanced at our Negro tenant's protruding stomach. She kept her hair up in a kerchief and rolled up her dress sleeves, exposing her strong, glistening forearms. Aside from her growing belly, she was thin and wiry, her neck so long, her head floated above her body. She lumbered behind her man, cutting leaves and throwing them to a hand-pulled sled. With no mule to bear the burden of the load, their work would last until nightfall.

"Daniel's not happy that y'all have Negro tenants." Susannah finished a hand of tobacco and placed it on her pile.

"Don't suppose Daniel has a say."

"S'pose not." Susannah clasped a bundle of leaves and used another tobacco leaf to wind around the stems and bind the hand. "Mind you, I don't make excuses for Daniel, but he was at home when their slaves ran off. His father was mad as a hornet. Daniel hasn't liked the Negroes around since."

Daniel had been at home during the War, as I had been. He hadn't witnessed the death, blood, and broken bodies on the battlefield, but he may have faced fears no child should experience. A memory of grabbing Jennie's hand, running toward the hayloft, and Pa shouting 'Hurry!' came on me. I shuddered.

"My parents' one slave ran off during the War," I said. "He tended the animal pens."

"My pa stayed at the Harris Inn on his drives. He had his favorites and your family's inn was among 'em."

"That pleases me, Susannah," I said. "The Union troops finished us." Our inn remained after the War, but the soldiers destroyed our fields and pens. The crops were lost. Union soldiers made off with our tools, livestock, and food stores. The War changed everything.

"Us too. Union troops stole a large herd from my father, left our family to scrape by with the land we lived on. All the children, includin' me, sought a way out."

"Is that when you married?" I could ask such a pointed question of Susannah. She'd certainly asked me plenty.

"My father led old Mr. Carter's herds to the coastal markets. It was his herd that was lost." Susannah's words flew out as fast as her tobacco tying. "Father brought my sister and me along to negotiate the loss. Didn't realize that we were compensation."

More than likely, the proposed marriages allowed her father to unload two more mouths to feed.

"I have some notion of being bought and sold," Susannah said.

My jaw slackened. *Surely Susannah wasn't comparing herself to a Negro?*

Across the field, our colored tenant held one hand on her lower back and leaned over to pick. She threw the leaves to the sled and wiped her brow with her smock, never lifting her bulging form from her half-bent position. A sympathetic ache coursed up my spine.

"Solomon said I'd suit Zimri. Jasper was just back from the War and not married, but he didn't take to his father's suggestion to marry my sister." Susannah looked up at me. "Not that she did anything wrong. Jasper couldn't bind his heart so soon after losing Garrett."

"One more disappointment for their father," I said.

"Ah, you've been told about the land."

"Where do you and Zimri stand?"

I hadn't thought Susannah's hands could twist any faster, but her movements quickened.

We shared more than a sharp tongue. Insecurity brought both of us to this family. Every day, I worked to shore up my standing by building a bond with my husband, seeking a way into my stepson's heart, sweating and straining to ensure a successful tobacco harvest.

"I like your ways, Alice. Not another one of my Carter sisters speaks her mind like you." Susannah smiled. "Solomon gave Zimri seventy-five acres just as he did Jasper. It all works for now."

"For now?" I asked.

"When Alvira dies, there'll be a reckoning. As executor, Daniel will settle the estate and even out the inheritances. Zimri's too kind-hearted to deal with him, so I s'pose I'll have to get involved." She tossed a tied hand on the growing pile. "I don't look forward to it."

My hands slowed, and I contemplated this newfound predicament. Susannah had sized up Zimri. I wasn't sure my husband would stand up to his younger brother or whether I might need to entangle myself in the family's business.

Chapter Fifteen

"Every Woman Knows Them ... The human body is much like a good clock or watch in its movements ... Hence it is that the numerous ailments which make woman's [sic] life miserable are the direct issue of the abnormal action of the uterine system."

The Asheville Citizen-Times

The men trudged in from the fields, leading the mules with the last of the tobacco. Soil and sweat filled the creases in their faces and necks, and sticky sap coated their hands and stained their forearms. My own arms and hands looked like brushes dipped in a tar bucket. Beyond the men's forms, the naked tobacco stalks wavered with the late summer heat and the bare fields longed for their burning and the ash to feed next season's seedlings.

The last of the crop cured in the barn on the second to last Sunday of October. I admired the fall colors on the ride to church. Throughout the year, I'd noticed the change in the flowers and plants that lined the road, and the birds that plied them for their seeds and berries. The familiar road brought contentment.

John and Caroline stood before the church entrance, with somber-looking faces.

"Good morning." I embraced Caroline.

She stiffened and pulled back from me.

"What is it?"

Caroline looked at John.

John held a letter. "It arrived early this morning from G.W. Cannon."

I could think of only one reason my sister's husband would write to me. My heart raced and my pulse thumped in my head. If there was a further exchange of words, I didn't hear them until Jasper said, "You all go on in. I'll stay with Alice."

Caroline corralled Robert and they left us.

My hands shook. My husband took the letter from me, opened it, and handed me the single page.

I read quickly through to the end. "Jennie is with fever. It's been three days and no sign of it breaking. G.W. says I should come to her." He didn't need to write in case she didn't pull through. I'd watched our brother succumb to fever. I cupped my hand over my mouth, concealing the pain and hampering my cry. Jasper's arms encircled me and I melted into him.

That afternoon at the Carter homestead, word spread of Jennie's illness.

"Try not to worry, my dear," Alvira said. "God will prevail."

He better. I bit my lip and nodded "Jennie has a delicate

constitution. I should be with her."

"Is it wise to expose yourself to the unhealthy vapors?" Daniel asked.

I disliked Daniel more than ever. While each of these men had the final say on their women's comings and goings, Daniel ruled over every woman in his vicinity. Bossy. Proud. Opinionated. I wanted to stuff his pocket watch down his throat.

Jasper's face appeared resolute. I wished I knew his opinion.

"Jennie is my closest sister," I said. "She would do as much for me."

Caroline encouraged the men to examine John's harvest in the barn, while the two of us walked through the orchard behind the house. The apples were ripe and ready for picking. My mind tussled with the mundane, the useless, and my worry.

"I must go to Jennie, but I think Jasper won't let me," I admitted.

"He'll fear you taking ill. Jasper blamed himself for Sarah's death." Caroline bore a pained look. "Childbirth comes with risks."

"I nursed my brother and survived. I can care for Jennie." My words faltered.

"It's not just you at risk. There's Robert and Jasper to think of." Caroline took me in her arms. I sank against the woman, who was more a mother to me than a sister-in-law. The scent of her flowery soap and the softness of her wrinkled skin embraced me. "Your love is strong, Alice. Speak to Jasper. He understands sibling responsibility and might approve of you going despite the danger."

We agreed I would travel Tuesday when the stagecoach stopped at the Carter Inn. It would take me as far as Asheville, where I would board a train for Hendersonville. I'd said some sharp words to Jasper when he hadn't allowed me to travel right away. He said it just wouldn't do, me traveling alone by wagon. I waited, worried, and cast a frosty eye my husband's way. If anything happened to Jennie before I arrived, I would never forgive him.

On Monday, I packed a bag and set the house in order in anticipation of being gone a week or more. On the porch that evening, I rocked back and forth insistently.

"Would you like your banjo?" Jasper held out my instrument.

I shook my head vigorously.

"S'pose not." He placed it on the porch floorboards. "Don't figure there's anything I can say to ease your worry."

I turned my face from him to swipe a tear away. He laid his palm on my shoulder.

Over breakfast on Tuesday, Jasper assured me he and Robert would get on fine, as they had done for many years. He realized what he'd implied and said, "Hurry back, Alice, when Jennie's better."

"Won't be the same without you." Robert's endearment brought me to tears again. I had grown fond of him, and now and again, he gifted me with a curt affection.

I burned the coffee and forgot to put butter on the table. Jasper left most of his runny eggs on his plate. I didn't care. *Serves him right for delaying my departure.* Before we could saddle the horses, a rider approached the house with a letter. Jasper paid the delivery boy a penny for the trouble. I broke the seal and sat down on the front porch steps to read my sister's fate.

I recognized her sloping handwriting. She was well enough to write.

October 27, 1882

My dearest Alice,

How worried you must be since receiving G.W.'s letter. Let me assure you that although I'm weak, I am on the mend.

Less than a week ago, I was taken by fever and a burning pain in the depths of my belly. For three days and nights, I slept. When I awakened, the household was quiet and I didn't know the day or time. A granny healer stayed at my bedside applying vinegar compresses to draw out the fever and feeding me willow bark tea. My fever broke on Sunday evening. I like to think it was your prayers that made the healing difference.

I'm most distressed to think of the concern my illness has caused you. Rest assured, I'm in capable hands. You don't need to come. I will remain in bed until I have regained my strength. I don't know what G.W. is doing for food, but I suspect he's not starving.

All my love,

Jennie

October 28, 1882

My dearest Jennie,

I was relieved to have your letter this evening sharing the news of your recovery. I wish you a speedy climb to health. Know, dear sister, that you are on my mind and in my heart.

As you insist that you are cared for, I will stay put for now. However, I will write regularly to bolster your spirits.

We leave for Asheville at the end of the week to take the

harvest to market. You may write to me in care of Cousin Mary and Stewart. They invited us to stay a few days to enjoy the city, their company, and to tend to business in town.

With loving wishes,

Alice

Chapter Sixteen

"ASHEVILLE TOBACCO MARKET. Prices are good, buyers are eager, and there is a general tendency under the eagerness of competition to continued stiffening of prices. Altogether, the outlook is encouraging."

The Asheville Weekly Citizen

Frost blanketed the earth when Jasper and his brother, Zimri, loaded the wagon with stacks of dried tobacco leaves caked together and tied into large square bricks. The curing had removed the cloying smell of the fresh leaves and our harvest would spread only a faint pipe smell on the road toward Asheville.

The air whipped up from the chilled ground, and I tucked the lap blanket snugly about us. Heavy lumber wagons traveled this road, carving ruts in the mud and slush. Overnight, they froze into hardened furrows. The wagon bobbled and jostled as we set off toward the city.

Jasper nodded at the tenants, and the man tipped his hat. His wife was close to birthing, which explained the old Negro woman sitting on the porch. Her mother, or his, had come to help.

I tucked my hands under the blanket and smoothed my skirt over my flat stomach. It'd been ten months and still no sign of a child. My courses were irregular and always had been. Would I not experience the joy of being a mother? Of holding our baby in my arms? If I were barren, would my husband regret our marriage? I squinted and looked away to watch the passing fields, hoping to leave my sudden melancholy in our wake.

Eighteen miles meant two hours of travel. My thoughts turned to Asheville. I couldn't wait to see the newest stores, hotels, and resorts that Cousin Mary had described in her letters. Zimri's wife, Susannah, and I planned to shop for Christmas gifts after the men sold the tobacco at auction.

"Our crop is fine and prices are holding this year," Jasper said. "Today will tell."

"It's been a good year. Perhaps we can find a new book for Robert?" My stepson yearned for words and stories. He had packed *Black Beauty* for his few nights stay at his Uncle John and Aunt Caroline's.

"A fine idea." Jasper pursed his lips. "I've heard there's a new photography shop in Asheville. I'd like to have a portrait of my wife. What do you say, Alice?"

I stared down at my rough, freckled hands. "In this state?"

"You've never looked more beautiful."

Since Jennie's illness and recovery, Jasper charmed me. Perhaps he regretted making me wait to attend to my sister when she'd been so sick. He should. Still, he was taking pains to apologize. I curled my arm through my husband's.

Tobacco-laden wagons jammed the roads leading to

Asheville's warehouses. I wasn't the only one worrying that other's harvests might fare better at auction. Jasper shifted as he eyed the loads. Our livelihood came down to the price offered, and as Jasper had explained, that had everything to do with supply and demand.

After the relative quiet of the farm, the warehouse was a tornado of activity and noise. Wagons rumbled up the wooden ramp, agitated horses snorted and whinnied, and gathering crowds added to the cacophony. The vast auction room accommodated eight or more wagons. Stretching from end to end and row upon row, mounds of dried tobacco awaited sale. Jasper corralled the workmen to unload our crop.

A tall man wearing a flamboyant suit, a green silk vest, and a top hat caught my eye. "Who is that?"

"The dandy? He's the auctioneer," Jasper said.

"He looks like he belongs on the stage." I watched the man twirl a brass-handled cane.

"Aye, it's fine entertainment," Jasper said. "His job is to attract farmers to the warehouse and flashy clothes help. The warehouse earns a commission on tobacco sales, so the more farmers—"

"The more product, and more profit," I said.

"That's right. The other part of the auctioneer's job is to move the product quickly. Once he starts, he watches for the buyers' signals, showing a raised bid. He squeezes out the highest price for the farmer and the warehouse."

"Are those the buyers coming our way?" I pointed toward a group of men working their way down the row of waist-high tobacco stacks. They huddled like penguins, waddling along in their dark suits, white shirts, and black top hats. Their inscrutable faces added to our worries about how we would fare today.

"Aye. Come along." Jasper moved from the auctioneer's side of the row to the buyer's side. The scent was overwhelming: sweet tobacco, horse manure, and the perspiration of too many men, boys, and women. As Jasper had promised, tobacco was work, and it required all hands.

"Mr. Miller, it's good to see you again." Jasper shook hands with a short round man sporting a bushy handlebar mustache. "Might I introduce Mrs. Carter?"

Pleasantries exchanged, Jasper continued, "I was showing my wife what an excellent color we achieved with the curing this year." He fingered the leaves, inviting the buyer to sample the crop. "Others cured too fast, which results in a greener leaf, but we stoked the barn stoves for a week and gradually increased the heat for a nice bright gold color."

Jasper's promotion drew the attention of more than Mr. Miller. The buyers fingered the leaves, pulling out samples to turn and inspect. Few spoke with one another, but then they were all competing for product. I gleaned a few satisfied faces. Perhaps our toil would pay off.

"It's a fine crop, Mr. Carter," Mr. Miller said. "You've done well again."

I hadn't realized I'd been holding my breath. Jasper's shoulders relaxed, and mine did as well.

The buyers moved along, inspecting the stacks and awaiting the bugle, signaling the auction start.

"Mr. Miller is one of the biggest buyers and has bought my crop two years in a row," Jasper said. "He works for Washington Duke out of Durham."

"I recognize the name."

"You should. If anything good came of the War, it was the Yankees finding our fine tobacco. Duke started filling Yankee orders by mail to become one of the biggest cigarette manufacturing businesses in the South." Jasper led me closer to our lot. "Never hurts to market one's goods. Might bring a penny or more per pound." He fidgeted and shoved his hands into his pockets. "Now, we wait."

The warehousemen cleared the sold product and filled the row again. The sold bundles of tobacco left the warehouse bound for train cars, taking them to factories in other cities. The warehousemen scurried about, clearing space for the incoming wagons to unload.

"My goodness, it's frenzied work," I said.

"Aye," Jasper said. "It's not only the farmers and warehousemen that want quick sales. The buyers need more product as the demand for cigarettes increases."

"That should mean a good price for us."

"You're a quick learner." Jasper's eyes gleamed with pride and I smiled in return.

The bugle blew and our row's auction steamed ahead. The auctioneer raised his cane and twirled it while chanting an incoherent stream of words. His sonorous voice echoed throughout the warehouse. With the buyers on one side signaling a bid and the auctioneer on the other side of the tobacco, the group edged closer to us. I didn't understand a bit.

Jasper tugged on his suit lapels. "It'll be over in a couple of minutes."

"That soon?"

"See the slips of paper the warehouseman sets on the stack? That shows the sale. Takes about fifteen seconds for a farmer to know whether he's made a profit."

The auctioneer stood before our lot and continued his rapid-fire calling.

"Hey-hey-give-me-seven-seven-seventy-five-now-eighty-I-got-eighty-five-up-up-up-hey-ninety..." The auctioneer's mouth opened and closed, spread wide and narrowed. His eyes bulged, darting left and right as he picked up the buyers' signals. The man moved constantly, waving his arms, pointing his cane, and dancing along the stacks.

Mr. Miller nodded at the auctioneer's call, followed by

another buyer tugging at his beard. Another touched the brim of his hat. Mr. Miller nodded again. With a sweep of the auctioneer's top hat, and whoops from the gathering crowd, I understood we'd received a notable price. Jasper tipped his hat to Mr. Miller, our buyer. The burden of worry lifted in a matter of minutes. Our year of toil resulted in a profit and we could now enjoy our few days in the city. I practically squeezed Jasper's arm off and he obliged the enthusiasm over my first market experience.

While we awaited our sales slip, workers hoisted away our row and unloaded more bundles for sale. A middle-aged woman dressed in a gray woolen skirt and drab white blouse stood apart. Her hair was reddish brown, braided, and tacked up across the top of her head in an old-fashioned, but practical style. While her wagon was unloaded, she braced her legs and rolled up her shirt cuffs, like someone in charge or someone who wished to be. A scrawny boy of about ten drove her wagon out and the woman shook a finger as a group of buyers walked by uninterested.

"I've got product to sell," she cried out to a passing warehouseman. "You've dealt with my husband in years past. Can't help that he's gone. A widow has a right to make a living."

Two men shuffled away to avoid the woman's outburst. The warehouse foreman beckoned a junior worker to his side, whispered some instructions, and the young man headed reluctantly toward the widow. After a brief exchange, he pointed to his logbook.

"I'll take my chances with the auction," she said. "Mine's good quality and I won't be taking your lowball price."

I hated to see the woman struggle on her own. I approached Jasper as he took our receipt. "Might you help this widow?"

Jasper hesitated. I'd seen him avoid conflict with his

brother over their differing opinions. The only thing to spur him into acting would be imagining my vulnerability. "I would be grateful for help if I were in such an unwelcoming situation."

With a pinched forehead and clenched jaw, Jasper pushed himself forward. "You've had a fine crop, Mrs.?"

"Corcoran. Mrs. Jared Corcoran." She lifted her chin, not haughtily, but rather to establish her right to be here.

Jasper handled a bundle. "The color is fine and the moisture content is just right."

The junior warehouseman looked over his shoulder for his supervisor but did not find him at the ready. Jasper excused himself to find Mr. Miller. The widow and I watched the two men exchange words. Mr. Miller looked down the row, nodded, and the two men broke apart. Jasper marched over to the supervisor. Mrs. Corcoran and I waited through the uneasiness, following Jasper's gestures toward Miller and us. The man waved at the junior laborer and the widow's product was added to the row.

The bugle blared, and the selling began. Within minutes, a sales slip rested on Mrs. Corcoran's harvest. She inspected it and did not fold down the slip's corner, signaling she accepted the bidder's price.

"Thank you kindly, Mr. ...?"

"Carter. I'm glad to be of service. Mrs. Corcoran, I'd like to introduce my wife, Alice. She deserves your thanks more than me."

I smiled with pride at my husband's actions and Jasper's face softened. My lingering resentment from Jasper restricting my visit to my sister, the stress of bringing our harvest to market, and the anxiety over our tenuous marriage dissipated. He didn't support my public school efforts, but he didn't hamper them. My outspokenness often caused him to bite his tongue. In our first year together, we'd had our difficulties, yet we were melding together and making it work.

I took my husband's arm as we turned toward the office to take payment. "That was a good thing you did back there."

"I reckon it was. Luckily, I have a wife who points out such opportunities."

Chapter Seventeen

"ATTENTION LADIES!—We have had a communication from Miss Anna Woodfin, of Asheville, who is Superintendent of the Flower Mission in N.C. She wishes a society organized here for work among the sick and destitute. We want all who are interested in this work to meet at the Academy at 5 o,clock p.m. [sic] Thursday the 18th."

The Carolina Mountaineer

My cousins greeted us like long-lost relations. We were fortunate to have Mary and Stewart in Asheville and avoid the cost of a hotel. A single man might sleep in the rafters of the tobacco warehouse, but a married couple could not. After a long day split between the dusty road and the fetid warehouse, I enjoyed a bath and a clean dress.

Soaking in the warm, sudsy water, I marveled at how not a year had passed and I was back in my cousins' home, feeling altogether more myself than the last time. I was settled in a marriage in which my opinions mostly mattered. Today marked another day in my education around tobacco farming.

I hadn't made progress with bringing a school to Democrat, but I planned to meet Elizabeth to hear of the public school effort in the city. Asheville's advancements encouraged me.

At supper, Mary relayed the progress of the Flower Mission.

"Anna Woodfin, bless her soul, founded our little group to deliver a little kindness and beauty to our shut-in neighbors," Mary explained for Jasper's benefit. "Now that we've been underway a little more than a year, we are collecting sufficient donations to start a hospital."

"Why, Mrs. Tate, will that come about?" Jasper asked.

"I'm working toward that cause. Asheville is growing and we must prepare for the future. We are looking for property."

My cousin's pretty smile and rosy lips accentuated her milky skin. Some exhibited pride by preening or swaggering, but not Mary. Her pleasure in helping others enhanced her grace like a fine brooch adorns a collar.

Stewart inquired about tobacco prices and the harvest. "There's talk in Asheville that the market will move to Durham following Washington Duke's investment in the cigarette-rolling machinery."

"Last year a girl rolled four cigarettes an hour and now with this machinery, output is twelve thousand an hour," Jasper said. "Cigarettes will be plentiful and popular."

"I say, I won't give up my pipe so soon." Stewart invited Jasper to his library for a smoke.

"Come Alice, let's sit awhile on the porch." Cousin Mary motioned toward the front of the house. This time there was no secretive message to the houseboy and the parlor window remained closed. Tonight, we wouldn't eavesdrop on our husbands, like we had when Senator Vance, Colonel Coleman, and Stewart discussed the future of the railroad. Too bad. I'd liked our little foray into spying.

The sounds of movement throughout the city—

whinnying horses, wagon traffic, various machinery, footsteps and voices floated onto the elevated porch. Those who came to shop or sell found ways to spend their money any time of day. The opera beckoned. Hotels offered entertainment. Taverns called. Asheville didn't sleep. It was a far cry from the moonlit porch back in Democrat, with only the crickets and frogs and fireflies as guests.

Mary patted the cushioned seat beside her. "Jennie and G.W. dined with us on their last trip to Asheville. She seemed well and G.W. very attentive," she said.

"In a good way?" I splayed out my skirt and sat beside my cousin.

Mary cocked her head. "Yes, of course."

"Right. How else would he be?" Jennie hadn't gone into details about their understanding, but I couldn't forget her letter following their wedding night. She'd been hurt, yet her husband had forced her to fulfill her wifely duties. Mary's firsthand account from their recent stay didn't assuage my concerns.

"Jennie visited Miss Shackton while here in Asheville," Mary said.

My sister hadn't mentioned this in her recent letter. I'd shared everything with her and specifically asked her to tell me of Elizabeth's school efforts. *Why hadn't Jennie confided in me? Why hold back about visiting Elizabeth?* The distance with my sister increased beyond the miles we were apart. My heart sank. "I'd hoped Jennie and G.W. would time an Asheville visit with ours."

Mary patted my knee. "Maybe next time, dear. She's still recovering."

Recovering from her recent illness and receding. My stomach twisted and burned. We hadn't fought—unlike Jasper and me over my need to care for Jennie when she'd been sick. No angry words were exchanged. Yet our promise to remain close slipped further away, flimsy or forgotten. *Perhaps Jennie's town friends with their fancy houses fulfilled her? Maybe she didn't need me?*

"What news did Jennie bring?" I asked.

"All the society news of Hendersonville. She's quite in the know, what with working in the store." She leaned in and spoke under her breath. "I have some ties there myself, so I enjoyed comparing notes with your sister."

"Hmm." I didn't care a whit about Hendersonville society. "I've been corresponding with Miss Shackton since my last visit."

"Is that so?"

"I like to hear of the progress that's yet to reach our small town."

Mary puffed up. "We are living in modern times. Did you know there's talk of telephones in Asheville?"

My cousin's question was a well-wrapped gift placed in my lap.

"My goodness, what a statement that would make to have a telephone," I said. My cousin did her best to keep up appearances. While Mary was more adept at calling cards and visits, a telephone would mark her as a modern woman.

"I will speak to Stewart, as I will surely want one to conduct business."

I seized the moment. "Times are changing."

"Hm." Mary relaxed on the loveseat.

"I admire your work with the many ladies' groups here in Asheville. The flower society, the new hospital ... why you're keeping up with changing times." I paused and then feigned surprise. "I don't know why I didn't think of it before! Cousin, I must introduce you to Miss Petersen and Miss Shackton. Your connections in society would help the public school campaign immensely." I widened my eyes and rounded my mouth. "Just think how far the movement would progress with you behind it."

I hoodwinked my cousin as a means to an end. If I could help move public schools forward in Asheville, perhaps I could figure out how to bring one to Democrat. Mary shifted beside me. I breathlessly awaited the next move. *Would she bite?*

Her response poured forth like molasses onto a biscuit. "I have a good number of contacts that might be of help."

"Of course you do."

"I have kept up with the talk, Alice. The current efforts are disorganized, and a powerful voice could bring groups together."

"Oh Mary, I can't think of a better person to be that voice."

She beamed, and I flashed her an innocent smile. We sat companionably and the lantern light offered a steady, insistent glow. Despite the long day of travel and selling our crop, I was alert and engaged in this pursuit. Until now my efforts to further the school cause had been as successful as a clothesline in the rain. The problem was all the action took place in Asheville. Elizabeth and Margaret were here. What could I do from so far away? If only I had a reason to visit Asheville more often, like Jennie.

"Alice, before you leave, I'd like to be introduced to Miss Petersen and Miss Shackton. Might you make those arrangements?"

"I'll send an invitation to tea for tomorrow afternoon," I said. It seemed my quest had only just begun. Later, in the privacy of the guest room, I penned a note to Margaret and shared my cousin's ambitions as a means to engage her.

"Mrs. Tate, it is a pleasure to meet you." Margaret curtsied quite low and Elizabeth followed suit.

Goodness, she's not a queen. My mind played through all the ways this meeting could go wrong. What if Elizabeth talked of her meager upbringing and lack of schooling? What if she compared her scanty living arrangements to Mary's sumptuous home? And if Margaret expressed some high-brow Northern ways? *Good Lord, why did I think this would work?* My apprehension diminished when Mary made a sweeping arm gesture and welcomed the women to her home.

Elizabeth took a seat on the sofa, perching on its edge as if she might be commanded to leave such a fine house, while Margaret exuded comfort in her surroundings. Not for the first time, I wondered what Margaret's upbringing had been like in the North. Her manners were impeccable, but her northern ideas might warrant my intervention. Once again, my mind whirled with the possibilities of what Margaret might declare and how I might keep a storm from brewing.

Elizabeth mimicked Margaret. She splayed out her skirt when she sat and held her hands on her lap, cupping her fingers together. Margaret's spine was ramrod straight and Elizabeth lengthened hers. Both women had taken great care with their appearance. Elizabeth had tamed her curly blond hair into a chignon and wore a tasteful navy-blue dress with fine stitching at the collar and cuffs. Margaret looked regal in a burgundy wool dress that complimented her clear fair skin.

Cousin Mary rang a small bell, and the maid arrived with a tea tray. She placed a cup and saucer in front of each woman without meeting their eyes. I couldn't remember the Negro woman's name, but I recalled her announcement at the missionary meeting and her fervent offer to help the school cause. No doubt she recognized Margaret and Elizabeth and would listen to our conversation through the kitchen door.

"Thank you," Elizabeth said.

My cousin wrinkled her nose.

I held my breath. I'd not anticipated this grave error, nor could I fathom how to rectify it without embarrassing Elizabeth or calling more attention to the mistake. Mary might preserve her position in society by condescending to one beneath her (without ever saying any such thing) or find a way to artfully excuse herself from this whole public school affair. I didn't blame Elizabeth. Her uncouth upbringing prevented her from knowing whom and whom not to thank.

Thankfully, Margaret drew Mary's attention away from the blunder. "Mrs. Tate, I've been following your work with the Flower Mission and the efforts to open a hospital with great interest. It's remarkable what you've achieved in such a short time."

Mary laid her palm atop her breast. "Well, I can't claim all the credit. It's a dedicated group of women. Although I will say that I mapped out our most successful donors, which helped expedite our fundraising."

"How marvelous! While I received teacher training, I find my skills at the art of fundraising lacking, and yet so important for the growth of public schools. And it is an art, isn't it? One must possess a talent for it, rather than hope to learn it." Margaret's resigned way of lifting her cup and saucer imparted a sense of giving up. Elizabeth watched closely.

I threw in a compliment, hoping we'd salvaged the situation. "My cousin not only possesses a talent for fundraising, but for promoting causes that better society," I offered.

"Like a hospital," Elizabeth said.

Well done.

"How many beds will the hospital have?" Margaret asked.

"Five to start." Mary waved the maid away. "And while we will serve the white population, we plan to add beds to administer to the health of our Negro population. The need is greater, but we must start somewhere."

"That is my mindset about public schools," Margaret said. "We are at capacity and yet the growth in jobs—why your hospital will require trained personnel and staff members that can read and write out doctors' orders and do sums to make accurate purchases of bandages and other necessities."

"Indeed." Mary sipped her tea and placed her cup and saucer on the pedestal table.

With the pause in conversation, Elizabeth surreptitiously surveyed the fine home, and I tried to see it with her fresh eyes. The sofa's green upholstery matched the striped silk curtains. The ceilings were high and the windows tall on both sides of the room, allowing breezes to circulate and cool this attractive sitting area. More than likely, Elizabeth had not seen a rug like the one beneath her feet. It stretched under all the furniture and the colors of its ornate design mirrored those in the room: green, blue, and cream with contrasting pinks and purples.

I couldn't relax, not when there was the slightest hope that Mary might commit to our cause. I stifled my desire to fidget by scrutinizing my mother's cousin. She sat rather stiffly, which might be a sign of discomfort or standoffishness. Her familiar dress told me she hadn't spruced up for this gathering. The maid had taken pains with her soft brown hair, coiling it in an updo that remained soft around the edges of her face. I couldn't decide if Mary was at ease and receptive to our message or unconcerned.

"I do not wish to impose," Mary said. "Perhaps I might attend one of your meetings and lend a hand where needed?"

"Oh, Mrs. Tate, I could scarcely ask for more." Margaret clasped her hands before her bosom.

I breathed out fully, relieved and already exhausted. The afternoon tea progressed with companionable conversation. I took a biscuit from the platter and finally sipped my now lukewarm tea. I'd orchestrated an alliance. Little ol' me from the country had linked together an improbable alliance: a poor illiterate dressmaker, a well-educated Northern missionary, and a respected Asheville socialite. Interlacing my fingers, I snuck a glance at Margaret and Elizabeth, while Mary exchanged words with the maid. One step closer, I tried to convey. One step closer.

Chapter Eighteen

"[Senator] Blair sees… the school fund is not large enough to be divided between the two races. He therefore urges that the fund be thrown into hotch potch; that the schools be thrown into one; that white and black children set on the same benches and sing out b-a-k-e-r in the same class … such commingGlement [sic] … the other side of Mason and Dixon's line could never effect, even in their own borders."

Asheville Citizen-Times

I lifted my boots and swayed on my cousin's porch swing, weightless, following the success of the afternoon meeting with Elizabeth and Margaret. Mary had joined our public education posse, and all because of me.

The cool evening air suppressed Asheville's often pungent smells. Breezes blowing down from the hills pushed out the stagnant remnants of turpentine and varnishes from the furniture factory and animal odors from the liveries. I wrapped my shawl tighter to ward off the encroaching chill. Cousin Stewart and Jasper had withdrawn to the library after supper to study the railroad maps, plotting the continued route through the mountains to Tennessee. Mary and I relaxed on the front porch.

"I enjoy meeting new people, particularly when I can offer help in some small way," Mary said.

"Now that you're involved in the school cause, I have high hopes." Like a mother feeds her child, I nourished Mary's pride.

She clasped her hands together. Whether she was emboldened at the suggestion, or surprised by how she'd been ensnared, I wasn't sure. Either way, Mary would tackle this cause with relish, as she did all her other civic duties. Her chest rose, and she took a deep breath.

"I'm glad married life suits you, Alice." She reached for my hand. "It's not always so."

I shifted on the porch cushion and slowed the swing. *Had Jennie confided in Mary?* I hesitated to express my concern, for my words might be carried through the grapevine telegraph of our family. "I believe Jennie is adjusting."

"Surely Jasper and Robert can do without you for a few days now that the harvest is over? Your sister would welcome a visit."

Did Mary know something I did not? Was her suggestion a plea? Would Jasper approve? The days were shorter, and the workload was lighter. I missed Jennie, and I wanted the truth about the state of her marriage. Perhaps I might discover what else my sister was holding back.

The next morning, while Jasper dealt with having a saddle stripped and reflocked, I met Susannah in front of the Buck Hotel. It was the oldest structure in Asheville, and it showed.

Neighboring storefronts had replaced the animal pens surrounding this old inn on the Buncombe Turnpike. The lumber siding resembled charred wood, and the painted trim peeled and flaked. It had no newfangled lighting, musicians on staff, or fine furniture in its lobby. Staying here confirmed Zimri and Susannah's frugality. With the colossal head and antlers above the pre-War building's entry, it was an easy-to-find meeting spot.

Susannah and I meandered the city streets, eyeing the marvelous goods in the storefront windows. We strolled by offices for lawyers, insurance agents, and banks. Signs for general merchandise, carpentry, publishers, and painters advertised their wares and services. There were cities larger than Asheville, but I couldn't imagine one. Everything a person needed was here.

One storefront caught my attention with a sewing machine on display in its window.

"Have you used one?" Susannah asked.

"No. Miss Shackton has one in her dressmaking shop. She pumps the treadle something fierce and that wheel spins. It's a mystery to me, but she makes good use of it."

Susannah huffed. "Seems like a lot of trouble, and a lot of racket." She turned toward the next shopfront. "Here's the bookseller." She entered C.M. Williams' ahead of me.

A clerk showed her their stereoscopes and views while I hunted for a gift for my twelve-year-old stepson. Shelves stretched from floor to ceiling, lined with leather- or cloth-bound books, some displaying gold-embossed lettering. I drew my finger across the row at eye level. There were more books than a person could read in a lifetime.

The bookseller helped me navigate the sections and shelves to find Robert's Christmas present. Our crop sale had left us flush, and I added a blank journal to my purchase. Jasper had placed extra coins in my hand, beyond what we had talked of as a budget. I accepted with grace, knowing Jasper attempted to buy his way back into my favor. He'd detained me from visiting Jennie when she'd needed me most. My thoughts towards my husband had softened after he helped the widow at the tobacco warehouse, but I would not let him off the hook. I rather enjoyed having the upper hand.

At our next stop, Lee & Childs Grocers, the aisles were full to the brim with those eager to spend their earnings. The farmers in town provided the last push for sales before the holidays. I was glad to have Susannah at my side. I'd made purchases for my family growing up, but those were at a much smaller country store or through a catalog.

A mound of citrus resembled a sunset-colored pyramid and the grocer's calls of "Fresh from Florida!" and "Just in on the train!" brought customers closer. He carved an orange into paper-thin slices and gave us a taste. Sweet, juicy and like no other fruit. Much to my surprise and enjoyment, my frugal sister-in-law suggested our two families split a half dozen oranges, a luxury for sure, but a well-earned one. Our three oranges would be a welcome Christmas gift—one for each of us.

We finished our shopping and planned to pick up the goods the following morning. The dressmaker's shop came into view.

"Miss Shackton is the one I mentioned—the one working to bring public schools to Asheville," I said. "She wrote that more normal schools are opening in the state."

"'Bout time we had proper Southern teachers rather than those Northern missionaries teaching their wayward notions," Susannah said.

"What notions?"

"That Negroes should have the same schooling as Whites," Susannah said. Her eyes followed a Negro man driving a wagon. "It won't do to have them rising above their station."

Susannah's concern for the pregnant tenant toiling in the field didn't mean she supported schooling Negroes. Heaven knows I wouldn't bring up mixed schools. That idea fueled many angry editorials in local newspapers. Margaret suggested it in one of her letters to meet the desperate need, but then she was 'one of those Northern missionaries with notions.'

I changed the subject. "My cousin Stewart has prospered with the railroads."

"Hm, yes." Susannah turned away and pulled her skirt in to avoid other shoppers.

"He studied engineering," I said.

"I sense where this is going." She raised her eyebrows and looked at me sideways. Shoppers swarmed the sidewalk, and we coursed our way forward, separating to weave through the crush of bodies.

I should have stopped, but all sense left me, and I plowed ahead. "Robert is a bright young man, and I'd like to see him have options beyond farming."

"Seems to me your past has more to do with it than Robert's future." She stepped away to peer through another window, ready to leave me and the conversation behind.

I ducked my head to hide the bloom settling on my cheeks. *Had she forgotten we'd both sought refuge in marriage because we'd no other means of support?* An education might have provided us another option. Perhaps it was a fortunate tobacco sale, or the distance from her father's marital bargaining, that fueled Susannah's sense of security. She admired my plainspoken ways because she, too, was blunt. *You get what you give.*

She faced me, not to make amends, but to reinforce her opinions. "Robert is bright, and he likes to farm. The Carter family looks after their own. Robert will be an excellent farmer."

There was no arguing with my sister-in-law on the subject. But she was wrong. One only had to look at the change surrounding us. Furniture, fabric, shoe and broom factories abounded. The railroad, hotels, and sanatoriums attracted many. Farming would play the poor brother to more modern ways of making a living. Asheville discarded its past and sought its destiny. I needed to be more persuasive if the Carter family, and the town of Democrat, would face the future.

Chapter Nineteen

"A mob at an early hour this morning lynched negro Bob Brachette, near the scene of his crime at Weaverville... Miss Henderson was present at the lynching, and shouted for joy when the fiend was swung aloft."

Carolina Public Press

The next morning, while the men collected our store purchases, I took extra care with my appearance in anticipation of visiting the photography studio. Mary offered me a strip of lace. While tying the bow gave me fits, it spruced up my dress. Her maid pinned up my hair under Mary's direction. She assured me this was the latest style, pulled high away from my face, pinned into rolls and adorned with more lace.

"I know just the thing." Mary bustled out of the room.

I took her absence as an opportunity to talk to the young Negro woman. "I saw you at the public school meeting."

Her hooded eyes widened. She dropped her hands to her sides as if I'd caught her stealing. "Yes, Ma'am."

"Have you been working for the cause with your people?" I asked.

Her eyes found mine. "I have. When it comes to a vote, we'll be out in good numbers. No matter what."

I knew well enough what might scare off Negro voters. The Klan might not parade through Asheville's streets, but it lurked in its alleys and skulked on the outskirts of town.

Mary returned with a pair of earrings and a silver disk. She waved the maid away and fastened the die-stamped coin pin to my bow.

"You will look every bit a lady of the times." Mary clasped the elegant earrings on. The moonstone drops hung alongside delicate enamel leaves.

"Oh, Mary, thank you. I hardly recognize myself." My initial reluctance at having my portrait taken evaporated and a curiosity at seeing my image forever captured on paper surfaced.

I'd seen photographs before. It was common for soldiers to pose in uniform and young women to send their true loves off to fight with their portrait in a pocket. My siblings and I had been too young for that.

Mary insisted I take the carriage to the studio. Riding in my finery on the streets of Asheville, I received quite a few appraising looks, and I enjoyed the attention. I patted my hair and clasped my ears to make sure Mary's jewelry remained securely in place. My cousin's house boy stopped the carriage and opened the door for me. A stranger tipped his hat at me as I crossed the sidewalk to the studio entry. The bell jingled when I pushed open the door.

A slender man in a trim-fitting suit fiddled with a large box atop a stand. "Good morning. Would you be Mrs. Carter?" he asked.

"I am. My husband has made arrangements."

When the photographer smiled, his cheekbones rose and his prominent chin jutted out. He was not unattractive, but his angular face and body reminded me of a marionette with its jointed limbs and jerky movements.

I glanced around the shop with its assortment of chairs and benches. A few garments hung on standing racks for those wishing to present a more refined look than their wardrobe allowed. Had Mary not loaned me several pieces, I might have perused the accessory collection of walking sticks, hats, fans and silk bouquets.

"Come right in. I am your photographer, W.T. Robertson, at your disposal." He gave a hasty bow. "Your husband ordered a portrait, which is an excellent investment to capture a moment in time." Mr. Robertson positioned a chair before the camera and dropped a dark curtain to serve as a backdrop. I hadn't noticed the mirror Mr. Robertson swiveled to face the front window. The light from the street bounced off it, illuminating the chair. He turned to look at me. "Perfect. Let's have you sit here, Mrs. Carter."

Mr. Robertson ducked under the black drape and reappeared to place a handheld mirror in front of me. I fingered my bow tie, spruced up the folds, and pinched my cheeks to add some color. The photographer darted into a small room in the studio's back corner.

"Just one more moment, Ma'am. I'll wet the plate and slide it into its holder," he called out.

He reemerged, and my nose crinkled at the unpleasant chemical odor. He studied me from all angles, and he considered the light and shadow as he played with the mirror. The light bounced too directly, causing me to blink.

The photographer lifted a metal piece to the back of my chair. "Push against the headrest to stay absolutely still."

Everything about this encounter fascinated me: the

intense man, strange equipment, odd smells, and plays of light.

Mr. Robertson dove under the fabric and the black hump behind the camera jostled like a shrouded swarm of bees. He emerged, slid the plate into the camera, and faced me.

"We are ready, Mrs. Carter. Hold still."

I stared into the lens, willing myself not to blink for the few seconds light poured into the camera, fixing my image for a lifetime or longer.

"Done!" He removed the plate and placed it into a box. "Your image is quite safe. After you leave, I'll take it to the darkroom. If you'll accompany me to the desk, I'll show you the options for card mounting."

I selected a buff-colored card with an embossed oval center.

"A favorable choice. I'll trim and mount your portrait to this card for a seamless look." The photographer scratched a note and tucked it along with the card in a desk drawer. "If you and Mr. Carter are in town a while longer, you might come along on one of my excursions. I bring a picnic and promise to show tourists the best mountain views, along with offering souvenir cards of the trip."

"We leave Asheville tomorrow, Mr. Robertson, and our journey home takes us along the French Broad River with wonderful views of those very mountains."

Mr. Robertson bowed. "Very well. You may collect your portrait tomorrow morning. Good day, Mrs. Carter."

The idea of a portrait made in a day astounded me. *Would I like the way I looked?* I'd find out *tomorrow.*

Already midmorning, I scurried to Elizabeth's shop. With the good return on our crop, Jasper had gifted me a new dress. I welcomed it, for I'd married with two day dresses and both had seen better days. Jennie's aprons couldn't cover the faded fabrics, and I'd darned one to where I had no hem left.

Following Margaret and Elizabeth's introduction to Cousin Mary yesterday, I'd returned with Elizabeth to her shop to select a fabric. This morning I entered her storefront to see my new dress on a mannequin.

"You must have worked all night to have this ready, Miss Elizabeth."

"Nonsense. I worked from your wedding dress pattern. This is a simpler style with its gathers and tucks. Please step behind that curtain and try 'er on, so I can check the fit."

While I tugged on the dress, I told Elizabeth the story of the widow at the tobacco warehouse, and her trial in getting the men to give her a fair shake. The woman's plight pressed on me like a hot iron to cloth.

Elizabeth pursed her lips and cast a wayward glance at me. "I feel we all have become more than acquaintances, Miss Alice. I consider you a friend."

"Likewise."

"Friends watch out for one another," Elizabeth said.

"Why yes, I believe so."

"It's just, you've an older husband. I hope you've planned for the unexpected."

I stepped around the curtain into the fitting space. Usually Elizabeth's ambition and large personality overcompensated for her diminutive size. Not today. She hesitated to say more.

The billowing green fabric of my dress floated just above the floor. "Please speak plainly."

"Does Mr. Carter have a will? I hope I'm not speakin' outta turn." Elizabeth knelt and checked my hem. "I see many a widow come to have mourning clothes made. The law's much improved since the War, but it doesn't benefit the wife when a husband dies without a will."

Old fears struck hard and fast, quickening my breathing. Jasper appeared fit and healthy, but I'd seen younger men die unexpectedly and without reason, my brother included. That tragedy had pushed me into marriage, and I saw the value of thinking about my precarious position should I be widowed.

Elizabeth circled the hem, while an uncomfortable silence filled the small dressmaking space. It wouldn't be an easy topic to discuss with Jasper. He avoided confrontation, whether talking about his relationship with his brother, Daniel, or his stance on public schools. I couldn't think of a way to introduce it. *Jasper, if you die suddenly ... or, Husband, when you die, what becomes of me?*

"You've given me much to think about." I smoothed the bodice of my new dress and hoped to exude a confidence I didn't possess. "I'll talk to my husband. He will have my best interests at heart."

Elizabeth sat back on her heels and surveyed her handiwork in the full-length mirror. Our eyes met, reflecting a desire to convince ourselves and each other.

"I hope so, Miss Alice."

December 10, 1882

My dearest Jennie,

Jasper and I were in Asheville last week to sell our tobacco harvest. This year's hard work paid off. We were fortunate at the market and made purchases for the coming year. Jasper bought seed, equipment, ammunition and such. Miss Elizabeth fashioned a new dress for me.

Jennie, my conversation with Elizabeth covered a sensitive topic. Given our husbands' maturities, we should plan for our security. I intend to discuss a will with Jasper. I encourage you to take precautions to secure your future, come what may.

We shall talk more when we visit late January.

Until then, with my love,

Alice

Chapter Twenty
Democrat 1882

"By 1868, [sharecropping] was the predominant capital-labor arrangement throughout the South ... it is associated with the kind of static, hopeless poverty and debt cycles that afflicted the entire South well into the twentieth century."

The Origins of Black Sharecropping, Wesley Allen Riddle, The Mississippi Quarterly

Within a week of returning from Asheville, the tenants walked across the field toward our front stoop. With the man's white shirt, clean pants and a colorful cloth knotted around his neck, he showed his finest attire. His bluish-black skin shone like a moonless sky. The woman wore a dark dress, and she'd replaced her daily kerchief with a cream-colored cloth tied above her forehead. She kept her large, wide eyes on the infant in her arms.

"Husband, you'd best come out. The tenants are coming," I called.

The screen door swung open. "Payment isn't due until Saturday, but I see he's carrying a money bag," Jasper said.

We watched the family's measured steps. The man's free hand guided his woman over the uneven ground.

"Afternoon, Mistah Carter. Missus Carter." Our tenant removed his hat. His eyes pierced the patch of yard between us. "I hope you well on this fine day."

Jasper's reply sounded short. "Afternoon, Hamilton."

"We is come to pay the rent." He stepped toward us, passed over the pouch to Jasper, and returned to stand by his wife and baby. "Was a good return on the crop. That's three quarters of the sale, like we agreed."

Jasper handed the money to me. "Mrs. Carter will make sure the terms are met."

An awkward silence ensued. The bag was heavy with coin. My thoughts turned to the Asheville shops and what I might splurge on.

"This be my wife Bettany and our son Adam," Hamilton added.

I nodded at Jasper and passed the bag back. "He looks like a fine boy," I said.

We remained on the edge of the porch under the shade of the roofline. The tenants occasionally glanced up at us, squinting in the sunlight.

Bettany beamed. "I thank you Missus. We are happy here."

"Do you wish to contract for another season?" I asked. This hefty payment confirmed they'd managed the fields well. Jasper ruffled next to me. I'd no reason to think Jasper wouldn't hire them again, but his brother Daniel didn't like Negroes and I wasn't about to give up this income.

"With the same terms, yes, Ma'am." Hamilton twisted his hat in his hand and never quite brought his eyes up to meet Jasper's.

I expected them to say their goodbyes and go back to their cabin.

Hamilton shuffled his feet. "My wife's mother come to

help with birthin' our baby. We'd like her to stay, and I be much obliged for an extra room on the home."

"Well now, I can't have any added expense," Jasper said. "Plenty of men would be content with the lodgings."

"Yessuh, we content." Hamilton's grip tightened on his hat.

"My Hamilton, he be a builder, too. If we were to git the lumber, maybe he build a lean-to for my mama?" Bettany rushed on, "A baby be getting up in the night and my mama sure appreciates some quiet space. Wouldn't cost you nothin'."

"I don't believe that would hurt anything." I looked to Jasper for the final word.

"Don't s'pose." Jasper's jaw hardened, and he stared straight ahead.

The payment had a pleasant weight, and Jasper wouldn't contradict me before others, especially coloreds.

"Next week you better start re-chinking the curing barn. Take a few days to mud and mortar to make it airtight." Jasper hefted the bag of coins. "You keep the weeds down this winter. I'll be providing seed the first of February for corn."

The conversation ended, and the tenants were dismissed. Hamilton set his hat on his head and touched the brim before they turned back to the one-room shanty. Considering the meager amount they'd kept, I didn't know how they could afford lumber. A change to the cabin seemed unlikely.

The screen door slammed shut behind me, like a crack of thunder before a lightning strike. My feet plodded across our threshold. Jasper stood in the hall with his back to me. I heard his grumbling roar before I comprehended his words.

"Alice, I am the man of the house. I will decide if we rent the land or not." Jasper delivered every word deliberately, punching me straight through. I quivered and my breath quickened.

"You've been teaching me about farming." My voice shook. "I figured with such a valuable payment, you'd want them to continue on."

Jasper turned toward me. His face was beet red, and a vein in his temple pulsed. "You know very well that's not the issue. I've put up with your high-falutin' ideas about education. I've protected you from those that don't see eye to eye. But I will not have you wearing the pants in this family!"

My eyes welled with tears, but I was determined not to show it. I stared at my husband. His clear blue eyes pierced me through.

"Well, you know who you married!" I stormed through the house and escaped out the back door.

I wandered in our orchard, dreading a return to the house. The trees surrounded me, but their bare branches didn't protect me. I swatted at them and they rattled. I'd done the right thing. The tenants were good for us. Why couldn't Jasper see that? I balled my fists, rubbed my eyes, and a low cry gurgled out. I'd exchanged one confine for another, with the course of my life controlled by men—first my father, then my brother, and now my husband. I wallowed in the old feeling of dependency, familiar as a worn-out coat.

I wept for losing all I'd worked for in this marriage, for my absent sister and vanished family, for my ineptitude, and for my hubris in a tenant negotiation. I sank to the ground, and my skirts ballooned atop the low-cut orchard grass. Less than a year ago, my dress had brushed against tall wet blades and Jasper had guided me through, introducing me to this land. He'd been proud of the well-tended fields and buildings. What of his pride now? I absorbed the views I loved: the creek running steady and strong along the property, the verdant mountains circling our plot, the rich fields, and the clean spare farmhouse. Did Jasper remain in the hallway? Maybe he'd taken his pipe to the porch and was thinking of me? My hand grazed the freshly mown grass.

I'd congratulated myself on learning to farm and, perhaps, I'd overstepped with the tenants. My gaze followed the path toward the house and the walk of shame awaiting me. What would Harriet preach? Proverbs 11:2: When pride comes, then comes disgrace, but with the humble is wisdom. An hour later, I hoisted myself off the ground, straightened my skirt, and readied to eat some humble pie.

Our reconciliation was like a newly cut mountain pass, with jagged edges and bumpy patches. I managed an apology for speaking out before consulting with him. Jasper's tone softened, and he admitted regret for his outburst. Neither one of us bridged the entire chasm, unwilling to travel the extra bit necessary to relinquish our pride.

A week later, I brought up the subject of a will. Jasper was happy with the profits from the market and our tenants were secured for another year. While the smoke from Jasper's pipe drifted and curled toward the porch ceiling, I skirted around the topic.

"Our trip to Asheville seems long ago. I look at my portrait on the mantel and I remember the peculiar smells of the photography studio."

"It's a pleasing picture," Jasper said.

I wasn't sure about that. My image surprised me. I'd held stock still and not blinked for what seemed like minutes, which resulted in a startled expression. The neck brace had pushed me forward, giving me a needy look. I couldn't deny Mary's accessories and my styled hair left an impression of a lady of leisure, which had more than once caused me to laugh, especially when on my hands and knees scrubbing floors or covered in ash making lye soap.

"It certainly is a modern age. Who knows what tomorrow will bring?" I said.

"Hmm." Jasper rocked gently.

"A sad situation with the widow at the tobacco warehouse. I suppose one can't predict such a loss."

"One never knows." Jasper laid his head back and closed his eyes. He sometimes dozed for a few minutes between supper and bedtime.

I broke into his reverie. "Jasper, should you plan for our security in case something happens to you?"

Jasper's eyes blinked open, startled and questioning. "I'm not planning on that."

"Of course not, but one never does."

"Aye." Jasper picked up his pipe and puffed. "What are you getting at, Alice?"

"Should you consider a will that would care for Robert and me?" If I'd waited minutes for my portrait to be taken, this felt like hours. I counted my breaths in and out, hoping to ease my churning stomach.

Jasper squinted, and he set his feet wider apart, ready to propel himself right out of the chair. "We'd better turn in."

I followed Jasper to the bedroom, where the air would be warmer than his embrace.

Chapter Twenty-One

"Many of our citizens appreciate not only the advantages but necessity of a graded public school in Asheville, and earnestly desire the early establishment of one."

Asheville Weekly Citizen

A week before Christmas, Jasper and Robert traversed the frosty ground to drag back a young evergreen. I cut trimmings and arranged the greenery and pinecones on the mantel, tucking in holly with its clumps of cheerful red berries. Jasper tacked the tree onto a stand and placed it in our front room.

Harriet and the children baked gingerbread men and women to decorate the tree. Popcorn crackled in a pot atop the stove and once cooled, we strung the kernels into a garland. While I helped the little ones make straw stars, Harriet threaded yarn hangers through the cookies.

"I swear we baked more cookies than this," Harriet said.

"Oh no, Cousin." Robert's cheeks bulged.

Harriet tilted her head. "You know your Ten Commandments, don't you?"

"I do. I also know the Lord's prayer. Forgive us our trespasses."

I stifled a laugh. At twelve years old, my stepson had a good command of scripture and a propensity for debate.

Harriet chuckled. "I suppose forgiveness is in order when it comes to the temptation of cookies."

Harriet's youngest, Cornelia, climbed onto Jasper's lap and they watched from the corner chair while we hung, and ate, our creations. Cinnamon, cloves, and sugar scents permeated the house, and the fire crackled and wheezed with each added log. Merry with decorations and filled with family, the house was a home, and just what I wanted.

Since our fight and the contentious discussion of a will, I'd treaded lightly and Jasper was quieter. I worried the rift would last. Harriet said nothing about the tension that hovered like rain clouds waiting for release, but I caught her watching us that afternoon. Forgiveness, Harriet would preach. *Had I forgiven him? Had Jasper forgiven me?* Cornelia snuggled against Jasper's chest, and I longed to take her place.

On Christmas Eve, I wrapped the book I'd bought for Robert in Asheville: *The Adventures of Tom Sawyer*, by Mark Twain. The bookseller assured me it was a splendid book for boys, full of adventure and mischief. I also wrapped the plain journal and hoped it would inspire his own writing. Along with an orange, Robert would have a fine holiday.

For Jasper, I'd purchased a tobacco pouch made of fine leather. From the market money, I'd put enough aside to buy him a dress shirt to replace his threadbare one. I folded the white fabric and pinched the wing-tip collar into place. Jasper wore his clothing past its time; he patched his boot soles, and I darned every sock, shirt, and pair of trousers. His only guilty pleasure was his pipe, in which he smoked his homegrown Brightleaf tobacco.

I admired my new dress and portrait, tangible gifts from Jasper that didn't obscure his many others. My much older husband, with his speckled skin and graying hair, exuded patience when guiding his son with a firm, loving hand. He cared for his niece, Harriet, and her children. In the hearth's light, I hummed a carol and wrapped my husband's gifts.

Christmas morning came like any other, with Jasper milking while I fed the chickens. Robert fetched the spring water, and I started breakfast. I kneaded and cut the dough, then slipped them in the oven. Smells of rich coffee and buttery biscuits competed with the sharp spruce of our Christmas tree. Over breakfast, Jasper told Robert to slow down or risk choking. We left the dishes for later and settled around the tree.

After unwrapping the book, Robert flipped to the first page and began reading.

"Alice gave some thought on what book to buy you, Robert," Jasper prodded.

Robert jumped to his feet and threw his arms around my neck. "Oh, thank you! It's just what I wanted."

I squeezed my stepson and inhaled his boyish scent. "You've got another gift."

Jasper handed Robert the journal, and he tore off the wrapping.

"You can practice writing, even create your own stories," I said.

Robert turned it over in his hands, flipped through the crisp pages, and clasped the blank book to his chest. "Thank you, Mother."

A tear rolled down my cheek. In all my years of mothering my siblings, I'd felt sisterly love. Well into my thirties, when I'd hardly expected it, I had the love of a son.

"Now, now," Jasper said. "This is to be a cheerful morning."

"Oh, it is." I wiped my eyes.

Jasper reached for a gift I'd missed under the tree. He passed me a small red package, no bigger than a teacup.

I fingered the precious box, outlined with gold and hinged. I lifted the lid to reveal a love brooch. My fingers went straight to my mouth, stifling a gasp.

Jasper smiled sheepishly. "I hope you like it."

I gaped at the rose- and yellow-gold overlays, and a center design of two lovebirds. "Thank you," I whispered.

I rose from the sofa and inched toward Jasper. His arms encircled my waist as he met me halfway. He held me like he'd never let go, and with his embrace, my every worry vanished. I'd married a careful farmer, a man I barely knew, and one almost twice my age. While we'd had words, and didn't agree on everything, he loved me. Jasper pulled back to search my face. Robert shifted on the sofa and cleared his throat. We each took a step back but remained within arms' reach.

"Oh, the oranges!" I fetched the fruit. The sweet citrus drew Robert away from his new book. After sectioning one orange, I popped one entire piece into my mouth. Jasper bit into a piece and juice burst forth, dribbling down his beard.

"Pa, you need a bib."

"I'm not the only one."

I laughed and cried at the same time.

Robert wiped his face. With the fruit consumed and the peels set aside for flavoring cake, we rested in each other's company.

Later, we were drawn apart and plunged into a larger, rowdier family gathering. At the Carter Inn, my mother-in-law, Alvira, reigned over the celebration. Each small great-grandchild took a turn with her by the red brick fireplace, telling her of their gifts. Some of her grandchildren were my age, and they hovered about like bees to honey.

Alvira called me to her. "How is your first Christmas with us?"

"I am well and happy."

"I can see one reason." Alvira nodded toward my collar. I touched the brooch, clasped to my lace bow. She patted the seat next to her, and I sat. "I've noticed a welcome change in my son. I am grateful to you, Alice."

She gripped my hands, and the room took note. Several of Jasper's siblings murmured to one another as they watched their mother take hold of me. Small and shrunken with age, Alvira loomed large in this home, loving, kind and pious. She'd been a widow for almost ten years, and I wondered if her stature had risen in that time or whether she'd wielded her own power in marriage. From what I'd heard of Solomon, I thought the latter unlikely, although perhaps she'd smoothed his rough edges and lessened his strict command.

Jasper stood in the corner, watching me with kind eyes and the faintest smile. The raucous commotion of the room fell away and a calm connected us, like a solid, permanent bridge. In our first year, we'd faced uncertainty, happiness, blunders, and success. We would steam ahead toward our unknown destination together.

Daniel appeared at his mother's side. "Mother, may I escort you to Christmas dinner?"

Alvira took her leave on the arm of her youngest son and everyone else followed to the dining room where roasted turkey, cranberry sauce, canned peas, mashed potatoes, and turnips filled the long table. For the centerpiece, candles flickered atop an oval mirror surrounded by fresh tree boughs. Their glow reflected off the shiny, veined glass, casting bands of light into the darkness.

"You have prepared a feast for us." Alvira clapped her hands.

Daniel pulled out his mother's chair at the head of the table. Harriet and Anna removed their aprons.

"Oh Grandmother, we worked ourselves to the bone." Harriet put the back of her hand to her forehead. Her sass brought a chuckle from her uncles, including Jasper. "Although I can't take any credit for the decorations. That was all Anna."

Anna sat to Alvira's right, with her husband, Daniel, by her side. Harriet took the other honored seat next to her grandmother, with her parents beside her, first Caroline, then John. Jasper, Robert and I lined up next, and the rest of the siblings, with their spouses and children, extended down the supper table. Alvira motioned for all to join hands in the blessing.

Robert's new book fell from his lap.

"What's that, Robert?" his grandmother asked.

"My gift from Mother and Father." Robert retrieved the book and showed it off.

My heart skipped a beat at Robert calling me *Mother*.

"Grandmother, Robert shows promise as a student," Harriet said.

"I'd expect nothing less. I look forward to hearing it, as *Black Beauty* was a treat."

We said grace, and I wondered if my mother-in-law could be a partner in my goal. I tested my theory. "On our recent visit to Asheville, I learned Reverend Pease offered land to the Home Mission Board for a new training school."

"Ah yes, the Methodist from New York City." Daniel's slicked back hair glinted in the candlelight.

"You've heard about his work at the Five Points Mission?" I glanced around the table and found many questioning looks. "Reverend Pease and his wife provided honest work for many and took in needy children. Now they are furthering education right here in North Carolina."

A few children picked up their forks, ready to attack their plates, but a steady stream of passing dishes impeded them. The adults sitting at the far end of the table stalled the steady flow, by craning their necks to listen in on my discussion with Alvira and Daniel. Over these months, the tension between Daniel and me had not gone unnoticed. Jasper, familiar with my passion on the subject, turned away to talk with his brother, John.

"What type of school will this be, Alice?" Alvira asked.

"A teacher training school," I said. "Public education is expanding across the state."

"Our subscription schools served me and my brothers just fine." Daniel held the platter of turkey for Anna.

Complacent and arrogant. I chewed my food to avoid giving Daniel an insincere smile. I wouldn't allow him to take over the conversation.

"I like school," Robert said. Cousins up and down the table agreed.

"My cousin's husband also grew up in the country, Robert," I said. "He trained to be an engineer and is building the railway over the mountains to Tennessee." I'd learned something from the Home Missionary Society's Mrs. Dawes, who'd preached her support of public education on- and off-stage. "Our farm goods will travel to new markets, which will benefit all of us."

"Indeed." Alvira's verdict drew the conversation to a close.

Harriet and Caroline both nodded along. John peered around my husband and studied me with an inscrutable expression. Daniel's face bore a sour look and his wife's, a cautious one. While my adversary was still in the game, I'd won this round. At least now I could count Harriet, Caroline, and Alvira in my camp.

Mince pie, dried fruits, and nuts adorned the table for dessert. The candles burned lower; the golden beeswax dribbled down the shrinking tapers. Anna lit the wall lanterns and the room's windows glowed. While the men smoked, Alvira led the children in singing Christmas hymns, and the young wives cleaned up after the meal. It was late in the evening when we started for home.

During the brief moonlit wagon ride, Robert leaned and slept against Jasper. I wrapped an arm around both.

"My mother is pleased with you," Jasper said.

"I'm fond of her. Can't say that your brother Daniel approves of me. I'm not sure what I've done to him."

He chuckled. "I think you know well enough."

Jasper was no fool. He hadn't objected when I steered the conversation tonight. He didn't always agree with my opinions, but my husband recognized my need to express my beliefs, or perhaps the futility of trying to staunch them. I gripped the love brooch and considered, once again, the intangible gifts of Christmas.

"A gentleman, traveling on one of the trains of the North Carolina Railroad overheard a conversation between two gentlemen from Pennsylvania..., one..., remarked to the other: "They have a very cute way of building railroads in this State. Whenever a 'nigger' steals a chicken, or a watermelon, they sentence him to the Penitentiary for four or five years, and put him to work on the railroads. I am told that in some of the Southern States they are hired out to work on farms and in the mines. If we were to try such a plan in our country, wouldn't there be a howl of indignation?""

Greensboro North State

January 14, 1883

Dear Jennie,

Thank you for the lovely Christmas gift. I shall think of you whenever I use the embroidered tea towel. Your fine hand shows in your work.

The new year has turned, and I can hardly believe it is 1883. Our anniversaries will be upon us before we know it. What a difference a year can make. Jasper will harvest the wheat and start the corn soon, and the fieldwork will continue. On these quieter winter days, I stay busy overseeing Robert's schoolwork and the occasional chores, like giving the smokehouse a thorough cleaning to prepare for the hogging this coming week.

Jasper's brother, Zimri, will join us, bringing his hogs over for the butchering. I do not relish this dirty job, but I look forward to a good supply of ham, pork cuts, and sausages. Our tenant will help, with payment being some lumber accumulated from the pull down of an old shed. The tenants plan to build onto the cabin.

I believe I have told you of our tenants who work the field adjacent. They are Negroes—a man, woman, babe, and grandmother. The latter came for the birth of the child and stayed on. Last week we heard a terrible keening and took to our porch to see what in heavens was the matter. The older woman kneeled on their porch and wept fiercely. The younger woman joined her in crying out. It was a sorry scene.

Jasper learned from Hamilton that his wife's brother drowned in the Tucksagee River while working on the railroad along with twenty-nine other convicts. I had no idea that these tenants had a criminal in their family. The crew was working on the Cowee Tunnel. I mean to write to Cousin Mary and inquire whether this has slowed Stewart's work on the rail expansion.

With this bit of news, I shall end.

I wish you and G.W. a happy new year.

With love,

Alice

January 20, 1883

Dear Alice,

I gladly received your letter last week. Yes, losing the convict crew has been a setback for Stewart's work. He is negotiating with the jails to deliver more workers as the railroad must progress westward.

Speaking of progress, our recent Hospital Benefit was widely attended and a great success. Stewart enjoyed the evening, laughing himself silly at the pantomime act. I have been hosting meetings between the various churches and interest in a hospital is growing amongst the congregations. I feel confident that once we build this network, I can extend the cause for public education.

My beliefs are changing on education. You may think Miss Petersen and Miss Shackton cause for this change, as they are both of a mind that the colored badly need education. Perhaps there is some truth to it. However, the greater influence is the need for Asheville to be the face of the New South. The more I know of the Northern visitors, whether Miss Petersen, immigrants such as Reverend Pease and his wife, or the many tourists who flock to our fine city, the more I realize the stigma of slavery sticks like tar. If Asheville is to attract tourists and grow its economy, then we must portray a sense of calm and content among our residents. I will include in my efforts to further public education, teachers and schools for both Whites and colored, although they will, of course, be separate.

With fondness,

Mary

Chapter Twenty-Two

"Every shovelful of dirt thrown on a railroad bed, every bar of iron laid on a railroad track, and every mile of road built in this State has been done by the use of convict labor…, [if not for] putting these thousand idle hands to work, your children and your children's children would have seen their hair turn gray."

Extract from Governor Jarvis's speech as printed in The Greensboro Patriot

On an early winter's day, we prepared for the hot, hard work of slaughtering hogs. Jasper and Zimri built wooden platforms on either side of the scalding trough, while Robert hauled the firewood needed to keep the water boiling long enough to dip four carcasses.

"Son, stand back. I'm adding some kerosene to the fire," Jasper said. "We want it to burn fast to get a good bed of embers. Your job today will be to feed wood to the fire."

Robert took instruction, like every other man helping. My stepson's frame had filled out over these last months, changing from a scrawny eleven-year-old boy when Jasper and I married to a young man with some fuzz above his upper lip.

His Aunt Susannah and I had started early with carrying water across the yard. Pail after heavy pail from the house to the trough reminded me of the convenience of a spring house just off the kitchen. My arms ached, and it wasn't yet nine o'clock.

Tapping the beast's haunches with a wooden pole, Zimri guided the first hog up the ramp to its death. Jasper drew a knife across the throat. The animal collapsed and blood poured through the boards, pooling on the ground. I covered my nose and mouth with a handkerchief to stifle the overpowering smell of iron and earth.

Hamilton tied ropes about the hog's legs and the men lowered the carcass into the steaming water, where it bobbed and floated. Our tenant stood half a head taller than Jasper and his brother, and his broad shoulders bore the brunt of the labor. With sweat dripping off his face and glistening arms, Hamilton grabbed a pole and rolled the hog in the simmering bath to blanch its skin.

"Keep it moving." Jasper directed the turning of the animal. "Don't want it cooking on any one side."

Steam and smoke enveloped the men, layering their flesh with grit and moisture. Robert joined them with the poles, plunging the hog and flipping it side to side.

"Hairs are loose," Zimri called out.

With a heave, the men hoisted the animal onto the other platform and fell to work, scraping with relentless motion to remove large patches of hair. Damp pants and shirts clung to their bodies, sticky with hog bristles and skin. I didn't look forward to laundry day.

I hovered near the men, holding a pail of water and a ladle for them to quench their thirst.

Jasper accepted the ladle and drank deeply. He wiped his mouth with his sleeve. "Dirty work."

"I'm used to it. Plenty of drovers paid their inn fees with an animal, although my father and brother did the slaughtering." My mother and sisters had been too squeamish to help, and my other brothers were too young when we still had the inn. I'd hauled water, kept the fire going, sharpened the blades, prepared the salt beds, and stored the pork cuts.

Jasper nodded and rejoined the men. Hamilton wiped his brow and licked his lips. He eyed the bucket but didn't make a move toward me. He wouldn't. I left the pail and ladle in the yard and returned to the house for another container and a cup. With a basin full to the brim, I crossed the yard and placed it on the platform near our tenant.

"Thirsty work. Best not get overheated. We've a long day ahead," I said.

"I thank ya, Missus."

Several pails of scalding water and subsequent scrapings later, the hog's smooth, white skin gleamed like a ghost. Hamilton cut the heels and bound the hog to hang. I was glad for our tenant's help, because it took all the men and a pulley system to lift the animal for carving. Hamilton stepped in and soon his hands were slick with blood.

Susannah and I wore a path in the yard between the springhouse and the trough, carrying water to replenish the bath and to clean the hairless carcass. Robert fetched more wood to keep the fire burning. I would have pitied him with his sweat-soaked hair and sagging shoulders, but I suspected he longed to prove he was man enough for the job.

With one hog ready for butchering, the men dropped another into the steaming tub.

"Robert, finish with that wood and join your uncle with the poles while I start the carving," Jasper said.

Jasper jumped off the platform as Robert threw a log on

the fire. An ember flew out, struck Jasper's leg, and his pants ignited in a whoosh of flame, causing Robert to reel and tumble to the ground.

Whose cries I heard, I don't rightly know. I picked up my skirts and ran toward the sound, fire, and movement.

Hamilton dropped his pole, jumped from the platform, and knocked Jasper to the ground. He laid his torso across Jasper's legs, rolling back and forth, smothering the flames. Jasper lay inert, on his stomach, with his arms spread eagle.

Zimri lowered himself to the ground, strode to Jasper, and rolled Hamilton off his brother forcefully.

Hamilton kneeled and coughed up dust and ash, beating his chest to stop the flames flaring on his flesh-splattered shirt. "Sorry, Mistuh Carter, didn't mean to hurt you none."

I knelt at Jasper's side, helping him to roll onto his back. Dirt smudged his face. His eyes rolled upward before finding their balance. "Are you hurt?" I asked.

He sat up and pulled up the shreds of his pant legs to reveal his reddening skin. "Must have splashed myself with kerosene to have lit up like that."

My husband looked weak, unsteady, and older than his years. My breaths came quick and shallow. An image of a woman in a drab dress with braided hair tacked over her head passed before my eyes; it was Widow Corcoran from the tobacco warehouse. No, it was the widow's body with my face. A sudden wave of dizziness threatened to topple me. Susannah wrapped her arm around my backside and steadied me.

Zimri helped Jasper stand, keeping a grip on his elbow. Jasper took measure of his burned trousers, and his reddened shins, already showing signs of blistering. He hesitated before extending his hand to help Hamilton to his feet. "I expect I'm a lot better off than I might have been."

Our tenant lurched to his feet, nodded at Jasper while keeping his eyes downward.

Robert stumbled forward. His voice cracked. "Pa, are you okay?"

With a curt nod, Jasper signaled he was all right. "Best turn the hog in the water." He brushed off his front, picked up his hat, and strode away toward the hanging hog.

In varying states of upset, we all returned to our work. Susannah led me to the carving station, and her soothing tones calmed me. "He's okay. It's alright, now."

Jasper stood before the lifeless animal and picked up a knife. With shaking hands, he put it back down.

My hands trembled and my breathing quickened. A few more minutes and the burns could have been fatal. I'd almost lost Jasper. *Without a husband, what would happen to me?* Anger burned within me at my helplessness. I yanked my hands away from the knives, uncertain whether I could lay them out without cutting myself. With my palms on my stomach, I closed my eyes and breathed deliberately.

Jasper went to the porch and drank deeply from the water ladle. My husband's shoulder blades rose and fell as he exhaled. With averted eyes, he stalked back to the carving station. Without any further hesitation, Jasper cut away hams, shoulders and middling, and tossed the trimmed fat into a bucket.

We pretended to go on as if nothing had happened. I distracted myself by preparing the beds to cure the pork cuts, wincing when the salt burned the blisters on my hands. Susannah set a cauldron over a fire to stew the fat into lard. Both of us kept a surreptitious eye on Jasper. Robert disappeared into the woodshed, and we all let him be. After a time, he returned with a slower cadence and laid more logs on the fire.

With the chops cut, I left to prepare dinner. My body relaxed in the familiar kitchen, away from the bloody visions and persistent taste of iron in the air. I'd prepared the potatoes the night before and brought the pot to boil. Pickled vegetables from the pantry and biscuits rounded out the meal. Fresh pork cuts sizzled atop the stove.

"Smells delicious." Susannah came into the kitchen. "I don't think I've ever been so hungry."

The outside scene invaded, and I twisted away from her. My shoulders shook and Susannah stepped forward to lay a palm across my back. I clasped my apron to my face, dabbing at the tears and sweat.

Robert hesitated in the kitchen doorway. "Pa sent me to help."

I cleared my throat. "Robert, dear, will you put glasses on the outside table for tea?"

The men broke for dinner. Jasper and Zimri sidled up to the porch table where a platter of crispy pork cuts awaited.

Hamilton wandered off toward the tenants' shack, his shirt charred black as his skin, his broad shoulders rounded after the morning's hard work. I watched him through the kitchen window, paralyzed with the mixed emotions of fear and gratitude. I grabbed a plate and speared three chops. Hustling outside and down the back steps, I caught up with him and shoved the plate into his hands.

"Thank you, Missus." Hamilton's eyes widened before he ducked his head and studied the ground. "My family sure do appreciate this." He tipped his hat and limped off.

I didn't care if the others judged me. Though I had no more food to bring out, I returned to the kitchen and stood gripping and releasing my apron, the tension spreading through my forearms to my shoulders.

"Everything all right?" Jasper was at my side. I sensed him before I heard him, the heat from his body, the pungent odors from the yard.

"Oh, Jasper." I turned to take in his blistering legs and his weathered face.

"You've a kind heart, Alice." He gripped my arms and let out his breath. We leaned toward one another, our foreheads touching. "S'pose I'd best buy our tenant a shirt."

I settled my head on his shoulder. His clothes were singed. He smelled of fire, smoke, and blood. But he was alive, and I was safe in his arms.

We returned to the outside dinner table. If the others considered the gift of pork ill-advised, so be it. Jasper did not object to my kindness.

"Thought I'd never want to see a hog again, but this chop has changed my mind," Robert said. With his hands on his belly, and his plate licked clean, he leaned back in his chair.

"Good thing, because we got two hogs left to dip, butcher, and salt," Jasper said.

Robert groaned. "I'll fetch some wood."

Chapter Twenty-Three
Hendersonville, North Carolina 1883

"One unique feature given to the town [of Hendersonville] during its design was a 100 foot wide Main Street. It is written that the goal was to have a Main Street wide enough to turn a team of horses and a wagon without having to back up."

Caption for the photograph: Main Street, Hendersonville, N.C. by Jody Barber from the UNC Library

We arrived in Hendersonville in the late afternoon and checked into our room. Robert marveled at his first stay in a hotel, wondering what they'd serve for breakfast and did they really make up the beds for us. I welcomed his endless questions. Since my family had once run an inn, I delivered answers as we strolled over to the Cannon Mercantile.

"At last!" Jennie rushed around the shop's counter to embrace me, and I inhaled the familiar scent of my sister. It'd take more than a year away from her to forget it.

Jennie's husband finished with a customer and stepped over to shake Jasper's hand, then Robert's.

"You've grown half a foot since last winter, young man." G.W. arched his back, emphasizing his rotund form. He looked like he'd widened half a foot. *He must like Jennie's cooking.*

Robert put his hands in his pockets and puffed out his chest.

"Beware! He'll eat you out of house and home." Jasper tousled Robert's hair, causing him to weasel away to inspect the store's dime novel collection.

Jennie laughed. "Come and tell me the news from your last Asheville visit."

We'd turned up near closing time and when the last customers departed, G.W. flipped the hanging sign to 'closed' and locked the entrance. Following them through the back storeroom, we climbed the staircase. My curiosity over living above a store matched Robert's about hotels. In Asheville I'd seen tenants open second- or third-level windows and imagined life above street level, but I'd never been inside such a home.

"Alice, come see our view." Jennie dragged me to the window overlooking Hendersonville's main street. Her letter had described the wide dirt road. Steady horse and wagon traffic bustled along and kicked up dust that clung to the windowpane. A woman glanced up at us, and I stepped back out of sight. Jennie pulled me forward.

"That's the first bank in Hendersonville. Over there is a pharmacy offering every cure you can imagine," she said. "Isn't this something? We see everything going on in town."

It didn't compare to our country home with its privacy and beautiful surroundings, but I wouldn't deflate Jennie's enthusiasm. "My goodness!" I said.

We settled in the parlor and Robert showed G.W. his newest book. I tempered my sentiments toward Jennie's husband. Ever since my sister's letter following their wedding night, I'd recognized my brother-in-law to be an insensitive brute. From more recent letters, I'd gathered he maintained a hold on the purse strings and exerted his will with some frequency. Knowing my sister, she sat back and took it, rather than confront her husband. Today he was on his best behavior, acting the kindly uncle toward Robert.

"What does Stewart Tate say about tunnelling through the mountains?" G.W. asked.

"Oh, he's proud of the Swannanoa Tunnel," Jasper said. "It only took twenty years to build."

I raised my eyebrows at Jennie. "We learned all the details."

"One thousand eight hundred and twenty feet long!" Robert exclaimed. "At its deepest, it goes one hundred twenty-three feet underground. Can you imagine?"

I didn't mention the cost of at least three hundred convict laborers. That information had not come from my cousins, but through the seamstress shop and talk amongst Asheville's religious leaders.

"You've a head for numbers, young man," Jennie said.

"Mother had me tested by a teacher in Asheville. I'm hoping to go on with my schooling," Robert looked sideways at his father, "if we can make the arrangements."

Delight drew a smile on my face when Robert addressed me as Mother. A rush of warmth filled me while in the company of Jasper, Robert, and Jennie.

"You remember Margaret?" I asked. "She tested Robert and found him able with his sums. Plus, he has a fine hand." I claimed responsibility for Robert's change of heart regarding school. While he had admitted to loving books and receiving high marks in penmanship, Robert had not always seen the value in more education.

"Alice, do tell what you have up your sleeve," Jennie teased.

"Aye, what are we in for?" Jasper smirked and laughter filled the room.

"Why, you all know me better than I do myself."

"I mean to find the land for a school." I confided in my sister in the privacy of the parlor.

Downstairs, G.W. showed Jasper his inventory system and the storeroom, while Robert picked out a dime novel for the long ride home.

Comfortable furnishings appointed their living area, and my sister's touch was in every embroidered pillow cushion or table doily. I couldn't get over a home suspended in the air, despite the dark wood floors beneath my feet and the solid brick walls.

"Will Jasper give up farmland?" Jennie asked.

"I haven't said I'd found the land. I mean to find it. Margaret says Reverend Pease offered his lands to the Home Missionary Society to develop schools in Asheville. I need to find another Reverend Pease."

"Who is he?" Jennie asked.

"He moved from New York over ten years ago after retiring from mission work. He and his wife believe providing education and employment opportunities are essential to improve people and bring them to the Lord."

"Well, an empty stomach is an impediment to focusing on scripture," my sister said. "How do you expect to find a wealthy Northerner in little ol' Democrat? The wealthiest landowner would be your family, and you said yourself that Daniel Carter takes a dim view on educating people beyond their needs."

"I must bend another Carter family member, or two, to

my way of thinking." I followed Jennie through a swinging door to fix supper.

Jennie grabbed the coffee pot from the stove and filled it with water from a wall faucet.

"You have running water?" I'd never seen such a thing. Mary and Stewart had it, but I'd not been in their kitchen.

"Oh yes, and an ice box. It's a very modern kitchen." She pulled a milk bottle out of the icebox. "The ice factory in town delivers daily. We get ours every Monday."

"Imagine that," I mumbled. My sister also had the convenience of milk without a cow.

Jennie put me to work at a narrow kitchen table. Unlike my own, this one was just for preparing meals. We would dine at the round walnut table in the parlor. I sliced bread and admired the kitchen's warm brick walls and high ceilings. With the kitchen as a separate room, my sister prepared meals in quiet solitude without a husband tromping through in muddy boots or a child racing about. I wondered if Jennie filled the kerosene lamps on the walls or if G.W. did. She didn't have to carry lanterns from room to room, bring water from a springhouse, or gather eggs from the coop.

Jennie unwrapped a new bar of soap and washed her hands at the sink.

My sister didn't make her own lye soap. "You seem to have everything you need here." I sniffed the soap and wrinkled my nose.

"Oh, I do Alice. I'm so happy to have you here and to show you." Jennie was pleased as a fox in the hen house.

I stifled a snort. "Have you discussed a will with G.W.?"

Jennie assembled a platter of meats and vegetables. She pulled fresh butter from the icebox. *Milk and butter delivered. How convenient.*

"G.W. thinks it's an unnecessary expense. He believes the Lord will provide."

I abandoned the knife. I blurted out, "Like He did when our father died?"

Jennie stood with her hands on her hips. "Yes, and you know it." We faced off across her worktable, and I imagined my sister's grim expression mirrored my own. "We both have a roof over our heads and husbands that provide for us."

"And what if that changes?"

"Alice, you are my sister and I love you, but I manage my household and my own life now." Jennie picked up the platter, pushed through the swinging door, and left me and the conversation behind in the kitchen.

Chapter Twenty-Four
Democrat 1883

"The present floor area of Asheville's four brick [tobacco] warehouses is about 25,000 square feet, and the sales during the last season (1882-'83) aggregated 1,500,000 pounds, at an average price of $11.75 per cwt. The coming year it is anticipated that not less than 2,000,000 pounds will pass under the hammers of Asheville's glib-tongued auctioneers...."

The Asheville City Directory and Gazetteer of Buncombe County

Snow covered the fields like a white woolen blanket, insulating the earth, protecting it, and hiding it. I should've taken comfort in this silent time on the farm, with the larder full from our trip to Asheville, our garden's bounty put up in jars, and the hams and pork cuts curing. But I'd been uneasy since our return from Hendersonville.

On the few occasions when my sister had chastised me growing up, I probably deserved it. This time was different. I'd tried to help Jennie, and she'd rejected me. She'd talked of her town friends, showed off the many conveniences in her home, and openly admired G.W., which I refused to believe. Jennie's first letter after their wedding night told me everything I needed to know about that man. During our visit while I'd helped her with supper, she'd said the words I found impossible to forget: *I manage my household and my own life now*. Well, if my sister no longer needed me and wished not to confide in me, so be it.

Through the spring and summer, our letter writing continued, laced with a noticeable distance. She talked of the store and their trips to Asheville, but did not mention seeing Elizabeth, as Mary had revealed. I wrote of life on a tobacco farm and family members without divulging my true feelings. As much as it hurt me, I wouldn't let her see my broken heart.

The end of summer arrived bearing an atmosphere that bristled, thick and palpable. Insects hummed and crawled through the dense air while sparrows and warblers rested on tree branches, fat from the bounty of berries, seeds, and earthworms. We pressed on to finish the harvest with long days, aching backs, and sticky stained fingers. With the last of the tobacco cured, we extinguished the stove fires, threw open the barn doors so the moist air plumped the leaves, and removed our product. The men climbed through the rafters and carefully detached the poles, pulling down the dried tobacco hands to be unbound, sorted, graded and stacked.

Susannah turned each leaf, determining the correct sorting pile. I struggled to judge the color and consistency of the grades. We filled the same stacks, so my meager contributions were less noticeable.

"Comes a drummer," she called up to the men.

I spotted a young man tying his horse to the porch railing before striding toward the curing barn. "What's a drummer?"

Susannah threw down a leaf and grabbed another. "Come to drum up business."

"Good morning, ladies." The fidgety man removed his hat and turned at the approach of Zimri, who pressed his lips together in a tight line.

"Good day to you, Sir. I'm Abraham McGill, representing the American Tobacco Warehouse. I commend you on the bounty of your crop. You'll be expecting a good return. Rest assured, American Tobacco offers the best price."

"That so?" Zimri asked. "Are you promising one today?"

"Well, *eh,* no. Only, our auctioneer commands the best prices in Asheville. A fine man, he is." He twirled his hat and faced Zimri with his feet spread apart wider than his shoulders. "I can offer you a first sale when you bring your crop to us."

I whispered to Susannah, "What's that?"

"With a first sale of the day, a farmer is done and paid and can return home without delay. It appeals to many who live a good distance from town." Susannah kept the leaves moving from the bundles to the stacks. I followed suit but kept an eye on the men.

Zimri rubbed his whiskers. "Last season, a warehouse promised our neighbor a first sale that didn't come about. Of course, after he'd unloaded his product, it was too late."

"Unfortunate circumstance, for sure." Mr. McGill mopped his brow with a handkerchief and changed tactics. "American Tobacco values its farmers and I'm recruiting new suppliers because of the growing market. In fact, if you were to bring in your product and convince your neighbors to, there could be a nice commission for you."

"Could be, huh?" Zimri said.

Susannah sniggered.

Mr. McGill looked at us and his arms hung at his side, his hat limp against his leg. "What will it take for you, uh, Mr. ...?"

"Carter."

"What will it take, Mr. Carter, to win your business?"

"Mr. McGill, my brother and I are longtime customers of Banner Warehouse. They've earned our patronage through honest dealings, and I see no reason to change. I thank you for coming all this way. Good day to you." Zimri touched his hat's brim, turned on his heel, and returned to the rafters.

Mr. McGill slammed his hat on his head and marched toward his horse with slumped shoulders. He mounted and rode off at a gallop.

"I'm surprised we've only had one this season. Usually, see more come 'round to drum up business for the warehouses. I wouldn't want his job," Susannah said.

I tried to judge the grade of the tobacco leaf in my hand. "Think he has more success than me?"

Susannah took it from me and laid it on the correct pile. "Hard to say."

I washed up outside the kitchen, scrubbing away the grit and grime. Cleanliness might be a virtue, but it was near impossible with tobacco harvesting. I was weary with the thought of making dinner, and nothing in the pantry appealed to me. Willing the air to move through the house, I propped open the front door and flapped my apron. During harvest I'd withstood the sickly-sweet smell, but now the faint odor of the dried leaves had me rushing to the porch's edge and emptying my stomach. *Heavens, I'm rarely ill.* I braced my hands on my knees, anticipating another round of sickness. I staggered and crouched on the steps.

The Negro woman rushed to my side, grasped my arm, and helped me to sit. The assumed familiarity jarred me, but I was too weak to protest.

"Oh, comes on fast them first months," she said.

Bettany's words carried no weight or meaning. *First months*. Hamilton stood in the field, holding their infant son. A child. In my exhaustion these last few weeks, I'd lost track of my monthlies.

"You be fine, Missus." Bettany's broad white grin prompted mine. She backed away toward her family.

I watched our tenant cross the field and take the child from her husband. In some months, I would hold my child. Bettany kissed his cheeks, and he snuggled into her neck while she wrapped the cloth that bound him to her chest. I stood up slowly and gathered myself, breathing deeply to settle my stomach and gain my balance. Gripping the porch pillar, I watched the family, bound together by their child.

Bettany's work went on and so would mine. My skirts swished as I bustled into the kitchen, ready to tackle the dinner preparations with a newfound energy. I might not feel like eating, but I would, for I was feeding two. I tried to recall my last monthly and calculate when the child would come. My mind was a whir of possibilities—a girl, a boy, blue eyes like all my family, wiry and strong like the Carters?

Jasper, Zimri, Susannah and Robert washed on the porch before coming in for dinner. They tucked into the table and Jasper said, "This sure smells good." He froze, either on account of my uncharacteristic silence or the grin on my face. "What is it? What's happened?"

I cupped my belly. Jasper rose and kicked out his chair. "Are you?"

His brows knitted together, Robert looked back and forth between us.

I nodded eagerly. Jasper lifted me off my feet and spun me around the kitchen.

On an autumn Sunday when the red leaves covered the road like a carpet rolled out for royalty, Jasper drove the wagon to church and rested his hand on my knee. While my husband had admired my work in the house and shared endearments in the privacy of our bedroom, he now treated me like a queen, asking if I needed anything in the evenings or how I was feeling, even demanding more of Robert so I might rest. I wrapped my coat tighter around myself and hugged my thickening waistline.

The child growing within me solidified my place in this family. Jasper didn't favor Harriet's sons over her daughters. In fact, he prized his great niece, Cornelia. Even so, I wished for a son, one with a claim to the Carter land and the security it offered.

Robert had warmed to the idea of a sibling and scooted closer to me in the wagon. I draped my arm around his shoulder.

"What shall we call him?" he said.

"What makes you so sure it's a *him*?" I asked.

"Well, what good would a girl do?"

"I beg your pardon." I shifted to meet him eye to eye.

Robert's shoulders rose to touch his ears. "I mean, how'm I supposed to teach a girl to hunt rabbits, skip rocks, or climb in the barn?"

My stepson straddled childhood and adulthood, just as likely to advise me how things were done around the farm as to run off and play with his cousins. His shoulders were broadening with the field work and his voice had deepened. I longed to hold on to Robert and stop him from growing up. This new child was playing with my emotions, plunging me into fits of nostalgia.

"You do all those things with your girl cousins. I imagine a sister might like a strong older brother to show her just such things," I answered.

"That settles it then. We will welcome a girl or a boy." Jasper flicked the reins, and the horses picked up their pace.

Chapter Twenty-Five
Asheville 1883

"DEMOCRAT. Farmers post-office 18 m N E of Asheville, on the Burnsville road. Mails daily from Asheville and Burnsville—Jno {John} A Carter, P M {Postmaster}"

The Asheville City Directory and Gazetteer of Buncombe County

Our trip to Asheville offered a much-needed distraction from my consuming thoughts on motherhood. Across Main Street, an enormous banner read 'Welcome Farmers' and storefronts advertised special sales. Merchants understood the importance of the tobacco auction and welcomed the farmers itching to spend their money. I counted myself among those people. Although Harriet had given me everything I'd need for the baby, I wished to purchase something brand new.

I also needed to restock my paper and ink supplies. Since I'd shared my good news with Jennie, our letter writing had increased in frequency. The stiffness since my visit to Hendersonville had somewhat lessened without either of us acknowledging the argument. My sister wanted to know everything about my pregnancy. Was I eating properly? Had I been sick in the mornings? Were my ankles swelling? I was more than willing to satisfy her curiosity. I would find a stationery shop in town. First, we would sell our harvest.

The flashy auctioneer with his silk striped vest, top hat and twirling cane welcomed us into the warehouse, where the sights and smells assaulted me again. Thankfully, I'd brought a clutch of mint, which blocked the vile odors of horse manure and pungent tobacco. I chewed a bit to settle my stomach.

"Good day to you, Mr. Miller. You'll remember my wife?" Jasper said.

The buyer lifted his hat and the two strode off to look more closely at our tobacco.

Jasper promoted our crop by pointing out the fine color and texture of the leaves, and other buyers took notice. He pulled the product off the stack and thrust it into the men's hands. My husband surprised me with this confident, talkative manner, so different from his reticence amongst family. Of course, if I had a brother like Daniel, I might not be forthcoming. Jasper shook hands with several buyers and returned to my side, with his chest puffed up. I was proud of our harvest and him.

The warehouse's central corridor managed the wagon and horse traffic as before, but this year space was cleared on both sides, enabling two lines of product instead of one. Our tobacco stacks completed a line. Listening to the auctioneer work the other row, I marked the rapidity with which the buyers moved along, placing their bids and confirming prices. Business was brisk, demand was high, our product was fine. I predicted a good return.

The farmers looked comfortable, but not extravagant. The women dressed a tad better, likely eager to visit Asheville's shops, as I was, and wanting to look their best. Widow Corcoran was nowhere to be seen, and I wondered if she dared face the market again alone. Perhaps she had married or found some male relative to assist her this year. I'd not forgotten her plight or the vulnerability it provoked in me. I stroked my rounding stomach and resolved to discuss a will again with Jasper.

Horses chomped at their bits, with heads held high, eager to dispense their wagon's load and leave the confines of the large wood-framed building. Men cleared the purchased product from the other line, making way for the newly delivered. The bugle blared and drew my attention to the race toward our tobacco. Buyers jostled along in tandem with the auctioneer, bantering back and forth with words, nods, waves and tics. I could now decipher the auctioneer's call, but only with the utmost concentration. Jasper stepped forward to inspect our receipt. When he let the slip of paper lie atop our stacks, I knew we had a favorable price.

With our business at the warehouse completed, Zimri and Susannah checked into the Buck Hotel, and Jasper and I made our way to my cousins' home.

"Come right in." Mary pushed her way past the maid and waved us inside. "We are not a hotel, but I do hope you'll be comfortable here."

"You've a fine house, Mrs. Tate, and we're much obliged for your hospitality." Jasper removed his hat and smoothed his gray hair down. I was glad he'd trimmed his beard. The close cropping was more the fashion in town.

"Family is always welcome and as this is your second stay, I insist you call me Mary." My mother's cousin bustled into the parlor and invited us to sit.

After standing in the loud, smelly warehouse, reclining on the soft chenille sofa with my feet propped up would have been divine. I restrained myself by stretching my legs outward and sinking back against the cushion.

"Did you notice the number of hotels downtown?" Mary asked. "And the big news is the building of a health resort."

"Another one?" I asked.

"It will be listed in the new city directory when next published." Mary handed me a bound volume.

I paged through advertisements, resident listings, and background on the city and county. Honestly, I didn't give a hoot about it, but I'd read whatever she gave me if I didn't have to move.

"It's a testament to the progress Asheville is making. Just look at all the commercial listings." Mary beamed. "When we have our telephone, I can search for names to give to the operator."

"Jasper, it lists farmers in Buncombe County," I said.

"Well now, little ol' Democrat made the directory." He leaned over to scan the page. "I don't much like each Carter family member listed with our acreage for all to see." Stark lines etched across my husband's forehead.

The maid brought the tea tray and attempted to serve until Mary edged forward on her chair and took over. With a slight nod my way, the girl scurried out of the room. I'd look for an opportunity to ask her about the public school campaign amongst the Negroes of Asheville.

Mary poured tea. "Besides your marketing, what plans do you have?"

"Miss Petersen will introduce me to the minister at her church school. I hope to learn about the requirements in setting one up."

Mary handed me a cup of tea. "I've had the pleasure of viewing Miss Petersen's classroom, and I'm impressed with her abilities. However, the real force behind pushing public education forward is your friend, Miss Shackton."

Mary held another cup and saucer. "Forgive me, Jasper. You must remind me how you take your tea."

"Just milk, Mary. No apology needed. It's been too long." Jasper took the cup. "I thank you."

Mary liked Jasper. She didn't put on airs or act coy with him, rather, she talked of her interests and asked of ours. *Perhaps she could tell I was happy with him? Or she liked him because my husband and hers had hit it off?*

"Is Stewart in town?" I sipped the sweet hot tea.

"Yes, he'll join us for dinner." She nodded at Jasper. "He'll want to show you the planned stations on the northwestern line."

"I'd find that mighty interesting. We'll have crops to ship when the railroad reaches us."

The drone of their conversation and the sweet milky tea lulled me. I slouched and my head fell back against the sofa. Jasper nudged me.

Jasper cleared his throat. "Alice plans to see Miss Shackton for a particular dress."

I wasn't the only one consumed with thoughts of our child. I smiled weakly and sat up. "We are pleased to share the good news with you."

Mary's cup clattered on the saucer as she set it on the side table. "Oh my goodness, can it be?"

Jasper laughed and affirmed it. Mary clapped her hands together and lifted them to her lips.

"My mission to have a school in Democrat is even more urgent," I said.

"Good morning, Miss Elizabeth." I greeted my friend before the door swung fully open.

"Mrs. Carter, I am pleased to see you again." Elizabeth rose from her sewing machine and whisked around the front counter to grab my hands. Despite the familiarity in that touch, she'd greeted me with my surname. I did not feel slighted. I'd expected it, since my sister-in-law accompanied me.

"May I present Mrs. Susannah Carter?" All introductions made, I came to my actual business. "I need a certain dress." I hadn't written Elizabeth of my impending motherhood. When I shared the news, I wanted to see her expression.

"Alice is to be a mother," Susannah said. "She needs a looser gown for the coming months and after." Besides the time spent with Susannah in the fields, we had become close because we shared the belief that one should get to the point. Although I was disappointed that she'd been the one to share the news.

Elizabeth reached for me, guiding me toward her workspace and expressing her joy with a squeeze to my arm and her warm smile. "Come this way. I've designed many to include the latest advances." Elizabeth measured me and explained that the fan-pleat design could be adapted for wear after the birth. The gathers from the shoulder to waistline could be cinched up with the drawstring now and loosened as the baby grew. Once the child arrived, this upper bodice style accommodated nursing.

Susannah excused herself to run a few errands. Elizabeth and I caught up on the past few months. I talked about our life on the farm and tobacco harvesting, answering the questions she hadn't posed in her letters. Elizabeth spoke of attending the temperance meetings with Mary to speak about public education.

"Your cousin has been mighty helpful. She finds common goals between our cause and the many ladies' groups," Elizabeth said. "Like the temperance movement. It wants to better society, 'specially the lives of women and children, by outlawing alcohol. Education helps those very people."

I twisted around as she took measurements. “I’m surprised Mary attended those meetings. She serves wine with supper every time we visit.”

“Oh, yes.” Elizabeth chuckled. “She said her husband’s too fond of his whiskey to let such ideas in their home. But that Flower Mission she works with spun off from the Women’s Christian Temperance Union.”

“I’m glad the introduction proved helpful.”

I looked around the familiar space and regarded the lonely settee resting against the wall. My sister had witnessed my wedding dress fitting from that empty spot. My eyes tingled, and I squeezed them shut. I‘d endured months of banal letters with Jennie. If my sister were here now, she’d say, *Enough!* She’d reprimand me and I’d deserve it. Two years ago, we’d left this shop together, and I’d promised we’d remain close. One argument had festered, but this wound could be healed. I resolved to write to Jennie.

I chose a green calico at ten cents a yard, a prudent choice compared to gingham or bleached cotton.

“Just think, Miss Alice, y’all’s child, he might get a proper education.”

“What makes you think it’s a *he*?” I asked.

“He or she will be educated.” Elizabeth unfolded the bolt of cloth.

Where would I be with a proper education? Grandmother’s lessons on becoming a well-to-do wife left me wanting. Without the means to earn a living, Susannah, Jennie, and I had relied on marriage for survival. Miss Elizabeth, while a business owner, felt the sting of illiteracy. Last year at the tobacco market, Mrs. Corcoran had been at the mercy of a well-meaning man to ensure a just payment. I was determined to give our child every opportunity.

“Might you join Miss Margaret and me tonight to talk about the cause?” Elizabeth asked.

Here was an excuse to avoid another snore-filled evening in the parlor. "I'll see you this evening." My hand grazed my belly and smoothed the dress fabric across the child growing within me. Perhaps in bringing public schools to Asheville, I would learn to do the same in Democrat.

Chapter Twenty-Six

"To Dr. J. G. Hardy, of this city, more than to any other man, does Asheville owe the organization of this elegant library."

The Asheville City Directory and Gazetteer of Buncombe County

The closed sign hung on the inside of Elizabeth's shop door. Lamps lining Main Street glowed through the front window. On my first visit to have my wedding dress made, the shop had struck me as austere. Now in the company of Elizabeth and Margaret, and with the corner stove radiating heat, the dressmaking area was warm and cozy. Admittedly, I was in a much better place almost two years later, contentedly married and expecting my first child.

Elizabeth tidied the shop, placing bolts of cloth under the counter and remnants of lace and cloth in a cubby. "Tomorrow I'll call on Dr. Hardy."

"The librarian puts aside a collection of newspaper articles and government documents related to North Carolina public schools," Margaret explained. "Dr. Hardy is very knowledgeable and willing to help us."

An occasional shadow darkened the shop window as someone ambled along, perhaps going home after a long day's work or moving on to a restaurant for a late supper. The volume of people in the city fascinated me. *What did they all do? Where did they go at all hours? Did they enjoy the swirl of progress around them?*

Elizabeth poked needles in her wrist pin cushion before removing it and storing it away. "I hope for better news. Last week's report was a might troublin'."

Margaret grabbed her notebook to review the list of barriers identified in the State Superintendent's annual report.

"I'm pleased you could join us, as we could use some new ideas. First, some background," Margaret addressed us as her students. "In 1868, in response to an illiteracy rate of fifty percent, North Carolina emphasized the need for education in the new state constitution, which called for a public school system, free to those six to twenty-one years of age, operating four months per year."

"Which didn't come about," Elizabeth said.

"Correct." Margaret paced the floor. "Lack of funding has been an issue from the start. The people and industry abhor taxes. Particularly the wealthy, who send their children to private academies."

I perched on the edge of my seat, looking between the two women. Biting my lip, I recalled my debate with Senator Vance over the school funding issue. Two years later, the same old problem stared us in the face.

"But the legislature raised taxes in 1881. That was s'posed to help the schools," Elizabeth said.

"Only to come back this year and strip the county superintendents of funding and restrict their duties, as you discovered in the superintendent's report." Margaret nodded at Elizabeth. "Those cuts mean an end to the teacher training institutes. Without those, the quality of teaching will decline."

"And faith in the public schools will fall," I said. It was like a giant puzzle, pieces fitting together only to have one go missing for an incomplete picture. "It all comes back to money."

Margaret waggled a finger in the air. "Only when we understand their arguments can we build a case."

"Thanks to your cousin Mary, we've talked with many women's groups in Asheville and asked why people resist fundin' education," Elizabeth said.

When Elizabeth spoke about schools, her enthusiasm enlarged her whole being. She joined me on the settee. Her dress held no stray threads nor dust from kneeling to adjust a hem, and her blond curls didn't stray. I considered the many hours she'd labored today and yet she maintained a vigor to work into the evening hours for this cause.

"The women shared their desires, and distrusts, for public schools," Margaret said. "What seemed an obvious advantage to me was not clear to others. In fact, some viewed them as detrimental to society."

"Speakin' plainly," Elizabeth said, "property owners are white and they don't wish to pay taxes for colored schools."

"We might appeal to their Christian ideals. The colored people need to read and write to further their spiritual learning and improvement." I recalled Mary showing me the Freedmen's Chapel and explaining its founding for just that purpose.

"That's good," Elizabeth said. "Reverend Dusenberry's parochial school teaches the Negroes cookin' and gardenin' and Asheville's resorts want that."

Margaret continued pacing alongside the counter, her hand tracing a line across the glossy, dark wood. She paused and pointed her finger in the air. "How about this? The fifteenth amendment gave Negroes the right to vote. They need an education to make smart political choices."

"Stewart Tate said something similar. He told me the Negroes in the eastern counties needed schooling to govern better." I related the story of elected Negroes running up debts.

"What else?" Margaret asked.

I had a good sense of how Margaret kept her students in line. Until now, I'd only seen her polite, serene side. Here was a commanding woman ready to take on Southern society: male, female, White, Negro, Republican or Democrat. She was inspiring and frightening.

"A woman at the quilter's circle read in the newspaper that large public schools bring 'bout crime," Elizabeth said.

Margaret scowled. "I sent the Home Missionary Society the clipping from the Citizen-Times and asked for their help."

I raised my eyebrows. "What did the clipping say?"

"The writer claimed that education enabled more forgery, embezzlement and crimes associated with breaches of trust."

"Learning to read and write makes criminals?" I asked.

"I know it's absurd, but the newspaper printed it as fact and it's an idea our opponents accept, as it preys on people's fears. We must prepare to speak to it and hopefully the Society will provide the ammunition we need."

Elizabeth tilted her head and cleared her throat.

"What?" Margaret stopped pacing and faced her. "I've known you long enough to recognize you've something to say, but you're afraid I won't like it."

"Some don't like the Northern ways," Elizabeth said.

"Say more." Margaret crossed her arms.

"Southerners are proud. Some think it's bad enough we lost the War, now the North sends in their teachers and ideas about schoolin'."

Margaret's shoulders sagged. "I see."

Elizabeth had voiced what I'd heard from Susannah. She was right, and it wasn't just about schooling. Southerners resented the years of federal occupation and the barring of former Confederates from office. During this visit, I'd read a newspaper column calling for developing manufacturing in the South, rather than shipping our commodities off to far-flung factories and making the Northerners rich. Margaret faced a lonely battle, far from home and surrounded by hostiles.

The standstill continued, with a silence that bounced between the three of us. I glanced between the deflated missionary and the fiery Southern dressmaker.

Elizabeth crossed her arms. "I don't feel that way myself."

"I know." Margaret slumped onto a stool. "I sometimes question why I try so hard."

On that solemn note, we said goodnight and agreed to meet the next day to visit the library together.

"Good afternoon, Miss Shackton, ladies." The librarian stood behind a wide oak desk adorned with slips of paper, writing instruments, an adjustable date stamp, ink pad, and a towering stack of books.

Dr. Hardy turned the register around and jotted down Elizabeth's name, Margaret's, and mine. I presumed this courtesy extended to Elizabeth and others hesitant to write their name, although I wondered how many illiterate people visited a library.

He motioned for us to come along. "I've something interesting to show you."

We followed the librarian, tall and slender and unmissable in his solemn black suit, with a silver mane framing a pale, angular face. Dr. Hardy looked over his wire-rimmed glasses at two women in the free reading room and they stifled their whispered conversation.

"Asheville's population stands at greater than four thousand." Dr. Hardy thumbed through a binder to the appropriate page. He stopped to admire the modest library occupying the entire third floor of the courthouse. "Hard to believe that Asheville has doubled in size since we opened four years ago. I remember when our townspeople relied on reading circles."

"Thanks to you, Dr. Hardy, we have a fine library," Elizabeth said.

He removed his glasses and wiped them with a handkerchief. "There are many friends of the library, Miss Shackton. Donations come in steadily." He set his glasses back on his aquiline nose. "Did you know we accumulated one thousand books in our first year?"

"I believe you mentioned that," Elizabeth said.

Dr. Hardy stuck his hands in his pockets. "Forgive me, if I appear boastful."

"Not 't'all. You should be right proud."

Elizabeth and Dr. Hardy carried on, and Margaret followed the chit-chat with interest. I, on the other hand, tapped my foot under my skirts, eager to get back to whatever idea Dr. Hardy had to sway the citizens of Asheville to our way of thinking.

"I'll be more proud when the library is free for use," the librarian said.

"What? No more subscription fees?" Elizabeth asked.

"I'll propose that to the Board of Aldermen next month. With the city's recent incorporation, the library can be a municipal institution supported by taxes."

Was this a way for the town of Democrat to raise money?

Maybe I didn't need the Carter men's support. "I don't understand."

"Of course, forgive me. I sometimes ramble on in my excitement without explaining." Dr. Hardy placed his palms together. "With incorporation, a town gains more control over its own governance instead of relying on the county. There are some hurdles to jump, but our city now has its own charter—its own set of laws, and an elected government. Here in Asheville, those are our aldermen. It's the government closest to the people. They pass local laws, create a budget, and select the services and programs people want."

"Like a library or public schools," Margaret said.

"I'll be at the meeting to support you, Dr. Hardy," Elizabeth said. "Although a dollar fifty a year is not a hardship. I get my money's worth."

"That you do. You're a frequent and welcome patron."

"You were telling us about the population growth?" I asked.

"Right you are. I digressed." He turned to the binder and flipped the page. "Asheville has over four thousand people. When the city reaches five thousand, it has the legal right to vote on a special levy tax supporting schools."

"That's wonderful," I said. "Funding has been a struggle."

"That it has," Dr. Hardy said. "The incorporation of the city with wider boundaries gives the board of aldermen a broader base to serve."

"And tax?" Margaret asked.

"It's a little more complicated," he continued. "The legislature passed a law in 1877 allowing cities over five thousand to put to a vote a school tax supporting an eight-month graded school, with a petition of one hundred voters."

Elizabeth's brow went from smooth to lined as she mulled over the librarian's words. "If Asheville continues to grow, and if we can get a petition, and if we can present it to the Board of Aldermen ..."

"Then the citizens of Asheville would be a step closer to public schools," Dr. Hardy said.

Elizabeth took a deep breath. "Looks like I got my work cut out for me."

November 5, 1883

My dear Jennie,

We've just returned from Asheville, where I called on Elizabeth to fashion a dress that will accommodate my growing waistline in the months to come. Standing in her shop, I was reminded of the last time we were there together. Your absence weighed on me, as did the promise I made to you about remaining close. I am sorry for breaking that oath. These months since I visited you in Hendersonville have been filled with distant letters and strained hearts.

My stubbornness got the better of me and I was reluctant to admit that you did not need me any longer. Perhaps envy of your life in Hendersonville factored into it. You moved away from the farm and have every convenience living in the city offers. I should not begrudge you that. Forgive me, Jennie, and let us renew our sisterly intimacy.

Your loving sister,

Alice

P.S. I hope you will experience the gift of motherhood soon. I can think of no better mother than you.

November 10, 1883

My dearest Alice,

How happy I was to receive your last letter. Perhaps we are more alike than we thought, for I too have a stubborn streak. Forgive me, Alice. I know you were looking out for me and meant no harm. I wanted to show you I am making my own way after years of working in your shadow. Those years with you guided me toward my own independence.

The way you mothered me and our sisters and brothers convince me that you will be a natural mother. How happy I am for you! Write soon and tell me everything you are feeling.

I confess I have kept a secret from you. At first because I feared failure. Then I was ashamed of my pride. On a trip to Asheville, I sought Elizabeth's advice on selling my embroidery work. My quilting circle acquaintances had admired my collars and asked where they might buy one. Elizabeth agreed to carry them in her shop, taking a commission for each one sold.

She selected my favorite patterns of magnolia blooms and leaves, saying the Northern visitors like the Southern flora and fauna, plus the white and green colors complement many dress colors. Elizabeth also mentioned that decorative collars are an easy sell to stout women as they draw the eye away from oversized waistlines.

G.W. fancies having the latest products in our mercantile and agreed to display a few under the counter. This provides me nice pocket change and I relish seeing my creations about town and imagining them in faraway places.

You worry that I no longer need you. I once told you there is a difference between needs and wants. We may not need one another as we once did. However, I do want my sister. Consider us reconciled.

Your loving sister,

Jennie

November 17, 1883

My dearest Jennie,

Your letter filled me with laughter and tears. You stubborn? My sweet, sensitive sister? I never would have thought. Thank you for your kind sentiments. I hope to be a good mother and your faith in me sustains me.

With the air cleared between us, let me share more of our trip to town. Cousin Mary filled me in on the recent happenings.

The Flower Mission is making strides in accumulating the funds needed to open a hospital. An important benefactor is Mr. Thomas Patton, a man known for his service to the community.

You will recall "Patton Avenue" in Asheville. His father built that road. Mr. Patton is the owner of the Eagle Hotel and a large hotel in Warm Springs. Along with his sister, Frances, Mr. Patton has contributed to the hospital's founding. How pleased Mary appeared when telling me of the Patton family's interest.

While in town, I visited with Margaret and viewed her classroom of Negro children. Margaret was in good humor following the school term's closing exercises the previous week. The new term started Monday. There are many pupils, although attendance does not always match enthusiasm. Fearful of sounding like my brother-in-law Daniel, I question whether the resources should be offered to a group that does not value education enough to show up for class.

All my love,

Alice

December 1, 1883

Dear Alice,

This is my first letter in my hand.

Mary invited Margaret and me to another Women's Christian Temperance Union meeting. Margaret used the ideas we all talked about. We found many women agreeable. While men may dismiss us, we know women will lead the change.

I wish you a very merry Christmas!

Elizabeth

Chapter Twenty-Seven

Democrat 1883

"The negro is a neighbor. Perhaps there is little or no intercourse between the cabin and the mansion, or between the cabin and the cottage, or even between two cabins, a white family in one and a colored family in the other."

Our Brother in Black: His Freedom and His Future, by Atticus G. Haygood, Southern Methodist Publishing House

Everyone around the holiday table joined hands for Alvira's prayer. My mother-in-law dipped her head and closed her eyes. "As we bless this gathering and praise the birth of our Lord, let us also celebrate the coming life within our very own family. In Jesus's name, Amen."

Jasper and I traded looks at the mention of our growing family. All seemed right in the world until I noticed his brother Daniel's clenched jaw and vacant eyes. My Christian upbringing advised me to love my enemy, but I found that tenet difficult when mine scowled at me from across the table.

Following a boisterous meal where everyone had their fill

and then some, I joined the women in cleaning up the dishes. Despite our objections, the cooks—Harriet and Anna, joined in.

"You've done quite enough," I said.

Anna took plates from Robert as he cleared the table. She lingered at my side. "Alice, you'll be blessed with a child. What a gift."

"We are excited." I'd worn the dress Elizabeth fashioned for me, pleased to wear something new and to show off my status. Motherhood arrived at the ripe old age of thirty-two and I couldn't be happier.

Daniel and Anna had married six years ago and remained childless. I'd witnessed her happiness tending to any Carter child, followed by an air of sadness brushed away. She delivered her heartfelt remarks with a forlorn smile.

I broached the subject with Jasper on the ride home.

"You're not the first to earn Daniel's displeasure," Jasper said. "Every brother's wife that bears a child is a reminder of what he doesn't have. Best pay him no mind."

"I'm sorry for them. Perhaps a baby will yet come."

"Aye, Harriet tried to console them. Mentioned God's will. Reminded them of Rachel, Rebecca, and Sarah, how God granted them motherhood. I suspect Anna holds on to that hope."

"But not Daniel?"

"He did for a couple of years. They visited the circuit of Asheville doctors and one said she was making too much violent movement, advised rest and all. On further examination," Jasper cleared his throat, "the doctor said it was a mechanical problem and nothing to do."

Perhaps too much violent movement explained Daniel's firm grip on Anna's arm after she'd danced at our play day.

"Harriet confided Anna wished to adopt, but Daniel would hear nothing of it. The Carter family is a stronghold to be *preserved*—and only Carter blood qualifies." Jasper shook his head.

I cradled my growing belly. Carter blood flowed in my veins. With this child, I hoped to preserve the name and my place within this family.

With the days getting longer, I grew larger, more tired, and worked at a slower pace. Jasper tended next year's seedlings. He did not bring up a will during our evening hours together and I let the matter lie, for now. Once the baby was born, I'd have more leverage.

In late spring we planted the fields. The air shimmered and insects buzzed as we trudged along the mounded dirt rows. I perched the wide flat box on my rounded belly and the men reached up to grab the tobacco seedlings, stepping toward me and saving me the back-and-forth movement. I wiped my sleeve across my forehead. With the child growing within me and the sun's strengthening rays beating down, I was an oven.

When my time grew closer, the midwife came.

"When the pains start, you count the minutes in between. It's your first one, so you'll have plenty of time. Send word to me when they're an hour apart. Until then, you have your husband's niece ready the boiling water and linens." For as long as the months of pregnancy lasted, these instructions seemed impossibly short.

On a hot July day while I tended the chickens, a gush splashed between my legs, soaked my stockings, and trickled into my boots. My back ached, but I didn't notice any pain. I gathered my wet skirts and found Jasper in the milking barn. With no mind to the advice we'd been given, he dashed off on the horse to fetch Harriet and send his brother John to collect the midwife.

I lumbered to the house and directed Robert to put the water on to boil. A pain gripped me. I cried out and placed a firm hand on the wall. When it passed, I stepped out of my soiled underskirt and fixed breakfast.

"Shouldn't you lie down?" Robert's forehead creased, and he hovered in the kitchen.

"It could be a while. Best to go about our chores until the pains are closer together. I'm glad I have my helper today." I ruffled his hair until a pain caused me to bend in half. A sharp stab sucked the breath out of me.

Robert braced my upper arm. "That seems mighty soon since the last one."

He'd paid more attention to the midwife's visit than I'd realized. "Your pa will be here soon." Another pain wracked my belly and wrapped around my backside. I cried out, scaring Robert even more. "Fetch Bettany and her mother. Just in case."

"I'm not leaving you." His voice broke, and he gripped my hand with both of his. Robert had matured in the short time since I'd joined the family. *Would this child grow as quickly?*

"Yell out to Hamilton in the fields. Have him bring his women." I squeezed Robert's hand and gave him a weak smile. "I'll be fine."

With that task done, he guided me to the bedroom. The pains bore down, and I sank to the floor beside the bed.

"Missus?" Bettany called from the front porch.

"Come in. I'm in the bedroom." *Thank God. I cannot do this alone.*

"Will she be all right?" Robert's lips trembled.

No doubt, he recalled the story of his mother dying after his birth.

"Git that water, Mistuh Robert, and git me some clean rags," Bettany said.

I nodded at Robert, encouraging him to go on. He didn't need to observe what was coming, and I didn't want to witness his anxiety.

"Missus Carter, you needs out of all those clothes. By the looks of it, this baby won't be waiting." Bettany's mother motioned me into bed. I hauled myself up and collapsed.

Through the next pain, Bettany mopped my sweaty brow. She wrung the rag out and dipped it in a bucket of cool spring water. The old woman raised her hands and pointed to my swollen belly. I nodded, and she ran her palms over me, pressing and prodding at various angles.

"That baby jus' right. Won't be no trouble coming out."

Relief flooded me, only to be nipped by a searing pain. I moaned and stifled my whimpering when I saw Robert's worried face in the doorway. Bettany piled the pillows behind my back and urged me up into a sitting position. Robert edged into the corner, staying as far away as possible.

"Mistuh Robert, you go be a lookout for your pa," Bettany said. Robert skedaddled out of the bedroom. Not one hour had gone by when Jasper returned with Harriet and the midwife.

"You go on now." The midwife waved the women from the room.

Jasper ushered Bettany and her mother out. He lingered in the doorway and his lips parted as if he wanted to say something to me. My husband dipped his head and backed away.

Time went by, measured only by the dimming light in the room and the increasing frequency of my pain. Harriet stayed with me, mopping my brow and encouraging me. I welcomed her occasional prayer and wanted to add a personal plea to God to speed this along.

My belly tightened and a ring of fire erupted between my thighs.

The midwife pushed my legs farther apart. "Push now!"

Jasper's footsteps pounded the porch floorboards.

Harriet clutched my hand, and I nearly squeezed it off. My stomach had a mind of its own, contracting, squeezing, expelling this baby. Sweat rolled off me and my hair clung to my neck and face, while I grunted and pushed.

"The head's out. Now one more push." The wizened old woman bent between my legs, cradling my emerging child.

Harriet held my hand in both of hers. "You're almost there."

Our child's bawl filled the room. The screen door slammed shut and Jasper slid into the doorway. His concern melted away when he glimpsed me—worn out, disheveled, but well. After the midwife cut the cord, cleaned the baby, and wrapped it in a fresh cloth, I held my baby for the first time. The small bundle felt impossibly light. Jasper knelt by the bed and pulled back the blanket to peer at our son. With his scrunched-up face and eyes squeezed shut, he was the most beautiful child in the world.

"Husband, meet your son, Claude Eugene."

July 9, 1884

To the gentlemen of the board of the Home Missionary Society of Boston,

I am pleased to write of the progress achieved here in Asheville, North Carolina. My teaching at the Freedmen's Chapel is nearing two-and-one-half years, and in that time, I have seen our classroom grow in numbers. The children are eager to learn and well-behaved. Many are instructing their parents at home, as these family members were in former years denied educational opportunities. In this way, I feel I have many more students. Is that not proof that our mission is much needed?

The classroom is made up equally of girls and boys, ranging in age from six to twenty years. Early in my service, I added a Sunday afternoon class, as the children often work jobs during the week. On Sundays, I can divide the students into two groups, and a colored teacher, Miss Mary Jane Dickson, admirably manages the younger set.

Sincerely,

Margaret Petersen

Chapter Twenty-Eight
Democrat 1884

"Now 'the facts' are these: 1. Southern white children, as a class, wont [sic] sit at the same desks with negro children; 2. Southern black children, as a class, don't want to sit at the same desks with white children. And this gives trouble to no soul of man, except to a small class of fanatics, who feel that all things human must yield to their fancies."

Our Brother in Black: His Freedom and His Future, by Atticus G. Haygood, Southern Methodist Publishing House

During my one-week confinement, Harriet came every day to help with the housework and to tend to me and Claude. Robert peeked into my room, eager to see his baby brother, to hold him, to play with his tiny fingers and even tinier toes. Jasper spent as much time as he could with us at dinner and dropped in throughout the day to *check on things*. Evenings we passed Claude around and rejoiced aloud at how this one little person had stitched together our family.

I healed and walked the farm to keep myself awake during daylight hours. Claude didn't have a sense of time, as eager to be awake when moonlight streamed through the bedroom window as to sleep when the sun warmed the earth. I carried him along in a basket as I fed the chickens, weeded the garden, or cooked a meal.

As summer ended and his work in the fields lessened, Robert showed Claude the farm, read him a book, or just rocked him to sleep. His wish for a baby brother had come true.

"When will he walk? When will he talk?" Robert asked.

I answered Robert's questions while rocking Claude on the front porch. Across the field, Bettany and her mother tended their garden, while her son toddled at her side. Bettany stretched with her hands on her lower back, then shielded her eyes and glanced my way. I nodded, signaling a tenuous bond between us. The comfortable distance between our shelters may have been breached, but the barrier remained.

Margaret wouldn't understand that my son and Bettany's child wouldn't play together. For all her time in the South, she couldn't accept that our past weighed upon us, forever marking us with our beliefs. If I could start a school in Democrat, Elizabeth wouldn't approve of it only serving white children. She was a Southerner, but one outside the norms of class and society—an orphan and a businesswoman, a single female and a force in her community. As much as I admired them both, neither understood the way of things.

"What's my fine fellow been doing today?" Jasper wiped the mud off his boots and the scraper's wiry hairs stood stiff and unbending. He climbed onto the front porch, and I handed Claude to him. Our marriage took on heft like the infant in his arms.

"Why, he's slept, fed, and gurgled. It's been a busy morning."

"That's a good morning, I'd say." Jasper took me in his arms and planted a warm kiss.

"Whatever is that for?" I asked.

"Can't a man kiss his wife?" Jasper blushed and leaned down to put Claude in his basket.

Robert fixated on his dinner plate.

"I should think so." I smiled. "Let's eat before this food gets cold."

One fall evening when the air still hung heavy, and the morning promised dew, we sat for a spell on the porch. Claude had gone down an hour after supper. At four months old, he woke just twice each night, and my memory of earlier sleepless nights faded like an echo. Robert had retired to his room to read, taking the lantern with him.

"I've been thinking 'bout a will." Jasper laid his hand atop mine. "When you first brought it up, I was not amenable. I s'pose my father's stuck in my craw, the way it favored some."

"Daniel."

"Aye. My father divided his lands after the War between us brothers. He rewrote his will, detailing the gifts, and he added a clause."

"I take it that clause was contentious." I sat up straighter and turned toward Jasper. Susannah had disclosed that Alvira's passing would bring a reckoning. I needed to understand just what that meant.

"It will be. When Father died some twelve years ago, it all stayed the same. Mother kept his remaining lands. When she passes, the entire estate, including those earlier land grants, is to be divided equally amongst all the children."

I chose my words carefully. "Isn't an equal division fair?"

"Depends on the appraisals. If our land is valued at over one-thirteenth, then we will owe the others. Coming up with a cash payment might be difficult. Again, it all depends on the land valuation. Daniel will be the executor, and he determines how it's done."

I pondered how that could go wrong. Daniel had an air of importance, instigated by his father's favoritism. While he'd never shown malice towards his older brothers, his arrogance might lead to unfair decisions. As much as I wanted to steer our conversation toward a will, I'd long wondered about this family's divisions.

"How does John figure into this?" I asked.

"He set his own path and didn't rely on Father," Jasper said.

"He'll get one-thirteenth?"

"Aye, but he's done well for himself and doesn't need it."

"I'm sorry, Jasper. I meant no harm by suggesting a will." It'd been more than a year since I'd asked Jasper to protect me and Robert legally.

"You've raised a subject needing discussion. I've spoken with Zimri, and we recognize the need to care for our families."

The rockers creaked against the floorboards, accentuating the stillness between us. I thought of Jennie and her acceptance of her husband's word as final. Jasper might have had a more malleable wife. I wanted to ask him why he'd chosen me, when I'd brought nothing more than a few belongings and myself to our union. He was a kind man. *Had he pitied me? Had Harriet pressured him?* He'd lived on his own for many years and had an heir. He didn't need a wife.

As if in response to my thoughts, Jasper continued, "You might have had a younger husband, Alice. Had your father not died, you might not have married. You've entered our marriage with hope and goodness. Now you've given me a son." He rubbed his beard, and the gray wiry hairs sprang back into their familiar place. "I want to do right by you, Claude, and

Robert. I'll make a will when we go to Asheville. You three should have this land when I die. I'm an old man. More than likely, you'll have many years after me."

I sucked in my breath. We'd only had two and a half years together. Although I liked to think I could be independent, the risks of living alone as a woman were apparent. The widow at the tobacco market, my mother's downfall as innkeeper, my sisters' (and my own) rush to marry had shown me as much.

"You'll soon know how to run this place better than me," Jasper said.

I gave my mother credit; in my short married life, I'd come to love this man. My eyes moistened. I clutched his hand and held on tight. "Here's to many more years."

"Three million women in the United States work for money. Of these, 600,000 are agricultural laborers, mainly in the cotton fields of the South; 640,000 are employed in manufactories, while 530,000 in the laundries of the country insist that the 'Chinese must go;' 280,000 are milliners and 200,000 find employments as dressmakers; 60,000 earn their bread in the tailor shops and 690,000 are saleswomen, teachers, telegraph operators, type writers, bookkeepers, typesetters and nurses. There are 2,500 female physicians."

Asheville Citizen-Times

October 10, 1884

Dear Alice,

We've just returned from Asheville. While in town, I met with Elizabeth, who said to tell you hello. I was quite surprised (and pleased) when she ordered more embroidered work. Last year my collars sold out before Christmas. For the upcoming season, Elizabeth requested ladies' handkerchiefs and purses from me. She had several cuts of silk and velvet prepared, and she showed me where to place the patterns on the material. I'll return these cuts and she will construct drawstring reticule bags.

The pattern for the velvet Chatelaine bags will be ornate but smaller. Elizabeth says that's to let the richness of the fabric shine. I am glad for that, as embroidering the thicker fabric will be more difficult. I will have my thimble at the ready!

The pattern for each bag will match a linen handkerchief. Elizabeth insists a lady will not want one without the other. I am learning much about business. I bargained with her to get samples for our Hendersonville store. G.W. bragged about me over dinner with Mary and Stewart. I feel quite the modern woman with my work.

Please give a hug to my nephew - I can't wait to meet him!

All my love,

Jennie

. . .

October 25, 1884

Dear Miss Margaret and Miss Elizabeth,

It's been four months since our son's birth, and I can't remember what life was like before Claude. I will soon be running after him. Robert assures me he will be his brother's protector.

Claude's birth and Robert's lack of educational opportunities here in Democrat drive my determination to improve the schooling for my own children and others.

My meeting in Asheville with the Methodist minister was informative. Unfortunately, the nearest Methodist church here is not a viable option, as the building is in use for various groups throughout the week. I continue my search for a suitable location and for a benefactor.

I look forward to seeing you next week when we come to town. You shall meet my Claude. Please plan to update me on your workings toward our shared cause.

With perseverance,

Alice

Chapter Twenty-Nine

"After the body has been prepared, the body is placed in the handmade coffin for viewing and placed in the parlor or funeral room. The custom of 'sitting up with the dead' is also called a 'Wake'."

'Sitting Up With the Dead: Lost Appalachian Burial Customs', Unmasked History Magazine

Claude cooed and babbled in his basket near the warmth of the kitchen stove. The sun edged over the horizon and its light streamed through the window, blinding me as I glanced across the snow-covered yard toward the barn, where Jasper milked the cow. Harriet and the children would arrive mid-morning and I welcomed the company as Jasper and Robert would be away the entire day, mending Zimri's fences.

My thoughts shifted to Claude's first Christmas in a couple of weeks. He kicked his blanket loose, and I tucked it back in. Light snow drifted outside, while I poured myself a coffee.

"Well, those chickens will be hungry." I drank down the warm brew and threw my shawl on. My boots were thin and ill-suited for the sudden wintry weather, but with knitted wool stockings my feet stayed warm. I pulled the scarf across my face as the icy breeze prickled. At least the snow put a damper on the smell of chicken manure. The hens roosted in silence as I spread their feed. Gathering the basket, I turned toward the house. Alongside my footprint trail lay Jasper's, leading away to the barn. He'd be in with fresh milk soon and wanting something hot to eat. I scurried up the steps and back into the warmth.

"Mornin'." Robert made faces at Claude, urging his brother to smile.

"No sense starting breakfast until Pa comes in," I said.

I edged two chairs closer to the stove, an invitation Robert accepted. Just as the fire warmed our bodies, Claude's arrival had thawed our relationship. My stepson had welcomed me into the home, read with me, done the chores that I'd asked, but before Claude, he'd not confided in me, sought me out when hurt, fallen into my arms for a hug or a kiss. With this baby, I'd become a mother and that qualified me to be a mother to Robert. My stepson leaned against me and we peered down at his brother, his face squishing up and his little limbs attacking his covering.

I nursed my fussy Claude. Once latched, he drank greedily, and a surge of milk coursed through my breast. When he drifted off, I laid him in his basket.

The sunlight flooded the yard and the snow's crust glistened. The tenant trudged across to the curing barn to mud the cracks today. My chores called. I stood at the window, searching the path in the yard. It was unlike Jasper to be this late. Perhaps the cow was unwell.

"Robert, go see what's keeping your pa."

Minutes later, the barn door banged open, knocking repeatedly against the planked wall and slowing its rhythm with each strike. Robert bolted toward the house. He stumbled and fell, picked himself up off the frozen ground and ran toward the house. I met him at the back door, pushed it open, and heard the words that changed my life.

"Pa's dead!"

No tears fell from Robert's glassy eyes, and his mouth slackened. I bundled him in a blanket before the stove and ran to the barn.

The horse, the mule, and the cow shuffled inside. A clatter startled the animals, and the metal pail rolled out of a stall, fresh milk seeping into the loose hay, and pooling on the dirt floor. I ran to where Jasper's boot stuck out, listless and lonely. Edging around the cow, I found my husband lying on his side, eyes open, one leg twisted around the milking stool.

"Jasper!" I sank to my knees, touching his face and shaking his shoulders. "Oh, Jasper!" I fell back against the stall's planked wall and my chest heaved, my breaths coming sharp and quick. Other than the slight shuffle of the cow, there was silence. I burst into tears, coughing and sneezing until my face was slick. I reached forward and caressed his cold, lifeless cheek.

The yard stretched interminably long, as I lumbered toward the house. My shawl lay in the barn, but the cold had no claim on me, and the sudden warmth of the kitchen didn't either. The motions came familiar and unwanted. I'd dealt with death before, my father's and my brother's. I gave Robert instructions to care for Claude, for there was no one else to send for help. I saddled the horse and raced across Ivy Creek to Zimri and Susannah's home. They were on the porch as soon as they saw me approach.

"What is it?" Zimri grabbed the reins as I slipped from the saddle.

I collapsed in Susannah's arms. "Jasper's gone."

She held me, while Zimri galloped off to find his brother, lying cold on the barn floor.

Standing in front of Jasper for the last time, my thoughts tumbled through all that had happened since yesterday morning, when Robert had found his father dead in the barn. The church bells rang within hours, calling our women neighbors to prepare his body. John, Zimri, and Daniel had carried their brother's body to our front room, while Samuel fetched a board and a coffin from the mill. The women of the church had laid him on the cooling board. They'd washed him, trimmed his beard, combed back his hair, and dressed him in his Sunday suit.

I'd stumbled along, fetching a clean collar, a comb, or a pair of scissors. I'd cooked for countless people, remembered to milk the cow, and sent Robert to feed the chickens. The day had passed like gossip, spilling forth and spreading quickly, while I stood with the body of my husband. Family and neighbors approached with condolences I wouldn't recall. I turned toward each person, nodded, murmured some words, and lapsed again into silence.

Coins rested on Jasper's eyes to take into the afterlife, some believed as payment for the crossover. They spared me from the sudden opening of his eyes, a cruel trick of the body to those that grieved. A white linen cloth tied around his head secured his jaw. Someone had fastened his ankles to the fabric-covered board. Tears coursed down my cheeks.

Robert had taken care to look his best. He'd slicked down his hair and dressed in his Sunday clothes. I placed a hand on Robert's shoulder, but he moved away in search of his Uncle

John. I knew he would never forget what he'd seen. He'd likely blame me for sending him after his father.

A young neighbor yawned in the corner of our living room. He'd had the night watch. It wouldn't do to leave a departed person alone before burial and this job rarely landed on a family member.

Propriety called and I pulled myself away from Jasper's body to greet neighbors. Harriet tended to Claude, allowing me my grief. A steady stream of visitors filed through the house. Kind words. Tears. Condolences. Exhaustion.

When dusk arrived on the day following his death, the women wrapped the body in linen and the men lifted him into the pine coffin. The heavy box traveled to the graveyard and a procession of wagons and buggies followed. Just as the church bells had called the women, so had the town's men been called to duty; they'd dug the hole that invited Jasper to his permanent sleep. I watched as Jasper's coffin and then earth filled the gaping hole. He laid within the Carter section of the cemetery, surrounded by generations of family members, each headstone a testament to this family's hold on the land.

On the morning after the burial, I woke to a half empty bed, stared at the blank ceiling, and listened to the stillness of the house. The reality of my situation set in. I was a widow with a baby and a stepchild. Jasper started a will but had not completed one. Jasper's land—my land, was part of the Carter estate, subject to the equal partition upon the death of his mother and Alvira was not young.

Yet again, I faced a family split apart and an uncertain future. The life I'd made with Jasper, the home I'd managed, the fields I'd labored in, all of it thrown into the chaos death brought. Sobs erupted from my chest. I balled my fists and beat the bedding. My lamentation woke Claude, who wailed in unison.

Days, then weeks, then one month passed, all measured by Jasper's absence. I went through the motions, rising each day, caring for Claude, managing a minimum of chores, and falling into bed each night. Robert spent more time with his Uncle John and Aunt Caroline, sleeping over at the Carter Inn, where life resembled something close to normal.

It was the quietest time of the year, but there was always work to do. The wood pile should have been higher, the curing barn re-chinked, and the fence posts mended. My unwashed hair hung in clumps and I tucked it behind my ears. My apron displayed days of spatters and dirty handprints.

Daniel turned up, waltzing onto the porch like he owned it. "In this period of grieving, we must not lose sight of practicalities, especially where you and Claude's welfare are concerned."

I braced myself in the doorway. He was not interested in my welfare. It was not a Christian thought, and yet, I questioned Daniel's grieving. Jasper had transformed these infertile fields into profitable farmland. With his death, his youngest brother saw an opportunity to grow his holdings.

"I appreciate your concern," my words choked out. I didn't ask him in, nor did I invite him to sit down.

"Your sister is in Hendersonville. Might you go to her? Family is all we have." Daniel smiled tenderly.

I didn't believe his gentle appeal for a minute. "My Carter sisters will help me. I know this family will respect Jasper's wishes. I find it impossible to leave the farm when he wanted it to provide for us."

"Do we know what his wishes were?"

Jasper had not mentioned the will to his youngest brother.

Daniel fiddled with his pocket watch, turning the gold

piece over and over in his hand. "Our father recognized the importance of keeping land and family bound. He tasked me with that goal." He spread his arms out and leaned back against the railing. "Robert and Claude have claim to this land, though they're too young to run the farm."

Daniel thought he would manage this farm. Perhaps he'd take in the boys and provide his wife with children. It wasn't unheard of for a childless couple to raise a family member's child and, in this case, under the guise of helping.

"I shall farm. Jasper taught me well. From purchasing seed to selling the tobacco at market, he involved me, and I intend to continue here." I enunciated every word.

"Alice, you might find negotiating labor or selling at market to be harder on your own," Daniel said.

The widow at the tobacco market had proven that. I lifted my chin, projecting a confidence I didn't feel. Claude's timing was impeccable. He woke from his morning nap and cried out. "Those are my intentions. My son needs me, so I must bid you a good day."

In the days that followed, I labored hard during the day and dropped into bed most nights after settling Claude. Thankfully, the fields waited through the wintry weeks. Hamilton minded the barns and winter chores. Harriet's daily visits resumed, and Robert helped. Between caring for Claude, keeping house, poring over farm accounts, and grieving, I was plumb worn out.

My siblings sympathized by letter. Most lived too far away to attend the viewing. Jennie arrived as soon as she could.

"I don't know what I'd do without you," I said. Farm

chores, laundry, and keeping the house clean, all went much quicker with my sister minding Claude.

"I'm glad to be here." Jennie bounced my son on her lap. "G.W. can manage the store without me."

I had my suspicions about Jennie's marriage. "You're good with Claude."

"I'll visit more often to see my favorite nephew." Jennie lifted Claude up in the air and kissed his tummy, making him laugh. "I know you wish to ask, so I'll tell you. I won't be having my own children."

I moved to my sister's side. "It's only been three years. There's still a chance."

"It's not for want of trying." Jennie blushed. "After our first year together, G.W. took me to a doctor in Asheville. He said I lacked the vital force of blood necessary to stimulate reproduction."

"What does that mean?" I asked.

"It means the doctor prescribed Mitchella compound, the nastiest drink around." Jennie bounced Claude on her lap. "After a year of drinking it morning, noon and night, and still no baby, G.W. tired of the expense of it."

"I'm sorry."

"G.W. married me to continue his family name. He wanted a son to inherit the store. He'd married twice before me and both women died, although not from childbirth." Jennie placed Claude face out on her lap. My son leaned into her and grabbed his toes.

"He wanted to try again?"

"Yes, and I complied. I didn't want to give him a reason for divorce. We'd been to the doctor, and I feared he might appear in court claiming I was the problem."

Jennie had learned more than business. She was right to fear divorce. The scandal would've left her unmarriageable.

Without a husband, she'd be homeless or rely on charity to put a roof over her head.

"But that didn't happen?"

"No. I told you about my business dealings with Elizabeth?" Jennie acknowledged my nod and rushed on. "Well, I'd gone to her shop to deliver more stitchwork. I had the doctor's prescription with me, and she had her own opinions about the situation."

"What did she say?"

"Elizabeth questioned whether G.W. might be the problem. After all, he'd married three times with no resulting children."

"No!"

"She asked where he'd served in the War. When I told her he was from Tennessee and had served around Nashville, she said large numbers of soldiers got the clap there."

I gasped. My polite, proper sister talked about the sexual misconduct of her husband. If she'd done cartwheels across the room, I wouldn't have been more shocked.

"It took careful maneuvering with G.W. to convince him to see a doctor." Jennie lifted Claude and laid him in his basket.

"How did you?" I asked.

"I pleaded with him to seek medical attention so we might have a child." She smiled, one corner of her mouth lifting higher in a mischievous smirk. "If he'd suspected I might use it against him in a divorce, he wouldn't have gone. The idea of a public trial is distasteful."

I didn't know what to say to my wily, scheming sister, so I said nothing.

Jennie arranged her skirt as she sat back in the kitchen chair. "The problem is as Elizabeth suggested."

The big burly G.W. could not father children. His manly

ways and enthusiasm in the marital bed would not bring the results he desired. "No children then?"

Jennie nodded and looked longingly at Claude. "But, no divorce either. I gained favor with G.W. by expressing sympathy for his condition, plus I believe he values my place in the store. I've a knack with the women shoppers in Hendersonville, as many come to see my latest designs. They purchase other goods, and that makes him happy."

I touched Jennie's hand gently. My sister would be childless through no fault of her own.

"On the bright side, I have appealed to my husband's strong Christian faith. Relations are for procreation. If we have no hope of a child, then ..."

Recalling Jennie's tender condition after the wedding, I decided she'd negotiated a satisfactory outcome under the circumstances. My younger sister had gumption. I stifled a chuckle and refilled our coffee cups.

"Will you manage here?" Jennie asked.

That question dogged me day and night. "I must try."

Jennie nodded. "If anyone can do it, you can, Alice."

My sister's faith bolstered me. I'd run our family's inn, managing the kitchen, preparing the bedding, ordering provisions, and handling payments. With three seasons of tobacco farming behind me, I understood the rhythm of planting, harvesting, and curing. I'd stood by Jasper's side in the warehouse, watched him market our product to ensure a good sale price. I stretched, rolled my shoulders, but the stiffness from weeks of stress remained.

While washing the breakfast dishes, I listened to the joyful sounds of Claude and my favorite sister. There was much to do before Jennie returned home, and I traveled to Asheville to file the death certificate. I would ask Zimri to oversee the farm and Robert to handle the chores. I needed to pen a letter to Cousin Mary requesting her hospitality.

After seeing Jennie off to Hendersonville, Claude and I left for the Buncombe County courthouse.

Chapter Thirty
Asheville 1885

"Col. W. B. Baird is helping to keep things straight in the clerk's office at present."

Asheville Citizen-Times

I presented the death certificate to the spry man behind the desk bearing the nameplate: William Bedent Baird, Clerk Superior Court. His bright blue eyes twinkled above a snowy beard climbing halfway up his cheeks. When his head bowed to read the document, I glimpsed speckles on his exposed scalp and the rim of white hair circling it.

Mr. Baird signed the paper with a flourish. "If you'll have a seat, Ma'am, I'll fetch the necessary forms."

I sank onto a bench. The dark wood walls exuded calm and comfort. I wanted to stay all day in this room, letting it infuse me with its serenity, rather than trudge through the wet wintry air pushing Claude about in his perambulator.

The elderly clerk returned and waved me forward to a

chair opposite him. “Mrs. Carter, my condolences to you. As you are widowed and your husband died intestate, that is without a will ...”

“He wanted to write a will.”

“Yes, Ma’am. That may be, but it appears not to have been signed nor filed.”

My shoulders sagged and my brow furrowed.

“Mrs. Carter, I shall walk you through the process.” His whiskers twitched upward, signaling a sympathetic smile. “Our first step is to recognize the death of your husband and file a petition for dower. The law entitles you to one year’s provisions from your husband’s family before the estate is divided. The dwelling and outbuildings are protected from creditors, and you own these for the rest of your life. After the dower, the estate is divided with one third to you and the remainder divided amongst the heirs.”

I sighed with relief, knowing the law worked in my favor. Now I had to figure out how to earn a living on my land. “What if something happens to me? Do I need a will?” Besides Claude, there was Robert to consider.

“Upon your passing, your dower is divided between the heirs of your husband.” The court clerk drew forth another sheet of paper. “We will take the next step in naming you as the administratrix of his estate. If you will kindly give me the names of his heirs, including this little fellow.”

Claude slept the entire time we spent completing the paperwork. After receiving the document and instructions to return with the estate accounting, including all debts owed, I thanked Mr. Baird and we took our leave. I expected many more late nights poring over receipts and numbers by the oil lantern at home.

Claude and I walked across Court Square. The first time I’d visited this gathering place, I’d been with Jennie in a situation I didn't think could be more dire. I'd been wrong—about so many things. Gripping the carriage's handle, I maneuvered it around fast-stepping townspeople, all eager to be a part of a city pushing toward its future. I meandered out of step with these people and at odds with myself. They strode forward with purpose, while I roved the public square, unsure of the fate I faced.

We crossed Main Street and ambled toward Mary and Stewart's house. Upon my arrival this morning, Mary had greeted me with pity. She'd offered sincere condolences, then launched into valid concerns. *How would I carry on? Poor Claude, to be raised without a father!* I'd escaped my cousin's sympathy by walking to the courthouse, which allowed me to stretch my legs after the two-hour drive from Democrat.

With every step drawing me closer to my cousins' home, I prepared myself for Mary's bundle of emotions: sadness over my loss, anger at Jasper for leaving me, compassion for young Claude, upset at the Carter family designs, and love for me. I didn't blame her for those feelings, rather, I wanted to delay seeing mine mirrored in another.

I climbed the Tate home's steps and Mary greeted me on the porch by taking Claude and passing him to the maid. She embraced me. The tension in my body eased as she led me into the parlor and called for tea. Her usual chatter about the hospital or what new businesses were coming to Asheville was absent. Instead, she became the mother I didn't know I'd needed.

I soaked up the comfort and compassion she offered, and I talked. In the hours that followed, the maid brought Claude for a feeding, a tray of food appeared and disappeared, and the lanterns were lit. The parlor's fire was stoked, Claude's basket returned with his sleeping form, and still, I talked. My cousin listened and held my hand. When I yawned, she led me upstairs to the guest bedroom, where my nightgown lay on the bed and my traveling bag rested by the door. She placed Claude in his basket nearer to the fire's warmth, kissed me on the forehead, and left me to sleep my troubles away.

The following morning, before leaving for Democrat, I visited Elizabeth. While I waited for her to finish with a customer, she cast concerned glances my way, for my black veil conveyed everything. The doorbell jingled as the patron departed.

Elizabeth drew me into her arms. "I'm sorry for your loss."

I shoved the court document into Elizabeth's hands.

She cleared her throat and slowly read: "Alice Carter, being sworn, doth say: That J.S. Carter, late of said County, is dead, without leaving any WILL and TESTAMENT, and that C. A. Carter is the proper person entitled to Letters of Administration on the estate of the said J.S. Carter."

I collapsed onto the waiting bench and Elizabeth joined me. Silence weighed like a rain cloud, ready to release its burden.

She clasped my wrist in a tender embrace. "What will you do?"

"Carry on, I suppose." I wiped a tear away and straightened on the seat.

"That you can do. Jasper didn't leave a will, but you and your children are heirs before Jasper's siblings."

"I believe Jasper's brother will make a claim. He's already said I should move to my sister's. He means to get me off the family lands."

"And you plan to stay?" Elizabeth asked.

I had thought of nothing else. "I do."

"If you've been to the courthouse, you've met the Colonel," she said. "He'll be a help to you."

"The Colonel?"

"William Baird fought with the Buncombe Rifleman. He's known 'round town as Colonel."

The no-nonsense man with the sparkly blue eyes and snow-white beard had helped me today. I didn't know then how much more he would offer.

Chapter Thirty-One

Democrat 1885

"While the population in thirteen years has increased about 200 per cent., the wealth of the city has in ten years been augmented 400 per cent. Truly this is a sign of abundant prosperity. And still the boom continues. . . ."

The Asheville City Directory and Gazetteer of Buncombe County

Not long after my return to the farm, the tobacco needed starting. I readied the beds, spread the seed, and laid the linen cloth. Scooping the soil in my hands as Jasper had done, I determined it would be some weeks before it would be warm enough for transplanting. The earthy smell clung to my skin and reminded me of Jasper walking into the kitchen from the fields, the odor following him in and lingering. The clumps of dirt crumbled to the ground and were lost to me.

Claude cried, and I knelt beside his basket to console him. I picked up our son and held him, knowing I had to go on, yet uncertain if I could. I'd prided myself on managing a home, even bragged about my abilities, but I'd never grappled with it all by myself. Before Jasper, there'd been Jennie. Claude settled, and I framed the blanket to shade his face. Dirt smudged my sleeves, covered my forearms and lodged in the crevices of my hands and nails. I was sun worn and beat down. When the tobacco seedlings needed moving, I would need help.

I hitched the horse to the wagon and drove to Zimri's house. Susannah greeted me and her anxious eyes spoke to either the grief of losing Jasper, or the fear that such a loss could befall her.

Zimri came in from the field. "A couple few weeks."

"Yes, I think so," I said. "I'd appreciate your help in planting my fields."

Silence surrounded them like a broken wagon wheel, unwelcome but needing addressing.

"Alice, I'd like to help, but Daniel asked me to lend a hand at the mill. Besides getting my own fields planted without Jasper, I'll not have a spare minute."

"We will hire a tenant to oversee the planting this year. We've never done that before." Susannah did her best to excuse their inability, or perhaps unwillingness, to help.

Daniel was exerting his influence through different avenues. His goal was apparent.

I watched them teeter backward under my insistent gaze. Silence endured, and yet they didn't vacillate with the unspoken pressure. "I suppose an opportunity at the mill is favorable," I said.

"Ah well, he says it's temporary. He won't be needing me more than this year." Zimri rubbed his hands together. "I'm awful sorry. Speak to John. He has tenants for his fields and might spare some."

The family had shown their colors. Daniel had suggested I leave. By hiring Zimri, he left me high and dry with the fieldwork. If I couldn't produce tobacco, I'd have no income, no way to support myself.

My thoughts spun as I contemplated how to continue on the farm. There was one remaining option. Smoke rose from the tenants' chimney as I strode across the field. I knocked on the uneven door and Bettany kicked aside the hay stuffed under the entry.

"Missus?"

"Bettany." I nodded curtly. "As you know, Mr. Carter has passed. I intend to farm these lands and would like to hire your man. He's familiar with my late husband's way of farming, and seeing as the fields are side by side, I thought we might come to an arrangement."

Hamilton stepped into the doorway alongside his woman. For three years I'd looked out on this ramshackle outbuilding, but I'd never been inside. The couple blocked my view and the dim light didn't help. A fire crackled within and Bettany's mother hummed.

They accepted the additional fieldwork under the same conditions as the existing tenancy. I'd realize seventy-five percent of the field's income, while they took twenty-five. The cost of seed would come out of my share, but the loan of our equipment cost me nothing extra. Hamilton gained the use of our equipment for his rented field. He'd double his income, a quarter of the income from his rented field and a quarter from mine.

"I planted the seedlings. Tomorrow you'll need to clean the barns, ready the equipment, and chop wood for the flues."

"Yes'm," Hamilton said.

"If you require more men, then I expect to approve of the workers." While I had no reason to question the couple's ability, I could not forget they'd had a criminal in the family.

Bettany's brother had died in a chain gang working the railroad. Elizabeth claimed the convicts were Negroes rounded up for simple offenses such as being without work or vagrancy, but I wasn't so sure.

Bettany smiled. "We be seeing you first thing in the mornin'."

I walked back home and logged an entry into my farm journal. Studying the income and expenses for the last three years, I'd concluded that renting both fields was my only option. I couldn't work the fields alone and wouldn't work alongside men other than my husband, certainly not a Negro man. I would keep the house, the garden, take on the animals that Jasper had managed, and be a mother to Claude and Robert. Though the income would be twenty-five percent less after paying the tenant, it would be enough. It had to be.

Spring came earlier than usual. While the weather remained cool and the fields awaited the seedlings, I returned to the courthouse.

Mr. Baird's low, slow drawl welcomed me. "Good morning, Mrs. Carter."

"Good morning, Colonel."

"Ah now, you've asked around town about me, have you?"

My cheeks flushed at the impropriety.

He delighted in my embarrassment and edged forward on his chair, tugging at his jacket lapels. "I suspect you have documented the estate value." The Colonel adjusted his pince-nez glasses and took the list of my worldly goods.

My pulse beat in my head while I awaited the court's verdict. He skimmed the paper, a statement on the slimness of my inheritance.

"I knew your husband, although he was younger than my cousin Zebulon and me. We ran wild about Democrat before one of us became respectable."

"Zebulon Baird Vance, the senator?" I asked.

"He always was the biggest toad in the puddle. He's made a name for himself and yet he hasn't forgotten his people." The Colonel copied out the listing and signed it. "This all seems in order. I will file it here at the Buncombe County Courthouse should there be any challenge to the inheritance."

"Is that it? Are we to carry on, Claude and I, on my late husband's farm?"

"I advise it, Mrs. Carter. There is another heir, Mr. Robert Swain Carter."

"My husband's first child is staying with his uncle." Although Robert returned daily to do chores, he didn't seem inclined to move back. He avoided our parlor with its abiding odor of pipe tobacco and his father's upholstered armchair. Grief was a thorny companion appearing suddenly with a sight or sound or smell to pierce one's heart.

"Robert Carter is still a rightful heir. May I ask, do you have a good relationship?"

"He's a young man, just thirteen years old," I said.

"A boy on the verge of adulthood." The Colonel leaned back in his chair. "As long as you live and take an interest, you have the legal right to manage the property. When Robert comes of age and if he were to make a claim ... Well now, I suggest you let sleeping dogs lie." He winked at me, and warmth spread across my cheeks again.

With business attended to, I retired to my cousins' home. Stewart stoked the fire, Mary cross-stitched, and I sank into the horsehair chair, while Claude slept upstairs.

"You and Claude are welcome here." Mary poked the needle through the fabric and drew the thread into a neat, fine stitch. She peered over her floor stand.

I smiled at Mary, then Stewart. "I appreciate your hospitality. You've been so kind to me and Claude. But now that I'm finished with the court filings, I must go home and carry on."

"Can you?" she asked. "Life in the city would be easier. Stewart and I would welcome having a child running through this old, quiet place." Mary waved her hand. "Claude could get a proper education in Asheville as there are several good fee schools."

Here was every wish for my child — an education, a fine home, and security. *I need only say yes.* I pictured Claude growing up in this comfortable house, attended to by servants, and dressed in fine clothes. *Could I deny him that life?* Then again, here in Asheville, we wouldn't catch water skippers at the creek, or listen to the cicada in the evening. We wouldn't pick the fruit of our orchard. Nor would we feel the land we owned under our feet. More importantly, Claude and I would miss Robert terribly.

Mary's face held a sanguine smile, and her eyebrows lifted. Stewart's silent nods made my response all the harder. "I thank you both. It's a generous offer. But Jasper wanted nothing more than to provide for Robert, Claude and me. By us staying on the farm, he's doing that."

Throughout my life, I'd passed from one caretaker to another, first my father, then my brother, my mother, and Jasper. Each time I'd been forced to carve out my role, fumble through the uncertainty, and work to secure my place. I didn't need to beg. I could determine my future and, while uncertain, I chose my own home.

Stewart propped an arm up on the fireplace mantel. "We respect your wishes. You know how dear you are to us—you and Claude. Should something change, the offer stands."

I didn't know that change was coming.

Chapter Thirty-Two
Democrat 1885

"The Buncombe-County court-house..., was completed in 1877, at a cost of $33,000. The United States Circuit and District Courts are held within its walls, in addition to the regular courts of the county."

The Asheville City Directory and Gazetteer of Buncombe County

Within a week of my return from Asheville, Daniel and Anna rode up to the house in their buggy. The unexpected call and her stiff posture told me everything I needed to know about this visit.

"What a surprise," I called out and strode into the yard.

It'd been a few weeks since I'd seen my sister-in-law. Although the Carter family continued meeting every Sunday, I'd been too busy for a day of rest. My absence probably caused tongues to wag. Let them. They'd taken sides, from what I could tell.

"It's been far too long." Anna kissed me on each cheek.

"Hello, Alice." Daniel removed his hat. His mouth was set

in a firm line of feigned concern. "Thought we'd talk business."

"Please have a seat." I motioned to the front porch rockers. After my visit to the courthouse, I was confident in my position, backed by the law in my inheritance claim.

Anna picked up Claude from the porch floor. "My, how he's grown!"

"And he's walking."

She placed him on his feet and held his chubby hands. Claude pranced toward me, wobbling along on his tippy toes. My son tottered into my arms. His aunt clapped and my child beamed. I kissed Claude and positioned him to walk back to Anna.

Daniel remained standing, leaning against the porch rail with his arms outstretched and towering over us. "About time to plant the fields."

"Not quite. The soil isn't warm enough," I said.

"Won't be long. You'll be needing some help."

"I've hired our tenants."

He snickered. "Jasper always said you had a head for business."

Goodness sakes. Did he think I'd cry and beg for help?

"Jasper taught me well. I've started the seedlings and when the soil's ready, I've contracted sufficient labor to plant, tend, and harvest the crop." I smoothed the folds from my skirt. "Plus I settled the inheritance."

"There's the matter of Robert," Daniel said.

"I've listed him as an heir." My hackles were up with the unexpected visit, questions about the inheritance, and the mention of Robert. Daniel had proven himself a gifted manipulator by hiring Zimri in the mill, so he couldn't help me with the fields. *What was he up to now?*

"My nephew will be fourteen next month. It's time Robert came into the family business."

I didn't like where this was headed.

"John and Caroline will file for guardianship of Robert," Daniel said.

Claude babbled and screeched with enthusiasm. His joy at his aunt's attention cast a darkness over me, a cloud of guilt. *Had I tended to the farm, the courts, and the chores at the expense of Claude and Robert?*

I snatched my son from Anna and hoisted him in my arms, twisting my body to keep him from them. The law would side with the Carters. Robert was not my blood, even though he called me Mother. While Claude was my very own, he was also a Carter.

Anna backed away and Daniel stepped forward, putting his arm about his wife's waist to calm her quivering. The two stood together against me, staring at me like a stranger. I bounced Claude on my hip and rubbed his back. My eyes darted to their empty buggy in the yard, willing them to see my unspoken invitation to take their leave.

My brother-in-law's forehead creased and his eyes squinted. "Guardianship protects Robert and combines the family interests."

Anna fussed with her dress cuffs and shame settled on her like a nightdress, from head to foot.

"I see." My thoughts swirled on their next move. Robert could claim one third of the land. As guardian, John could exert influence over him and my property. I'd mentioned that my stepson was not old enough to manage the farm, and they'd solved that problem.

"Let us know how you're getting along." He put on his hat, motioned to Anna, and they left. I sank onto the rocking chair, pushing it back and forth, with my thoughts moving the same way.

Throughout that spring and summer, Harriet came often with Robert and her children in tow. I appreciated her help but could not forget that it was her father who'd taken my stepson from me.

On a mid-summer's day, we worked side by side in the shade of the house preparing the bounty of our orchard. Harriet washed the fruit and piled it in a never-ending mound. "We've missed you at Sunday suppers."

"I've not had time." With every plum I grabbed, another rolled into place. I cored, sliced, and set the plum and peach pieces on the outdoor table to dry in the sun.

"We all recognize what a burden you're left with." Harriet knelt to play peek-a-boo with Claude under the table and I bristled. The Carter family's ploys with my stepson and son left me wary.

"Do you now? All of you?" I wielded the knife with more force, knocking it methodically against the tabletop. "Daniel encouraged me to leave the farm. Zimri withheld his help. I reckon no one believes I can make it on my own."

She stood, her eyebrows pinched and her bottom lip jutted out. "The family wants to support you and the boys."

"Funny way of showing it." I tossed the knife down on the outdoor table. The clattering caused Claude to cry, and I picked him up.

"I know the pain you feel, and it breaks my heart. Believe me when I say this too shall pass." She reached for my hands. "Let's pray together." Harriet bowed her head. "The Lord is my shepherd. I shall not want."

"I *want*, Harriet. I want to know why your father and mother filed to be Robert's guardian."

She jolted backward. "What?"

My voice rumbled. "Your family never accepted me. I'm finding that out now."

"That's not true, Alice." Harriet's face flushed. "And we're all grieving. Remember, Jasper was my uncle before he was your husband."

We squared off in the yard, our words thrown around like fruit pits scattered on the ground, hard and unforgiving. Claude cried, and I balanced him on my hip while wiping the juice on my skirt. As the purple and red juices spread over Jennie's stitching, I realized too late I'd picked too fine an apron for this work.

I yanked the stained cloth off and threw it on the table. "You'd best go." I whisked Claude away and marched into the house, slamming the door on my way inside. With the Carters attempting to force my hand, I needed a plan. I knew just the person to consult with to be ready for battle.

The interior of the Buncombe County courthouse, built solidly on the laws of the people, exuded durability and tranquility. Getting into the building was another matter. I wormed my way in and eased onto a bench outside the clerk's office. While I waited, boots stomped in and out, doors swung open and clattered shut.

My turn came, and I greeted the gentleman I'd come to rely on. "Good morning, Colonel."

"Good morning, Mrs. Carter. Why, that young lad must be heavy to tote. Why don't you give him here?" The grizzled war veteran took on a fatherly countenance as he lifted my son over the desk and jostled him on his knee. Claude smiled and showed off his new teeth.

"You're wonderful with children. As often as we've met, I don't know whether you're a family man."

"I'm afraid I was not fortunate in that regard. The War took my younger years."

I wondered if there was more. Some soldiers returned wounded, reluctant to burden a marriage with their physical or emotional scars. "That's a shame Colonel, as you're right good with this one."

He wiped Claude's face with a handkerchief. "I get some practice with my sister's grandchildren. Susan is a mother hen, constantly fussing over her chicks and her old coot of a brother."

I liked the way he talked with no pomp, as if we were familiar friends.

"Colonel, I wonder if I might call on your legal advice, since you have kindly advised me before?"

He mocked a salute. "At your service."

I laughed. "Are you always so friendly?"

His blue eyes twinkled. "Only with those I wish to be."

If I didn't know better, I'd think he was flirting with me. I pressed on with my business. "I'm afraid my husband's family will undermine my claim."

He straightened and cupped Claude to his side protectively. "Do tell."

"My husband's first child, Robert, turned fourteen and my brother-in-law seeks guardianship."

"You think this could be a move against you?"

I nodded.

He leaned back and glanced upward, seemingly studying the ceiling. Claude followed his gaze, then became enamored of the Colonel's wiry white beard. Claude poked his fingers in and gave a tug. The Colonel pried my son's hands from their target and occupied him with a game of pat-a-cake.

The county clerk's playful nature turned serious. "If you

were to struggle in managing the farm and they could prove that Robert's assets were at risk, your in-laws could move for rights to manage."

The Colonel leaned forward on his desk, the fine wool of his suit jacket brushing the surface. I wondered who pressed his shirt, if he lodged alone or lived with a relative. Perhaps he had a landlady to prepare his meals. The Colonel lifted his eyebrows, waiting for my response.

"Is that possible?" I asked.

"Possible, yes, probable, no. The law is clear about a widow's rights. Since the 1868 constitutional convention, our state has recognized a widow as the rightful owner of much of her late husband's property for as long as she lives. Proper management of the estate would lessen the risk, giving the Carters a weaker argument."

Colonel Baird shared typical arguments suggesting poor handling: upkeep of a farm, ensuring a good harvest, getting a favorable market price. Some were successful in overturning the legal owner's property rights. I would do my darndest to give the Carter men no cause for complaint.

Claude whimpered and squirmed with hunger. When I'd arrived, sunlight streamed through the window, now it crept over the sill.

"I've taken too much of your time, Colonel." I reached for Claude. "Thank you for your help. I feel better after speaking with you."

He rose and grasped my hand. "Anytime, Mrs. Carter. I can't imagine a better way to spend an afternoon." He let go only when I pulled away.

With autumn's cool nights, the apples in our orchard ripened. I cored, sliced and threaded them to hang and dry in the October sun. I stewed some on the stovetop for a rich soft applesauce. Claude lapped up the treat, and more ended up on his face than in his belly.

Eleven months after Jasper's passing, grief visited less often, only occasionally stirring me in my sleep. On those restless nights, I'd rise and find my way to the porch, to witness the moonlight and shadows, the crisp air and the warmth of my shawl, the silence of the dark and the tremor in my heart. I'd sit in the rocker until the lulling motion drew me back to the bedroom.

Days blended one into another, with the tenants managing the fields, Robert helping with farm chores, and the frequency of visits to the courthouse diminishing. I spent peaceful hours with Claude, reading, singing and playing with him. Every moment with my son restored me.

With the harvest finished, Hamilton tended the fires in the barn. He dried the tobacco to a rich golden color that would yield a good return. I worried about going to market alone as I'd been a witness to a single woman's attempt to command a fair price. I had a bold idea, one I kept to myself. That evening after dinner, I drafted my first letter to Colonel Baird.

October 10, 1885

Dear Colonel Baird,

Thank you for your honest and valiant efforts to support my inheritance claim. I need some assistance when bringing my crop to market next month. Might I enlist you to accompany me to the tobacco warehouse? I feel your presence will ensure a fair price and negotiation.

Sincerely,

Mrs. C.A. Carter

October 15, 1885

My dear Mrs. Carter,

I thank you for your kind words. As to your request, I have no experience in farming tobacco, nor in negotiations of its business, and so I suspect the presence needed is strictly of the male kind. I can deliver that, and I will oblige to accompany you on one condition. I request the honor of your company for supper at the home of my sister, Susan Reynolds, on the eve of the market day.

Your humble servant,

Colonel William Bedent Baird

Chapter Thirty-Three
Asheville 1885

"The market yesterday was in a condition almost of exultation. The warehousemen were all jubilant at the good sales they were making for their friends, the planters.... We quote sales...,

ASHEVILLE,

Sales 6,255 lbs. Mrs. C A Carter, 3 lots, 17 ½, 10 ¾, 10;"

Asheville Citizen-Times

"It is a pleasure to meet you." Susan Reynolds appraised me. Her eyes considered my hair and adornment, and with a sweeping glance, she looked over my dress.

I resisted the urge to smooth my bodice and straighten my skirt. I lifted my chin slightly and imparted a serene smile. "Good evening, Mrs. Reynolds."

"Allow me to introduce my son, William."

"Welcome to our home, Mrs. Carter." He moved across the entryway in two quick strides. "Please come in."

We entered the parlor with its rich taupe walls, crown molding, and wood floors gleaming around a lush Oriental rug. A grand piano stood in the corner of the room. With the lid propped open and song sheets on the music rack, I recognized this as a played instrument and not merely decoration. I'd seen such fine instruments in Asheville's hotel lobbies, but never one in a private residence.

William Reynolds extended his arm toward an auburn-haired woman sitting before the fireplace. "May I present my wife, Mamie?"

"Forgive me, if I do not rise, Mrs. Carter. It's a pleasure to meet you." She was in the last stages of pregnancy and looked unable to move from the sofa.

"The pleasure is mine."

The Colonel, his sister Susan, his nephew William and wife Mamie circled me in the expansive room. The feeling of being on display caused a shiver, which I disguised by turning toward Susan Reynolds. "Thank you for the invitation. You have a lovely home."

It was one of the oldest brick homes in Asheville, constructed before the War. The Colonel had explained that his sister and her husband, Daniel Reynolds, had raised ten children here—five girls and five boys, including their eldest son William, the Colonel's nephew and namesake. I admired the floor-to-ceiling windows, promising views across the property's fifteen hundred acres. In the fading light, I glimpsed the silhouette of hills and woods through the glass panes.

"My dear sister, I think a toast is in order. Earlier today your esteemed brother has, by his mere presence, enabled a satisfactory price at market for Mrs. Carter." The Colonel winked at me.

"Do tell, Brother." Susan rang for a servant, who brought glasses and a decanter of sherry.

"My introduction to the tobacco warehouse was remarkable. I considered my attire carefully. One must not appear above or below in station to those one deals with in business. I chose a fine suit and a modest cravat. I visited the barber yesterday. In other words, I presented my best self." The Colonel puffed out his chest and rocked back on his heels. "Then I let the lady do the talking."

The room erupted in laughter.

"You assisted me more than you know," I said.

William and Mamie Reynolds cast sidelong glances at one another.

"After today, I'm fixing to hang up my fiddle at the clerk's office and offer my silent male presence to smart businesswomen across the city." The Colonel raised his glass. "To Mrs. Carter and her success at the market and my new profession."

My face ached from smiling. In the Colonel's company, I'd laughed more than I had in years. Besides the business of the market, we'd spent the day amicably talking and getting to know one another better. I sipped the sweet sherry and admired the exquisite room. The fire crackled beneath a wide oak mantel, above which hung an enormous portrait.

"What a fine-looking man," I said.

"Our father, Israel Baird," Susan said. "His father, Bedent, was one of the first landowners in Asheville."

I recalled the commemorative plaque in Court Square. Three years ago Jennie and I had stood before it, anxious, worried, and soon to be brides. With the Carter family challenging my inheritance, insecurity riddled me yet again.

The mantel clock struck seven, and a servant announced supper. Back in Democrat, Harriet would put Claude to bed about now. She continued to help me, but our argument had strained our warm, easy relationship. *Would exerting my legal rights rectify the situation or cause more fall out?* I shoved the concern aside to enjoy the evening.

We lingered over the meal. My cousin's offer to live with them in Asheville floated on the periphery. *Claude would have access to school. I could have a social life. Elizabeth and I could work together on the public education cause.* Throughout the evening, such thoughts swirled in my mind, like waltzers' skirts. After hours in their company, I thanked my hosts, and bid them good night.

The Colonel escorted me to the Tate house. We had exhausted all talk and sat companionably within the carriage as it rumbled into town and stopped before my cousins' home. He offered me his hand and held me as I climbed down.

"I had a fine day in your company, Mrs. Carter."

"I am grateful for your help, and I had a wonderful time this evening. Thank you."

"I imagine we've given my sister and nephew something to talk about," he said. "I wouldn't presume Mrs. Carter ..."

The sharp-witted gentleman focused on me with no mind to the hour or the neighbors. It'd been so long since anyone had seen me as someone other than mother, worker, or widow. I welcomed his attention and it emboldened me. "Colonel, friends address each other by their Christian names. After today, I expect we might be more than acquaintances?"

"I'd like to think so, Miss Alice." His whiskers climbed his cheeks. William kissed my hand and took his leave.

I listened to his carriage pull away and caressed the skin where his lips had touched. I wasn't ready to go in and face Mary's prying questions. I didn't have answers. Easing onto the top porch step, I kicked my skirts out and leaned back on my hands to stare at the stars—distant, brilliant, each offering a beautiful, distinct light. *If I had to choose just one, which one?*

October 28, 1885

Dear Alice,

I find myself thinking of our evening together and how easily we found conversation. I hope I am not too presumptuous in writing to you, as I would like to continue our friendship through correspondence.

This week I read of the successful fundraising effort by Joseph Pulitzer, the New York World publisher. He raised one hundred thousand dollars for the construction of the pedestal on which the Statue of Liberty will sit in New York City. This must be something to see, a giant statue of a woman to greet all those immigrating to this land. Those French were smart to choose a woman as we both know it is the fairer sex.

Perhaps Asheville will build a similar monument to welcome the crowds of people descending on it. Between the railroads and the new industry, I swear there are unfamiliar faces every day. New people mean new land grants and business licenses and other such legal documents, which keep me busy.

I hope you will think kindly of me and write to me something about your country life. If I do not hear from you, I will not pester you further.

With kindest regards,

William

November 9, 1885

Dear William,

I was happy to receive your letter. While I enjoy the comforts of home, I miss the lively conversation of adults. Claude is talking, but it shall be a while before we have riveting discussions.

Although the harvest has been sold and winter stretches on, the work on the farm is never ending. There are the animals to tend to, the house to keep, and so on. You may think me silly when I tell you I have named our milk cow. Clementine is a great producer and I declare it has something to do with my singing to her while milking. Her favorite song is "Oh my darling Clementine," in case you wondered.

Lest you think I am all work and no play, Claude and I went to the creek yesterday to plunk rocks.

Now I must put this aside and deal with my accounts. I hope this finds you well and that I have not bored you with my bit of news.

Sincerely,
Alice

November 21, 1885

Dear Alice,

How welcome your letter was, and I think you could never bore me with your comings and goings. I recall the joy of creek-side play when I was a young boy and can just imagine young Claude's expression.

My sister Susan inquired as to your well-being just the other day. It seems you have a mutual friend, Miss Elizabeth Shackton. Besides complimenting Miss Shackton on her dressmaking abilities, my sister was impressed by her efforts to further public education. Miss Shackton mentioned that you and she share this interest.

It occurs to me you might enjoy meeting my cousin Zebulon at his upcoming rally at the Carter Inn. Zeb has been reelected to the Senate and departs for Washington in January. Susan and I plan to attend, show our familial support, and wish him well in the larger political arena.

I would gladly introduce you, so you might make your case for improving education. He values hearing people's concerns, and I feel sure that you would leave a lasting impression with him as you have done with me.

Your humble servant,
William

Chapter Thirty-Four

Democrat 1885

The mountain winds blew down and swirled around us on the short drive to the Carter Inn. I perched Claude on the bench at my side, bundled up in blankets to fend off the biting cold. Claude's pink cheeks poked out of his scarf and his high little voice called, "Rob-rob."

"Yes, we'll see Robert, Harriet, and all the rest of Pa's family." I jiggled the reins and kept the horses moving. It had been more than a year since Jasper passed, and we seldom attended family dinners. I told myself I was too busy. In truth, I'd avoided them. Like all families, this one came with the much-loved members and the few dreaded.

Harriet had been on my mind, and I still hoped to mend the rift between us. She'd acted oblivious to her parents seeking guardianship of my stepson. As Robert continued to live at her parents' house, I found her ignorance unbelievable. Still, I regretted my outburst and the lasting tension between us.

I prodded the horses on to John and Caroline's, for it was on this stretch of road when I most missed Jasper. Away from the farm, our conversations had drifted to diverse subjects, often scripture, sometimes family history. We'd shared more of ourselves. I'd thought his absence would hit hardest in the evenings with the emptiness of the porch, but I spent more time inside writing letters, logging farm expenses, and reading the paper to keep abreast of tobacco prices.

Claude pointed out landmarks on our drive. "Twee! Crick! Horsey!" I don't know if he or I found more joy in his naming things.

This time of year, the talk always centered on crops and prices. I dreaded Daniel's remarks about my successful tobacco harvest. No doubt he'd find some way to belittle my accomplishments. At least I had the women of the family backing me, including my mother-in-law, who'd grown fond of Claude. Alvira enjoyed his occasional overnight stay when I tended to business in Asheville.

We pulled into the yard and Harriet lifted Claude from the wagon. "I'm glad you could join us. Both of you. Come inside before we freeze to death."

I grabbed the basket of cornbread and followed Jasper's niece into the house. A fire crackled in the gray stone fireplace and the children knelt before it, playing games. The women in the family sat in the vicinity, ready to stop any roughhousing. My brothers-in-law stood about the room, chatting in small groups.

Alvira reached for Claude. "You needn't have brought anything. This little one is enough. Oh, I'm glad to see my grandson." An expression of intense pain crossed her face, and she reluctantly handed him back.

"Are you unwell?" I asked.

"Just a strain." Alvira rubbed her upper arm, shook her head, and turned toward the kitchen. "We're all here, so let's pull the meal together."

The Carter women prepared a feast of pork, mashed

potatoes doused in butter, pickles, cornbread, and pies—apple, nut, and chess.

Daniel sidled up next to me. "I hear you've had a lucky take at the market this year."

Luck had nothing to do with it. "I'm managing the farm well."

"Had a little help, did you?" he asked.

I placed a plate of pickles down with a little more force than necessary. "When dealing with men, it's wise to understand their prejudices and take the necessary steps."

"Ah well, is that all it is?"

Alvira linked her arm through mine to lead me to the dinner table. "I'd like to hear thoughts on today's sermon. Daniel, why don't you say grace and lead the discussion."

From Daniel's startled look, I presumed he'd slept through the reverend's never-ending preaching this morning, as had a good many in the congregation. I breathed a sigh of relief that Alvira had directed the conversation away from Colonel Baird and me.

Was there something there? William's letters were cordial, often flirtatious, but not romantic. He had never married, though he'd had ample opportunity; there were many more women than men in the years following the War. He came from a prominent family, held a good job, and could offer security to a wife. I didn't think I was being naïve in deducing that he was just being friendly. He'd asked to call on me, but that was regarding my interest in education, and his sister would accompany him. *Was I mistaken in his intentions? Did I need what he could offer? Did I want it?*

Many widows sought another husband for want of security. In the year since Jasper's death, I'd proven I could manage the farm, and the law supported my property rights. I had Claude and Robert, both of whom would take an interest in the farm. I didn't need a husband.

"Why the smile?" Anna watched me from across the table.

I fumbled for an alternative explanation. "Just thinking how much Claude resembles Jasper."

"He's certainly a Carter," she said, "hungry all the time." She hovered the spoon in front of him and Claude leaned in for a bite. I regretted our last interaction on my front porch when I'd torn my son from her arms. She'd shown nothing but kindness to us, and I wouldn't deny her a chance to be a mother for an afternoon.

"He would be proud of his little boy," Anna said.

"I'd like to think so," I said. "I hope he'd be proud of me."

She turned her attention from Claude to me. "He would be. You've shown all of us what it takes to survive and thrive. I can't think of a better example for your son." Her eyes had an uncommonly fierce look, dark and penetrating.

I looked down and away, wanting her words to be true but uncertain all the same. Claude reached for the spoon, pulling his aunt's attention back. My son Claude, my joy. At one-and-a-half years old, he walked and talked, smiled and laughed. What would come next? I laughed when he blew bubbles at Anna.

Robert and his cousin Rollelia elbowed one another at the table. This family made it clear that Robert was not mine. My chest fell, and I wished for the umpteenth time that I'd gone to the barn and found Jasper instead of my son. Maybe then Robert would still be with me. Harriet spoke in a hushed manner to her father and reached an arm in the opposite direction to quiet the two children. The sign of a diligent single mother—eyes in the back of her head.

Over dessert, Robert showed me his latest book. This made today's visit worth the trouble. I missed reading together, perched on the sofa in front of the fire. Robert still called me Mother when he came to work at the farm every day. With the chores done, he often stayed for dinner and played with Claude while I washed up after the meal. Yet ever since Jasper's death, he'd lived with his uncle and aunt. And he didn't mention school anymore.

My mother-in-law gathered the children by the fireplace with the promise of a story. She winced while pulling her shawl up.

I helped clear away empty dishes and mingled with my sisters-in-law in the kitchen. "Is Alvira unwell?" I asked.

"She's aging and slowing down," Caroline said. She scraped plates and passed them to another for washing.

Caroline saw her every day and perhaps didn't notice the change in pallor, Alvira's slowing steps, or her more frequent wincing. Susannah's words echoed: there will be a reckoning. *When Alvira dies, the Carter lands will be divided equally. What was Jasper's portion worth? Would I owe the others? How would I pay them when I was barely getting by?* I grabbed a towel and dried a plate, going round and round and round.

January 7, 1886

Dear Alice,

You will meet Senator Vance once again. I got your letter asking for the latest news on school funding. I quick closed the dress shop to visit the library and ask Dr. Hardy for his advice. He writes -

Senator Vance supported Henry Blair, Republican Senator from New Hampshire, in his efforts to provide millions of dollars to the South in federal aid for education. This cross-party cooperation is unusual, but both have their reasons. Senator Blair would like to help the southern arm of his party, which has faltered since federal occupation ended and the Redeemer Democrats resumed power. However, there are many Northern Republicans who oppose such help as they consider their party a lost cause in the South. They've shifted their focus to the western states.

Senator Vance supported Blair's bill because he knows the South will find it difficult to raise enough taxes to support building the educational system it needs. He's at odds with his own party in the North—the Democrats, who believe Blair's bill results in an unfair geographic distribution of funds. It seems no one likes taxes, especially when it benefits someone else. But I digress....

Senator Blair has made concessions and brought the bill up multiple times for debate. He conceded to state oversight of the aid, he's decreased the amount of aid over ten years, and he's agreed to segregated schooling.

Mrs. Carter, I hope this gives you the background you need. Let us know how your conversation with the formidable senator goes.

W. G. Hardy,
Librarian
Best wishes,
Elizabeth

Chapter Thirty-Five

"CARTER'S MILL, N.C..., The first question asked is, does the same enthusiasm prevail all along the line for Vance. The answer is that he has met with shouts and greetings from large crowds of men and women at every town and in almost every rural district he has been."

The Wilmington Morning Star

Susan Reynolds took her brother's hand and descended from the carriage. "Mrs. Carter, how nice to see you again." Even away from her grand home, she had a regal air. Her slender neck graced a narrow set of shoulders, and she clasped her hands before her waistline in a natural, composed way. I could imagine her commanding any situation and, according to her brother, she rather enjoyed doing just that.

I motioned for my guests to follow me into the house. "What a pleasure to welcome you to my home."

The Colonel climbed onto the porch and got down on one knee to shake Claude's hand. "There's that fine young man!"

"William, don't frighten the child," Susan said.

"Nonsense. Claude and I are well-acquainted."

Claude puffed up and shook William's hand vigorously.

"Please, come inside. I have tea ready." I'd wrapped a cloth around the teapot's chipped handle and arranged my finest cups and saucers on the front room's table. I couldn't disguise how small and simple my home was compared to the Reynolds's mansion.

"You keep a well-appointed home." Susan moved to the mantle, perusing my few decorative items. "I see you've had your portrait taken. It's very pleasing." Turning to her brother, Susan said, "Remind me to tell William and Mamie it's high time they had a family picture taken."

"How are your son and his wife?" I asked.

"Busy with their newborn daughter, plus the two older ones. You're familiar with that, aren't you?" Susan smiled at my two-year-old son and turned back to the portrait. "I cherish the photos I have of my late husband, Daniel."

William had shared that his sister and her husband had been married thirty-four years and from Susan's wistful smile as she spoke his name, I gathered it had been a loving marriage. Jasper and I had so little time together, and without a portrait, how long would it be before I forgot the look of him when he smoked his pipe, his unhurried smile, or the gentleness in his eyes when he held me close?

Claude distracted me from my pained thoughts by climbing onto William's lap. How good they were together. During my many court visits, Claude sought the indulgent gentleman, who offered a bouncy knee or sugary sweet.

Susan's keen eye roved the room. I hoped it passed her inspection.

"William tells me you're managing the farm on your own," she said.

What else had he divulged to his sister? "Yes, although we were married less than three years, my husband taught me much about farming."

"It's unusual for a widow to act alone." She sat on the sofa, swept her skirt and petticoats outward, then leaned forward to accept a cup of tea.

I wasn't sure this was a compliment. *Was this a commentary on her own situation and her five sons managing her life?*

William handed a cookie to my son.

"You've always been good with children," Susan said to her brother.

When Harriet arrived to mind Claude for the afternoon, I breathed a sigh of relief. I wanted to end the conversation that was beginning to feel like an auctioneer's call with me on stage and William bearing a bidder's card.

"Harriet, allow me to introduce Mrs. Susan Reynolds and her brother William Bedent Baird." Turning to my guests, I said, "My husband's niece, Mrs. Harriet Carter Swain." All rose, and the women curtsied, Harriet rather more deeply than Susan, given the older woman's social standing and her age.

Susan eased down onto the sofa. "Mrs. Swain, my late husband had business dealings with your father. They also shared an interest in politics."

Harriet picked up Claude. "We lodge many politicians as they travel this part of the state."

"Yes, Mr. Reynolds met a few at your family's inn and the mill." She sipped her tea. "I've not had the pleasure of making your mother's acquaintance."

Harriet shifted Claude to her other hip, drawing his hands away from the enticing combs holding her hair in place. "She'll be in attendance today. She doesn't miss an opportunity to hear Senator Vance speak. I hope I haven't delayed you." Harriet looked toward the carriage outside.

William rose and offered his hand to his sister. "I suppose

we'd best be on our way. Zebulon likes a crowd." William nodded at Harriet. "Mrs. Swain, a pleasure."

The drive passed easily in the broad-based brougham. Its cushioned leather seats withstood the bumps and divots of the road better than my wagon. Susan and I sat side by side and William entertained us.

"You and Zeb were terrors," Susan said.

"I know not of what you speak." William raised his eyebrows and his mouth formed a perfect 'o.' "We were curious, energetic boys exploring our world."

"Which included spying on me and my friends."

"Learning about feminine ways at an early age and recognizing the superiority of women." William placed his palm across his chest, as if taking an oath.

"How you escaped marriage, William Baird, I will never know." Susan mimicked exasperation.

Yes, how had he remained a bachelor? He was so charming. The hours we'd spent together at the courthouse, the tobacco warehouse, or with his family had passed easily. I'd grown to count on his advice and companionship. He wrote frequently, and I stopped at the post office twice a week now in anticipation of his letters. Court happenings, current events, social outings, the progress in Asheville—they took on more meaning when William and I discussed them.

"What will we hear today from Senator Vance?" I asked.

"I suspect Zeb will speak to the farmers in the crowd, how currency contraction and high tariffs hurt them." William rubbed his beard, reminding me of Jasper.

"Expect a good bit of humor," Susan said.

"That's a given," William said. "And sincere thanks from the people going back to his days as governor."

I recalled the help and hope Governor Vance had offered during the War. He'd organized food depots, relief agencies and blockade running to bring in supplies, so North

Carolinians hadn't starved. Few thanks would come from any Negroes, if there were any in the crowd. Vance fought for the Confederates and his family had owned slaves.

"And you intend to speak with Zebulon about education?" Susan asked.

"I do." I'd given some thought to this conversation and corresponded with Elizabeth in preparation. "The benefits of improving education are clear."

"I believe you'll find a receptive audience in Zeb," William said.

"What remains is how to fund it equitably, from cities to towns, for whites and Negroes," I said. "The state legislature has approved taxation, but the collections don't meet the needs. We must look at a tax on business to support educating the workers of the future."

"The railroads are the biggest concern," Susan said. "Zebulon has been instrumental in their expansion and I doubt he'd support taxing them. What do you think, William?"

"Well now, he pushed through completing the railroad to Asheville and on to Knoxville. Even leaned on the Penitentiary Board for workers. He made it a personal crusade to see the rail brought to the western part of the state with the goal of promoting trade and helping farmers." William drummed his fingers on his knees. "Suggesting taxes on railroads to support public education—well, he might use that as a bargaining chip."

"Isn't that contradictory to supporting the railroad?" I asked.

"It would seem, wouldn't it? But then Zebulon's purpose was to help farmers move crops to new markets. Now that the rail lines are there, he's doing everything possible to benefit the farmers by removing tariffs and regulating freight pricing."

"So Zebulon might support taxing the railroads to fulfill

two goals—as a lever to keep the transportation costs in line and to fund public education," I said.

"I told you Mrs. Carter was a bright one." William's eyes sparkled.

"I see that for myself." With a sly smile, Susan turned to me. "Mrs. Carter, may I remind you that your cousins' livelihood is the railroad? Should your efforts today prevail and Stewart or Mary Tate get wind of it ... well, just know that you'll be welcome in my home when you visit Asheville."

The rally drew hundreds of people to the Carter Inn. Horses, carriages, and wagons lined the road and circled the yard before the entrance. The elderly and women with small children perched within their wagons and carriages. In the yard, an able-bodied crowd stood awaiting the most prominent politician in the state's history.

Senator Vance stood firmly on John Carter's front steps, having worked his way through the crowd shaking hands and accepting the gratitude of his constituents. He had a slight roll to his walk, from a childhood injury to his foot. Otherwise, his thick gray hair, gleaming eyes, and large stature affirmed his vigor.

"My friends, my neighbors," Zebulon spotted William and Susan in the crowd, "and my family, I thank you for this warm welcome. It gladdens me to be with you—my people. I am about to venture to our great Capitol for another term in the U.S. Senate."

Applause broke out. "Hear, hear!"

Senator Vance acknowledged the cheers with a nod. "Now, I know from experience that when there is no hope, when only impossible actions lie ahead, I am suddenly very popular."

The crowd roared.

"And when things appear easy and the job is clear, my enemies emerge. I know not which lies before me, but I know for whom I work—the good people of North Carolina. And I thank those who've written to me with their concerns."

William whispered, "He may outpace you in terms of correspondence. Zeb answers every letter."

I scanned the crowd and wondered how the senator had time to attend rallies. During the periodic applause, he waved at familiar faces and lifted both hands to tamp down the crowd's outbursts. It worked about half the time.

"I will work to support our farmers in making credit more available, in limiting the railroads to only the land they need and to prohibit alien ownership of property in our state." The senator paused until the clapping died down.

"Many of you have prospered with access to the rail lines to move your crops to market. I intend to ensure that continues, that you will not be subject to protective tariffs nor exorbitant shipping prices."

The rally carried on, with the senator gathering more strength from the questions and comments directed at him. The weather was pleasant, and I was used to being on my feet. Susan begged off to sit in the carriage. John Carter appeared at her side and offered his hand as she climbed to take a seat. They leaned toward one another in discussion. My brother-in-law looked our way, his gaze moving from me to William.

I turned my attention back to Senator Vance. At least one of us enjoyed being the object of others' attention. After hours on the stump, the senator finished and mingled with the crowd. People clapped his shoulders and shook his hand. He stopped from time to time to address an attractive woman.

William offered his arm. "Are you ready to meet your senator?"

I pursed my lips and gathered my skirts, determined to make a good impression. Senator Vance spotted his cousin and moved through the crowd.

"William!" Zeb said. "By God, you've aged."

"Better than a dirt nap." William shook his cousin's hand.

"It's been too long," Zeb said. "You've brought a companion a sight fairer than you."

"Senator Vance, allow me to introduce Mrs. Alice Carter of Democrat. I had the pleasure of meeting Mrs. Carter through my work."

Zebulon glanced at my ringless hand.

Few women presented themselves alone at the Superior Court office unless widowed. My presence in the company of William Baird confirmed my status.

John appeared at Zebulon's side. "Senator Vance, Mrs. Carter is my brother Jasper's widow."

Senator Vance conveyed his condolences. "I never forget a face. Mrs. Carter, I believe we've met before."

John cocked his head.

Yes, John, Senator Vance knows little ol' me. I recalled my introduction to the senator at the Tate household prior to my marriage. His premonition that we would meet again had come true and I would show him I knew more about the state of schooling in Buncombe County.

"Senator, you've captured the crowd today," I said.

"And you, Mrs. Carter? Were you captured by anything I said?"

"I had hoped to hear more of federal and state efforts to fund education. I applaud your support for the Blair bills, but not one of those bills has made it through the House."

"Ah yes. I'm afraid the Blair bills divided both parties. Southern Republicans support federal school aid as an appeal to the many illiterate Southerners, while Northern Republicans don't like their party's chances in the South and therefore refuse to give it aid. In my party, the division is equally strong."

A small crowd gathered around us. The senator perused his followers and continued, "Northern Democrats are adamant that one state should not fund another's educational efforts. They also reject the tariffs that provide the surplus used as federal school aid. Southern Democrats, such as myself, are receptive to the federal aid despite disapproving of the tariffs making the aid possible. It is a perplexing and likely unwinnable piece of legislation, Mrs. Carter."

"If the federal government will not take a stand on education, then the state should address the current dysfunction of schools." I acknowledged the nods amongst the crowd.

"William, you've brought an admirable debate partner."

"Indeed I have, Zeb. Watch yourself."

The crowd chuckled. I detected John's almost imperceptible nod.

"Mrs. Carter, I agree with you. In the words of Senator Blair, government can only survive if the people read and write. But Blair's proposal funnels funds to areas with the highest illiteracy."

"Shouldn't it?" William asked.

"That results in seventy-five percent of funds going to the South and that will never get by my northern brethren in Congress. State and local funding is the way forward for education." Vance tipped his hat and moved on through the crowd.

"You held your ground with the great North Carolina senator." William placed my hand in the crook of his arm and walked me toward the carriage. His jaunty gait contrasted with my dragging steps.

I separated from him and, with hands on hips, surveyed the yard where I'd been thwarted. "Then why do I feel I've failed?"

"That doesn't sound like the Alice I know," William said. "The Alice I know runs her own farm. She raises her son. She takes her crop to market. The Alice I know is a fighter."

"Thank you, William." Emboldened by William's comments and maddened by my inability to influence the senator, I gathered my skirts and moved toward the carriage. "You're right. If Senator Vance won't give me what I want, I must make my own way. It seems I can only rely on myself."

Chapter Thirty-Six

"You will agree with me that we in the Southern States are not now able to educate them and our own children. They were set free as a necessity of the Union. You so regarded it. Then it is proper that the union should come forward, and with its vast resources aid in their education."

Our Brother in Black: His Freedom and His Future, by Atticus G. Haygood, Southern Methodist Publishing House

Spring brought forth the rains, wrapping the smoky blue haze around the mountains like ribbons on a gift. While awaiting a drier, warmer soil, I ensured my tenant managed tasks such as cleaning the barns, watering the seedlings, and maintaining the farm equipment.

Robert came to the house every day to help with chores. I wished my stepson would return home, but suspected that since his father's death, the farm held an air of loneliness he couldn't abide. The Carter Inn, filled with his cousins, Uncle John, and Aunt Caroline, was a livelier home, missing the grief surrounding me and the barn, where Robert had found his father. We didn't talk of Jasper, but rather found conversation in the books we read, the farming tasks, and his little brother's antics. On the days when Harriet didn't come by, my sons were my sole companions. My loneliness ebbed and flowed. My only solution was to keep busy.

Once a week I made entries in the farm journal, noting the progress of the crop, the temperature and rainfall, and listing the expenses of labor, seed, and materials. My meager savings worried me. A poor harvest would mean cutbacks. The hornworms were especially bad this year, and my tenant had hired extra labor to save the tobacco from hungry vermin. That labor would cut into my profits, but it couldn't be helped if I was to salvage the crop.

At least Zimri had managed the hog butchering this year, hiring Hamilton and the other farmhands. My meat supply would carry us through another year. I'd lost a young sow in the woods to a hungry bear out of its winter sleep. I feared Robert venturing out into the woods, but he gripped a rifle and assured me that at fourteen years of age, he was man enough to deal with a bear.

One summer morning, the drumming of horses' hooves neared and dust billowed on the road. My heart lurched. Robert hadn't shown this morning, and I'd milked the cow myself. *Could something have happened to my son?*

Strong, capable Harriet slid from the saddle, hanging on to the pommel as if her life depended on it. I'd never seen her in such a state—tears rolling down her cheeks, and her normally neat hair coming out of its braid. She leaned against her horse, as if her knees would buckle.

"Grandmother's passed."

My arms enveloped her shaking shoulders and Harriet leaned into me and sobbed. Our argument over Robert's guardianship was forgotten. Any distrust between us dissolved like sugar in tea. I embraced the one person who'd first made me feel like family.

It would be some days before I realized the impact of Alvira's death on me.

Daniel wasted no time. A month after my mother-in-law's funeral, he rode his chestnut mare to my front porch. His fine gray jacket covered a dark green vest, reminding me he was a man of business, not of toil. I pulled another item from my mending basket. He glanced at the fields where the colored men labored. His nostrils flared and his forehead creased.

"Mornin', Alice." He slid off the saddle and tied his horse to the railing.

"Morning, Daniel. What brings you by?" I got straight to the point, hoping to keep this visit as brief as possible.

Daniel grasped his hat in both hands as he climbed the porch steps. "With Mother passing, I'll be settling the will, which brings us back to my father's wishes."

I knew my late husband had met the stipulations of Solomon Carter's will. Jasper had installed a dam on the creek to keep the land allotment. I stitched a sock, anticipating Daniel's real purpose.

"When Father divided his property, it was with every intention of being equal to all his children. Mother's death requires me to value all assets." Daniel leaned against the porch railing, calm, cool, and ready to pounce.

I didn't ask him to take a seat. "And what might that mean?"

"Jasper's lands ..."

My lands.

"Are likely worth more than some other portions,

requiring a payment to the executor—that being me, and settlements paid out. I'll be getting land assessments, making calculations and returning with a full accounting." He checked his pocket watch and snapped it shut.

I tied off a knot and poked my needle through my apron as I stood. "I expect you will. Good day, Daniel." I left him standing on the porch with a bewildered look as I turned on my heel and went inside, closing the door behind me. Through the window, I watched him turn his hat in his hands and stare at the porch floor. He donned his hat, mounted the mare, and rode off toward home. I gazed out over the fields and wondered what it would take to hold on to what little I owned.

"I need your help, William."

He glanced up but would not meet my eye.

"What may I do for you, Mrs. Carter?"

William's formal greeting startled me. He smiled down at Claude but did not shake his hand or invite him behind the desk. I held Claude back, unsure if I had offended my friend in some way. I'd written to William and his sister after the trip to hear Senator Vance and thanked them for the excursion. He'd sent a brief reply acknowledging that I'd convinced him *I alone was equal to the task*. I found it odd—task seemed a trivial term for funding education. Months had gone by and our letter writing became much less frequent. I'd chalked it up to both of us having more work than we could manage.

I explained my circumstances, including the bill delivered by my brother-in-law.

His brow creased and he rubbed his jaw. "The law is clear regarding a widow's rights. I must pull Solomon Carter's will to understand your brother-in-law's claim. Will you be staying in town, Mrs. Carter?"

I confirmed Claude and I would lodge with my cousins and asked him to call on us that evening. He stiffened, and I thought he might refuse my invitation, perhaps request I return to the court office the next morning.

"Stewart and Mary would surely enjoy your company."

His face softened and his whiskers edged up with his tepid smile of agreement.

I wanted an explanation for my legal situation and to William's unexpected coolness.

We settled on the porch, where the lanterns cast a warm glow.

William shifted uncomfortably in his seat and drummed his fingers on his leg. "Ah-hem. I've wondered how you were getting along on the farm with young Claude."

"The farm keeps me busy."

Silence hung between us like ripened fruit on a tree, ready to drop and sour the ground. The street's newly electrified lamps fired, breaking the stillness and illuminating our uneasiness.

He cleared his throat. "Mr. and Mrs. Tate enjoy your visits."

"Yes, they especially like having Claude about. I think my son reminds them of their own grandchildren, who live some distance away."

They also welcomed William. Stewart had pumped his hand and offered him a drink. Mary fawned over him, asking if he'd had supper, insisting on calling the maid to bring something as he must be famished after a long day's work. How glad they were to see him again. How kind of him to call. I blushed at their attention. After staying an obligatory hour in their company, I excused us to the porch by mentioning we shouldn't keep the Colonel working until all hours of the night.

I rambled on, offering little of interest. I couldn't read William's face. He might have been bemused or annoyed or tired. I hesitated to ask what I wanted most to know—what happened to our friendship?

"I reviewed Solomon Carter's will," William said. "It's a complicated affair, which is to be expected given the size of the estate and the number of heirs. Mr. Carter divided the land amongst the children in uneven parcels many years ago. That's not unusual, as land holds varying values and uses."

"Jasper mentioned his father held some above others." I hesitated, unsure whether to divulge more of the Carter family secrets. I couldn't offer it as a fact. It was Jasper's understanding and not acknowledged by all family members. Perhaps this legal document substantiated Solomon Carter's favoritism.

"The initial gifts appear uneven. However, upon the death of your mother-in-law, Alvira Carter, the will requires a settling up."

"That is what Daniel wants," I said.

"I suspect so. If your brother-in-law were to get fair appraisals of the land and present a comparison of value for each beneficiary before the court, old Mr. Carter's will would give him the legal means to demand payments to even out the inheritance."

"And if I can't pay the settlement?" Just when I thought I could make my own way, Daniel Carter meant to show me otherwise. Vulnerability stuck to me like feathers to tar. I turned away from William and bit my lip. I would not sob in front of the man who clearly wanted to be anywhere else but here. His constant shifting and inability to hold my gaze showed me that.

William dug into his suit pocket and handed me his handkerchief. "Ahem. I would advise you to retain a competent representative of the courts, one who knows how to fight."

I dabbed my cheeks and straightened in my seat.

William leaned forward, resting his elbows on his knees, bridging the gap between us. His eyes softened. "Fortunately, I know just the man."

I smiled and found myself ready for a fight.

Cousin Mary raised her eyebrows when I entered the breakfast room the following morning, whether in response to my cheerful humming or the Colonel's evening visit, I wasn't sure.

"Good morning, Cousin." I took my seat, and the maid poured coffee. I was ravenous.

"You've a letter on the sideboard, delivered this morning from Susan Reynolds. It seems your visit has been a productive one." Mary lifted her eyebrows.

"It's unopened. How did you know it's from Mrs. Reynolds?"

"Honestly, Alice, everyone knows the Reynolds family and their staff. One of their servants delivered it." Mary sipped her coffee.

I skimmed over the note requesting I come to tea that afternoon. I hoped to avoid further inquiry from Mary by asking after Cousin Stewart.

"They called him out for another emergency on the western line." Mary buttered a scone but stopped short of eating it. "I swear I've eaten more breakfasts alone than with my husband over the course of our marriage."

My coffee cup rattled on its saucer and I released it to clench my napkin and still my hands. I let go of the cloth in my lap, but the memory of Jasper wasn't so easily discarded.

Mary dropped her scone. "Oh dear, I apologize for my lack of sensitivity. You've experienced the true loneliness of dining alone."

I looked toward the kitchen door, where the maid fed my son. "I have Claude."

"He is a charming little boy." Mary recounted the previous afternoon spent with Claude and his exploration of the back garden, naming every color he saw, and pointing out all the bugs.

I longed to leave a conversation about what I had and what I didn't. It's all I'd thought about for years. "You have a new maid."

"Vina, yes. I let Amanda go to the Mission Hospital," Mary said, "which was no small gift, as it takes some time to train good staff. Amanda's making herself useful and shows an aptitude toward nursing the Negro patients."

Amanda. The colored maid, who held her tongue in her daily work, and used it to fight for public education. On my first visit to Asheville, she'd stood during the Home Missionary Society's meeting and advocated for rallying the Negro population. For the cause's sake, I hoped she'd been more successful than me.

"Does it take some education to be a nurse?" I asked.

Mary lowered her voice. "It does, and I was surprised when Amanda approached me, expressing an interest in hospital work. One must watch what one says around the staff." Mary pointed her butter knife in the air and helped herself to a second scone. "Once the hospital opened, Amanda asked if there was a spot for her."

"You've done so much for the hospital," I said. Mary got things done. Elizabeth pushed forward with the public education crusade. Margaret carried on teaching. *What was I doing?*

Mary batted her eyes. "One does what one can, my dear." She filled both our cups and posed the question she'd been wanting to ask. "Will you move to Asheville? My invitation stands. You could leave this fight with the Carter family behind."

That would be the easiest choice. Live in this fine house, join in Mary's charitable efforts, and raise my son. Our future would be tied to Stewart and Mary's fate. I would own nothing and we would always be guests. The bitterness from giving up would fester in me like a wound.

"Thank you, Mary, but I must fight." *For what's mine, for public education, and whatever else I needed. Or wanted?*

"You and Claude would be very welcome here and Asheville offers educational opportunities not seen in Democrat."

"Claude will need schooling in four more years." I sipped my coffee. "Times are changing. Who's to say public schooling won't extend to Democrat?"

Mary dabbed her mouth and spread her linen napkin across her lap. "I wouldn't bet on that in our lifetime. Who would spearhead such an idea? The Carter family? From what you say, they rather like ruling the roost out there. Education brings new ideas, and I doubt very much they'd welcome that."

Mary spoke the truth. With Alvira's passing, the Carter men held the positions of power like army commanders and ordered the entire family's way of life. Daniel was their general. Might the Carter women mutiny?

Chapter Thirty-Seven
Asheville 1886

"Valuable Land for Sale!

We will sell at private sale, on reasonable terms, the Baird property known as 'Forest Hill,' situated on South Main street, containing about 42 acres, with a house of 21 rooms and all necessary outhouses; also a half interest in 9 acres on Bailey street; and one-ninth interest in 10,000 acres on Craggy Mountain."

Asheville Citizen-Times

I joined Susan Reynolds on the back veranda overlooking her rose garden, an idyllic spot to spend an afternoon. From the rounded porch railing, I absorbed the expansive view. The tree-covered hills flowed down to Asheville some miles away.

"Mrs. Carter, I'm so glad you could come," Susan said. "Please sit down. Tea?"

I swished my skirt outward and sat on a white wicker sofa. The pink pin-striped cushions matched the color of the roses blooming around the garden perimeter. Deep green woods in the distance capped the shock of color. *What would it be like to see the beauty surrounding one's home instead of the work calling out from every parcel?*

"I'm delighted to see you again, Mrs. Reynolds." I accepted a cup and saucer.

Susan poured herself tea from the bone china teapot with its pink and purple primrose design. I made a mental note of everything, as my cousin would demand details.

"I do like to rest here on a warm afternoon. It's a quiet, protected space, although the city encroaches."

"Asheville is growing," I said.

"Yes." Her smile evaporated for a moment. "My sons convinced me to part with some of our lands with the argument that demand is rising and so are prices. I was reluctant to sell any portion of this gift from my father."

"Your property is lovely, especially the rose garden."

In the few times we'd met, Susan Reynolds's poise never faltered. Her no-frills dress with its high neckline and her uncomplicated hairstyle befitted an older woman and widow. She didn't need one of Jennie's embroidered collars. She owned her modest, dignified appearance.

"With my children grown and raising their own families, I sought something to care for." Susan gave me a conspiratorial wink and continued, "and roses don't talk back." She sipped her tea and looked longingly out across the blooms.

Her devilish look reminded me of her brother. Through our two years of friendship, William had made me blush, think, debate, and laugh. A heaviness settled over me. Our conversation yesterday evening had been stilted. Our last words held the promise of working together over the legal matter with Daniel. However, a return to our former closeness remained elusive.

Susan placed her cup down on the table. "I met my

husband right here, on these lands, when he worked for my father. I was very young and impressionable, and I fell for him right away." She gave me a sideways glance and her smile showed the youthful beauty she'd once possessed.

"Years later, I realized how unusual my parents' blessing had been, given the times and the propensity to marry for all the right reasons—by that I mean class, social circle, and binding families together for business reasons. My mother gave me valuable advice. She said to never let love pass me by. Grab hold of it. Life brings challenges and facing them with a loving husband makes them bearable. Sharing life's joys brings greater happiness."

I'd discovered that with Jasper in the smallest and largest ways. In our brief marriage, we'd faced insignificant challenges because of my outspokenness or his stubbornness. We'd had words and come through stronger. We'd shared many joys, the greatest being our son, Claude.

"My brother mentioned you were in town attending to legal matters. Let me assure you, I don't wish to pry, and William keeps confidences. However, my inquiries to your well-being were met with, shall we say, a stiffened countenance."

So I was not alone in noticing William's cooler approach. She offered me a plate of cakes and cookies.

"I gathered I would have to make a more direct inquiry. I invited you here today so we might continue our acquaintance," Susan said.

Like Alvira Carter, Susan Reynolds exercised the matriarch role and the right to have her say. Her prestige and force disarmed me. I leaned against the sofa back, shoring myself up for words I wasn't sure I wanted to hear.

"We find ourselves in unenviable situations. When my husband Daniel died, I was unprepared for the role of widow."

"I don't imagine that's a role many prepare for," I said. The molasses cookie remained untouched on my saucer.

"No. I suppose not." Susan surveyed her home and garden. "Daniel built this house intending to fill it with children. We were blessed with five sons and five daughters, and many happy years together. We often sat on this veranda in the evenings and discussed our blessings."

Although Susan Reynolds gave me an opening, I was reluctant to share my memories of Jasper, those evenings spent on our porch in Democrat, talking about Claude, the farm, faith, family, any number of things. Our shared words led to admiration, fondness, and finally, love. I guarded my memories, afraid that by letting them out, I might lose them forever.

The rose bush stems swayed in unison and brushed the canvas sky with color. Petals floated to the ground, to dry and darken and dissolve.

"When Daniel died, our children were grown and living on their own. I focused on my grandchildren, I gardened, and I joined a woman's club or two to occupy my days."

"My cousin, Mary, keeps busy with civic organizations. I imagine such good works provide fulfillment."

"To a point." Susan sipped her tea. "I find the evenings rather empty."

The breeze shifted, bringing the scent of roses. I breathed in the sweet smell and swept a dry, brown-edged petal from my skirt, hoping to brush away the melancholy that settled upon us. I didn't like the conversation but couldn't politely steer it in another direction.

"I shall never marry again." Susan stared at me. "If I was younger, I would consider it. Life is long and more enjoyable with a companion by one's side."

I had no retort, no counter to her argument. Susan's heartfelt sentiments resonated with me, and I pictured the empty porch at home, the quiet bedroom, and no companion with whom to share my days and nights. Since Jasper's death, I had occupied myself with a multitude of tasks, allowing little time to think. Here in the quiet afternoon, I glimpsed my lonely future in the woman at my side.

Chapter Thirty-Eight
Asheville 1886

"LOCAL EXLAVIGATIONS.

—Circus here October 1st.

—Oh, those Mulligan letters.

—Several marriages in town last week.

—Tobacco said to be curing finely this year.

—Tobacco sales are a new feature at Raleigh

—Don't forget that we want a Graded School in Asheville."

The Exlavigator

My frequent trips to the court in Asheville that autumn allowed me to take part in the graded school campaign. Elizabeth had organized the petition for a tax, working with Cousin Mary's former maid, Amanda, to canvass the Negro neighborhoods. Now we had to present the signatures to the aldermen and request the matter be put on the ballot for a public vote.

Elizabeth shuffled her papers and addressed the city council. "Good day, gentlemen."

"She's nervous," Mary whispered to me.

No wonder. Small, young, and alone, standing before the Asheville Board of Aldermen and about to reveal what she'd hidden for so long.

"Three years ago, I could not read the words on this paper," Elizabeth said.

The aldermen not paying attention abandoned their distractions. They knew Elizabeth Shackton as a prominent businesswoman. From the few raised eyebrows, I gathered her admission of illiteracy took them by surprise.

"I was born poor, like so many during the War. My mother and my grandparents could not pay the school fees. Yet I have learned."

The shame Elizabeth had borne through the history of her birth and her illiteracy fell away. *Would the aldermen catch the mention of a mother, but no father?* She'd confided in me the story of her grandparents whisking her mother away from their country home a few months after the soldiers came through and burnt their farm. They'd told their Asheville neighbors their daughter's husband was lost in the fighting. Elizabeth had never seen a wedding band. When she asked to see something of her father—a portrait, watch, comb, some possessions, they told her it was all lost. She drew her own conclusions.

Elizabeth turned to her written words. "A teacher explained, illiterate does not mean unintelligent." She pronounced unintelligent with care, emphasizing each syllable.

Margaret beamed and nudged Mary's shoulder. Margaret had taught Elizabeth to read, and Mary coached her on speaking before the aldermen. All three of us sat in the audience to support her.

"I can read the catalogs to order fabrics I need for my business," Elizabeth said. "I write the money order for my tax payment. I read the newspapers at the library to follow state governance. I can do all this, because I am educated."

She paused and peered into each alderman's face, insisting they see and hear her. Several of the board members leaned forward.

"How did you come by your education, Miss Shackton, if not through the subscription schools?"

"From Miss Margaret Petersen and the Home Missionary Society at first. I've also bartered for lessons," Elizabeth said.

"Your dressmaking skills?"

"Yes." Elizabeth knew several of the aldermen's wives as her customers. She looked down at her paper and I recognized the statement Mary helped write. "The days of scraping together an education are long past. Asheville is a modern city, with industries, a water system, telephones, the railroad ..." At the mention of the railroad, she looked back at us.

Mary nodded in encouragement.

"The ways of the future are upon us, gentlemen. Asheville requires a new citizen—an educated worker and an informed voter. Public education is the solution. I submit to you a petition of one hundred signatures, and I ask you to put to a vote a school tax for the betterment of our city, our county, and our people." Elizabeth folded her speech, took her seat, and the men passed the list, divining the names of their fellow townspeople interested in public education.

Mayor Harkins, sitting at the center of the aldermen's table that spanned the length of the room, responded. "Miss Shackton, I thank you for your submission. You have the required number of signatures. As Asheville's population stands at five thousand, and the state law grants such communities the right to vote on school taxes, I authorize a school tax ballot to be presented to Asheville's voters."

Whoops and hollers rang out in the audience, including more than a few from Mary.

The mayor banged his gavel on the table. "Ladies, please!"

Two months later, I found myself again in the company of these women, awaiting the tally of the votes.

"My feet ache." Elizabeth flexed her feet and extended her legs before her. "I believe I've walked near a hundred miles in the last six weeks."

She'd marched up and down city streets since the aldermen's meeting, visiting every business and many homes to encourage voters to support the school tax.

"Thankfully, along with Amanda, Mary Jane and her father covered the colored neighborhood," Elizabeth said.

"Who?" I asked.

Elizabeth looked at me with surprise. "Mary Jane teaches with Margaret. Her father, Isaac Dickson, owns a grocery and other businesses near the corner of Eagle and Valley."

"They can read?"

"Yes." Elizabeth laughed. "Some do, and many more want to."

Margaret chimed in. "The Dicksons helped bring voters to the polls by speaking at the Negro church services, at neighborhood functions, visiting Negro businesses and even going door to door."

"Will it be enough?" Mary asked.

Townspeople crowded the courthouse, and even more milled around the square outside, awaiting the outcome of the vote. Mary twisted her gloves in her hands.

"Whether the Negro population will support the tax, I don't rightly know," Elizabeth said. "They all support public schools, but many earn so little, getting them to pay a poll tax is a might hard sell."

"How much longer?" Margaret bit her lip.

She wished this tax would pass as much as any of us. After five years of teaching Negro children in the Freedmen's Chapel, Margaret would soon head home to Boston. Her Northern ways had softened and Asheville society had come to embrace her. I wondered if she'd picked up any Southern notions that might bother her Northern family and friends.

"It must pass," Mary said. "We have worked too hard." She bristled as she turned to Elizabeth. "I told Stewart this morning he must vote for the tax or else he would eat dinners at hotels for the next month."

I smiled at the thought of my mother's cousin berating her husband.

Elizabeth laughed. The first time she'd met Mary, she'd feared offending such a fine Southern lady. Since then, the two had bonded while speaking to ladies' quilting clubs, reading circles, church groups and charitable organizations on the need for public schools. Both women were passionate, fierce and relentless.

"Ladies and gentlemen, please be seated for the reading of the vote," Mayor Harkins said. The aldermen sat down, and the audience members shuffled to their seats.

The mayor stood and read from the summary. "As to the referendum put to the voters of Asheville to support a property tax and poll tax ..."

"Good Lord, spit it out, man," Mary whispered.

I would have laughed had I not been thinking the same thing.

"To support a public school system with a term of eight months per year, to serve all peoples, both Negro and White, from the ages of six to twenty-one ..."

"I shall strangle the mayor, be put in jail, and never see

Stewart again," Mary said under her breath. She shook her gloves.

Mayor Harkins looked down at the tally. "The referendum passes with a vote of 722 for and 718 against."

The room erupted in applause. A few landowners stuffed their hats on their heads and stomped out of the meeting. We'd expected them to oppose additional taxes to educate the poor.

"You've done it!" I said to Elizabeth. Mary marched off to speak to the mayor. Margaret was nowhere to be found.

"He did it," Elizabeth said. She motioned to an older colored man in the back of the room. The Negro crowd clapped and cheered. "That's Mr. Dickson. With the vote that close, it was the Negroes that made the difference."

Margaret shook Mr. Dickson's hand and turned to celebrate with the young woman at his side. The white attendees paid little attention to the back of the room and missed Margaret's familiar ways with the Negroes.

"That's his daughter, Mary Jane. She'll be the colored school teacher." Elizabeth strode toward them.

The throng of White and Negro citizens continued to celebrate, with some pumping hands and others slapping backs. *Another step forward for this city.* Instead of sharing the cloud of excitement, a wistful air swept over me. A colored school for Asheville and still no school for Democrat.

Chapter Thirty-Nine

Democrat 1887

"THE BOARD OF ALDERMEN

Met last night in regular session. The following Graded School committee was elected:

For six years—H.A. Gudger, D.T. Millard.

For four years—W.W. West, S.R. Kepler

For two years—J.R. Randolph, Isaac Dickson. (col)."

Asheville Citizen-Times

I returned to the farm, eager to shake the loneliness that stung me like a hornet—piercing, aching, lasting. That feeling had sharpened since meeting with Susan Reynolds last fall. Our conversation had upset me, and I wanted to deny understanding why. We led different lives, yet we had much in common. Her portrayal of the lonely widow's life rang true.

As I collected eggs, milked the cow, did the laundry, and swept the porch, I replayed our conversation. Toppling over Susan's words was the echo of my sister Jennie's: wants are different from needs. Someday you'll understand the difference. *What did I need? What did I want?*

The settling of the estate dragged on with Daniel seemingly tied up with various land appraisers, plus correspondence with his siblings near and far. William wasn't surprised. He explained that the larger estates typically meant more complexity.

On this long summer day, Hamilton and the men worked the fields. Robert helped his Uncle Zimri with his tobacco harvest. I'd missed Harriet these last few days. I hefted Claude in my arms and placed my cheek against his soft curls. Summer's humidity brushed moisture across his brow and plastered his blonde hair against his soft face.

I inhaled the indescribable smell of my three-year-old child, hoping never to forget it. Yet I couldn't recall the volume of his cries in those first days, nor remember the exact moment he first smiled. His funny gait with his first steps made me laugh, but I could only describe it imperfectly. Memories faded despite my best efforts to recall them. Had Jasper lived, we would have mined those moments, pieced them together, and brought them to life.

While my son napped, I returned to my desk and the papers on which I'd scratched out figures. Strong crop prices and the tenant agreement solved the issue of my daily living, but it wouldn't be enough to pay the estate. *Could it be that other family members faced a similar situation?* Thirteen Carter children meant each inherited one-thirteenth of the estate. Zimri and Susannah's farm appraised at more than that amount, and like me, they would owe a settlement. With Zimri farming and working at the mill, I expected they had more put by.

I listed the things I could do: talk to Susannah about their plans, and await word from William. I rested my chin in the cup of my hand. *Think, Alice, think. Who else would be affected? Jasper's eldest brother had gone his own way early in life. What did John and Caroline stand to gain from the settlement?* I chewed on the end of my quill. Talking to Harriet about her parents' sentiments might bring up our argument over their guardianship of my stepson. Nonetheless, it had to be done. I added 'Talk to Harriet' to my list, tucked my journal in the desk drawer, and returned to my afternoon chores.

I was outside beating rugs, when a horse and rider came up the lane. A delivery boy jumped off the animal, away from the dust bloom I'd roused. I paid him a penny and tore open the letter.

July 17, 1887

Dear Mrs. Carter,

I hope this finds you and Claude happy and well on the farm. Upon further consideration of your circumstances and given the invoice presented to you by your brother-in-law, Mr. Daniel Carter, I would advise that I issue a summons on your behalf. Calling Mr. Carter to court to review his claim against your widow's rights would show your willingness to fight for what's yours and might convince him to compromise regarding his claim.

With your permission, I will prepare the paperwork and instruct the sheriff to deliver it to Mr. Carter.

Your presence would not be necessary in court, but I advise it and I would be glad to see you again.

Sincerely,

William B. Baird

I wrapped one arm around my waist and with the other I held the letter aloft, reading it a second, then a third time. *Glad to see you again. Was our friendship fully restored? No. William still addressed me formally. Something stood between us.* I gave great care to my reply.

July 20, 1887

Dear William,

I thank you for your continued legal advice and your work on my behalf. I approve of the summons, and of course, I will make myself available to the court. Do advise when I am needed, and I will write to my cousins to request their hospitality. I expect they would like to have you call again. Stewart spoke kindly of you and enjoyed your insights on the railroad and its effects on land purchases.

With warm regards,

Alice

Awaiting William's correspondence took all my patience. I found excuses to visit John's store for little things like a spool of thread or a newspaper, and while there, I asked after the post. My brother-in-law made no mention of the more frequent visits, but each time I left, he assured me he'd send a delivery boy along to the house with any post.

August 1, 1887

Dear Alice,

The sheriff returned with the summons, claiming that Mr. Daniel Carter was not to be found. I find this ridiculous given the size of Democrat. One could throw an ax from one side of town to the other!

I will proceed with an alias summons for the sheriff, requesting he return the sixty cents paid him and that he be fined one hundred dollars for neglect to serve. Further, he should explain himself to the court.

The summons for Daniel Carter is thus delayed.

Forgive me for my short temper, but I do not suffer fools who think they are above the law.

Kindly,

William

The following Sunday morning, William's letter rested in my skirt pocket. Although he'd not yet delivered the summons to Daniel, he and I had made progress in restoring our friendship. His use of my Christian name was evidence of a thawing. *Kindly. Kindly, William. I would have preferred 'fondly.'* I shook my head. What was I thinking? I busied myself getting Claude fed and readied for church.

Yet my mind returned to the letter. By the time we reached the churchyard, I contemplated William's temper and how it reminded me of my own toward Harriet and the rest of the Carter family since Jasper's death. Shame washed over me as I sat on the wooden pew.

The sermon on Job held new meaning. Five years ago, Jasper and I had discussed the devil's trickery within the story. Today my focus turned to Job's friends questioning his innocence. They asked whether he deserved his afflictions, and he responded with sarcasm, hiding his impatience and fear. *Hadn't I responded to Harriet with impatience? With fear?*

I was afraid of losing the farm, but even more so this family. Years ago, I witnessed my parents' farm fail, and I'd left the only family I'd ever known. At that time, I couldn't imagine the love I'd feel for Jasper, Robert and Claude, or for that matter Anna, Susannah, and Caroline. My closest bond was with Harriet and yet I'd snapped at her, offering biting retorts to her words of compassion and understanding. We'd parted in anger over her parents becoming Robert's guardians. Though we'd carried on and Alvira's death had partially restored us, I'd been unwilling to revisit our argument and my role in it.

After services, I joined the other congregants collecting picnic baskets from the wagons. Claude held his brother Robert's hand and ran off with the other children. I walked toward the creek with a blanket over one arm and my basket on the other, greeting my neighbors along the way.

My thoughts returned to Jasper on our first Sunday of married life. I'd expressed my belief that God tested Job's faith through trial. Since then I'd suffered more losses: Jasper, Alvira, and in a way, Robert, who preferred living with his uncle and aunt. Losing my land and my independence might be another misfortune, another test of my faith.

"May we join you?" Harriet asked.

"Harriet, John, of course." I motioned for father and daughter to sit.

"I understand I owe you an explanation, and it's a long time coming." John eased on to the ground and removed his broad-brimmed hat. Harriet gave her father a nod, encouraging him to continue. "My daughter tells me you've the impression I moved against you when I applied for guardianship of Robert. While I had an ulterior motive, it wasn't to cause you pain. Harriet recently informed me it did, and for that, I am truly sorry."

In all the time we'd spent at family suppers, eating, visiting or making music, John Carter hadn't said half as many words to me. "I don't understand."

"Well, I've got you started. Don't stop." Harriet stood up, brushed off her skirt, and looked at her father like a teacher instructing a pupil. "Alice needs to hear it and you need to tell it. Blessed are the peacemakers, for they shall be called sons of God," she pronounced and strolled off.

"Sometimes it's hard living with a minister's ghost," John said.

I would have laughed, but I could see he was serious. My faith was easy. Living with Harriet's faith might not be.

John leaned back on one arm and propped the other over his knee. "Daniel didn't fight in the War like the rest of us. He was young and Father relied on him."

"Your father favored him."

"No, although that's a common misconception amongst my brothers. Our father held fast to the things that were important to him—family, land, faith. When the Union came through, Daniel watched, helpless, as the soldiers burned our fields and barns. They took what they wanted. Our slaves ran off. The War destroyed everything Father had worked for. Then our brother Garrett didn't return. It nearly killed him."

"He divided his lands. Are you saying he didn't do it to punish some?"

"Punish? For what?"

I hesitated. "For not bringing Garrett back."

John's face tightened. "Did Jasper think that?"

I nodded. "And that you saw the way of things and plotted your own course."

John twirled his hat between his hands. "I'm the eldest son. I had more to prove. Caroline's family had been innkeepers, so we came to that naturally. Her father wished us to take over their business, but I couldn't leave Father and Mother after all they'd lost. We bought our land and built the Carter Inn to stay in Democrat, close to home."

"That's the only reason you didn't remain at the homestead?"

"The homestead wasn't ideally positioned for travelers, plus Mother, Father, and several of my brothers and sisters still lived at home."

Over the past two decades, the Carter family epitomized

steadfastness when continuity was a rarity. Family suppers, shared businesses, and preserved lands had held this family together. However, the War created lasting effects, the Lost Cause dogma drilled into minds as indelible as gunshots through bodies. Solomon Carter had imparted those beliefs in his actions to reestablish order and maintain the South's old values.

"Your father gave your brothers land," I said.

"To get started. We were all busy rebuilding after the War. Father hoped the work would tamp down our sadness. Holding on to the remaining family and working our land became the Carter way."

"I understand." I pulled back the basket towel, and I laid out my picnic.

When I offered sliced ham and bread, John waved it away. "I don't think you do. Daniel isn't the devil you've conjured."

A rush of heat inflamed my cheeks. I'd labeled Daniel many things: hurtful, insensitive, arrogant, though never a devil.

"What I'm trying to tell you is that you and Daniel are more alike than different."

That hurt. Does John think so little of me? "And just how are we alike?"

"You both care about the land and this family."

"Then why is he trying to push me off?" I shoved the food back into the basket, hastily trying to end this failed picnic and conversation. "He suggested I move to my sister's."

"Daniel worried you'd lose the land. Frankly, he was surprised—we all were, at how you've turned a profit."

Barely.

"He planned to farm your land on your behalf and share the proceeds with you, Claude, and Robert. His goal was to keep the land in the family, to not lose it to creditors."

When Daniel had shown up at the house a week after

Jasper's funeral, I'd cut off our conversation before hearing him out. I hadn't invited him in or offered him a seat on the porch. Daniel had feared I would fail. Given my state of dishevelment at the time, it wasn't a bad assumption. My father had run up debts and my grieving mother had lost our farm. *How had I gotten it so wrong?*

"I don't suppose he considered what a move to Hendersonville might mean for you." John rubbed his whiskers.

I mulled over my beliefs about Daniel. I'd presumed he resented my motherhood because he and Caroline were childless. That as a businessman, he abhorred taxes to support schools. By living in the family home, I supposed him to be his father's favorite. His dapper appearance meant he didn't toil like the others, didn't it? And my biggest mistake was assuming he wanted to get rid of me after Jasper's death. My head hurt, wrapping my mind around all the ways I'd misconstrued his intentions and my situation.

"And I suppose I didn't think how you'd feel about Robert becoming our ward. He'd practically lived with us after his mother died. Harriet raised him like one of her own until Jasper found himself. Legally, I wanted to protect Robert, rather than leave him an orphan. He is so fond of you. I never thought you'd question that."

In the distance, Harriet scooped up Claude and swirled him in the air. She occupied my sons, knowing her father's story wasn't finished.

John stopped twirling his hat. "Daniel has a responsibility as executor to see my parents' assets evenly distributed."

"My profits are slim. I don't know how I can pay what's owed," I said.

"You're not alone." The lines on John's brow deepened. "It's likely to tear this family apart."

This family. Every member wanted something different. Or did they?

The children played by the creek as children had done for decades. Church bells rang every Sunday. Every year, the land gave and took and gave again. I'd been focused on the future without considering the importance of the past.

Maybe we all wanted the same thing: to hold on to family and place while facing the coming change together.

"John, I have an idea."

September 1, 1887

Dear William,

I appreciate you delivering the court paperwork yourself to ensure that Daniel received the summons. With that done and the court date arranged, I find I have a related situation that may be vital to our court appearance and resolving my inheritance.

Would you be so kind as to call on me at my cousins' home this coming Tuesday evening?

Fondly,

Alice

September 1, 1887

Dear Elizabeth,

A surprising development here in Democrat means that I'm closer than ever to our shared goal. Would you and Margaret come to court and bolster me this Wednesday? I do hope that we will have cause to celebrate as we did in Asheville earlier this summer.

Alice

Chapter Forty
Asheville 1887

"On occasion of its [the Swannonoa Tunnel] opening for passenger transit..., this day marking the triumph of a long cherished idea, the breaking down (of) the physical barrier between eastern and western North Carolina, and the linking together the two extremes of the State by imperishable bars of iron."

The Asheville Weekly Citizen

I jostled the reins to keep the horses on pace along the dusty road to Asheville. My eagerness to resolve the dispute with the Carter family see-sawed with my anxiety over the outcome. Could I hold on to the land I'd come to call home?

Harriet murmured a Bible verse. "I have fought the good fight, I have finished the race, I have kept the faith." She pressed her shoulder against mine. "Alice, do you think we'll win?"

"You know your Uncle Daniel. Will he take the deal? Or will he continue to fight?"

Harriet bit her upper lip and shrugged.

Claude perched on her lap. "Horses go fast! Mama, look trees!" he cried.

Whatever happened, I would have Claude. I smoothed my son's curly blond hair and tucked a stray piece behind his ear. I would do anything for him, anything to secure his future and mine. Gripping the reins, I turned my attention to the widening road.

The French Broad River appeared to our right, lined with trees bending over to graze the water. A train ambled over the iron bridge, announcing its arrival with hissing steam and a shrill whistle.

Claude's incessant babbling continued, but our conversation stopped as we regarded the city streets leading to my cousins' home. Unlike Harriet, I'd witnessed the city's rapid growth on my frequent visits to court or to the tobacco warehouses. Every visit brought some new marvel: resorts, sanitariums, telephones, waterworks, and electric streetlights. Although the school vote had only just passed, it wouldn't have surprised me to see masons laying bricks for the city's first graded school.

Mary and Stewart had graciously offered to host our large group while we plotted our strategy for tomorrow's appearance in the courtroom. We arrived at a household bustling with activity. The maid took Claude to the kitchen, and we joined the others in the dining room, narrowly avoiding the serving boy hustling in to replenish drinks and refreshments. The room's candlelight added a festive air, but not enough to erase the palpable nervousness of the guests. Harriet and I moved to greet her father, John. I tried to overhear the topic he discussed with William, but my approach stifled their words. After perfunctory small talk, I moved away, aware of William's furtive glances trailing me.

I rubbed my neck, kneading the tension away. *What was William to me? Counsel? Friend? Something more?* Some months ago, I'd done something—most likely said something that had offended him. I missed his teasing, his playfulness with Claude, the deep discussions we'd had. Tea with his sister hadn't revealed the cause of our ruptured friendship, but rather laid out the lonely life I faced as a widow. I shook my head and put aside my feelings for William. Figuring out my inheritance was more than enough for tonight.

Once we were all sitting around the supper table, Zimri started the discussion. "As executor, Daniel must settle the estate now that Mother has passed. Isn't that right?"

"That is correct," William said. "Your father's will states that all property be evenly divided between the children. The earlier land grants, including yours, mean the property is now unevenly divided. According to the will, some children must pay their siblings. So the question is, where does the money come from to pay the claims?"

"I can't sell enough land to settle and still make a living," I said. A week ago, I wouldn't have admitted this vulnerability. Harriet reassured me with a nod, and I was reminded of my sister, sitting across from me at this very table five years ago, encouraging me as I spoke to Senator Vance about public education.

"We're in similar straits," Zimri said. He looked at his wife and Susannah nodded in agreement. "So, what can we do?"

"That's where I come in." John commanded the room's attention. "I stand to gain. I've none of Father's lands. Bought the land for the inn on my own."

Ever since that day in the churchyard when John explained Daniel's true motivations, I'd realized my judgments flew fast and sometimes false. My Carter family didn't want me to lose the land any more than I did. I might not win in court, but I'd have them alongside me for the battle.

"Are you making a claim?" Susannah asked John.

"Only to serve a broader purpose," he said.

Mary rang the dinner bell. "Now, this sounds interesting. I'll call for more candles," she said.

This discussion would go deep into the night, as we weighed the arguments to make tomorrow.

"All parties rise," the clerk announced. "Judge Merrimon presiding over this court."

I stood and took a deep breath, absorbing strength from William standing next to me at the defendant's table and from my family in the gallery. Today would decide my fate and ultimately that of Jasper's siblings, including Daniel. If my brother-in-law, as executor, persisted in collecting cash payments from me and the others to make the inheritances equal, then I would be forced to sell my land. I'd lose my home and my family.

Boots shuffled and bodies squeezed into the tight rows of seating.

Claude called out, "Wee-yam!"

William turned and waved at my son, who stretched his arms out toward us but remained firmly within Harriet's arms and surrounded by other Carter family members. I suspected the audience was rather large for a probate trial. My sister Jennie and her husband had timed a trip to town to coincide with the hearing and to show their support. Cousin Mary sat with my friends Elizabeth and Margaret, who'd come to cheer on my inheritance deal-making and my convoluted attempt to bring a school to Democrat.

Daniel stood across the aisle on the plaintiff's side.

The court clerk announced the case. "Mr. Daniel Washington Carter, as executor of Solomon Carter's estate, makes a claim of Alice Carter, widow of Jasper Shuflin Carter."

"You may be seated," Judge Merrimon said. "The audience will obey the rules of this court and keep conversations to a minimum."

Anna gave me an almost imperceptible nod from her place behind her husband on the plaintiff's side. As my opponents, they had not been present at the previous night's dinner, where we'd hashed out a plan for today. My sister-in-law had never been my adversary and, while we planned to ambush her husband, it hadn't felt right to surprise her, so late last night I'd sent a note to the Eagle Hotel, where she and Daniel lodged. I worried about her reaction. More importantly, I wondered whether she'd kept the details of my note private as I'd requested.

The judge addressed William. "Colonel, I see you are representing Mrs. Carter."

"Yes, Your Honor."

"And Mr. Daniel Carter, you are without counsel?" the judge asked.

"Your Honor, my father's will is perfectly clear." Daniel stood and held the document up, his arm stretched high above his head.

"Mr. Carter, I hope you do not presume to do my job for me." The judge peered over his half-rim spectacles. "I will determine whether this is a clear-cut case."

"Yes, Your Honor." Daniel placed the will on the table.

"Mr. Carter, please state your case," Judge Merrimon said.

Daniel splayed his fingertips on the edge of the table. "With my mother's passing, my father's will calls for an equal inheritance for their children. One thirteenth of the estate is to pass to each." Daniel rustled his papers. "As executor, I ordered appraisals of the lands given to myself, my brothers and my sisters."

"Has the Defense seen these appraisals?" the judge asked.

William stood briefly. "We have Your Honor, and we do not contest them."

"Very well. Carry on."

"My brother Jasper's land is valued at more than one-thirteenth of the estate. Therefore, his widow, Mrs. Alice Carter, owes the estate," Daniel said.

William stood. "Objection! This does not consider the amount owed to Mr. John Carter."

"Is Mr. John Carter in attendance?" Judge Merrimon asked.

"I am, Your Honor." John stood, smoothed his shirt, and promptly sat back down.

Daniel blustered and shook the stack of appraisal documents at me. "What is this about? John will get a fair share. I've made the calculations."

"Silence!" The judge banged his gavel. "Colonel, what argument are you making and how does this involve John Carter?"

William puffed up, his personality filling the open courtroom like tobacco in a pipe. "The Defense has invited Mr. John Carter to this courtroom, as under Solomon Carter's will, he is owed money from the estate."

"Damn straight," Daniel murmured.

The judge stared down at Daniel. "Mr. Carter, you will watch your language in my courtroom."

"Yes, Your Honor." Daniel bowed his head and clamped his mouth shut.

"Now the calculation lies in question." William held firm to his suit jacket's lapels. "And here is the complicating factor. Mrs. Carter falls subject to widow's rights. The primary home and outbuildings belong to her for the rest of her days. The remainder of the property is divided with one-third belonging to her and two-thirds to their children."

Daniel jumped to his feet. "Mrs. Carter inherited lands subject to my father's will."

"Mr. Carter, one more outburst and I will have the bailiff remove you from my courtroom!" The judge turned away from Daniel and spoke to William. "And what say you to the Plaintiff's claim?"

"I say that a widow's rights versus Solomon Carter's will becomes a question for the court. Perhaps Your Honor could illuminate us on the timeliness of a decision should an appeal go forward?"

I held my breath at William's bold question.

The judge clasped his hands in front of him on the dark wooden bar. "Do I understand, Colonel, that you will appeal a verdict on the outcome of this trial should it not favor your client?"

"You've hit the nail on the head, Your Honor." William hooked his thumbs in his vest pockets and rocked back and forth on his feet.

Here was the William I knew.

Judge Merrimon leaned back in his chair and braced his hands on the arms of his chair. "Given that the appeals log is rather long in Buncombe County and assuming that Mr. Daniel Carter would like to resolve this inheritance and get back to his normal business, then I would advise mediation."

"An admirable suggestion, Your Honor. We have a compromise to propose." William ceded the floor to me.

I rose, nodded at William, and wiped my clammy hands on my skirt. The courtroom took on a stillness of anticipation. "Your Honor, instead of payments, I would like to build a school for the benefit of all the children in Democrat. My brother-in-law Zimri Carter agrees to source the lumber from his lands, and his brother Samuel will mill it."

John Carter stood in the gallery. "Your Honor, I'll lodge a teacher at our inn to support the school."

The judge raised his eyebrows and glanced down at Daniel from the bench.

Daniel gaped at his brother. John had suggested we catch Daniel off guard, anticipating that he would decide quickly whether this proposal was a challenge to his authority or a compromise speeding up his duties as executor. I hoped my letter encouraged Anna to sway her husband to the latter.

"Mr. Daniel Carter, what say you?" Judge Merrimon asked.

"What of the rest of the payments to square up the inheritance?" Daniel turned to John. "You're only talkin' about the payment you're owed. What of our other siblings?"

Harriet stood and addressed Daniel. "Uncle, I've spoken with all of your siblings, and they favor a plan that saves them education fees for their children and grandchildren."

"You've not spoken to the spouses," Daniel ranted. "You've not spoken with me about this, Harriet." His reddening complexion signaled a fight ahead.

In the gallery Anna Carter stood slowly and resolutely. "Your Honor, may I address the court?" From her gentle, lilting voice, I couldn't tell if she was about to throw daggers in our plan or ask the judge to dance.

Judge Merrimon nodded. "By all means, Madam, if you can resolve this situation. Please state your name and your business."

"Anna Carter, your Honor, wife of Daniel Carter. There appears to be a missing piece to the compromise."

"It seems many in the court today mean to do my job. Pray tell," the judge said.

"The defendants offer a school building, land, and teacher accommodation." Anna swept her arm toward me and the others. "However, my husband and I also owe the estate." She turned toward him. "Daniel, should you choose to offer the land for the school, instead of our payment, it would be a grand gesture toward family reconciliation and community charity."

A hush fell over the courtroom. I held my breath.

"Mr. Carter?" Judge Merrimon asked.

"Excuse me, your Honor, I have more to say," Anna interrupted.

The judge threw up his hands. "By all means."

Anna lifted her chin. "I offer my services to the new school as a music teacher."

I'd judged Anna wrongly as I had so many others, assuming her quiet ways implied subservience. Harriet gave me an 'I told you so' look. Daniel wilted in his chair, and his eyes wandered the room like a moth looking for the light.

"Might I also suggest the school be named for the Carter family?" Anna asked. "What a fine legacy that would be, Husband."

I left the courtroom giddy after the auspicious outcome of the probate hearing. I'd offered a non-arable plot for a school instead of the cash needed to comply with Solomon Carter's will. It was a measly offer on its own, but with the support of other Carter family members—Zimri with the lumber, Samuel milling the wood, John housing a teacher, and all of us providing the labor, we'd successfully ganged up on Daniel. But then Anna had suggested their land for the school and Daniel acquiesced. My farm would remain intact, and Democrat would have a school.

I pushed through the tall double doors and paused to wait for the others on the courthouse steps. Court Square lay before me, much more crowded now than five years ago, when Jennie and I had walked its paths, grieving and despondent. I pondered Asheville's past and its future. Once a stop on the drover's road, slave auction site, battleground, manufacturing center, and travel destination, the city had experienced many ups and downs, just like me.

Jennie and G.W. approached. She slipped her arm through mine. "My sister's done it again."

"What exactly?" I asked.

"Gone head-to-head with a powerful man."

I blushed and managed a tepid smile at my sister's husband. After Jennie's revelation about their childlessness and marital arrangement, I found it difficult to look him in the eye.

"Good thing I have a sister who's always there for me when I need her," I said.

"You'll always have that." Jennie hugged me before taking her husband's arm and walking away.

Harriet came up behind me. "You've done it."

"Not without your help. Thank you." I placed my hand over hers and hoped to convey my gratitude for more than just today.

"It took very little to convince Father after he heard you and Senator Vance sparring at the rally. He recognized a fighter when he saw one, and he didn't want to lose the banjo player in the family."

I laughed. "I'd better get back to practicing."

"I've spoken to Uncle Samuel," Harriet said. "He'll send some men to clear the trees from Zimri's woods next week."

"It pays to have a sawmill in the family," I said.

John joined Harriet and me. "And an inn," he said. "I'll make inquiries for a teacher."

Elizabeth and Margaret came to stand on the steps below us. "We can help with that, Mr. Carter," Elizabeth said. "Why don't we head over to the Normal School right now to post the position." John tipped his hat at me and scurried after the dressmaker and the missionary.

The courthouse doors swung open behind us, and Daniel walked out, looking far less stunned than he had inside. His usual swagger had returned and he offered his arms to both Anna and Caroline. Perhaps Harriet had been right, Daniel convinced himself that our surprise ambush was what he'd wanted all along.

"Brother, your charity will go a long way to better all the families in Democrat," Caroline was saying. "Imagine! Carter's Hill School. The goodwill might follow you to other opportunities, perhaps political ones?"

"Indeed." Daniel looked out across Court Square. "Perhaps this will be the first of many improvements to our town."

Caroline and Anna smiled at us as they passed.

Harriet lowered her voice. "Remember my boast at your wedding?" She squeezed my arm and flounced down the steps after the others.

How could I forget what she'd said five years ago at my wedding to Jasper? *Don't let him tell you any differently. I'm responsible for your match.*

I felt William's presence before I saw him beside me. "Thank you, William." I rested my palm on the sleeve of his topcoat. Months of letters, planning, and scheming had paid off. My land and my life were secure. With the others off to celebrate, we lingered on the steps.

"It has been my honor." William took my hand from his sleeve and held it. "Now that you've secured your future and the children's in your fair town, what will you take on next?"

I blushed. "You think too much of me."

"I think not." He gazed at me, his bright eyes asking, almost imploring. "I know from a previous conversation that you are determined to make your own way."

My fingers moved to cover my mouth and I looked down and away. William had repeated the words I'd uttered after my failed meeting with the senator. Yet again, my outspokenness had proven detrimental, and my boasts of independence had pushed away those I needed, including William. I glanced at our hands firmly together and placed my other hand atop his. Doubts about myself, my place, what I needed and what I wanted vanished.

"I've been thinking that solo ventures are rather lonely." My heart raced. *Could I win him back?*

"Might you be interested in a companion?" he asked.

I squeezed William's hand and inched toward him.

"Miss Alice, I think we've proven to be a fearsome pair here today," William said. "Will you do me the honor of becoming my wife?"

October 2, 1887

To Colonel and Mrs. William Bedent Baird,

My hearty congratulations on your nuptials. William, you've chosen wisely. Mrs. Baird, you have your work cut out for you.

I hope to call on you when I visit Asheville for President Cleveland's brief stop on his goodwill rail tour. While I approve of the President's choice of bride (like you, William, he has married a much younger, more beautiful lady), I cannot say that we agree on politics.

I expected more alignment once we had a Democrat back in the Oval Office, but the President continues to defy the working man, thwarting trade by supporting the gold standard and desiring to repeal the silver coinage act. I digress into my favorite topic, politics, when I should instead say that I look forward to your company later this month.

Mrs. Baird, word came to me that you intend to raise Carter's Hill School in Democrat. Well done. It is a testament to the power of the female resolve and a fine tribute to your Carter family. My wife, Florence, wholeheartedly approves and invites you to visit us at our new home, Gombroon, at your earliest convenience. She looks forward to making your acquaintance.

Sincerely,

Senator Zebulon Baird Vance

September 22, 1890

Dear Jennie,

This week we celebrated Claude starting school. He walked proudly across the field all by himself with his primer and pencil. He turned and waved to Bill and Charley, and oh, how they longed to join their big brother.

It's hard to believe we have one starting and another leaving school. Robert completed three years at Carter's Hill School, and while I had hoped he would consider furthering his education, he is drawn to the farm and the life his father loved. He now farms our two fields and has built his own home where the tenants' shack once stood. He's still an avid reader and I often see him in the evenings on the porch with his nose in a book.

Your loving sister,

Alice

September 4, 1898

Dear Alice,

All the news in Asheville is of Mr. Vanderbilt's marriage to Edith Dresser. We know what she wears and where she goes. I've never been busier, fashioning dresses the likes of the new Mrs. Vanderbilt.

I met the Vanderbilts' estate manager, Mr. McNamee, while touring the new colored kindergarten at the Young Men's Institute. What a fine organization for our colored community. About every week it hosts a concert or lecture. The library is fine, and the gymnasium and meeting rooms get put to good use. George Vanderbilt's contributions have been a boon for Asheville.

Mr. McNamee invited me to attend Mrs. Vanderbilt's arrival at the Biltmore Estate, following their European honeymoon. It was a fine day, and crowds of people awaited Mr. Vanderbilt and his new wife. The couple got off the train in Biltmore Village and rode in an open-topped carriage to their house. Mr. McNamee and I stood alongside a line of servants to welcome them. When Mrs. Vanderbilt climbed down from the carriage, I was surprised to see she stood a head taller than her husband. That had me thinking fondly of you.

I look forward to seeing you, William, and the children when you come to the Biltmore.

Your friend,

Elizabeth

P.S. I had a letter from Margaret. It's been ten years since she returned to Boston. Her husband is a lawyer, and they recently welcomed their third child. She is recovering well.

Epilogue
Biltmore Village 1899

"I have traveled in many of the countries of the world, ... If you wish to save time, expense and trouble in looking for the beautiful places of the earth come to Asheville."

Asheville Citizen-Times

The wagon rumbled over the snowy road leading to the rail terminus in Biltmore Village. I squinted at the sunlight reflected off the sparkly crusts of ice, and breathed in the crisp, clean air. I tugged the lap blanket up and around our children.

Bill and Charlie jostled under the blanket, each making a grab for more cover. At twelve and ten years of age, they competed in everything.

"How much longer, Pa?" Charlie asked.

"Not much farther than I could spit."

"Honestly, William." After twelve years of marriage, this man still made me smile and laugh.

This trip today reminded me of my first trip to Asheville

seventeen years ago. Maybe it was Bill, who was almost the same age as my brother Ralph had been when I'd left home to marry. Yesterday I'd said another goodbye to Ralph, waving him off on a train bound for Oregon. I brushed aside my tears and cupped my rounded belly. This pregnancy kept a grip on my heart and wrung out memories like it was laundry day. At forty-eight years old, this child would surely be my last.

William held the reins and guided the horses around the spectators arriving by train. It would be three more miles along curvy lanes and through thick forests before the grand home came into view. My girls–seven-year-old Mary and five-year-old Cynthia–joined in Charlie's excitement when George Washington Vanderbilt's mansion appeared.

"Cynthia dear, close your mouth before you catch a fly," I whispered. I closed my own.

Although I'd read of the Biltmore, nothing prepared me for the spectacular chateau or the enormous lawn before it. I didn't know where to look first: the home's arched entry encased in a stone tower, its steep-pitched roof that grazed the sky, the decorative stonework surrounding its windows, or its countless chimneys.

Bill rubbed the back of his neck. "One family lives here?"

"I reckon it's a big family," Charlie said.

The rolling cadence of his voice reminded me of his father. I glanced over Charlie's head at William. His white hair had thinned over the years, his skin was more mottled, but his eyes remained bright and they missed nothing.

He tied off the reins and helped each of us out of the wagon. "Mr. and Mrs. Vanderbilt are just married," he said.

Cynthia fidgeted. "That big house for two people?"

We followed the other spectators coming to visit the Biltmore and its occupants. On certain days of the month, the Vanderbilts opened their grounds to share their splendid home. It had taken twelve years of acquiring lands, and employing architects, builders and artisans to create the largest personal residence in America. In that time, Asheville had grown from a sleepy mountain town to a burgeoning tourist destination, successful manufacturing center, and modern city.

I'd grown as well. From an apprehensive bride to a confident wife, mother, and school organizer. The security I'd desired had manifested itself in ways I couldn't have imagined. I walked with my family along the gravel path to the entrance, lost in my thoughts of the sureties in my life: friendships with Elizabeth and Margaret; the support of Harriet and my Carter sisters; and my lasting bond with Jennie. Cousin Mary and Stewart. Jasper's legacy of the farm, my stepson Robert and our son Claude. Most of all William and the children. My feet kicked up the pebbles before me. In this life, I'd traveled over bumpy and smooth lanes, down roads I'd never planned on taking, to arrive home to a family I'd never expected.

I stretched and twisted, trying to find some comfort after the long wagon ride. Smoothing my coat across my middle, I willed the child to change positions. William wrapped an arm about me, recognizing that with this one, I tired more easily.

"Is this a castle?" Mary asked.

I herded my daughter along. "With two hundred and fifty rooms, I'd say so."

Mary wiggled away. "It must've taken forever to build."

"Six long years or thereabouts," William said. "I was still at the Superior Court office when Mr. Vanderbilt started buying up land—early on, very quietly."

Not long after I first visited the courthouse. Little did I know that years later I'd be married to that clerk, managing my farm, and chasing after five—soon to be six, children.

"Alice!" Elizabeth strode toward me, Mr. McNamee attempting to keep up. Although I had speculated about some attachment between the two, Elizabeth had assured me they were business associates with a common goal of providing opportunities to all of Asheville.

"You look in good health." Elizabeth kissed my cheek. She was older than I'd been when I first stepped into her dressmaking shop as an unhappy bride-to-be.

"And in fashion." This dress had seen me through my first pregnancy with Claude, and every child since.

"How much land did Mr. Vanderbilt buy?" Claude's voice broke, and he cleared his throat. At fourteen years of age, Claude was becoming a young man, working most days alongside his brother Robert in the fields or helping his Carter uncles.

"One hundred and twenty-five thousand acres," Mr. McNamee answered.

"How many do we have, Mama?" Cynthia asked.

I brushed a blond curl away from her face. "Seventy-five."

"Golly." Charlie sighed. "One man did all this?"

"It took more than one man to create this. One thousand men worked six days a week for six long years," Mr. McNamee said.

William winked at me, inviting me to follow his gaze as it landed on each of our children. "It takes at least two people to make something so worthwhile. And it often takes a long time."

I slipped my arm through his. "In my experience, it's worth the wait."

Chapter Headings and Periodical Sources Listing

(In order of appearance)

1. The Farmer and Mechanic, October 7, 1880
2. Asheville-Citizen Times, December 7, 1890
3. Our Brother in Black: His Freedom and His Future, Atticus G. Haygood, Southern Methodist Publishing House, 1887
4. The Biblical Recorder, September 19, 1883
5. The Asheville Weekly Citizen, August 26, 1887
6. The News and Observer, January 7, 1880
7. The Rutherford Banner, February 17, 1882
8. Asheville-Citizen Times, November 4, 1890
9. The Raleigh News, January 29, 1880
10. The Asheville City Directory and Gazetteer of Buncombe County, 1883-1884
11. The News and Observer, February 13, 1884
12. The Asheville City Directory and Gazetteer of Buncombe County, 1883-1884
13. Asheville Citizen Times, May 5, 1886
14. The Asheville City Directory and Gazetteer of Buncombe County, 1883-1884
15. The Asheville Citizen Times, October 11, 1887
16. The Asheville Weekly Citizen, October 31, 1883
17. The Carolina Mountaineer, November 15, 1884
18. Asheville Citizen Times, July 29, 1887
19. Carolina Public Press, 1897
20. The Origins of Black Sharecropping, Wesley Allen Riddle, The Mississippi Quarterly, vol. 49, no. 1, 1995
21. Asheville Weekly Citizen, September 6, 1883
21. "A gentleman traveling on one of the trains ..." Greensboro North State, January 1, 1880
22. Extract from Governor Jarvis's speech as printed in The Greensboro Patriot, August 25, 1880
23. Caption for the photograph: Main Street, Hendersonville, N.C. by Jody Barber from the UNC Library
24. The Asheville City Directory and Gazetteer of Buncombe County, 1883-1884

25. The Asheville City Directory and Gazetteer of Buncombe County, 1883-1884
26. The Asheville City Directory and Gazetteer of Buncombe County, 1883-1884
27. Our Brother in Black: His Freedom and His Future, by Atticus G. Haygood, Southern Methodist Publishing House, 1887
28. Our Brother in Black: His Freedom and His Future, by Atticus G. Haygood, Southern Methodist Publishing House, 1887
28. "Three million women in the United States work ..." Asheville Citizen Times, October 19, 1887
29. 'Sitting Up With the Dead: Lost Appalachian Burial Customs', Unmasked History Magazine, September 21, 2019
30. Asheville Citizen Times, September 7, 1888
31. The Asheville City Directory and Gazetteer of Buncombe County, 1883-1884
32. The Asheville City Directory and Gazetteer of Buncombe County, 1883-1884
33. Asheville Citizen Times, May 6, 1886
34. Photograph of the Carter Inn, listed on the National Registry of Historic Places, located in Democrat, NC, taken by the author
35. The Wilmington Morning Star, August 27, 1876
36. Our Brother in Black: His Freedom and His Future, by Atticus G. Haygood, Southern Methodist Publishing House, 1887
37. Asheville Citizen Times, July 9, 1887
38. The Exlavigator, September 28, 1884
39. Asheville Citizen Times, August 6, 1887
40. The Asheville Weekly Citizen, January 1, 1880
Epilogue. Asheville Citizen Times, December 17, 1890

For Discussion

1. The story opens with Alice facing a hastily arranged marriage. What does Alice want? Does she get it?
2. Missionaries arrive from the North to aid the South in educating its people. What obstacles must they overcome?
3. Cousin Mary shows Alice and Jennie the Freedman's Chapel but doesn't go into the Negro neighborhood. Alice thinks: *She'd drawn her boundary, taking us to church, but not beyond.* What boundaries are depicted between Whites and Coloreds? Where does Alice stand?
4. Elizabeth Stanton tells Alice, "Women got more opportunities. Single women got the right to earn a living. Need that same right for married women." The women in this story have varying levels of independence. How did some of the female characters exert their independence despite legal, economic and societal limitations?

5. Is the marriage between Jasper and Alice a happy one?
6. Alice is initially quick to judge and often wrongly. Discuss her appraisal of Cousin Mary, Daniel, her cousin's maid, and others. How do Alice's presumptions change throughout the story?
7. The Freedmen's experience is portrayed through several minor characters and always seen through the eyes of Alice. Did any of their experiences surprise you? Did any surprise Alice?
8. What similarities and differences (political, economic, social) do you see between America in the 1880s and today?
9. What historical topics or events mentioned within the novel were new to you?
10. How does the past influence the future? Alice and Asheville attempt to leave their pasts behind and forge a new future. Are they successful or not? In what ways?

Afterword

Two colliding forces prompted me to write this story: a family mystery and an unfamiliar history. Genealogical research uncovered the mystery. At thirty-years of age my great-great-grandmother, Cynthia Alice Harris, married a much older Civil War veteran, *and* her three sisters married very near the same time. Why? Further digging revealed their father and eldest brother had died within months of the weddings. Intriguing, but not an untold story.

Then George Floyd was murdered.

The African-American experience in America was front and center–in the media, on the streets, and in my son's university Sociology class. On a visit home my son complained he'd learned so little about African-American history; his previous lessons jumped from slavery and emancipation following the Civil War to the 1960's Civil Rights Movement with nothing in between or after. His statement rattled me, but I had to agree, for that's what I remembered from my own schooling. I wanted to understand the experiences of Whites and African-Americans after the Civil War and in the post-

Reconstruction South. Writing Alice's story offered a means to do just that.

Prior to the Civil War, the Harris family (and the Carter and Baird families) owned slaves. What did these White families experience after Emancipation? What kind of life did the Freedmen have in western North Carolina? The more I read and researched, the more I found probable intersections. The critical involvement of Asheville's African-American community in the graded school vote was a lightbulb moment. The public education movement would be a vehicle for Alice, the Freedmen, and Asheville to show their fighting spirit.

Asheville became a character in my novel, and like Alice, it wanted to leave its past behind and find a new future. When the railroad arrived in 1880, tourists seeking the healing mountain air followed. Hotels and sanatoriums sprang up. Farmers gained access to faraway markets. Industries such as tobacco, furniture and textile developed. Asheville flourished.

Yet not everyone benefited. The Drovers' Road was abandoned when the railroads transported livestock to market faster. Farmers abandoned subsistence farming for commodity crops and didn't always come out ahead. It's quite likely these downturns affected Alice's family, since they'd operated the Harris Inn on the Drover's Road.

Several legal documents I uncovered showed Alice to be a fighter. She claimed $104 in widow's support from her husband's family (North Carolina law stipulated a year's sustenance for widows). Then shortly after Jasper's death, two other events complicated Alice's life: her brother-in-law John Carter filed for guardianship of her stepson Robert and Jasper's mother Alvira died. Upon her death the will demanded that all thirteen Carter children receive an equal inheritance. Previous land gifts valued above 1/13th meant remuneration to the other siblings.

Alice turned to Superior Court Clerk William Bedent Baird (my great-great-grandfather) for help. Family lore had it that William wooed Alice while she settled the estate. He did more than that. William applied his legal handiwork to issue a summons for relief against the estate's executor, Daniel Carter. Further documents revealed that the sheriff was *unable* to deliver the summons. Alice sought restitution from the sheriff —return the delivery fee paid or be fined $100! My great-great-grandmother was no pushover.

Neither were the Freedmen who sought an education and a better way of life in Asheville after Emancipation. Many found work in the growing service opportunities in hotels and resorts. They filled the colored schools, eager for the education they'd been denied during slavery. Some, like Isaac Dickson, prospered; he owned a grocery, coal yard, and taxi service. He was instrumental in rallying Black voters to support the first publicly funded graded schools in Asheville, and for that effort he was named a school board member–the only African-American school board member.

Other Freedmen were not so fortunate. Many farmed as tenants or in sharecropping arrangements. Segregation persisted. Black codes restricted African-Americans labor and activity. Violation of the codes ensured a steady labor force for the railroads. Though the 15th Amendment passed in 1870 and promised the right to vote regardless of race, Black codes and the Ku Klux Klan offered a different reality throughout the South.

Yet in Asheville in 1887, African-Americans turned out to vote and the school tax passed *by four vote*s. Asheville's Black community ushered in a new era for education that benefited Blacks and Whites.

In this novel, I imagine that my great-great grandmother put her fighting spirit to work in furthering public schools, in promoting education so other women might avoid hasty marriages as the only means for financial security. Maybe she participated in a women's organization (like the Flower Mission or the Women's Home Missionary Society), which were on the rise during this era. Historical documents indicate there was a Carter's school, although nothing remains of it. The suspected location near the Carter Inn makes sense as this hub offered other services, including a store and post office.

The Carter Inn still stands and is a private residence. Once owned and operated by John Carter, it served as a stopping point along the Asheville-Burnsville thoroughfare for circuit riders, drummers, judges and lawyers. The Carter-Swain House is recognized on the National Register of Historic Places.

For the sake of the story, I took liberties with the following historical events. John Swain (Harriet's husband) had retired from his saddlebag ministry and was at home when he was killed by a falling tree. I changed the circumstances of his death to insert a plausible way for Jasper and Alice to come together in marriage. Alvira Carter died in 1885, just a month after her son Jasper. I extended her life within the novel to make sense of the legal story that followed. Finally, the Biltmore did not open to the public until 1930.

The newspaper and periodical quotes are written as they appeared, with all spelling and punctuation errors intact. To avoid any confusion with the timeline of Alice's story, I only included dates for the quotes within the Chapter Headings and Periodical Sources listing.

For more information, pictures, and anecdotes about *Brighter Than Her Fears*, join me on my Facebook page or author website.

Acknowledgments

A novel is a collaboration of efforts and I hope that I recall everyone that helped make this one. Historical fiction novels demand research to bring accuracy to the time, location, and characters portrayed. A special thanks to Katherine Cutshall and the staff at the Buncombe County Special Collections in Asheville for answering my numerous questions and for access to maps, books, and online articles that allowed me to build Alice's world. To Gene Hyde, Head of Special Collections, University Archives, Ramsey Library, UNC Asheville, my gratitude for providing reports and documents to answer my questions and for pointing me to others who could do likewise. To Darin J. Waters, Ph.D., thank you for your illuminating work: *Life Beneath the Veneer: The Black Community in Asheville, North Carolina from 1793 to 1900.* To my local library, the Cedar Mill Library at Bethany, thank you for providing numerous interlibrary loans from around the country to support my research.

My search for Alice's story was accelerated by Susan Corcoran Hayes, a second cousin I connected with on Ancestry.com, who had extensively researched our family and kindly shared her findings with me. To Larry and Joyce Buckner, who found me wandering around a church and helped me find the Carter graves, gave me a tour of Democrat, and invited me into their home, you proved that Southern hospitality remains a real thing. Thanks to Russ Carter, who answered a *You don't know me, but* voicemail and graciously invited me to his home to read his genealogical research on the

Carter family. And to his mother, Bunny Carter, thank you for filling in the gaps in the Carter family and on life in Democrat, North Carolina.

Thank you to Tom Holm and John Farrauto, who reviewed the documents I found related to Alice's property struggles and provided legal expertise. While I have attempted to interpret these documents accurately and portray the legal proceedings that followed, any legal errors within the novel are my own.

The Reynolds Mansion is now a wonderful bed and breakfast and the owner, Paul Manshon, gave me a tour inside and out, describing the history of the home and the work that goes into maintaining a historic house. Greg Goins spent an hour on the phone educating me about tobacco and the selling of it, even giving me a taste of the auctioneer's call. What a treat!

The writer is only as good as the other writers who fastidiously critique their work. To Mark Barbour, Joni Blecher, Bobbie Calhoun, Marty Castelao, Michael Colvin, Kevin Johnsrude, Melissa Owens, Cathy Rittenhouse, and Mike Weedall, a big thank you for reading and improving Alice's story. And to my online group on Critique Circle, thank you for the improvements, suggestions, and encouragement. To Suzi Swartz, Martha Taylor, and Jamie Campbell, thanks for listening every other Thursday night to Alice's story and providing valuable feedback and support.

Thank you to my daughter Molly Ard for the beautiful magnolia branch artwork that appears throughout the novel. I can imagine Jennie (your 4x great aunt!) stiching it.

A special thanks to Jean Lowd and the publishing team at Creative James Media, who put it all together and got it into the reader's hand, showing dedication and persistence in delivering the best book possible. I'm so pleased with the outcome. Thank you!

To my readers, thank you for reading, reviewing and spreading the word about *Brighter Than Her Fears*. There's no greater pleasure for an author than to know that their work has been read and enjoyed.

Finally, to Tony, Holden, and Molly, who cheered me on the entire way.

About the Author

Lisa Ard is the author of the adult historical fiction novel: Brighter Than Her Fears, and three children's books: Fright Flight, Dream Team and Saving Halloween (a Kay Snow Award Finalist). When not writing, you'll find Lisa leading bike tours in Palm Springs, golfing, or curled up with a good book.

Printed in the USA
CPSIA information can be obtained
at www.ICGtesting.com
LVHW090802220124
769094LV00006B/572